Charles W. Jeschke

Diversity

The Lost Child

authorHOUSE®

AuthorHouse™
1663 Liberty Drive
Bloomington, IN 47403
www.authorhouse.com
Phone: 1-800-839-8640

First published by AuthorHouse 5/19/2011

ISBN: 978-1-4567-3694-1 (sc)
ISBN: 978-1-4567-3693-4 (hc)
ISBN: 978-1-4567-3692-7 (e)

Library of Congress Control Number: 2011902687

Printed in the United States of America

To all the teachers in the world, this is for you with my heartfelt thanks.

MONDAY

Morning

On a clear night with numerous stars, a bright Milky Way and a full moon, a young boy plays with toy spacemen figures between two mounds of dirt on the edge of a short grass oval meadow. Tall evergreens with a few interspersed deciduous trees surround the veldt. A slightly taller streak of lavender meanders through the short yellow grass along the longer axis with a couple short breaks.

Like a ghost, a thin fog fills the area opposite the boy's position. Moonlight brightens the top of the fog bank making it look like a cloud hanging centimeters from the ground. Otherwise quiet, only the irregular sounds of owls, sparrows and black birds fluttering among the trees, punctuate the air.

He sits in the dirt, a meter from the edge of the forest, wearing dirty blue jeans and a musty short-sleeved yellow shirt with scuffed tan loafers. His black hair is ruffled and mangled. Streaks of dirt line his face in patches on his cheeks, forehead and chin. Dry mud still attached to his hands and lower arms sporadically falls off as he moves the toy figures.

With a frown on his face and cold gray eyes, he looks up at the full moon at its zenith and smiles. He watches the stars as they slowly rotate through the sky. The major and minor constellations are visible in this northern hemisphere. The moon's gravity distorts the placement of many of the stars close to the edge. He marvels at how bright the moon appears against the black of the sky. As it moves across the sky, stars appear and disappear.

Returning his gaze to the toy figures between the mounds, he moves two of the tiny figures to the top of the right mound. As he places them in position, a small twig snaps somewhere in the forest behind him. Ignoring the sound, the boy keeps playing with the space figures.

Moving another figure up to the top of the left mound, he pushes a pebble down the side of the same mound into a group of figures in the valley. The pebble hits all the figures knocking them over except for one who was shielded by one of the containers away from the path of the pebble. The boy maneuvers that last standing figure carefully around each of the other fallen figures, one by one, as if he were checking for life signs.

After examining all of the fallen figures, the boy moves the last standing figure to the center of the valley between the two mounds. Using his other hand, he brings the right hand of the figure up to its mouth.

The boy says, "All of the scientists have been killed by a tumbling rock."

The boy moves the two figures on the right mound to look down into the valley and leaves them there. He does the same for the lone figure on the left mound. Using both hands, he holds one of the figures from the right mound and the lone figure on the left mound. After a moment, he returns the figures to their original positions. He grabs the right figure again and brings the left hand to its mouth.

Wriggling the right figure, he says, "Roger, that. We'll be right down. We'll return to base for further evaluation and analysis. This will go down as the worst accident resulting in deaths for this three month project."

On the other side of the meadow, a field mouse scurries out of the forest, and seconds later, right back into it. A brown fox with a white tail and front paws follows the trail of the mouse out into the veldt and back into the forest. Soon the regular sounds of the forest return.

For a momentary time, quiet reigns within the forest and the meadow. Even the wind no longer blows through the tree tops or rustles the grass in the meadow.

To break the momentary quiet, an owl hoots, sparrows fly from the top of the trees up into the sky, and a surge of water babbles along a brook through the edge of the meadow below the fog. The boy remains focused on his figures.

Within the dark forest, a man walks, trying not to step on any more dry twigs as he maneuvers over the mantle of fallen leaves, broken branches and accumulated flotsam. Between the trees, he spots the boy, playing with his space figures with the background of fog and mist at the other end of the meadow.

Moon light runs through the trees, highlighting moving apparitions. They only appear to move with his movement as he walks closer to the edge of the forest. When the man steps out of the forest, he stops to allow his eyes to adjust to the brighter light of the full moon.

The man wears black pants, a short-sleeve pale blue shirt. His black shoes shine in the moonlight. An emblem in brown and white seems to float on his left chest. The rest of the emblem is indefinable in the moonlight. His face remains just as unrecognizable.

Brambles, wet leaves, and stickers cling to the lower portion of his pants and his black shoes display scuff marks from branches, roots and the occasional broken twig. He disregards all of that and keeps his focus on the boy.

Without looking up, the boy says, "You may sit down for a while, if you want.

"My parent's won't. They would like me to play by myself in my room."

After cleaning the lower legs of his pants, the man moves closer to the boy and sits in the grass in a yoga stance. He pulls his pilo out from his right pants pocket.

The man's pilo displays, "Monday, June 7, 2483 1:15 A.M. Prestige, Filmore."

He says, "Bryan, we'll have to leave pretty soon. Your parents are expecting you to be home before 2: 00 A.M. We've been through this before, several times, and you know the kind of reaction you'll get."

Bryan says, "Karl, why would they want me home when they aren't there most of the month. When they are there, they don't want to listen to me. It makes me so mad that I throw a tantrum. My mother doesn't know what to do except cry. My father waits until we're both spent and orders me to my room. I usually miss dinner, but my mother always brings me something after Dad has retired to the library."

"Parents can be mean at times. They don't always know how to handle their own children. You're a single child that means your parents get to take all their frustrations out on you, even when they don't mean too. I know you don't understand what's happening to you, but later on you will grow into it. It's going to take some time." says Karl explaining.

"It's always my fault. I sometimes wonder why I am even there. They never want to talk to me and they don't ask me any questions about school or my friends. My father only issues commands and my mother does all of the explaining. Sometimes, I think I would rather be in a circus."

Karl replies, "Between you and me, we are a lot alike.

"We both grew up without brothers or sisters. You have a choice to always run-away or stick it out."

"Then why do they want me back?"

"The three of you will make a decision about your welfare," responds Karl.

"Yes, that's why I ran away. They want to send me away to a military academy until I turn sixteen. That's eleven years from now which is twice as long as I have lived. Knowing them, I'll never see my parents again."

Karl says, "I will try very hard to change that course, if at all possible. Your father is a stubborn man who has other concerns, besides you."

"And my mother follows him implicitly. I don't understand how she does it. I've heard them arguing, but it's always my father who punishes me."

"Parenting is not an easy task for any adult although getting older has advantages. Some retreat into their own internal thoughts. I don't even know what my parents were like. But I made it and so can you," says Karl.

The boy places all of his space figures in a small blue bucket along with the space vehicles, their miscellaneous cargo and equipment. Smoothing the two mounds and the valley, he removes all of his tracks.

Karl stands up and extends his left arm towards Bryan. Bryan stands, brushing off all the dirt off his shirt and pants. He rubs his hands and lower arms together to loosen the caked on dirt which falls into the short grass. After looking down at the two mounds and the valley between, he looks up at Karl. Like a giant, the man towers above him, making him feel even smaller and less capable of responding. He sees Karl's smile and smiles back warming his heart, making him realize he is only a child and shouldn't feel so responsible.

Without looking, Bryan grabs the black handle on the blue bucket with his left hand and Karl's left with his right. Bryan rotates around Karl's left side as Karl turns towards the forest.

Seconds later, they are at the edge of the forest. Together, they walk into the forest, where they soon disappear allowing the night creatures to return to their exploits in the meadow.

Bryan says, "Karl, you're much better than my parents. You should adopt me and take me away from this place."

* * *

Karl and Bryan walk out of the forest onto a broad plain, stretching east and west. Mountains to the west have rolling hills, leading right up to the forest. To the east, the plain extends to the horizon with sporadic rolling hills and mounds throughout. Streams join to form rivers and lakes. Short and tall grasses populate the plain along with tumble weeds and gnarled withered trees, where fruit never grows.

The forest behind them goes east and west for about two kilometers, before curving out of sight, leaving a broad plain, extending southward and northward to the mountain ranges.

They remove the wet leaves, stickers and small branches which cling to their lower pant legs and shoes. Their shoes have scuff marks primarily on each side with only a few on top. Cleaning their lower legs, they wait for their eyes to adjust to the moonlight, before walking forward.

Before them, about thirty meters away, nine meter cubes, sixteen levels high, wide and long blot out most of the mountains to the north with only the white covered peaks showing. Sixteen cube arrays to each side, they seem to fill the northwest part of the plain. Stairs and elevators are near each corner and the middle of each array.

Bryan says, "It looks like a large prison. I wonder what the prisoners do with their free time."

Karl replies, "Many young adults feel the same way, especially those who have returned from group vacations on Diversity. It takes a while before they calm down.

"The cubes aren't for everyone and there's a growing consensus to get rid of them entirely. Most haven't taken it seriously, yet."

"That's why my parents are not home that often. It's not their work they enjoy; it is outside, away from the cubes that they spend most of their time."

To the right of the module in front of them, an exit door comes into view on the ground floor. In between two cubes nearest the corner of this module, above the lowest level door and on each of the levels above are smaller central rectangular windows with the shades closed.

Lights shine through all the windows where stairs and elevators would be, but the rest of the complex has only one or two lights on in the cubes.

The bottom three meters of each cube are reserved for service maintenance including: HVAC, sewer reclamation, water purifying and recycling and garbage maceration. Where power for the cubes resides is not obvious from the outside. Within each section of cubes, a central open oasis receives sunshine, and in turn with the ability of hidden solar panels, electricity flows to each cube.

* * *

Karl walks through the darkened hallway to the door of his Personal Activity Room (PAR). Light panels every five meters provide the only internal light. Moonlight filters through the partially open window blinds at the end of the hallway.

He palms the outline of the door on his left. It opens, sliding upward through the wall, into a modest nine meter cube of which he only has the upper six meters. The ceiling light panels bathe half of him in white light.

Sixty-eight with graying hair, twelve centimeters short of two meters tall and a less than svelte body, he wears a broad smile. Wearing the black and blue colors of a private detective with a brown and white emblem on his left chest, illustrating a silver shield and a similar patch on his right arm, he walks into the room which is twice as long as wide.

His black shoes still show the scuff marks from the forest.

A bathroom/closet fills the left corner next to the door with the bathroom in the corner and the closet next to it on the left wall. A small kitchen fits on the same side in the far opposite corner.

A wall bed seam on the left wall surrounds a large rectangular screen monitor. Outside the wall bed seam on the right near the middle of the monitor, a green button with a red button below are indented into the wall. The red button glows softly, pulsing three times, getting brighter every few seconds. The green button remains unlit.

A pale blue sofa abuts the right wall. A small two shelf bookcase filled with rows of e-books hangs from the wall above the sofa.

He moves quietly to the sofa.

A large picture window fills the middle of the wall straight ahead centered within the outline of the bed.

The internal blinds are currently closed to help retain heat within the room.

Per some internal command the blinds open, filling one third of the room with light from a twinkling field of stars and the last quarter moon.

The inside wall color matches the outside wall's grey-white.

A short hair beige carpet covers the floor with tile in large black and white squares of grouted tile at the door, the kitchen area and the bathroom. The off-white walls are offset by the wood cabinets and stainless steel appliances.

Open blinds show a pristine clear night sky, a slice of the Milky Way and the big full moon. The lights slowly dim, plunging the interior of the Karl's cube into the light from the moon.

He sits on the sofa, removing his shoes and socks. With his eyes drooping, he decides to lie on the sofa. He brings his feet up and soon falls asleep.

Low on the horizon, the big full moon, slightly larger than earth's, casts an eerie light into one half of the room.

Shadows of items on the counter shimmer, when a few clouds intervene between the moonlight and his cube.

The blinds close tightly, shutting out the night sky's starlight brightness.

As the light panels turn completely off, only low-level spots on the kitchen counter and the bathroom mirror remain.

Karl's snoring begins and the sofa vibrates until he stops. Karl turns over and within minutes is snoring away, once more. The sofa vibrates until his snoring stops.

Karl's monitor displays, "Monday, June 7, 2483 1:55 A.M. Prestige, Filmore," centered at the top of the screen with white letters on a black background. The monitor measures a meter and a half along the diagonal. The rest of the monitor is completely black with a green light on the right bottom corner, indicating the device is active. The outer edge is two point five four centimeters in width with a three millimeters black indented band.

The monitor serves three main purposes: a rotating scheme of local scenes in various picture frames, a video phone service and a data terminal. It is the front end to a sophisticated computer system that maintains the cube and everything in it. Besides being multilingual, it can also do Braille or text depending on the type of disability, which among the population is minimal.

As a data terminal, it can exchange information with any other monitor or pilo. In this way, knowledge is exchanged to maintain the population and prevent any catastrophes from happening. Events which would upset the norm are discouraged.

* * *

Within the tall grass between a one story school and a sidewalk on the lower edge of a grid of sixteen one story homes, two guards rest in wait hidden within the stalks of long grass. They watch children arrive at the one story hexagonal shaped school, walking from their homes through the tall grass. They each check their pilos every few minutes.

Both guards wear gray habits with gray pants and black shoes. They've rubbed their shoes with dirt from between the grass stalks to take off the shine and blackness.

Likewise, their hands and face are grayer matching their surroundings.

One guard has two white strips on his left shoulder, while the other has only one.

Neither has any other insignia, decoration or honors.

So well hidden, they can see the children on the sidewalk, but the children can't see them. Lying entwined within the tall grass stalks, they blend in to the gray and brown ground cover from decaying and broken stalks.

They are a meter apart, laying between stalks parallel to the sidewalk but well back so as not to seen, facing each other about four meters to the left of the sidewalk and six meters from the east end of the tall grass. They carefully watch the sidewalk as it enters the tall grass.

Kids of all ages, singly or in groups small and large, walk along the sidewalk through the tall grass to the school.

The guard with two white stripes takes out a red cloth from his pocket and folds it in half twice. He takes a small bottle of green liquid out of his left pocket and wraps the bottle in the folded red cloth.

The first guard says, "The boy will be here very soon."

"What's the exact time?"

"7:30."

"Wow, that's not too much time—until he gets here."

"It's enough or I would have mentioned it sooner."

"Then we should probably get into position."

"Get fresh face paint on your face and don't forget your hands. Wait for this next bunch of kids, especially the tall one."

"Will do! This should be the last group through, until our boy arrives."

"Except that it's Monday, and more kids always arrive late on Monday."

Adamantly arguing about some teacher's attitude, a small group of kids walk along the sidewalk.

They get ever closer to the tall grass. The tall boy keeps his full attention on the blond girl, walking next to him. The rest of the kids maintain their separate conversations, blissfully unaware of the guards on either side.

Whispering into his mike, the first guard says, ""Now you take the right side and I'll take the left, but wait for this group of kids to come through, before we make our move."

They watch the group of children come off the sidewalk. They enter the tall grass crossing into the school's perimeter. Moments later, the children find their friends and associates on the other side of the tall grass near the school.

After the kids are through the grass, the guards slither between the stalks, avoiding bending any stalks, which would give away their positions. They each move from their hiding places, within the tall grasses closer to the sidewalk, but still well hidden among the tall grass, a good three meters from the edge.

They slither like snakes, slowly moving between the stalks. The second guard moves to within two meters on the far side of the sidewalk near the right side while the first guard does the same on the left. Their habits blend into the lower gray of the grass stalks.

* * *

Karl wakes up at 7:30 a.m. After sitting up, he rubs his eyes and runs his right hand through his hair.

Karl's monitor displays, "Monday, June 7, 2483 7:31 A.M. Prestige, Filmore."

He remembers what he wanted to do first thing.

Karl commands, "Let's see a typical housing grid near the kidnapping on Diversity.

"It's part of a very well planned network of homes, schools, parks, shopping centers and businesses."

His monitor responds, "Processing, please wait for approximately five minutes."

Karl stands trying to decide what to do next. He leaves the sofa and walks over to the kitchen counter.

He opens an upper cabinet, selecting a tea bag from a box on the lower shelf, which he places in his favorite cup on the counter. For the briefest of moments, he only looks at the tea bag in his cup. He puts the cup under the hot water dispenser near the back of the sink and fills the cup with hot water. He sets the cup on the counter with a lid closed on top.

Five minutes later, Karl gets off the sofa again, walks over to the counter and pulls the tea bag out of the cup, squeezing it dry. He places the tea bag on the spoon holder in the design of a gingerbread cookie boy and returns to the sofa as the monitor announces, "Display ready."

After sitting on the sofa, Karl responds, "Display."

The monitor displays and says, "Sixteen one story homes, in a four by four square, form a grid of houses, surrounding a modern one story shopping and business office center with additional space on levels underneath."

Rotating the grid to a side view, the monitor displays, "The houses, shopping center and businesses have more levels, extending underground. Each section maintains a geothermal substation for heat and electricity."

Dotted lines below the surface outline single levels for most of the houses, while the shopping and business centers have some dotted lines extending many levels underground.

Karl commands, "Expand to show girds around the farm." Expanding to a plan view, the monitor displays and says, "Four grids of houses to a side surround a forest of tall evergreen trees that happen to be four rows deep. The trees are even alternated to give them plenty of room for sunshine with an occasional deciduous tree replacing an evergreen. The forest surrounds a large farm with a variety of fields that are fallow, half way to harvest, in harvest, or recently planted."

Karl commands, "Show a typical house."

Zooming in to a house in one of the middle rows, the monitor displays and says, "The house has a long slopping roof with glass on the southeastern side. It is rotated on the center of the lot by forty-five degrees. Extending past the ridge line of the roof, solar collectors turn with the sunlight as it arcs through the sky.

"The houses have various pastel colors with no two exactly alike. While the house's trim on each compliment the main color, no two houses within a grid have the same trim color."

Karl commands, "Show city orientation."

After zooming way out to show the three closest cities around the previous, the monitor displays and says, "The closest grid cities are two hundred kilometers away, in three equiangular directions. All of the grid cities are built in the same way. All populated cities are at indices of a hexagon structure, put in place by the previous civilization all over the planet. That civilization used geothermal heating and electrical for government, business and housing."

* * *

One particular home, three houses west of the southeast corner of this southeast grid, has a pale blue clap board siding, a medium brown metal roof and white trim. A bountiful flower garden separates the grass and the hedge which in turn separates the houses.

The low trimmed hedge, common throughout the grid extends around the perimeter of the grid. The garden is a meter wide from the hedge in front of the house around the left side to the back and around the back edge of the property. Singular and group flower plantings in a bed of multihued bark are evenly spaced from the driveway to the flower garden along the front sidewalk along the roadway.

Bushes and small fruit trees separate the garden into unique and colorful representations. Small fruit trees are also placed in the corners and at the ends.

The sidewalk, curb and roadway are basic gray stonework with concrete binding them together to a smooth surface. The short grass has hexagon patterns with different shades of blue-green grass in the front yard. The side and the back yard are a Kentucky blue-grass variant.

A medium sized oak tree stands between the front porch and the sidewalk, the meandering walkway and the driveway next to the right side of the house. It provides all of the shade on the front porch during the spring and summer seasons. During the fall and winter months, sunlight streams through the bare tree, bringing additional warmth and comfort to the house.

The house's porch extends around the left side of the house to the back door. It has a shake roof, using tall white tapered columns with a white painted wood railing, using similar short tapered columns, every other one with filigrees. A white trim surrounds the windows and doors.

From the front porch to the sidewalk, the meandering walkway consists of hexagon white stones in a bed of small pebbles with red brick edging two and a half centimeters above the white stone, using a herringbone pattern. The grass on either side has been recently mowed and edged along the walkway with the cut grass removed. The stone work looks almost as if it was recently laid. A closer look would reveal some stones are depressed among their neighbors. The pattern continues throughout the walkway.

* * *

Inside the house, no lights shine, no one is stirring, at least, not on the upper floor. After the entry, the living room is modest with the usual number of pictures on the walls and nick-knacks on the two bookshelves on either side of the fireplace. To the right, the kitchen has windows surrounding the dining room table with the bay window facing the front lawn. A smaller breakfast table borders the side of the kitchen with another bay window facing the rear. The breakfast table monitor displays and beeps, "Monday, June 7, 2483 7:30 A.M. Bridget, Diversity."

At the end of a short hallway, a set of stairs lead down to the lower level. The sound of a downstairs door opens and closes softly. Footsteps at first tentative and then bolder echo from the hallway up the stairs to the upper level.

They are irregular with random spacing, as if some alien being were stalking through the hallway on its way up the stairs. Footsteps go up three steps and back two, up four and back one with a mad rush up to the top, where a five year old boy brings himself up to his full height of one meter, stopping on the top step.

He wears a pastel yellow shirt not tucked in with a disheveled collar, unfastened. An unbelted dark green pants and shiny black shoes complete the unusual ensemble.

Two black female Labrador retrievers sit at the bottom of the stairs watching the antics of the boy even though this has been repeated many times.

He looks around the room to the right at a den with desk, chair and small half-bath, straight ahead to the hallway, leading to the living room, and on his left, the kitchen's breakfast table with a bay window, jutting out into the back yard. The floor consists of large black and white tiles throughout the kitchen. The hallway from the living room to the rear bathroom and the back door uses smaller black and white tiles in a herringbone pattern.

Tarcey, his mother, is leaving the kitchen, heading for the dining room and doesn't ever notice him, although he knows for certain that is not the case.

He quickly tucks his shirt in, fastens his pants, pulls the seams straight on his pants, and adjusts his collar.

He stands at attention, keeping his feet together, his shoulders back, his arms at his side and his head forward.

Although, the shoe laces of the left shoe are untied, he waits. He waits some more and then. . .

Tarcey, from the kitchen, says, "Cliff! Your lunch is in your backpack. Put it on, before you leave the house. I don't want to bring it to you later. You'll get in trouble with your teachers for not bringing your homework."

Cliff walks over to the breakfast table, removing the backpack from one of the nearby chairs. Putting it on like a full space suit, he reaches down to tie his left shoe. Sitting down on one of the chairs, bending over to pull on imaginary boots, he sits up after pulling on each boot.

He puts on invisible gloves, pulling them tight along his wrists. He fastens the gloves to his imaginary sleeves and checks the seal. He stands and turns towards the breakfast table. He places the pretend helmet on his head and twists it until it locks in place. The make-believe laser pistol snaps into place along his right leg. After checking his left forearm, he looks down the hallway.

Cliff says, "All systems go."

Cliff walks slowly, bouncing off each foot, moving from side to side through the hallway. He draws the pistol.

"Ka POW, Ka POW," comes from his mouth.

He shoots the daffodils and ferns in the flowered vase on the three-leg table in the short hallway.

He pumps three more shots into the front door, before he gets there.

"Ka POW, Ka POW, Ka POW.

"New alloy. I'll have to send a sample to base."

After getting to the door, he removes an imaginary clear plastic bag from one of his outer pockets. Using a knife from his right pocket, he pretends to scrape chips from the door into the plastic bag. After three scrapes of material, he seals the bag and puts it and the knife back in his pockets. After checking his status, he returns to taking a last look around the living room.

He opens the door. Sunlight bathes him from head to toe. He reaches up and lowers the heat shield over his faceplate. He steps out to the front porch.

The two retrievers at the bottom of the stairs turn around, running into the boy's room, hopping on the still warm bed, lying side by side on opposite sides falling fast asleep.

Meanwhile, the small monitor, above the breakfast table, beeps every fifteen minutes on the hour and the quarter hour. A similar one exists above the central console that divides the main dining room from the kitchen.

The breakfast table monitor displays without beeping, "Monday, June 7, 2483 7:40 A.M. Bridget, Diversity."

* * *

The front door of a pale blue single story house opens. Cliff walks out the massive black door, down the porch steps, onto the meandering path from the house heading towards the sidewalk along the wide roadway.

A garden of bountiful multihued roses together with primrose, black-eye susan and upright sedum, boxwood, camellia, lavender and bright colorful *Festiva Maxima,* surrounded by sea foam blanketing a meter of ground parallel to the fence on his left.

He shoots the oak tree in the middle of the yard and several roses on either side.

"Ka POW, Ka POW, Ka POW, Ka POW."

A small light green shack with a bright red metal roof near the front left corner of the house serves as a tool shed.

He turns left onto the sidewalk and walks past three similar houses two with flower gardens and all with similar hedge fences.

After shooting various trees and bushes along the way, he gets to the edge of the housing grid community.

Before he gets to the grass, the sound of the children gets increasingly louder as a soccer ball goes high into the air above the grass. Sides are chosen; older children become referees. The ball is placed in the center of the field between the tall grass and the edge of the school building. The captains come out, the whistle blows and the game begins.

Cliff stops, before entering the tall grasses to watch which way the ball goes.

It is tossed into the air and goes to the left in one head butt, but before it gets any further it switches direction. For several seconds the ball bounces one way and then the other. Soon a score rouses both teams

The ball is kicked out onto the field and play time resumes.

Holstering his imaginary weapon on his right hip, he walks through the tall grasses.

* * *

The first guard spots the child coming along the sidewalk towards the tall grass. He motions to the second guard to get ready.

The second guard unfolds the red cloth and removes the bottle of green liquid.

He opens the bottle and pours a third of its contents onto the middle of the cloth, as the boy arrives. The second guard gets up on one knee, waiting for Cliff to get closer. The first guard also gets up on one knee to grab the boy's legs.

Cliff walks into the tall grass. As he takes his second step through the grass, he is lifted off his feet and a wet cloth is put over his mouth held by a large hand.

He struggles to get free, but his breathing becomes shallow. His limbs become limp and his head falls to the side.

He soon loses consciousness.

As he nods off to dreamland, he remembers hearing the school children, laughing and playing on the other side of the tall grass as he drifts off to sleep.

The second guard keeps the red cloth on Cliff's face as he opens the bottle and adds a couple more drops on the cloth.

The first guard removes Cliff's backpack and tosses it closer to the sidewalk.

He holds Cliff's head and shoulders up off the ground with his left hand.

He hands a large black plastic bag with multiple small holes on the top half to the second guard. While the first guard holds Cliff, the second puts the plastic bag at Cliff's feet, arranging the bag so that his feet are within.

Temporarily, Cliff is lowered to the ground. The first guard brings the black bag over the boy's feet and lower legs up to his knees. While the second guard removes the red cloth and puts it back in his right pants pocket along with the closed bottle.

The second guard takes over wrapping Cliff from the first guard. He pulls the plastic bag over Cliff's upper legs, using his left knee to hold Cliff's head and upper body, bringing the bag over his torso, arms, shoulders and head.

He ties it off as the first guard gets down on the ground, moving south carefully through the tall grass.

A smile comes to second guard's face as he watches the first guard snake his way between the tall stalks of grass not even touching a single stalk. He only wishes that his own exit with the boy will be as graceful.

After the first guard's soles disappear into the stalks of tall grass, the second guard returns to his duties silently cursing the first guard for leaving him once again to clean up after their escapade in the tall grass. He calms down realizing the first officer probably went through the same routine when he was second.

After checking the boy's breathing, the second guard puts Cliff across his back, carefully slithering between the tall grasses behind the first guard.

As he gets past the sidewalk and slithers deeper into the grass, he hears the sound of more children on the sidewalk behind him, hurrying to cross the tall grass.

They rush through the grass to get to the school, before the bell rings. Two more bunches of children skip along the sidewalk and run into the tall grass never noticing the green and black backpack off to their right. They talk and laugh, trying to do as many nonsensical words or actions as possible.

A bell sounds, calling all the children into their appropriate classrooms. Soon doors are closed and through the windows, sounds are muted with children walking, skipping, jumping and running to their seats. Later, the kids write, read, ask questions and the teachers attempt to explain and try to maintain a semblance of order among chaos.

Although not all of the children are paying attention, they exchange notes and glances. For some, their eyelids are heavy. Others are distracted by the slightest movement outside or inside.

Outside the school, the soccer ball sits on the short grass field, waiting. The school yard and the apparatus of climbing, jumping and exercising wait for the next break time.

Much later, the two guards with Cliff on the second guard's back arrive south of the tall grass far away south from the houses and the school.

A few deciduous trees with cops of tall grasses rise in the distance, but otherwise the plain is dotted by short grass and reddish-brown open ground.

They stand up with the first guard, placing Cliff over his right shoulder as they follow a well-worn path south towards an older civilization's shopping center in the far distance. It has a tall central spire above the trees with shorter spires connected by bright banners, using all the rainbow colors except black and white.

* * *

Through the clear window of Karl's PAR, the morning sun rises out of the clear blue sky. His monitor displays, "Monday, June 7, 2483 8:30 A.M. Prestige, Filmore."

Karl sits on the sofa opposite his large screen monitor, but his attention is not on the monitor. Wearing the same clothes as this morning, Karl reads from his pilo, sipping a hot tea from a well-used favorite cup. He punches a button on his pilo and reads some more. He contemplates the meaning of what he has read and adds notes to remind him of things to check. He gets to the end, turns off his pilo and puts it back in his right pants pocket, contemplating his next move.

He sets the tea back on the edge of the coffee table.

He looks out the window for a moment.

Out the window, the morning sun hangs above the horizon, casting long shadows of bushes and trees outside his PAR.

The monitor, using a computer male voice, says, "A Mr. Dradsole is calling."

Karl responds, "I'll take it. I've been waiting for this call since last night."

Mr. Dradsole appears on the monitor dressed in a dark brown robe with pink slippers that have black soles, lying on a lounge chair.

A big man, he overfills the extended chair with layers of fat on each arm rest. He lies back with his head barely above his gut and a smile on his face. He keeps his hands behind his head, until he begins talking.

An e-book two centimeters thick rests on the wooden end table next to his right hand, while part of a dark brown leather sofa on his left abuts the chair. Behind him, a plain white wall has not even a hint of missing pictures or bookshelves.

Hoping to make his point early, Karl begins, "Mr. Dradsole, I hope you had a pleasant night. I thoroughly enjoyed talking with

Bryan during the time I was bringing him back to you. He has quite an imagination and tons of creativity. You and your wife must be very proud."

Dradsole comments, "Thanks, for the compliment, Karl, but he can also be a headache at times.

"Thank you, again, for finding Bryan and returning him so soon. My wife and I are in your debt."

Karl responds, "I have received your payment and it is what we agreed to, so I won't be asking for any more."

Dradsole returns the compliment, "You are a very kind person, Karl."

"Have you decided on Bryan's welfare?" asks Karl.

Dradsole answers, "Let me give you a bit of background.

"As you know, Bryan has been attending school on the planet Diversity, near a city called Bridget."

"Why so far away? That a good days trip, using our fastest freightliners," asks Karl, thinking this could explain his reasoning.

Dradsole answers, "Of all the schools on any of the four planets, it is the best.

"Not only is it a good education, but the school is in a clearing, where the kids can play outside.

"He comes back for some weekends and between sessions. We're not always home when he is, which causes some grief. Enough of background.

"We had a serious family discussion last night after you left.

"We're all agreed that our decision is sound and proper.

"My wife, Bryan and I have decided to put Bryan in a military academy on Diversity, until he reaches sixteen at which time he can make his own decision."

Karl asks, "Do you think that is best for Bryan?"

Dradsole explains, "I told you last night that both my wife and I are very busy people constantly away from our PAR.

"It would be almost impossible to return in an emergency.

"Bryan wants to be around kids his same age with lots of discussion, debates, arguments, playtime or harmonization.

"The academy groups candidates together by fours with individual bunks. And each candidate has their own corner of the room for personal items. He will learn certain duties that we have not been able to impart.

"They'll be his age, of course. The school is the best of the four planets. A private tutor is also available. He'll be on bivouacs during most weekends along with basic camping, learning the compass, first aid, and survival skills."

Karl counters, "You are well aware of the ability to change careers and provide a home for Bryan, where one of you is constantly home.

"I don't believe in non-parenting a child.

"Studies show kids are healthier and better adults with good parenting.

"That doesn't mean around the clock parenting, but there has to be some kind of normal routine in order to the child to feel security and to learn responsibility. Being there for your child can be a blessing as well as a curse. It all depends on how you want to handle it.

"There are so many opportunities you will be missing. You will miss out on many years of growing up, attaining goals, being responsible, learning compassion, training athletically and those competitive college years."

Adamantly, Dradsole responds, "Nevertheless, my wife and I enjoy our careers and fully expect to enjoy them through our one-hundred and twentieth birthdays or beyond. We never expected to have a child. We are not prepared for the responsibility. We have our own lives to live and the child is becoming a nuisance."

Trying harder, pressing forward, Karl retorts, "There are courses you can take, either through your pilos or monitors.

"You can take sabbaticals each taking a turn of six months.

"Parenting has its ups and downs.

"Your child needs your guidance and feedback whether he says it or not."

Not backing down for anyone, Dradsole says, ""Karl, we made our choice. No matter what you say we are sticking to it.

"Thank you, again, for finding Bryan and bringing him back to us safe and sound. You will be in our thoughts for a very long time."

Dradsole ends the call.

As the monitor turns black, Karl slams his right fist on the coffee table, causing an immediate reaction with several items responding awkwardly.

He knocks his hot tea onto the beige rug where it spills. The tea cup bounces on the rug fibers.

The spill fades away by action within the rug.

The last drop of tea hits the rug suspended, where it becomes sliced and diced into many parts and then disappears. The last few drops of tea still in the cup, including tea leaves, disappear as well.

Karl turns off the monitor, using the remote, walks calmly to the fridge, opens the door, and grabs a beer, drinking half of the contents before removing it from his mouth.

Closing the door, he returns to the sofa and sits down.

He places the beer box on the coffee table and leans back on the sofa, trying to figure out his next opportunity for Bryan's benefit. Like so many times before, he realizes his limitations. This isn't the first time he's had to figure out a way for a child to get what he/she needs. At it probably won't be the last although he's getting too old.

Bryan visits a certain family on Diversity and has a buddy relationship with another boy. Perhaps I could spend more time on Diversity for the next several years.

I could set up a temporary office for seminars and training. I could install a monitor and do everything remotely, training even more officers. After training a few, I could select the best to do the same training for new officers and keep them up-to-date. This could turn out to be a blessing for the entire planet enabling us to have instant communication. But on the other hand, it will have to

have some kind of security to keep the general population away
from unnecessary attention.

* * *

Two guards walk through tall grasses to a short grass clearing with a tall evergreen forest rising high above them.

The first guard carries Cliff in the black plastic bag over his right shoulder.

As they approach the forest edge, the first guard places Cliff on the ground about three meters from the edge of the forest and removes the black plastic bag, while the second guard continues on to the edge of the forest.

The second guard removes a dull black helmet from behind a meter and a half diameter tree.

Unconscious Cliff lies very still in the short grass. The first guard checks the boy's pulse and breathing.

Walking back to the first guard, the second stops off near an area of several similar stones arranged in a hexagon. He pushes the central one. It depresses and then rises back into position. Gears below ground rumble smoothing the soil.

An opening appears showing a stairwell going down into a dark space.

The displaced slab recedes horizontally underground, until the stairwell is completely exposed. The distinct steps at the top of the staircase merge into indistinct steps in the middle.

After walking over to the first guard, he hands the helmet to him as the second waits and watches for any movement in the tall grasses behind them.

The first checks the inside of the helmet, reading the small screen inside, before placing it back on the boy.

The helmet covers the boy's eyes and over his ears.

The first guard turns the key on the back of the helmet. He removes the key and puts it in his right pants pocket.

They walk down the steps into the maze with the second guard holding Cliff over his shoulder, fireman fashion. The first guard turns on his pilo light, casting a strong beam onto the passageway's dirt covered stone floor.

The first guard moves through the passageway quickly marching, realizing their great accomplishment. The second guard follows a step behind, as they know for sure exactly, where they are going.

* * *

Outside the side kitchen window, Tarcey sits with her legs off to her side near her flower garden.

The sky is clear with the Diversity's sun shining as it rises above the horizon.

Birds chirp in the nearby trees and bushes. Their song is melodic and cheerful. Tarcey smiles and almost breaks into to song herself, but she decides against it as other sounds occur.

Dogs bark occasionally and cats settle down after their morning meal dreaming of their next opportunity to play with their meal. Dogs are more content with the chase.

A few people walk along the sidewalks getting their morning exercise and talking about the day's events. Flights of aircraft, mostly single passenger, cross the sky above at many differing levels and all compass directions.

Wearing work gloves, Tarcey pulls weeds and trims plants in her garden.

Switching positions, she moves to her left side and trims a rose bush.

Her pilo beeps.

Wearing a sullied flowered yellow dress with blue knee pads and blue and white sneakers, she removes her gloves.

She sets them on the grass near her knees and removes a pilo from its packet nearby on her left.

Her blond hair, blue eyes and soft pale skin hide her age from everyone except her, but she remains generous to a fault even under the most trying conditions possible.

She looks at the pilo and reads it twice.

Tarcey's pilo displays, "Monday, June 7, 2483 9:30 A.M. Bridget, Diversity.

"This is to notify you Cliff did not come into school today. We have searched the school and the surrounding area. We are concerned for his welfare."

Tarcey quickly writes back.

Tarcey's pilo displays, "Monday, June 7, 2483 9:33 A.M. Bridget, Diversity.

"Thank you for your concern. I will try to find out what happened. He has always been diligent in his routines. I'm sure it's something simple."

Tarcey rises quickly and runs to the sidewalk, looking both east and west.

She quickly runs east along the sidewalk past three houses to the school.

She watches for any signs of Cliff's travels as she follows along the sidewalk. Before she reaches the tall grasslands surrounding the school, she spots his backpack off the path through the tall grasses. She stops and looks through the tall stalks of grass, in case he is hiding out caught up in one of his many fantasies, as would be his usual pattern.

Walking into the tall grass, she retrieves the back pack and places it on the sidewalk, where she looks through its contents. Bending down on one knee, she hurriedly looks at his books and other paraphernalia.

Carrying the backpack in her left hand, she stands back up. After looking over the tall grass once more, she puts on the backpack and starts off with a trot, turning into a healthy jog as house after house recedes behind her. Her house comes closer with each bound. Reaching her house, she jogs through the meandering entrance, jumps up the steps to the porch and runs through the open doorway stopping in the middle of the living room. She regains her regular breathing with a few deep breaths as she tries to think of what to do next.

* * *

Tarcey heads straight for the breakfast table. She looks suspiciously at the monitor above the breakfast table.

Tarcey commands, "Call the Chief of Police!"

The breakfast table monitor displays and beeps, "Monday, June 7, 2483 10:00 A.M. Bridget, Diversity."

The monitor expands to a larger size to accommodate the video request.

Robert appears on the kitchen monitor sitting behind his desk, busily looking over his pilo. He reads one of the messages and responds immediately. He looks over others, some of which he deletes and others he saves. Noticing one which brings a frown to his face, he stands, pushing his chair back.

One centimeter short of two meters, a robust body, Robert strikes a gentlemanly pose with tints of gray and white around the edges of his short brown hair near his ears and traces throughout the back.

He wears the standard blue and black uniform with a red emblem with the letters PC in white in the middle.

The words *Police Chief* stitched in white are centered within the red emblem. A similar patch on his right arm contains gold stars around the words.

The plaque on the desk also identifies him as the Police Chief of Region 23.

He fails to recognize her call. A moment later, he looks up.

Recognizing the look from so many times before, he tries to be conciliatory as he sits in his chair. After straightening up in his chair and placing both hands on the desk flat, he composes himself while he thinks of what he has to say.

Robert asks, "How can I help you, Tarcey? I don't usually get this early of a call from you concerning Cliff.

"Don't tell me he skipped school. This would make the third or is it the fourth time away from school. That boy is going to be an adventurer."

Tarcey says, "Second guessing again, Robert. He wouldn't skip school; he loves it too much. He was sick the last two times and he didn't make it back home or to school. This is more disturbing though. Not like him at all. He has done some very good vanishing acts on the weekends, but he always turns up eventually.

"He didn't show up at school. I found his backpack at the edge of the grasslands. I looked all through the grass, but didn't see any sign of his presence.

"No sign of a struggle and no blood either. Thank goodness! But it doesn't make any sense."

Robert says, "I'll get right on it.

"You want the PID engaged? It would be a great help to quickly get his location. Besides that's what they were designed for in the first place. I can't even begin to count how many times my officers have found children who have become separated from their parents."

Tarcey says, "Yes, whatever it takes. Find him."

* * *

Karl gets up from the sofa and walks into the bathroom. His living room monitor displays, "Monday, June 7, 2483 10:30 A.M. Prestige, Filmore."

Karl washes his hands and face in the bathroom sink.

After grabbing a towel and drying off, he exits the PAR.

He heads to his right down a long hallway with brightly flashing advertising on all surfaces except the overhead light panels, including punctuating and decorous sounds.

Later he arrives at the entrance to "Murphy's Bar & Grill" and heads directly to a rectangular table in the rear. He passes the main bar, where several patrons are quietly drinking beers and wines, while others are engaged in animated conversations. He acknowledges a few hellos, but doesn't stop for any casual conversation. He walks on past the bar.

He arrives at his favorite table in the rear corner. *Who will be here beside me?*

Broad black and red striped cushioned benches are along each long side of a dark oak table.

Two chairs, one with wide red, black and red strips through the back and seat, and the other just the opposite colors, are at each end of the table with the usual condiments of salt and pepper, olive oil, hot sauce, ketchup and three kinds of mustard a third of a meter from each end.

The benches are long enough for four people.

Tables along the wall are separated by long leaf green plants that reach to the ceiling.

More people are gathered together around the bar, reminiscing with the bartender. A few others are at tables, discussing current events. Piano music fills the air.

After taking a seat in the far corner, Karl orders a dark beer as Ester, wearing a pink, brown and white blouse with pale purple pants, enters. Bill, wearing a cyan shirt and brown pants, follows Ester. As they exchange pleasantries, Johnathon, wearing a vivid yellow shirt and faded blue jeans, arrives with a broad smile on his face, taking his seat next to Bill.

Johnathon asks, "Any luck with Dradsole?"

A waiter arrives with a pilo in his right hand and says, "May I take your order," looking directly at Karl who ignores him for the moment staring off into space. He doesn't' even recognize that the waiter is even there.

Finally, Karl waits to respond, as Ester, Bill and Johnathon place their orders. While Bill's order is quickly processed, Johnathon, as usual, can't make up his mind for a good three or four minutes.

After Karl places his order, he says, "Nope, he won't listen to reason." Karl looks up to see Johnathon.

"What's with the smile?"

Karl smiles back, trying to figure out what this is all about.

"I got myself a promotion, but let's talk about Bryan for now. My joys as less than his concerns," says Johnathon as he takes a seat opposite Karl.

Ester asks, "That's bad about his father. What will happen to Bryan?"

Karl removes his smile and looks over at Ester.

"Bryan is off to a military academy on Diversity, until he reaches sixteen," answers Karl.

Bill asks, "Are you going to notify the authorities?"

"I won't in this case. They're too reasonable. If they were more unreasonable or addicts, I would."

Johnathon says, "The GHD takes care of that though, we haven't had any mentally or physically challenged nor any addicts since way before our ancestors boarded those ships which left Earth so long ago."

"That doesn't stop irresponsible behavior. Some are upset with our use of the cubes while others work to build other habitats, some individually maintained with many rooms. I'm in favor of both sides.

"Tradition still drives many of us while the young seek alternate possibilities and the information we continue to get from Diversity's planned neighborhoods doesn't help the cube side. Discussions throughout the other three planets have not reached any momentous decisions.

"However, certain events are occurring which will precipitate some wrong decisions. Hopefully they are few."

* * *

The guards march in step through a maze dimly lit with single light panels every ten meters and at intersections. One of the guards carries a boy over his shoulder. Traveling along the passageway, they pass several intersections, until they seem to turn at every intersection, alternating directions. At the next intersection they turn left to a short passageway dead ending to an intersection, where they turn right.

Having been awake for some time, Cliff tries to keep track of all the directional changes, but it is too much.

They stop for a moment to check their location on their pilos like they have already done several times.

After many other rights and lefts, where even the guards are not sure if they haven't doubled back, they check their pilos and turn left at the next intersection.

Cliff's head is spinning from all the misdirection and he decides to wait for other possible opportunities.

About a hundred meters away on the left side of the passageway, a set of vertical bars look like a solid sheet of steel from their current location. A couple blinking lights appear on the wall closest to the cell's location. Otherwise, the rest of the passageway remains the same.

A minute later, they approach a set of vertical bars, gleaming like stainless steel with a control panel, having a small rectangular LCD screen and six buttons below it.

The wall opposite matches the rest of the passageway.

A dark cave within the bars is constructed of the same materials as the passageway. As they come closer, they stop, before reaching the edge of the bars.

Centered over the passageway and the cell bars, a single light panel lights the path, the bars, the control panel and the interior of the cave, casting a dim shadow of the two guards against the passageway walls.

Overlapping shadows of the bars occur inside the back wall and floor of the cave.

The second guard punches three of the six buttons on a control panel at about eye level below a small screen, which shows the date and time.

The cell's monitor displays, "Monday, June 7, 2483 10:30 A.M. Bridget, Diversity."

The bars silently move upwards into the ceiling, leaving only a couple of centimeters showing.

The first guard walks into the cell and gently places Cliff on the dirt covered stone floor lying down. He walks out of the cell into the passageway.

He walks over to the second guard by the monitor panel and buttons. Motioning the second guard to go ahead with lowering the bars, the first guard watches Cliff sleeping.

The second guard pushes the other three buttons and the vertical bars come down, stopping mere centimeters from the dirt covered stone floor.

The first guard leads, followed by the second guard. They march through, in cadence, the passageway at a fast pace, except they turn the other way at one intersection, until their footsteps can no longer be heard from the cell.

Cliff stays motionless, trying to stay awake, but soon his eyes are closed.

* * *

With her chin on top of the rake handle and her hands around the top, Tarcey stands, taking a short break, before completing the installation of the fourth bush.

She looks out over the hedge, which separates her property from her neighbors. To the east is a well maintained green lawn with small separate circles of flower gardens on the far side of the property spaced about three meters apart.

Feeling ready to resume, she returns to her work.

Wearing a pastel cyan blouse, black pants, gold flippers and black knee pads, she scrapes the ground around a small tree and three bushes, two on the far side of the tree and the other on the near side, with a long handled three tine rake. Carefully avoiding the round hole next to the lone bush, she rakes the ground around it, keeping the rake as low to horizontal as possible; she builds a mound around the hole about ten centimeters above the ground level. She smoothly evens the slope on each side until the mound looks like a small mountain.

Pulling the rake head up to her waist, she removes lumps of dead brush, twigs and weeds from the tines. She places the rake on the grass. She walks over to a bush two meters from the edge of the garden with its root ball laying in the center on a yellow tarp. She pulls the yellow tarp over to the garden, pulling from the grass into her garden towards the hole she has dug. Avoiding the other bushes and the small tree, she pulls it into position between the back hedge and the hole. She folds the front part of the tarp underneath itself to give her more room to work on the hole.

She moves gracefully to the grass in front of the hole.

She pauses for a moment and removes the pilo from the work bag on her right.

Tarcey's pilo displays, "Monday, June 7, 2483 11:00 A.M. Bridget, Diversity."

Sitting sideways, she tucks her feet in close.

She replaces the pilo into her work bag.

After selecting several pebbles and rocks from different piles behind her on her left, she places the amount she needs on the grass to her right.

She places several small rocks and pebbles, which she puts in the bottom spreading them out evenly. Over those, she sets shards of flat stone on top of the rocks and pebble leaving some space between.

Pulling the yellow tarp with root ball closer to the hole, she lifts it over the mound and drops the ensemble into the hole.

Holding the root ball with her left hand, she pulls the tarp with her right until it is out from under the root ball and folds it into a manageable state, laying it on the grass.

Getting on her knees, she tilts the bush upright and turns it around to the best side facing out. Satisfied with the look, she sits back down in front of the bush on the grass. Holding the root ball netting, she resets the flat stones below, until they are once again well-spaced. She cuts off the netting, using a razor cutter. She pulls it off the root ball, setting it on top of the tarp. Untwisting the roots, they stretch to their normal position.

She pulls a bag of potting soil from behind her, opens the bag and pours enough to cover the bottom third of the ball supporting the bush upright.

She grabs the hose on her left side and adds water, until it is thoroughly soaked, freeing additional roots, that snap out as they come free from the root ball. She places dirt all around the mound until all traces of water have disappeared before watering again.

She does the same for the next two thirds, adding one third at a time until the soil around the root ball is thoroughly damp. Waiting for the remaining water to drain, she pauses for a moment.

Returning her thoughts to the work at hand, she pats in enough soil on top to cover the root ball, but not above the mound. The water slowly drains with additional roots springing free. She adds water and dirt until all the roots have vanished.

She stands to survey her work.

She walks backwards, avoiding the other tools scattered on the grass near the flower bed, until she is a good two meters from the new bush. She walks sideways to get a better look at the scene, before deciding that she likes it very much.

She keeps walking back.

When she gets to the meandering path, she looks over the front yard to decide what will go in beside that bush and the other three and the small tree.

* * *

Robert's office space is the largest room next to the larger conference room which is used primarily for lunch breaks. His monitor displays, "Monday, June 7, 2483 11:00 A.M. Bridget, Diversity."

Standing behind his desk, Robert watches a meandering path on his pilo, which is on his desk corner. It's on playback with the time display showing the time at each point in the progress along the path.

A large monitor hangs on the wall opposite his desk between two internal windows. Light panels cover the ceiling with only the center row currently lit.

Two high small windows on the outside wall provide outside light to enter Robert's office. The outer wall has bookshelves up to the ceiling going around the high windows.

E-books, old paper-back books and assorted knick-knacks fill every single space on the shelves.

The inner walls have windows over meter high walls except for the monitor wall which rises to the ceiling.

The windows are filled with transparent maps of housing grids with certain houses highlighted in different colors, depending on the type of recent altercation.

Roberts says, "Display on monitor."

Robert's monitor displays, "Monday, June 7, 2483 11:12 A.M. Bridget, Diversity."

The monitor shows an enlarged map south of Bridget. The old shopping center area is one quarter of Bridget's shopping center area. The map superimposes a maze below the center. It reaches west beyond the center to the tunnels.

Farther east it reaches below the old city to the old civilization's small space port, which has not been used by the current population since they arrived.

The maze is colored pink with yellow wherever there are unverified passageways.

It would appear, as in the old city and the shopping center, nanos maintain the areas in operational readiness, as if anticipating the old population's return. Although according to records in the old library, they didn't even indicate they were leaving.

Currently the old city and the shopping center remain tourist attractions that aren't visited as much as the rest of the attractions: water falls, farms, ice and stone caves, the old library, the hot springs, the glaciers, wide rivers, small streams and a variety of plant and animals, originating with the planet.

The path leads from the tall grass south towards the old shopping center.

It is surrounded with vines, brushes and tall evergreens. Doubling back several times for long moments, the kidnappers stopped at various times, where no other movement occurred. The path ends close to the center's northern boundary. The path's stopping point has a time of 9:33 A.M.

Robert looks through his pilo.

Robert says, "It's in here somewhere.

"The seminar on lost children on that planet, Filmore, on the outer ridge. Of course!

"I'll call him, later. This is way beyond being a typical lost and found."

* * *

Walking through a long passage, the two guards approach an intersection with a protrusion jutting towards them. The first guard moves to the right of the protrusion and hands something to the second guard. The second guard walks around him and places an emblem within a relieved surface, where it seems to fit snugly. It snaps into place.

The second guard turns the emblem a quarter turn clockwise. He turns it back and removes the emblem.

A door opens, regressing and moving up into the ceiling. A stairwell appears before them, leading up into bright sunshine with a few clouds in the sky. They walk up the stairs as the hidden door comes back down, sealing against the wall to leave no discernable seam to indicate there ever was an entrance to the stairwell.

They arrive at the top of the stairwell at the lower terrace of the old city, where children, wearing white habits, frolic along the lower terraces, playing games. Stepping out of the stairwell, they walk to the walkway, between the east gate and the terrace steps.

They turn to the terrace steps, going up to the upper terrace. The steps continue to a great height above them.

The city has a total of nine terraces each five meters above the lower. After eight sets of steps, they arrive on the top terrace.

The second guard waits at the edge of the terrace, while the first guard bows his head and bends his knee as he approaches Ingrider Butler, his master. Ingrider doesn't acknowledge the guard at first.

The second guard pulls out his pilo and checks for new unread messages.

The guard's pilo displays, "Monday, June 7, 2483 11:30 A.M. Bridget, Diversity."

Not finding any new messages, he turns of his pilo and places it back in his pants.

Keeping his head bowed, the first guard kneels on one knee, when he gets within a meter of Ingrider's gold lined stone throne with a cantilevered overhang and a padded seat next to the circular hub, waiting for Ingrider to respond. Finally, he acknowledges the guard's presence by tilting up his right foot.

The first guard says, "The boy has been captured as per your instructions and we were not followed."

Ingrider says, "And the boys health? He must be in perfect condition. No scratches, no convulsions, no bumps or bruises. No sickness or ill health is upon him.

"No effects from the drug induced sleep. His mind is sound; he's not mindless. He's clean without any stains on his body?"

The first guard says, "He is in perfect health. We placed him in a maze cell as you requested. He was still asleep when we put him there. Your plan worked perfectly without a hitch. It was almost intentional."

"You've been a good and faithful follower. Has the helmet been put on his head?

"Yes, master and we waited until it was securely on, before we went into the maze as you suggested."

"That will keep our enemies on their toes.

"Now we just have to wait to see if they take the bait. Keep the boy moving between the old city and the shopping center. Keeping them confused is our best defense. And keeping our enemies confused is our best offense.

"Our plan has worked so far, but our enemies are clever and devious. We will have to watch carefully to keep them away from the final ceremony. Keep a watch around the clock at all levels of the terrace."

Afternoon

Karl walks through a long hallway which ends with a window at the end and another hallway heading right. Arriving at the window with a door to his left, he places his right hand next to the door. Inside his PAR, his monitor displays, "Monday, June 7, 2483 12:00 P.M. Prestige, Filmore."

The door closes automatically as Karl enters his room. He heads for the fridge and opens a beer, looks out the picture window and walks towards the sofa.

Sitting on the sofa, he brings up a video on his monitor with the remote.

It's a very old movie, starring Charles Bronson and Henry Fonda, *Once Upon a Time in the West*. Watching the opening gunfire, he sips his beer. He intently watches Henry Fonda's bad guy character kill the boy. Later Charles Bronson's character plays on a harmonica a song which upsets the bad guy, giving him all kinds of grief, throughout the movie. Until at the end, Henry Fonda is shot by Charles Bronson.

Charles Bronson places the harmonica in Henry Fonda's mouth and watches him.

At that point Henry finally remembers the song.

Later, the closing credits role, Karl lies down on the sofa on his right side, keeping his eyes open. On the coffee table, the beer box lies on its side empty with the cap hanging off the side.

Karl says, "Wake me at 3:00 P.M."

He closes his eyes.

The blinds close and the ceiling light panels dim and go out, leaving the under cabinet lights in the kitchen and the lights around the mirror in the bathroom.

* * *

Robert's office lights brighten as his shakes his head. His monitor displays, "Monday, June 7, 2483 3:10 P.M. Bridget, Diversity."

Robert sits at his desk with a few decorations for meritorious achievement as a cop, detective and chief hanging across the wall to his left.

Robert says, "Call Karl P. Perkins on the planet Filmore in the city of Prestige."

The monitor goes black for a second displaying, "Calling Mr. Perkins."

Robert's monitor displays Karl sitting on his sofa with a small bookshelf above his head with several e-books with his name on them.

Karl waves at Robert and smiles as he takes another sip of hot tea.

Karl asks, "Robert, it's been a few years. How are you and the kids? Are you running for Precinct Director this year? I've been meaning to ask you about Diversity and what life has been like on that planet?"

Robert says, "Hi, Karl. The kids and my wife are fine. I believe they're doing a little shopping for summer clothes.

"We're probably going on vacation, before school starts in the fall, during the break between quarters. I'm thinking about applying for the regional Directorship, but not this year.

"I thoroughly enjoyed your seminar. The two men that I brought to the seminar are applying your methods to all my regular officers in this district.

"They have been teaching my crew for the last several years since your seminar.

"Other districts have been making inquires and I've been handing out brochures. I'm not sure why but the northern regions seem much more interested.

"I've never seen so much activity from our younger generation except when the traveling circus comes to town.

"You're going to have to hire some assistance, or you're going to be working around the clock for a long time, probably the rest of your life.

"It almost seems like a revolution is taking place.

"I'm getting more reports of mischievousness in my monthly inquires.

"More districts are going to be sending groups of people your way for this lost children training.

"We've got inquiries from the other two planets, as well.

"There's a general unrest from this current generation of children, wanting to get away from their homes."

Karl asks, "But something else bothers you?"

Robert asks, "I have finally run into the type of case you described once.

"Where it is beyond my ability to track without the PID.

"I am desperately in need of your skills in this particular area where your expertise comes to mind.

"You discussed this in one of your sessions, but you didn't go into much detail.

"Especially, since a cult of religious fanatics may be behind this. Which means, I have a kidnapping case?"

* * *

In a semi dark passageway, a set of vertical bars secure the entrance to a small cave. A single light panel shines through the vertical bars onto a helmeted kid lying on the dirt floor. A dull black helmet covers his eyes and ears. The child sleeps peacefully even though he is sleeping on stones covered by dirt.

The sound of running water flows through piping above his head and then stops.

To the left of the opening, centered within a single stone, a small screen panel has six buttons in a hexagonal layout below it. The rest of the passageway is made of stones, concrete and loose dirt with the walls, ceiling and floor all the same length.

The cell's monitor displays, "Monday, June 7, 2483 3:20 P.M. Bridget, Diversity."

The kid awakens and quickly stands up.

He touches the helmet and tries to remove it.

It doesn't budge.

He tries again.

He tries twisting it off first to the left and then to the right, but it still doesn't budge. He bangs the back of the helmet against the cave wall to no avail.

Giving up that task, he touches the stone walls, determining the size and depth of each stone. He walks around the small cave till he reaches the vertical bars. He measures the width and depth of the cell.

He leans his helmet between two bars, resting for a moment.

Cliff asks, "Is anyone out there? Why are you doing this? I want my mom."

* * *

Robert's office lights dim slightly returning to normal operation. His monitor displays, "Monday, June 7, 2483 3:30 P.M. Bridget, Diversity."

Wearing his usual uniform, Robert looks fairly composed behind his desk; the way he pushes buttons on his pilo only shows his frustration level is increasing.

Sitting at his desk, Robert punches more buttons on his pilo, occasionally looking out the internal windows. His officers are gathered around their desks, shuffling paperwork, reading and writing with their pilos, leaving and returning from important investigations and appointments and lying back in their chairs for a quick nap. It's their normal routine without any variation among all of his officers. Some are more motivated than others and they are in the minority.

Robert commands, "Check the signal again. Are you sure it's his? He's moving all over the place, towards the old sacrificial tower and beyond.

"Then they reverse direction and head back towards the old shopping center.

"The cult is probably involved and that is not good. I couldn't imagine trying to take the boy away from that group. I don't have enough officers in this district."

Robert's monitor, using Robert's voice, says, "Rechecked signal several times.

"It is verifiably his even though intermittent.

"Cult involvement is highly suspect.

"Your consensus is correct. The cult has more followers and guards than there are officers in this particular district."

Robert asks, "Then why do they keep moving him all around the maze?

"Perhaps when Karl gets here, he will have a more complete explanation."

Robert commands, "He's been moved a dozen times.

"How many times has he been in the same place, not necessarily only one place?"

Robert's monitor says, "They come back to three particular sites every few times.

"It can only be surmised that they use a different direction to confuse someone, probably the child."

Robert stands, putting his hands on his hips. He looks out again at his officers working at their desks.

Robert commands, "Call Tarcey. She'll want to know Karl is coming and the cult's involvement with her son's kidnapping."

* * *

Karl faces the window with his back to his monitor. It displays, "Monday, June 7, 2483 3:30 P.M. Prestige, Filmore."

Standing in the center of the room, Karl looks at his pilo in his left hand.

He reads for a few minutes. He writes a note to himself as a reminder, before shutting off the pilo and placing it back in his pants pocket.

Karl says, "Arrange a flight schedule for tonight for Diversity. Get all the information on the cult, including its origin and leadership on Diversity.

"Find any parallels with the birth of Cliff up to the present time using all sources on the four planets.

"Get a timeline on the leader, his current whereabouts and number of followers.

"Look for other articles related to cults, sacrificial offerings and the previous civilization's library. At least, the translated parts that have been done."

Karl's monitor, using a computer male voice, says, "Processing. Approximately fifteen minutes duration."

He stops for a moment to collect his thoughts, knowing that this will not be one of his easier cases.

Karl takes a few steps to his closet. Bending over, he pulls out a plastic hardcase backpack and after placing it on the coffee table, he opens it.

He walks back to the closet, selecting clothes for the trip. He takes some shirts and pants from the closet and tosses them towards the backpack, sometimes missing.

When he has gotten enough for the trip, he stops and reaches for the chest of drawers. Opening one drawer and removing several small boxes, he carefully places each in outer side pockets of the backpack. Before placing the next to last box in an outer pocket, he opens the box and removes a round container like a pillbox.

The label says attack nanos 1000. He puts that pillbox back in the box and removes the last container. The label reads lock nanos 100.

Placing the boxes in the outer pocket, he stands and walks into the bathroom. Half a minute later, he returns with two bath towels, two hand towels and several washcloths along with a bag of toiletries.

He walks over to his backpack and dumps everything on the coffee table. He starts folding clothes into the front part. He folds pants first then shirts, rearranging them until half the front part is full.

After most of the clothes are in the bag except for t-shirts, underwear and socks, he places the towels and washcloths on top of his regular clothes.

He brings the back over the front.

He opens the secondary portion soft outer pocket. He places his t-shirts, underwear and socks along with the bag of toiletries in that compartment.

* * *

The lights in the maze passageway dim and then return to their normal brightness. The cell's monitor displays, "Monday, June 7, 2483 3:40 P.M. Bridget, Diversity."

Cliff sits with his back against the stone wall.

He turns his head towards the vertical bars. Footsteps get closer and louder.

Stopping, the first guard facing the panel pushes three buttons below a small screen.

The vertical bars slide up into the ceiling, leaving a couple of centimeters. Two guards in grey habits enter and grab Cliff.

The first guard leads and the second guard follows as Cliff walks between them out of the cave onto a stone pathway. The two guards march through the passageways, while Cliff has to practically run in order to keep up.

They travel through several semi-dark passages, before they arrive at another cave.

The second guard pushes three buttons on that control panel. The vertical bars slide up leaving only the tips showing. Likewise the holes in the bottom fill with a material similar to the dirt of the floor. The second guard and Cliff enter the cell. Cliff almost tumbles to the ground, but the guard catches him.

The second guard turns Cliff around, until he can get to the key hole in the back of the helmet. He takes the key out of his pants pocket.

The second guard puts the key in the back of the helmet and the helmet comes off.

He examines the helmet's core, looking at the small screen within. He notices Cliff rubbing his eyes. Satisfied with the outcome, the guard waits for Cliff to finish.

Cliff squints, rubbing his eyes.

The second guard replaces the helmet on Cliff and pulls out the key.

The second guard leaves. The vertical bars slide down.

The two guards march through the passageway, until their footsteps can no longer be heard.

Cliff listens for quite a while, before he makes any moves.

This cell has none of the usual sounds; it must be outside the old city.

Noticing that the sound of water dropping no longer occurs, Cliff feels certain he is in a different cell.

After verifying the stonework is different from the other cells, he listens quietly without moving.

He remains motionless, listening for any unusual sounds to help him identify where he might be within the maze.

Unfortunately, it is extremely quiet without any other sounds, especially of people. *The only place I could be would be under the old space port or the old city or the shopping center. I only know I'm somewhere in the maze that I've never been before.*

Cliff touches the cold stone walls. The stones remain the same size but their placement is different.

He traverses the wall until he has circled the room. This cave seems slightly larger. It's wider and deeper.

He lies down, sleeps and awakes as the process of movement, helmet removal and relocation repeats several times, leaving Cliff sleepless, tired, confused, until he arrives at the cell.

Each time, he repeats the measurement and sound signature of the specific cell he is in until he has the measurements in his head. After a dozen times, he is certain, he is randomly moving between three cells.

* * *

Tarcey quietly eats a breaded pork chop with peas and carrots at the breakfast table. She drinks from a half glass of wine.

The monitor displays and beeps, "Monday, June 7, 5:30 P.M. Bridget, Diversity"

A plate of green salad is positioned to her right.

She takes a sip of red wine and listens to the quietness throughout the house.

Two female Labrador retrievers come snapping at each other through the back door and sit quietly at her feet underneath the breakfast table.

She says, "It is definitely not the same without him.

"I hope they're treating him well and he's not making too much of a disturbance."

She finishes the pork chop, leaving some meat on the bone and vegetables. She munches on the green salad, occasionally sipping the wine.

After finishing the salad and the wine, she clears the table, putting all of the dishes in the dishwasher, which is currently empty. Breaking the pork chop bone into two, she throws both pieces into the dog's bowl between the cabinets and the refrigerator. She cleans up the rest of the kitchen, putting away all the utensils, pots and pans that have been cleaned. Using a dry cloth, she wipes every surface until they all shine.

She retires to the den, where she finds a good e-book and curls up on the window seat as she reads. A light panel comes on shining its light to fill the window seat. She adjusts her position and the light follows keeping her e-book bathed in white light. Settling down with one leg under, she finds her last place.

After devouring the bones, the two female Labrador retrievers follow her to the den and lay at the base of the window. She looks down, seeing them curled up, facing each other.

They in turn raise their heads and perk up their ears. They keep their eyes on Tarcey waiting for snacks or a head pat.

Putting the book down by her side, she says, "I'll bet Cliff is wishing he had you two with him. T and L, you are so good for that boy.

"He'd be way out of trouble.

"You're the ones who got him out of the river and wouldn't let him cross the rope bridge right before it fell into the water.

"A blessing in disguise.

"And you're missing him too.

"Cliff would do anything for you and you're just as likely to do the same for him. And you don't even know what I am talking about.

"You're quite the kind of companions I wish every child could have."

She picks up the e-book and returns to reading it.

The two dogs lower their ears and heads onto their front paws, keeping their eyes open.

She presses a button to turn the page.

About half way through the page she looks up and out the bay window.

In her peripheral vision, she sees a white streak through the back yard.

The dog's ears bristle.

They both jump and run out of the room to the back door. In a flash, they jump through the doggy door and run into the back yard, chasing some unfortunate jack rabbit out of the garden.

Minutes later both dogs return to lie at foot of the window seat as if nothing at all had happened. They aren't even winded.

They face each other with heads on their front paws.

On the other side of the hedge, the jack rabbit huffs and puffs trying not to be frightened out of its skin.

Evening

Robert's office lights remain bright while the rest of the office space lights are dimmed to the lowest setting. His monitor displays, "Monday, June 7, 2483 6:00 P.M. Bridget, Diversity."

Robert sits at his desk watching his monitor display the old terraced city.

Robert commands, "Come in closer on the three lower levels at the east gate."

The monitor zooms in to the indicated area.

A quarter of the lower three hexagonal terraces fills the screen with a quarter of the circular wall around the lowest. Students in white habits are eating dinner at tables all around the lower three terraces.

Two guards watch outside the gate, while two others eat with the students. Older students wait for drink refills and clearing plates. Those students that have finished their meal gather together to play games within the confining spaces on the terraces between the gardens and the habitats. As the last of the students leave the tables, the older students clear the tables, including the table cloths and return everything to the closest habitat. Next the empty tables are folded and brought to the same habitat.

The terraces are cleaned of the usual scatterings of trash from eating, snacking and the usual leaves and flower petals. All of the garbage is taken inside each of the habitats on each level. Soon each terrace level is once again pristine.

A few students get books out of their habitats and walk over to the water falls, sitting near the gardens, where they can smell the fragrances of wild flowers.

The rest of the students play quietly with marbles, jacks, dominoes or cards. Even the ones playing rowdy games do so quietly without all of the usual yelling and laughing.

The east gate opens and two guards go out to relieve the two standing guards. The four guards exchange information with two signing in and two signing out. The other two guards return to the habitat, removing their outer clothing, washing up and grabbing a bite from the pots and pans on low heat.

Robert says, "Looks normal to me. No sign of the boy or any activity that would be out of place.

"He must be in the maze. This is going to be a rough and tumble extraction."

Robert commands, "Zoom out to the top of the hub."

The monitor zooms out to the indicated area.

It displays the circular hub top with banners between the six indices. Red sash acolytes busily remove accumulations of leaves, needles, bird droppings and the occasional nests displaced by the wind and rain.

Filled garbage bags are handed to white habited acolytes at the top of the stairs. The unadorned white habited acolytes walk down the outer stairs around the circumference of the hub to the upper terrace. They return with fresh black bags, walking out of the hub entrance, up the outer steps and back to the top deck of the hub where the bags are refilled. This continues until the top and inside of the hub is just as clean as the outside terraces.

More in depth cleaning occurs around the central stone. A couple of red sash acolytes clean the knives laid out on the top of the stone, while another sharpens the knives, using a whetting stone and a small bottle of water. After one knife is sharpened to his satisfaction, he returns the knife to the top of the stone.

One on each side cleans out the grooves in the stone, removing any accumulations.

*   *   *

The lights within Tarcey's house brighten with the waning sunlight. The kitchen console monitor displays, "Monday, June 7, 2483 6:30 P.M. Bridget, Diversity."

The sun sets in the west with several high clouds, looking like they are chasing it.

The waning sun's warm orange glow on the few clouds casts long indistinct shadows throughout the kitchen as Tarcey washes her hands in the kitchen sink. She turns off the water and dries her hands on a towel from the counter.

Wearing a blue taffeta blouse with white pants, she turns to face the kitchen's console monitor.

Tarcey commands, "Call Robert."

Robert appears behind his office desk, clearing paperwork off the desk and dumping it into a drawer.

Robert asks, "Tarcey, something come up?"

Tarcey asks, "No, but I've been thinking about this cult.

"Why now? It doesn't make any sense.

"Wouldn't they have done this earlier, like when he was one or two? I can't imagine why this birthday is so different from the earlier ones.

"His sixth birthday comes Saturday. I have certain plans in place. What would they do to him?"

Robert responds, "Good questions. I don't have all the answers and I have more questions than you do.

"This cult is very mysterious. It so happens that I became aware of it about the same time that Cliff was born. The cult recently started doing animal sacrifices, which is still allowable in their charter.

"Of course, those are only small animals like rabbits and squirrels.

"Occasionally, they have requested larger species, like goats and lambs.

"The council has approved almost all their requests on a case by case basis."

Tarcey asks, "They're certainly not going to sacrifice Cliff.

"That's not in their charter. Tell me more about this Karl and why you think he can find Cliff?"

Robert says, "Karl is a former highly decorated policeman with over forty-five years' service finding lost children. I knew him several years ago.

"Over the past twenty years, he has rescued more than a thousand lost children not all of which are returned to their original parents or guardian.

"He has written several books and conducts seminars year round on all four planetary systems.

"He currently is freelancing as a private detective for lost children not all of which are runaways.

"He is the best man for this job.

"And he happens to be the only one on the four planets with his expertise."

* * *

The passageway lights dim to a lower setting while still keeping a minimal light level. The cell's monitor displays, "Monday, June 7, 2483 7:45 P.M. Bridget, Diversity."

Cliff sits on the dirt floor, listening to water drops echoing in the stone passageway outside his cave cell. Two sets of footsteps come from his right.

He crawls to the bars and puts his helmet against them.

The first guard asks, "Up to the very top this time?"

The second guard answers, "That's what the chief wants.

"Training for those elite red sashes and the guards. He's expecting trouble and wants absolute readiness."

The first guard says, "That's what I thought. The real deal happens Saturday."

Cliff scoots back to the cell's wall as the steps get closer.

He lies down, pretending to sleep, keeping his hands between his legs. The bars slide up and two guards enter the cave.

The first guard says, "Wake up!"

The second guard grabs Cliff by the arm and lifts him up. Cliff stands acting groggily. The first guard shoves Cliff through the opening and leads him along the stone path. Cliff resists by stumbling at every chance. The second guard follows, punching Cliff occasionally.

Cliff's legs move twice as fast as the two guards and he is always out of step with them. He acts more tired than he really is. They walk past several intersections, occasionally turning right.

They stop at a "T" intersection with a protuberance, jutting into their passageway. The second guard removes something from his pocket, handing it to the first guard.

The first guard walks past the right side of the protuberance to the left of the slanted wall. He stops at that point and puts his left hand on the stone surface.

Cliff notices a different smell. At first it doesn't register and then he remembers it being similar to his mother's garden.

The first guard touches the surface, trying to find an indented space about eye level on his left side.

Keeping his right hand in the depression, he brings the hexagon shaped emblem up to the depression.

The first guard places the emblem on the stone wall in a recess to his left. It clicks into place. He turns the emblem ninety degrees clockwise. The door to the right regresses several centimeters. It slides up into the ceiling, revealing a rising stairway open to the dark sky above.

They walk up the stairs.

The door closes behind them, sealing the entrance as if no seam could be found. Likewise, the stone work slides into place over the stairway sealing the edge leaving no trace of a seam. No seems to notice as the guards and Cliff come out of the stairway as if it were perfectly normal for guards to enter or exit the stairway even though many don't know how the opening works.

* * *

The two guards and Cliff walk out of the maze into a night sky filled with stars and two full moons, barely peaking above the horizon. They arrive at the lower end of a high walled circular terraced complex with a central hub tower high above them.

Each of the eight terraces above the lower terrace is five meters high with five meter high habitats near each set of terrace stairs opposite the water falls beside the steps.

The stairs come out five meters from the previous level. The sides of the hexagon are one hundred and eighty meters on the lowest level decreasing by twenty meters, until the sides of the top terrace are twenty meters. Each level juts out ten meters over the lower, providing some shade except for the top terrace which has awnings on the longer side of the habitat.

Several single story habitats dot the terraces especially near the terrace steps.

The habitats come out of the terrace above them, except on the top terrace, five meters and extend under the terrace above them another fifteen meters.

The habitats height is the same as the terraces, providing room on the top for gardens. On the top terrace, one habitat exists for each of the six indices of the hexagon. The habitats provide sleeping quarters, dining facilities and training rooms.

A single wooden door to the left of center on the outer wall provides an entrance. A single arched window centered on the outer wall provides most of the interior light.

Two tall narrow four pane windows on each side are arranged offset so that the one near the outer wall is higher. The two side windows have blinds which restrict the light coming through them from the outside.

Continuing their procession, the trio walks up the terrace steps to the top terrace and on to the hub. The lead guard turns left and follows the steps around the hub, heading up the steps.

Pushed by the second guard, Cliff stumbles, regains his posture and continues up the hub steps. As they reach the top, a group of people in white habits and red sashes surround the central stone. Brought to the central stone, Cliff stops near the middle. A bird chirps as the wind rustles various habits. Lifted by two red sash acolytes and placed prone on his back, Cliff lies on a flat oval stone shaped as an elongated Omega symbol.

The two red sash acolytes return to their positions around the stone.

The guards head back down the stairs.

Cliff remains quiet, listening to his surroundings and to the touch of wind on his garments. The red sash acolytes circle the stone clockwise, chanting. The chant increases in volume as two full moons finally rise above the horizon.

When the two full moons rise above the horizon, the chant reaches a crescendo. A bell chimes.

Cliff feels a chill go through him.

Something wet with a funny smell lands on his mouth. He recognizes the smell from being kidnapped in the tall grass. In spite of the noxious smell, he remembers the smell of evergreens.

Soon he is asleep. His arms fall to his side as the red sash acolytes look directly at his form.

* * *

With the setting sun, several PAR's lights brighten including Karl's. His monitor displays, "Monday, June 7, 2483 8:00 P.M. Prestige, Filmore."

Sitting on his sofa with his pilo in his right hand, Karl scrolls through the text.

He says, "This is getting more and more interesting.

"Ingrider Butler is a very charming fellow with a sharp change in personality around the time that Cliff was born.

"Well enough of this for now. I'll make some notes and do some follow up on the space fight to Diversity. This is going to require many resources and quite a few officers. I wonder if Robert has considered that yet.

"I'll have to remind him that I can only do so much."

Karl takes another sip of hot tea as he relaxes back on his sofa as he thinks about something to reset his mind.

He commands, "Monitor, let's have some entertainment.

"With my mood right now I need some comedy."

He lays the pilo on the coffee table as it performs an outline consensus with notation from all the material gathered related to the boy.

The monitor displays a current film from his collection. The opening credits rolls over a scene of a normal city morning.

It has chosen a comedy about two garbage men and the cash they recover which gives them all kinds of trouble. It's more of a tragic comedy with an emphasis on material gains.

Later as the credits role, Karl turns off the monitor with his pilo. He places the pilo on his coffee table and then picks it up again. He stops for a moment to collect his thoughts and get his mind on duties at hand.

He looks over the results of the pilo's consensus.

He reviews the data, makes a few changes and adds a couple more notations for his own benefit.

He says, "He's concentrated his forces at the old city. Along with a bunch of students which I am not sure of.

"I'll have to work at getting in and out through the maze. Unfortunately, the library doesn't have enough information about the maze. Whatever it was for, it has long since survived its purpose. The old shopping center will have to be studied as well. So much is unknown and will require a lot of searching most of which will be right under their noses. It will take all of my resources, more so, than any other situation that I have ever been in. However, I can never pass up a challenge."

Karl reviews more of the material, until he notices the time.

Karl's monitor displays, "Monday, June 7, 2483 10:00 P.M. Prestige, Filmore."

Karl says, "Wow, how time flies. Good thing I'm already packed. I have to be at the space port at 11:30 P.M. I have enough time to freshen up and get on the subway."

He turns off his pilo and puts it in his pants pocket.

He stands and walks into the bathroom, removing his shirt.

He comes out of the bathroom freshly scrubbed in a light green robe. He walks past the monitor over to the closet and selects a shirt and tie along with a nice suit.

After dressing and putting on his best black shoes, he goes back to the bathroom.

Karl comes out of the bathroom with his pilo in his right hand with his hair trimmed and freshly shaved.

He checks his schedule on the pilo, turns off his pilo, places it in his pants pocket, and swings his backpack onto his back. He adjusts the back straps and the waist band until he has the backpack comfortably on his back. He reaches back with his right hand until he can feel his pilo in its pocket.

He fastens the straps and walks out through the doorway, which opens automatically and turns right.

Several stairs and passageways later, Karl arrives at the subway station. A train moves out before he gets to the gate. He puts his card in the slot and removes the slip acknowledging his ticket. The next train to the space port pulls into the station.

Karl climbs aboard when the doors open automatically. He finds a seat and settles down for the quick trip to the space port. A half a minute later the doors open and the few passengers disembark heading to the shuttle gateway.

Most head for the commercial shuttles which transport the business people to meetings and conferences on the space platforms that the companies maintain for offloading and on loading various materials from the moon and the asteroids.

Karl finds the shuttle he is looking for among the few public space platforms for space liners docking, transferring cargo or taking on cargo for one of the planets in the other three solar systems. The space liners are so much larger than the shuttles, there is not enough room for more than two to dock and then only at the two outer lying docks which were made especially for the space liners.

Shuttles also arrive and dock at the space station from trips to Filmore's moon or the fourth planet which are major jump points for travel. Scientists are usually the only passengers to the moon or the fourth planet. A few undertake journeys to the two inner planets without landing on either, but rather to relieve persons who are needed elsewhere.

After sticking his card in the appropriate slot and selecting the correct itinerary, Karl takes his shuttle ticket to the waiting area where he takes a seat and waits for the shuttle to be prepped.

Soon Karl is resting onboard the shuttle which is on its way to rendezvous with a freightliner.

TUESDAY

Morning

The freightliner jumps through various points in space, some near planetary bodies where supplies are exchanged, others near plasma infused clouds where it refuels and more jumps to empty space. Meanwhile, inside Karl's assigned space, his cabin's monitor displays, "Tuesday, June 8, 2483 7:30 A.M. Konectidy, Freightliner #43."

Coming out of the bathroom, freshly shaved and showered, in his underwear, Karl walks towards a soft brown pin-cushioned bench. A grey suit, pale brown shirt and abstract tie rest on its back. Through the three oval portals, the stars whiz by like streaks of lightening. As he sits, he brings up his monitor's analysis on his pilo which lies on the side table next to the bench. While dressing, he reads his pilo.

Karl's pilo displays, "The cult started by Ingrider Butler a week after Cliff's birth a former pastor of a minor religion in the northern region.

"In the five years, he has amassed about three hundred followers, although that number could be much higher.

"He traveled extensively around the planet, visiting every major city especially the ports along the coast.

"Ingrider has groups in all of the cities on Diversity with his red sash acolytes ministering to even more.

"Current translations of the library on Diversity show a parallel with sacrificial offerings. Apparently, a religion conceived by an undetectable rogue computer which promoted itself as their absolute leader. The reason for the mass exodus is unknown; the libraries last entry doesn't mention anything about the exodus."

The cabin's monitor, using a female voice, says, "Breakfast is being served on level three for all passengers.

"Currently, the ship is on schedule to arrive at Diversity's Space Station in approximately twenty-two hours.

"We also have routine scheduled stops for plasma replenishment which are already allocated in our time frame."

The monitor displays a map of Karl's current location and the fastest route to the mess hall which is one deck lower. Karl takes a quick glance and points his pilo at the monitor. He presses a button and the map is transferred to his pilo. He looks over his pilo one more time, getting the path in his head, realizing that his pilo could guide him. He saves the map to his pilo's memory.

Placing the pilo in his pocket, Karl walks to the hatch which opens automatically to a "T" hallway. Once he has cleared the doorway, the hatch closes behind him. He turns right and heads down the passageway, following the path as he occasionally brings out his pilo to check his memory. Once he gets to the central corridor of the ship, he turns left and follows the signs to the mess hall where all the noise is coming from.

He finds a table where the rest of the passengers are sitting. He grabs a tray and begins making his selections. When his tray is full, he finds an empty table and sits down. Several groups of people, including the off-duty crew in their obvious attire while the rest of the passengers wear standard issue.

* * *

The passageway lights remain dimmed before brightening for the new day. Quiet rules for the time being. The nearby cell's monitor displays, "Tuesday, June 8, 2483 7:30 A.M. Bridget, Diversity."

Cliff awakens startled. Getting up quickly from the shadow and walking into the light, he wears a black habit with a white emblem over his heart and stands on bare feet. He shivers. As soon as the shivering stops, Cliff traces the emblem with his right hand.

He tries to put either hand between the helmet and his jaw bone. No go. He tries the back without success. He gets two fingers, up either side of his nose, to the ridge between his eyes where the constriction is too tight.

He touches all his limbs, his chest and his neck feeling the length of the sleeves and the length of the habit at the hem. Startled, he stands quietly. Only water dripping on stone breaks the silence and that is very intermittent. He walks over to the bars placing his helmet against them. Distressed, he moves back and heads for the deepest darkest shadow in the cave. He stands for a moment going over all the details that he can remember about his kidnapping. He's still puzzled by the ease with which he was caught.

When he feels he had done nothing wrong, he becomes tired and ready for sleep, but he knows that won't happen.

Down on his knees, Cliff turns his right side, twists his hips and falls on the dirt floor, cushioning his fall with his hands and knees. He slows his breathing until he looks like he is sleeping. He twitches slightly, keeping his hands between his legs. He keeps his eyes closed even though the guards can't see his eyes because of the helmet.

The sound of multiple footsteps on stone comes quickly to his cave. The two guards stop by the control panel; the bars slide up. After entering the cell, the second guard lifts Cliff to his feet by his left arm. Straightening up, Cliff marches out of the cell. He hears the cell bars close behind him. Sensing the second guard behind him, Cliff hurries to catch up to the first guard.

Like before, the three go in several directions, arriving at another cell. Inside the cell, the second guard removes the helmet. Cliff doesn't even try to open his eyes. Replacing the helmet, the guards leave and the bars come down. The footsteps dim quickly as the guards turn right at the next intersection. After moving into the right back corner, Cliff sinks into the dirt floor and tries to go to sleep. This time he doesn't have to fake it. He no longer cares if they come to wake him up; he's too tired to care. After turning over several times, he finally drifts into sleep.

His present cell remains unusually quite from the other two. No water runs or drip. The mice remain quiet as well as any other animals. The outer lights in the passageway dim slowly until shadows are distinct. Even the passageway remains free of distant footsteps. Inside the cell, Cliff sleeps soundly.

* * *

Robert pauses for a moment as he sits at his desk. He looks through the windows to the many officers working at their desk. His monitor displays, "Tuesday, June 8, 2483 8:30 A.M. Bridget, Diversity."

Robert reads from his pilo.

Robert's pilo displays, "The leader of the cult disappeared last night out of the city of Presevo, southwest of Bridget where he had been conducting a three day seminar on his new religion and interviewing new acolytes.

"He was last seen south of Bridget near the derelict shopping center where he disappeared again without a trace. He was last seen in the central room of the center.

"A contingent of his followers masses in the hundreds at an old city/worship center southeast of Bridget. Most of the members are less than sixteen years of age, but he has plenty of his older acolytes with more experience. A major force of guards has arrived at the old city primarily guarding the outer gates and each of the terraces.

"No one has been near that area for fifty years except for archeologists, relic collectors and a few unscrupulous thieves. Ingrider signed a lease for ten years covering the derelict shopping center, but not with his name. We are following an extreme internet path to find which company has the actual lease. At this time, Ingrider has multiple companies, but not with the same name and none of them would appear to be the controlling company.

"The acolytes are busily cleaning the terraces and habitats of rats, dust and the remains of vagrants. They're bringing in supplies by the ton. With the amount of arriving food, they will be staying for more than a week.

"New flower starts, bushes and small trees are being planted in the old discarded gardens. Bark has been added to cover the ground around the plants.

"They've got the pumps restarted which enables water to flow down the terraces to all the garden areas to pool at the lower level before being brought back up the central hub to the upper terrace where the action repeats.

"Red sashes work within the central hub, removing broken branches, mounds of leaves, assorted bird's nests and dust collecting in all the corners from the inside and more flotsam from the outside which they bring through the entrance.

"The city terraces gleam and sparkle with their hard work. Habitats are now set up for education classes primarily on the three lower levels where acolytes rush to enter.

"The upper levels house the teachers which, in turn, have vacated and are busy preparing their classrooms and their libraries. They must be preparing for another one of their ceremonies which have been repeatedly done in the southern regions of Diversity, although the city council has yet not received any request for a permit. And the city council is a little miffed."

Robert says, "I want the leader's appointments and locations for the last three days. Do the same for his top twenty minions, the red sashes, who do all the work.

"Establish a fly-over with zoom, radar and infrared capability of the old city especially near the hub in silent mode every two hours. Find out what they are preparing and how soon it will happen. We have to get a handle on what their plans are since I have been unable to get an officer to infiltrate their organization. They are very thorough."

Robert's monitor says, "Processing requires about ten minutes. Where do you want the reports to go?"

Robert says, "Send the reports to my pilo. Provide both detail and summary."

* * *

The freightliner comes out of a jump into the black of space and a moment later enters another jump. The action is so smooth the passengers and crew don't even know. Karl's cabin monitor displays, "Tuesday, June 8, 2483 9:30 A.M. Konectidy, Freightliner #43."

Karl sits on a black bench in his room on the freightliner looking at the various pictures cycling through his monitor. The last few have been pictures of the north pacific continent of

Diversity. Various scenes of city layouts, mountains, deserts and the space port have highlighted the layout of the population.

Karl looks up at the time on the monitor, rubbing his forehead with his right hand.

Karl commands, "Call Robert, the Police Chief in Bridget."

The monitor fades quickly to black. A second later, Robert, at his desk, appears on the room's monitor across from the bench.

Robert asks, "Karl how's the flight?"

Karl asks, "So far very pleasant. And Cliff?"

Robert says, "I keep getting intermittent signals from his PID similar to what you described in one of your seminars as interference, something about a shielded helmet."

Karl asks, "Based on the information I have about the leader, anything is possible.

"However, I would expect something like that. They almost always repeat themselves or keep their prisoner in one place once the novelty has worn off. If you keep contact, we'll have a much better time trying to find him in a maze.

"What is Cliff's general location and status?"

Robert says, "There's a derelict shopping center, hasn't been used since we colonized this planet. It looks like they keep moving him through the maze towards the center and then back towards the old city, between primarily three cells.

"His status is normal, except for a slight lowering of skin temperature earlier this morning. The monitor states a change in clothing has occurred, but no reason is given. His other signs are within normal ranges except for higher adrenaline due to stress. Breath and pulse rate are within normal ranges.

"Based on the elevation, he's in a maze below the shopping center. My guess, it was used for supplies, at one time. The library does not have a complete map of the maze which I have always wondered about. They have all kinds of patterns for cities, schools and parks, as well as nano procedures for building each, but for some odd reason only a small section of the map of the maze."

"That means he must have read one of my e-books or, perhaps, one of his acolytes or guards has attended my seminars. Moving him around three different cells means he will be harder to extract. They could be moving him while I'm entering the maze elsewhere. The number of moves and the amount of guards in the various areas precludes getting him out of the maze, but the same can be said for the shopping center or the old city. This is not going to be easy," says Karl.

Afternoon

The steps echo through the passageway increasing in volume. Cliff's cell monitor displays, "Tuesday, June 8, 2483 12:00 P.M. Bridget, Diversity."

Standing, Cliff moves away from the bars and sits on the dirt floor, waiting for the expected guards. As usual, it doesn't take long, so they must not be too far away.

Footsteps come closer, only one set this time, which doesn't entirely surprise Cliff since the arrival of his breakfast early in the morning. Never sure of the time, his stomach seems to want another meal. He hopes they don't have any children of their own, otherwise, they would always come in twos.

The first guard says, "Here's your noon meal. A little chicken soup and half a tuna fish sandwich. Mm, very tasty.

"If you don't care for it let me know. There are many guards and acolytes who would love to gobble this up."

The bars slide up half a meter. Kneeling on both knees, the guard places the tray inside the cell on the dirt floor, sliding it a little past the bars. The guard stands, moving over to the controls as the bars come down. The guard walks back the way he came not quite marching but rather falling into the cadence from habit.

Cliff waits in the corner until the guard's footsteps can no longer be heard. He goes over the timing of the guard's actions from the time the bars went up to the time he stood after placing the tray on the ground. He uses his fingers to keep the time until he feels his plan will work. He meticulously goes over each detail until he is satisfied that he could do it blind.

Standing, he walks to the middle of the bars and bends down to grab the tray. Cliff brings the tray to the back of the cave.

He carefully sits down without tipping the tray. He puts the tray on top of his outstretched legs.

Finding the spoon, he tastes the soup. He shovels the soup into his mouth as fast as he can.

When the spoon doesn't pick up any more, he tilts the bowl, bringing the front edge right up to the helmet into his mouth and slurps the rest. After licking his lips, he places the bowl back on the tray. He feels around for the sandwich finally touching it in the far corner of the tray.

He grabs the sandwich and takes a small bite savoring the taste which isn't quite like his mother's but he decides he likes it. Swallowing slowly, he enjoys the taste of onions, celery, tomatoes and mayonnaise. Then he gobbles it in seconds, stuffing his mouth, which he enjoys immensely. When his mouth is empty, he finds the water box in the corner of the tray. Using two hands, he pops the corner of the box and tastes it first before taking a gulp and washing his face.

When finished, he walks to the middle of the bars, directly across from the passageway panel light. Cliff places the tray back against the bars on the dirt floor. After walking to the corner of the back wall, carefully counting the number of steps, he sits down against the back wall, contemplating his predicament and his many opportunities for escape. He's pretty sure that while the routes are random, the cells are the same in three different cases. At least the smells and sounds are the same in each case.

* * *

O utside the kitchen windows, Tarcey sits in the grass close to the garden. Inside the house, the kitchen's console monitor displays, "Tuesday, June 8, 2483 1:30 P.M. Bridget, Diversity."

Wearing a pastel cyan blouse and black pants with blue knee pads and dirty yellow loafers, Tarcey scrapes the ground with a three tine rake around a small tree and two smaller bushes on one side of the tree and two others on the other side. After pulling the dead leaves, broken branches and stalks towards the edge of the grass, she places the rake on the grass and sinks gently to the dirt on her knee pads.

She pulls weeds and dead leaves off the plants, and trims branches from her flowers, bushes and trees. Removing the handle, she uses the three tine rake to aerate the ground around her primrose, black-eyed susan and upright sedum, the boxwood, camellia and lavender which surround and intersperse the four bushes and the small tree.

After reattaching the handle, she stands, picks up the rake and walks over to a bush of flowers surrounding a single rose bloom. She kneels placing the rake to her side on the ground. For a moment, she does nothing else except stare at the single rose.

Tarcey asks, "How did a single crimson rose get surrounded by my much larger *Festiva Maxima* with the white flowers and crimson flakes around the edges?

"You look so out of place and lonely. I'll get you out of that bush and place you where you belong with the rest of your family. Although, it will take a lot of work to extricate you out of those bushes. It's a wonder you even made it to the surface. I'll have to remember to use my thicker gloves.

"I've looked after you with water, nutrients and care.

"My lost son is now surrounded by hundreds of fanatics. What are they intending to do to you?

"I will look after you, clothe you, feed you and watch over you, at least until you're eighteen.

"Return and I will give you the biggest birthday party you have ever had.

"Hopefully, that will be this Saturday."

She pulls another weed and continues to rake the ground, tilling the soil until rich dark brown replaces the lighter compacted tan mixing the nutrients which she had previously added on top of the packed soil. She scatters multi-hued bark over the ground until it is entirely covered.

Evening

The passageway's quiet is broken by distant footsteps. The lights are dimmed to indicate night time. The nearby cell's monitor displays, "Tuesday, June 8, 2483 7:00 P.M. Bridget, Diversity."

Cliff sits in the dirt with his back against the stone wall waiting for the arrival of the guard whose coming footsteps echo throughout the passageway, now far away, but getting ever closer.

His legs are stretched straight out in front of him. He clasps his hands together on his lap as if holding something between them. He waits, going over his plan step by step, until he can do it blindfolded which he happens to be with the helmet blocking his view. While going through the steps the third time, he hears footsteps coming.

The footsteps get closer and stop. The bars go up half a meter. The guard comes to the middle of the cell bars below the light panel casting his shadow into the cell along with the tray between his hands.

The first guard says, "Here's your evening meal. A little roast beef in gravy with mashed potatoes and carrots. Enjoy and if you don't, my second will be more than happy to have another meal. He's always hungry."

Kneeling, the guard slides the tray into the cell and begins to get up on his feet, one leg at time. He stops before getting to his feet. The boy is moving towards him and this has never happened before. He remains suspicious. The guard watches his every move trying to figure out what the boy is up to. But, he becomes distracted when the boy speaks.

Barely moving, Cliff asks, "I found something. Would you like to see?"

Lowering himself back to kneeling, the guard looks up from the tray. Getting up off the ground, Cliff walks right up to the bars to the left side of the tray. Cliff raises his hands up slightly above his mouth, tilting his head back ever so vaguely. He turns a little to face the guard whose eyes follow every move the boy makes. The guard follows Cliff's hands as they move towards him and the cell bars.

The first guard asks, "Well, what is it? I don't have all day."

Cliff opens his mouth and opens his hands somewhat flat.

Slowly taking a deep breath, Cliff continues to open his hands to a clump of dry dirt which quickly loosens and falls apart into small clumps onto his open palms with lots of loose dirt between. The always on-guard first guard looks at the loose dirt and clumps wanting to believe something is there, trying to find something in the dirt that's important, realizing that this is a diversion, but before he can speak, Cliff does something totally unexpected. Cliff blows the dirt, sending it into the face of the first guard. An instant later the first guard's face is plastered in dirt.

The cursing guard falls backward, losing his balance, striking his head on the stone surface which yields further cursing, trying to brush the dirt from his face and out of his stinging eyes.

The guard keeps his knees up in his face to keep further dirt from landing in his face

Grabbing the lower edges of two of the bars, Cliff slides under them on his feet to the outside of the cell. He straightens up, listens both ways and makes his decision. He races to his right, past the guard's flailing feet, disappearing into the darkness of the maze. He continues to run noting his steps and turning at appropriate intersections which he finds with his fingertips carefully listening at all the passages before proceeding until he arrives at his destination.

Before proceeding into the corridor, he listens to the sounds from the far end where more activity takes place at irregular occurrences. He follows the path in his head, stopping before every intersection no matter how insignificance, listening for the guard's footsteps or conversation.

Later, he arrives at the final intersection where the crossover to the south leads to his destination.

* * *

Robert sits behind his cleared desk looking at his pilo in front of him. He pushes buttons and the text scrolls up or down depending on which button was pushed. His office monitor displays, "Tuesday, June 8, 2483, 7:20 p.m. Bridget, Diversity"

He gets to the end of the text and pushes save on his pilo. He reads the last few sentences once more.

Turning off his pilo, he puts it in his upper right drawer. He sits back with his arms across his chest, pondering what he has read and how much he actually understands.

"I should never have let this get out of hand. The reports came regularly, but I ignored them. How foolish I've been. Well, now's not the time to feel sorry for something that I've already done and can't change. I shouldn't feel that way but it doesn't stop me from going through the emotions.

"It's going to get very hectic round here, until that boy is found. We only have so many days. Karl came up with some good ones though, so if we stick to it, our odds get better and better.

"Good thing he is so resourceful; I couldn't have thought of half of the things he has already done.

"Well, enough for today, we'll start early in the morning. Maybe, just maybe, we can solve this case before Ingrider and his guards get too involved."

He stands, pushing the chair behind him with his knees. Walking over to the door, he goes through and turns around. Closing the door, he listens as it latches.

Without his hand on the lever, after taking the key out of his back pocket, he pushes it into the deadbolt lock and then looks up. The lights are still on in his office.

Muttering to himself, he removes the key and opens the door. He says, "Lights off."

The lights dim until they are completely out, plunging the room into darkness except for the starlight which appears on the opposite windows displaying dust particles swirling through the air. Robert closes the door and locks it with the key. He turns toward the entrance through a now darkened Police Station. He can see no vehicles in the field outside except for his own flighter with its distinctive markings. He opens the outer doors after setting the alarm for the night crew. He walks down the steps and out into the field towards his flighter.

* * *

Hidden within a declivity in the passageway, Cliff listens as voices get louder. The stairwell's monitor displays, "Tuesday, June 8, 2483 7:20 P.M. Bridget, Diversity."

Cliff waits in a dark declivity in the left wall of the passageway meters from an intersection outside the secret stairwell to the old city.

The door to the stairwell has opened several times with guards and white habited acolytes walking right past him. He's on the long arm of the tee where he can hear the door regress away from the stone surface and slide up into the ceiling, the guards in the passageways and the acolytes who are assigned to the guards.

His black habit and helmet make him almost invisible in shadow. He has rubbed dirt over his chin, neck, hands and feet to further darken his light skin. Only his blue eyes would betray him, but the helmet already hides his eyes. The white emblem on his habit luckily doesn't glow in the dark and therefore doesn't give him away either. The guards and acolytes wouldn't even notice since they aren't looking for him to be there.

The door opens and a tall male acolyte with a male guard come out walking down the long arc of the tee. They are followed by two slightly younger female acolytes with another female guard and male acolyte bringing up the rear. They carry on a conversation concerning the ceremony that had begun on the lower terrace. They stop five meters past Cliff's position. The tall acolyte turns around as the young acolyte asks a question. "You must be fairly recent to this facility, because your question is the major reason we're here," he replies.

"Honored sir, I did not mean to offend. I was only curious and, yes, I arrived yesterday afternoon from one of the southern regions. I'm still getting acclimated. This is the first time I have been to this location."

"Then allow me the pleasure to answer your question. The boy is to be sacrificed in order to appease our master's wishes."

"When will that happen?"

"All preparations are leading up to the ceremony on Saturday evening.

"Rising above the horizon, the two moons escape the planet's grasp."

"I have been teaching and ministering to the young in the cities for the last two years. This will be my first time to attend a major sacrifice. This will be an enriching experience that I wasn't expecting so soon."

The tall acolyte turns around and the conversation turns to the various preparations taking place as they walk into the darkness of the maze. Soon their conversation has diminished to nothing and he can't even hear their footsteps.

Finally, the door to the stairwell stays open, hesitating for a few moments before beginning to close. He listens for only a moment before making his decision. Timing his entrance and carefully listening, Cliff rushes through the thinning opening and up the stairs mindful that someone could be coming down, but he doesn't hear anyone else on the steps.

* * *

Robert walks down his hallway and into his bedroom. He stands in his bedroom near the bed, packing his hardcase backpack which lies open on his queen sized bed. Most of the backpack is empty waiting for additional items to fill its empty spaces.

The room's three walls are painted a light aqua with the bathroom and closet wall painted flat black with mirrors across the wall making the room seem twice the size. The ceiling is composed of light panels with only the outer edges dimmed half way. The quilted down cover on the bed in green and blue triangles contrasts with the white tufted rug with a border of dark brown and deep green checker boards. The wall skirting uses the deep shade of green as the rug.

The backpack lies on the bed, open and half packed. Outside the faux bedroom window, the dark sky has a few clouds obscuring the stars with two moons shining between clouds. The clouds aren't moving but the stars are rotating around the axis of the planet bringing galaxies and clusters into view.

No other monitor or window is on any other wall of the bedroom. The faux window is really a plain monitor with picture capability when required.

After walking into the walk-in closet, he grabs a couple small boxes from a drawer in a white chest of drawers, walks back to the bedroom and puts them in side pockets of the backpack, packing them in tightly until bursting full. He zippers close all of the outer pockets.

He walks back into the walk-in closet. He opens the third drawer of a chest of drawers. A knife with a long broad blade and mother of pearl handle lies in the bottom. He starts to grab it and then releases. Closing the third drawer, he turns to the backpack on the bed.

After taking a few steps, he stops in mid stride, turns around, walks back to the dresser and opens the same drawer. He removes the knife carrying it by the handle, walks to the backpack and secures it in a scabbard on the back, fastening the Velcro strap around the handle to keep it in place.

He heads for the bathroom in the opposite corner next coming out with several towels, washcloths and bag full of toiletries which he dumps on the bed. Just as he starts to figure out where to place everything, his pilo beeps. Taking it out of his pocket, he reads the report.

Robert's pilo displays, "Tuesday, June 8, 2483 8:10 P.M. Bridget, Diversity."

"Increased activity around the hub. Several groups of guards and habits descend into the maze on the lower level terrace near the east gate. They haven't as yet come back out of the maze.

"At least a hundred have been counted so far. The rest of the acolytes continue in their normal routines, including the red sashes, although Ingrider has not yet been seen on any of the terraces or the top of the hub. The red sashes are only on the upper terrace. They come and go into the hub or the habitats."

Robert says, "Looks like something is amiss. They've been so orderly. With the gardens especially, someone has been here longer than we would have guessed. The younger acolytes have been faithfully attending their classes and the red sashes continue training in martial arts. The older acolytes have been preparing the habitats and the central tower with food stores, books, various posters and the appropriate games. The acolytes range in age from six to the late teens."

He pushes buttons and places the pilo back in his pocket. Shaking his head, Robert continues to pack his backpack finishing with a medkit and toiletries. Using his pilo again, he back checks every pocket in his backpack until he is satisfied that he has remembered everything. But never satisfied with these tools, he rechecks it one more time. Pausing trying to figure out if he is satisfied, he wonders if he can handle what is coming. This will be the biggest job, yet.

* * *

Before Cliff reaches the top of the stairs, he stops and tilts his head right and left listening for the sounds on the lower terrace.

Only running water from the lower terrace nearby and a few birds chirping in the neighboring forest trees interrupt the silence. He can hear a few voices but they sound far off out of sight probably as well based on the blackness surrounding him.

He rolls out of the stairs onto the path up against a five meter high building. Staying glued to the wall, he rises and walks left to the corner. Before turning, he puts his helmet against the building. Satisfied that no one is in the building or around the corner, he turns the corner, finds an open door and heads inside.

Two teenage white habited acolytes walk from the above terrace down the steps by the habitat. One is male and the other is female. They hold hands and look at each other from time to time.

"I thought it was one of the foxes from the middle terraces, but when he stood on two feet, I knew it wasn't, I can't figure out how he could get out," says the female acolyte.

"It's more than likely the young boy that stays in that habitat. The guards use it once in a while for training, but that won't happen again until next week."

They reach the lower level terrace and stop by the habitat.

"He must have been hiding near the stairwell to the maze.

"He was probably gazing at the stars as he has been for the last several nights.

"He can't reach the controls to open the door and anyone would recognize him out of place," continues the male acolyte.

The female goes to the front of the habitat and closes the door till it latches. She returns to the side of the habitat. They walk on around the lower terrace.

"Well with this little exercise, he won't be participating in the ceremony this weekend," says the female acolyte.

WEDNESDAY

Morning

S huttles arrive at and depart from a rather large space complex on the planet Diversity. The shuttle that Karl is on comes into a gate on the southern edge of the complex. The shuttle's monitor displays, "Wednesday, June 9, 2483 7:30 A.M. Bridget, Diversity."

Karl disembarks from the shuttle to the tarmac. He walks towards the terminal to the baggage area. Once inside, he finds the baggage carrousel and grabs his backpack from the baggage area and puts it on. He walks through and past the other baggage carrousels until he finds the escalator to the upper terminal level. Once there, he walks past groups of people still waiting for their tickets and boarding passes. Restaurants, delis and small specialty shops for local trinkets line the passage on both sides. Monitors display inboard and outboard times of the shuttles. He heads for the reception area of his arrival gate.

Robert waits in the reception area watching the incoming and outgoing shuttles. Three shuttles take off at once and right after they have cleared the airspace, two more shuttles come in for landings. Karl taps him on the shoulder. Robert turns and smiles. Robert stands and shakes Karl's hand.

Robert asks, "Welcome to Diversity. Did you get to see the layout as you were coming in? This particular Space Port is the largest on this planet."

They stop shaking hands. Karl looks around at the incoming and outgoing shuttles.

Karl says, "I did and I am amazed.

"Living under an open sky, watching a sunrise and sunset, breathing the fresh air, hearing the birds and feeling the wind against my neck, I was ready to throw up.

"I am almost overwhelmed."

Karl looks directly at Robert.

Karl says, "Only my training keeps me from running into the nearest PAR."

Robert says, "You won't find a single PAR on Diversity. We reconfigured each and every PAR, mostly into storage containers."

Karl asks, "What transportation do you have? I didn't see anything about subways."

Robert says, "No subways either. We use a flighter. It's part of our own design.

"A single passenger plane, using the old vernacular, with dual in-line rear props, snub nose, short wingspan and v-tail fins, it has fantastic flying abilities.

"The dual props and wings fold for storage. They're available for anyone over sixteen years of age.

"They have a medium range, primarily between two or three cities."

Karl asks, "You think you can train me on how to fly one of these flighters?"

Robert says, "While we are at the space port, I can get you up to speed in about a half hour."

Karl says, "This I have to experience."

* * *

About a quarter of the way above the horizon, the Sun shines in a clear sky. Inhabitants of the old city are beginning to stir with the usual sounds of children. But the lower terrace hasn't begun to awaken. Inside one of the habitats, a small child sleeps through the gathering noise. The habitat's monitor displays, "Wednesday, June 9, 2483 8:00 A.M. Bridget, Diversity."

Cliff awakens as warm sunlight comes through a high window, down the back wall, across the cement floor, reaching his helmet, neck and shoulders. He rises from the floor and stops for a minute to listen.

Tilting his head back, he faces towards some cabinets in the rear above a sink.

He walks towards the sink.

After opening some drawers below and alongside the sink, he uses them as stair steps to get to the counter. He stands on the counter near the sink.

He opens a cabinet and pulls out a box of cereal. Opening the box, he smells the inside and puts his hand inside to check the texture. He sits on the counter and munches away at the oatmeal flakes with nuts.

He walks to the end of the counter and opens another cabinet. Feeling around, he finds plastic drink glasses and takes one over to the sink. Pushing the valve, he holds the glass under the running water until it overflows.

After drinking that glass and then another, he quickly gets off the counter and runs to the closed doorway. He finds a chair nearby and pushes it beside the door. Standing on it he reaches along the wall until his hands touch the door lever. Pulling it down, the door opens. Sunlight streams into the room almost blinding him even though the helmet protects his eyes.

Before running out, he stops, placing his helmet against the doorway. He stretches his arms out the door. Sunshine appears on the left side of his bare outstretched arms. Walking out of the habitat, he turns right. He turns right at the end of the building and stops after going around the corner. Lifting the habit, he pees against the building while in shadow.

* * *

Karl's aircraft lands first with Robert following closely behind. Karl's cockpit monitor displays, "Wednesday, June 9, 2483 8:30 A.M. Bridget, Diversity."

Karl and Robert sit in the cockpit of their respective flighters on the ground. Other aircraft and shuttles fly above them, some landing and some taking off. Each of the student flyers have distinctive flyers depending on which school or instructor was training them. The sky looks filled with a rainbow of colors moving round and round the field.

A few aircraft taxi into hangers while many others are pulled into gates for offloading of people and cargo. The cargo trains are constantly delivering cargo to the baggage areas and off-loading cargo from the shuttles.

Robert's flighter has quite distinctive markings, red and orange flame stripes on a black background. All of the other aircraft nearby are pale blue, including Karl's. Some have markings related to missions accomplished or the crew's favorite pin-up, but none are as garish as Robert's flighter.

Karl says, "I'm getting the hang of this.

"It's really quite natural, except for my stomach which keeps trying to get out.

Robert says, "That will soon pass within the hour. You're really a natural.

"I've never seen anyone fly as well as you after only ten minutes of practice and you handle the controls so effortlessly."

Karl says, "It's probably all of this safety equipment. Putting the power interrupt on the bottom is ingenious. I never would have thought of that."

Turning his head towards a man and his wife together with a teenage son, Karl watches an instructor approach the family. After handshakes are exchanged, a short discussion takes place leaving the woman with a concerned face as the instructor and the teenager approach a flighter.

Immediately upon arrival, the teenager nervously runs through the standard checklist of fuel level, ailerons, rudder and elevators. The instructor smiles as the teenager climbs into the aircraft running through the instrument check and computer systems diagnostics and checking the controls for the ailerons, rudder and elevators. Once the flighter has been checked out as much as the teenager can remember, he looks over at the instructor waiting for that first moment of uninstructed taxiing.

Giving the teenager the go ahead sign, the instructor walks back towards the teenager's parents. When the instructor stops and turns around, the teenager starts the engine, runs a system check on oil levels, fuel balance and engine rpm before taxing onto the taxi way. After asking over the radio, he waits for clearance from the tower before taxiing to the main runway where he sets the brakes and runs the throttle fully open. The dual props spin until they virtually disappear with only the hub visible. The aircraft buckles against the brakes trying to overcome them and get off the runway.

When the brakes are released, the flighter zips along the runway, and moments later, it rises into the air reaching four hundred and sixty meters above the tarmac. After leveling out at that altitude, the teenager circles the spaceport and straightens the flighter for approach on the same runway.

The teenager radios for clearance and is immediately cleared for landing. He sets the flaps and adjusts the throttle to minimum speed without stalling. He lowers the wheels and checks they are locked.

He lands the flighter on the tarmac in a perfect three point landing. The teenager looks over at the instructor who signals another go around.

The aircraft surges forward as the throttle is pushed to its limit. When he's got clearance, the flighter soon rises again to minimum altitude, circling the field, landing back on the tarmac. The aircraft further reduces forward motion as it approaches the taxi way. Before long the flighter is secured back at the training center, being refueled ready for the next student's training. Both parents have wide smiles as they greet their newest flyer. He remains bewildered that he has even accomplished the flight.

Karl turns his head back towards Robert. Robert notices Karl interest.

Robert says, "We use our flighters for about anything. They're great for short hops to the other side of the city.

"Currently, we use them to carry the harvest from the farms into the cities."

Karl asks, "You'll have to tell about these farms another day. Shall we head for the maze?"

Robert says, "Good idea."

* * *

Ingrider Butler sits on his throne with several white habited applicants gathered around in groups, keeping a close eye and ear for what is going to happen next in front of Ingrider's throne.

He checks his pilo. His pilo displays, "Wednesday, June 10, 2483 9:30 A.M. Bridget, Diversity."

He wears a white habit with red sequins in horizontal dual stripes spaced every fifteen centimeters while silver threads run around the seams and hem line. Two guards run up the terrace towards Ingrider and his small group. Tilting his head downward, the first guard approaches Ingrider cautiously not wanting to upset any mediating he might be doing.

Kneeling a meter from Ingrider and bowing his head, the first guard says, "He escaped during his dinner meal. We did an exhaustive search during the night and this morning, but didn't find him."

Ingrider looks up at the guard with a face the guard dare not see for he has seen it more than once in his tenure with Ingrider.

Ingrider says, "I can promise you great rewards after the boy dies on Saturday.

"Unfortunately, I can't even think of the possibility of your punishment should he still be alive.

"I suggest you take a hundred of my best white habited acolytes to the lower terrace stairwell. Station one per intersection of the maze until all of the intersections have been searched.

"Bring lights, check every open cell; he has the ability to blend into the shadows with his habit and helmet. He'll be difficult to see except for his lower face, neck, hands and feet."

Ingrider dismisses the guard. Not having expected this turn of events, Ingrider broods as his sits on his throne. The rest of the white habited acolytes on the upper terrace in the vicinity watch Ingrider closely as they go about their regular duties, quietly dispersing to lower levels leaving him with all his troubles.

Standing, the guard turns walking towards the other guard, keeping his head bowed. After stepping down the first step after the upper terrace, the first guard brings his head back up. They both descend the terrace steps picking up acolytes along the way.

* * *

K arl and Robert get out of their respective flighters and walk through tall grass to a clearing of shorter grasses about ten meters away. As they get out of the tall grass, both check their pant legs for ticks and assorted flotsam which make them look like they were creatures of the forest.

After clearing off everything they can remove from their pants, Karl looks over the small short grass clearing before checking his pilo.

Karl's pilo displays, "Wednesday, June 9, 2483 10:30 A.M. Bridget, Diversity."

While they walk, Robert points straight ahead toward the far end of the clearing.

The forest of primarily evergreens with vines, broken branches, ferns, dead leaves and many animal trails and markings stands right at the edge of the clearing, going left and right around the perimeter of the shopping center.

Robert says, "Over there is where Cliff went in. It's the only entrance to the maze outside the old terraced city or the shopping center."

Karl says, "I suggest a bit of advice before we descend into the maze.

"Mazes are excellent places for ambushes because of their many dead ends and their few exits and their lack of maneuvering room. They are usually no wider than two people could easily walk side by side."

Karl hands him two small white canisters similar to a good cigar. In the middle of each is a opening shaped like lips that is very flexible.

Looking at the mouth piece on the side, Robert asks, "What are these?"

Karl says, "I brought a few canisters of oxygen. A word of caution though, keep your nose and eyes closed. Some strains of gas work on orifices getting absorbed faster.

"Our pilos will guide us to the closest exit. All we have to do is listen for their guidance."

Robert says, "I better check my pilo. I have an around the clock fly over the old city, in silent mode."

He checks his pilo and then looks up at Karl.

Robert says, "Interesting, two guards met with the leader, Ingrider near the hub.

"They left in a sudden hurry and picked up about a hundred older acolytes from the lower terrace levels. All of them descended into the maze at the lower terrace stairwell. A couple acolytes are guarding the stairwell entrance on the lower level."

Karl says, "Then we will have to be cautious. Something is definitely amiss."

Robert points at the opening to the maze. Karl moves first down the steps into the darkness. Robert follows.

When his waist dips below the surface of the clearing, Robert removes a paper wrapper with a depiction of a granola bar from his right pants pocket and leaves it half buried in the dirt at the top left edge of the stairwell. He descends the stairwell trying to catch up with Karl. The sliding door closes above him as he plunges into the darkness of the maze. After his eyes adjust to the minimal light of the maze passageways, he catches up with Karl who has his pilo light showing him the way through the maze. Just as Robert starts to say something, Karl quiets him with his finger over his mouth.

* * *

The first guard's group of acolytes arrives at a cell where the bars are closed. The cell's monitor displays, "Wednesday, June 9, 2483 11:00 A.M. Bridget, Diversity."

The first guard shines a pilo light into the cave revealing an empty cell. He moves past the cell and through the passage. Before long the next intersection comes into view. After even more intersections, the other cell comes into view.

He is followed closely by nine murmuring white habited acolytes to the next intersection where he leaves another acolyte as in the past four intersections. The acolyte quickly decides to use his pilo to search the passageways away from the intersection so that he won't have to keep looking every so often.

Turning right, he stops at the next cave. The bars are already up, but the floor of the cell confirms only the activity of several rats. The rest of the dirt covered stone surface remains untouched with a fine film of dust covering each and every stone that doesn't have rat trails.

Sensing something amiss up ahead, he walks to the next cell cautioning the acolytes to remain quiet. The remaining acolytes stop murmuring.

After that cell turns up empty, they reach the next intersection where another acolyte is left. This acolyte decides to use her own senses instead of her pilo so she walks past the intersection in each direction listening and watching for anything out of the ordinary while she waits for her replacement.

With the rest of the acolytes following resuming their murmuring, the first guard with his senses on high alert marches down the passageway to the next cell wary of something prickling the back of his neck.

Before reaching the cell, the first guard asks the acolytes to stop murmuring. He thinks he has heard other footsteps moving through the maze, but he is not sure. Not hearing anything while the acolytes remain quiet, he cautions them even though they totally ignore him and cautiously return to a lower level of murmuring watching the first guard carefully.

After shining his pilo light into the cave, the guard turns it off and stays quiet motionless for a short period of time. After putting a finger to his mouth, the acolytes stop murmuring.

Farther down the passage in semi-darkness, Karl and Robert cautiously move forward, not using their pilo lights. They don't want to give away their position too easily. They've heard the acolytes murmuring and are staying in the darkness between light panels in the passageway.

Robert snubs his toe on one of the exposed edges of a stone and nearly falls, stopping the fall with his left hand and arm. He grunts and rights himself. Looking over at Karl, he sees Karl's concern and Robert shrugs his shoulders and points to the raised stone amongst all the flat ones.

Hearing the grunt, the guard motions the acolytes backward. Looking back at every intersection, noticing the lighting and the dark spaces between of the passageway, he doesn't spot either Karl or Robert in any of the lights. He quietly follows the acolytes back through several intersections picking up the other acolytes, until they reach the passageway which leads to the secret stairwell.

* * *

The first guard arrives at the secret door to the lower level stairway along with his contingent of acolytes where the monitor displays, "Wednesday, June 9, 2483 11:25 A.M. Bridget, Diversity.".

He opens the secret door with the emblem and sends his acolytes up the stairs. A moment later, another group of guards and acolytes arrive and the first guard sends them up the stairs, while he waits for the rest of the groups to arrive. Yet another group comes and heads up the stairwell.

Soon the last of the guards and a hundred acolytes stream up the stairwell on the lower terrace. The first guard follows the last of the acolytes up the stairs. When on the lower terrace, the first guard sends all the acolytes back to their regular duties and dismisses the rest of the guards including his second most of which return to guard duty on the other terraces.

The acolytes and guards gathered on the lower terrace take some time to clear out of the area, not being too organized. After several miscues, the acolytes are on their way up terrace steps or along the lower level terrace to other terrace steps. The rest of the guards wait for the acolytes to clear. The guards return to their respective levels.

When everyone is clear of the stairwell on the lower terrace, the first guard reaches down to one of the stones near the west side of the stairwell, tilts it up and pushes the large red button underneath with his thumb. Gears start turning and the ground around the stairwell trembles.

A sliding stone shell slides over the stairwell entrance as if it were part of the regular groundcover blending into the surrounding ground leaving no trace of its existence. The trembling continues and as quickly stops.

Back at the entrance where Karl and Robert entered, a sliding stone shell slides over that stairwell entrance, too.

Opening another stone near the previous, the guard pushes three of the six multicolored buttons with different symbols on each in order and watches the LCD display indicate the status and readiness of each step of the process. When the LCD screen goes from red to green, the first guard pushes the stone back into position.

He removes his pilo from his pocket.

The first guard's pilo displays, "Wednesday, June 9, 2483 11:45 A.M. Bridget, Diversity."

The first guard looks at it and starts a half hour countdown. He sets a different beep for each five minutes and places it back in his pants pocket.

Afternoon

Green gas spews from outside the light panels in each passageway in the maze.

With an oxygen canister in their mouths, Karl and Robert close their eyes. Using one hand they hold their noses. They listen to their pilo's beeps as it guides them back out of the maze using several different tones for correct moves and for distress on wrong moves. Once they understand the code, they walk faster.

Karl and Robert arrive at the closed stairwell to the small grass clearing. The gas fumes have dissipated, leaving traces of white meandering along the walls and floor of the passageway. Karl's pilo beeps several times. Opening his tearful eyes, Karl punches several buttons.

The stairway monitor displays, "Wednesday, June 9, 2483 12:15 P.M. Bridget, Diversity."

After feeling the edge of the wall, he places the pilo on the wall near the stairwell. The stone shell slides back, revealing the sun high in the sky above them and lighting the stairway halfway down the side and halfway across the steps. With their eyes still closed tightly, they walk up the stairs.

* * *

They hurry up the stairwell, spit out the oxygen canisters and fall coughing as they collapse onto the shorter grass clearing.

Each of them tumble one way or the other bringing their knees up to the chest in coughing fits while they hold their head to keep it from exploding.

After the coughing subsides and their headaches have diminished, they sit up in the grass. They each take off their backpacks and remove water boxes from side pockets.

Washing water over their faces to remove any trace of the gas, they begin to recover lying on their backs, except that a few minutes later both turn over to their right side. Still coughing regularly, they spasm in silence with one feeling this is only a passing moment while the other is almost positive he is dying.

Karl sits up first with tears in his eyes and an occasional cough. He unfastens a side pocket on his backpack and removes a small box, popping two pills.

Moments later, Robert does the same except his remaining cough is more exuberant, knocking his cap off several times. Robert opens his mouth to talk, but nothing comes out except for a few squeaks.

Karl motions to wait and holds both hands up by the side of his face. Nodding is agreement, Robert lies down again. Their coughs persist gradually diminishing. Once their coughs resign, they both fall back onto the grass fast asleep with their water boxes by their sides.

Near the forest edge, a doe comes into the clearing to munch on the short grass. Her speckled fawn lies behind a bush in the darkness of the forest. The doe's head comes up and so do its ears. She quickly returns to the edge of the forest to lie down beside her fawn, hiding herself and it from view.

Birds fly from another short grass clearing high into the sky, forming a V-pattern to the south. A leopard settles back into its declivity in the same small grass clearing, enjoying the warm afternoon sun.

Twenty minutes later, Karl wakes, pulling his pilo out of his pocket and pushing several buttons. Robert wakes, rubbing his eyes and shaking his head.

"I thought they were trying to kill me. What was that stuff?" asks Robert.

Looking over his pilo, Karl responds, "Primarily a sleep agent, but some people could be allergic. Have your pilo check your vitals, just to see."

Robert pulls out his pilo from his pocket and points it at his heart. The pilo beeps and Robert looks over the results.

He says, "Wow, I barely made it. The nanos saved my life again. I was allergic to something in that gas.

"Without the nanos, I would have died and you would have buried my here."

"Well that's what nanos are for, to save and extend our lives from all kinds of viruses and bacterial attacks. Debilitating diseases can no longer affect us as they did back in the twenty first century on Earth," says Karl.

Robert looks long and hard at his pilo, barely heading Karl's words. His next words take another turn.

" How can we go up against this guy when he has these tools to keep us at bay?"

* * *

Ingrider sits in his throne by the hub with the second guard kneeling in front of him with his head bowed nearby. Ingrider occasionally stares at the guard as if trying to impart dark designs to him through his mind. The guard patiently waits.

Several red sash acolytes mill about talking among themselves, carefully watching the drama between their master and the guard. They stay a considerable distance away without leaving the upper terrace trying hand to maintain some semblance of dutiful endeavors. Ingrider consults his pilo.

Ingrider's pilo displays, "Wednesday, June 9, 2483 12:40 P.M. Bridget, Diversity."

Ingrider says, "I already know about those two. Their escapades are well known among the four habitable planets in the four solar systems.

"They can't escape my small security devices.

"As soon as the maze is clear of the gas you can get them and the boy. They will be totally incapacitated for several hours. Do whatever you want with the two men.

"Tell the first guard to find a better hiding place for the boy until Saturday. Since they already know about the maze, moving the boy no longer is an option, but we don't want them to know that. We have to keep them guessing right up to the ceremony which cannot fail.

"I'll make my final decision about his care, concern and responsibility on Saturday."

The guard rises keeping his head bowed as he retreats to the edge of the upper terrace at the east steps. As he passes the second step down from the upper terrace, he raises his head thankful to still have it on his shoulders. The guard leaves walking at a fast pace down the terraced walkway.

* * *

Robert sits cross-legged in the clearing looking at his pilo. Sitting with his legs outstretched, Karl goes through his backpack, checking several outside pockets, and rechecks his pilo.

Karl's pilo displays, "Wednesday, June 9, 2483 1:30 P.M. Bridget, Diversity."

Robert asks, "Still no sign of Cliff anywhere. If he isn't in the maze, then where could he be? If they stop moving him, we'll never find him.

"This maze extends from the tunnels in the west to the old space port in the east."

Karl says, "About anywhere.

"Since this morning's excursion, he could be on any of the old city terraces or in the old shopping center or the space in-between. It's not like he will be able to signal us.

"I seriously doubt he could get out of the old city pass the guards. They keep moving around on each of the terraces and they have six guards on two hour rotations at the gates.

"The gas attack was for our benefit.

"Ingrider knows we're in the maze and he's not taking any chances. The guards will be massing in the maze within moments. We just as well head for the shopping center. I'll investigate the maze myself later on."

Robert says, "Sounds reasonable to me considering the number of guards within the old city's walls as you just said. Ingrider has more guards and red sashes than I do officers for the entire region.

"A five year old can only go so far. At least, when I have found him out on the prairie, his trek has been within a reasonable area for a boy of his size to walk. He could be out in the open in the old city or above ground, but with that particular outfit, he would be instantly noticed. I would swear that boy knows more about this maze than anyone else I know. However, I can't say that because I have never caught him in here. However we don't have a very decent map of the maze and the hidden passageways are completely unknown.

"The shopping center west of the old city is a more likely place to hide with all of its stores and hexagons. And it has fresh food there, as well. It is accessible through the maze through a stairway in the central cone. I've had that particular entrance open more often than you would think."

Karl and Robert stand.

They walk past the stairwell through the short grass clearing. They reach their flighters and climb in. Soon the two flighters are in the air.

* * *

Sitting in his usual place, Ingrider faces the first and second guard on their knees with their heads down. He fidgets, shakes his head, taps his toes and drums his fingers on the arm rests of his throne. Shaking his head, he looks up and down, right and left as if searching for an answer. He checks his pilo.

Ingrider's pilo displays, "Wednesday, June 9, 2483 3:00 P.M. Bridget, Diversity."

Ingrider asks, "This brings me no pride. You can't find either the two men or the boy. It's only a maze. How are you ever going to protect me?"

Another guard walks up the east terrace steps towards Ingrider. As he nears the last step, he bows his head.

After kneeling and bowing two meters away, the guard asks permission from one of the red sash acolytes to speak with Ingrider. Ingrider consents. With his head bowed, the guard approaches to one meter and kneels. He whispers something into Ingrider's ear as Ingrider leans forward.

Ingrider dismisses the guard who rises; keeping his head bowed, he walks to the east steps.

Ingrider says, "What a fortunate change for you two. It would seem that our brat used an acolyte's habitat.

"Seal the city gates, close all of the other exits, triple the guards on all terraces and find that kid! Search every habitat and all the usual hiding places. I'm sure you know what I am talking about. You probably used them yourself at some time.

"You two take six of your best guards and head for the shopping center. If you don't find that boy, you better hope we find him in the terrace city."

The two guards rise and bow to Ingrider backing up to the edge of the terrace where they finally turn around to walk down the east terrace steps. After the second step, they raise their heads and hurry down the steps to the lower terrace.

They are both thankful for the questionable outcome. Removing his pilo from his pants pocket, the first guard sends a message to six of his best guards.

Finding the secret door open, the first guard closes the secret door to the maze, pressing his right foot on the stone midway along the stairwell's west edge, while the second guard briefs the six guards after they arrive out of the east and southeast habitats on the second level, reassigning them to new duties. After the briefing, the six guards return to their habitats for prepared backpacks for themselves and the two leaders.

Since two guards are assigned to each habitat, they just happen to be on the same terrace. So before long, six guards properly outfitted wait by the terrace steps. Before long, the two officers join them and they go over the plan until each has memorized all of the details.

* * *

Eight guards walk through the east gate. The two senior guards climb into their respective aircraft. Two other guards climb into each of the storage lockers in the nose cone. The last two wait for one of the flighters to return since no more than three people can travel in one aircraft without overbalancing the wings.

On the first guard's flighter, the console monitor displays, "Wednesday, June 9, 2483 3:05 P.M. Bridget, Diversity."

The first guard starts his engine and engages the turbo props in the wings. His aircraft rises into the sky where after reaching a suitable altitude the dual props in the rear are engaged, throwing the flighter forward toward the west. The second guard in the other aircraft does the same, heading in the same direction. The two flighters fly in formation past the central hub and onto the central tower of the shopping center.

The last two big guards sit on the short grass field, waiting for one of the flighters to come back for them. After one game each on their pilos, they hear the sound of the returning aircraft. Putting away their pilos, they stand up watching the flighter come to a stop above them, slowly sinking to the ground in front of them.

Once the second guard indicates it is safe, they walk over to the front of the flighter and open the nose cone with the turbo fans humming in each wing. They climb into the storage locker barely squeezing in, putting their legs between each other's legs. One of the guards closes the cover until it locks into position.

The flighter rises into the air, engages the rear dual props and heads west for the entrance to the shopping center flying directly over the central hub of the city. Not long after the old city is no longer below them the shopping center comes into view.

A couple minutes later, the flighter approaches the east end of the shopping center and starts to glide downward towards the west end heading almost directly for the central cone of the shopping center. The flighter uses the height of the cone to gauge his descent and glide path. He sets the destination into the computer and watches the gauges.

The central cone comes into view below the flighter as it continues its gradual descent. It glides over the central cone missing it by several meters.

Moments later, the flighter is hovering above the other aircraft on the ground, descending vertically. As the flighter lands beside the grounded aircraft, one of the two guards in the storage locker releases the catch which opens the nose cone and they both climb out onto the short grass. The second guard climbs out of the cockpit of the flighter after the turbo fans have spun down.

The eight guards gather at the west entrance. After the first guard relays cautionary intones to the others, they all head through the main west entrance into the west corridor, heading for the central room. They walk past many store entrances along each side of the main west corridor which connects the west hexagon to the northwest and southwest hexagons each of which have several stores within like all of the other hexagons in the shopping center.

* * *

With a dirty chin, neck, hands and feet along with a mucky black habit, Cliff arrives at an intersection in the maze where he stops for a moment to listen for any unusual noises within the passageway. He walks for several meters to his right where he begins a search along the wall on his left, using his hands to feel between the stones slightly above his helmet. He finds what he is looking for between two stones and pulls the metallic lever out. Gears are actuated and an opening appears in the middle of the wall revealing another couple of vertical doors behind it as the outer door regresses and slides up into the ceiling.

Cliff opens the dumb waiter doors and lifts himself up into the dumb waiter, using the space between stones to hook his toes. He crawls into the metal box that's big enough to be a good sized fort as he looks around the expansive space. After closing the door, he hears the outer stone door closing. He pulls the two centimeter braided rope inside the dumb waiter. It rises until it reaches a stopping place.

Cliff opens the dumb waiter doors and waits while he listens for any noises. Not hearing anything out of the ordinary in the shopping center's shops, he opens the wall door of the tower which slides up into the wall cavity. He climbs out of the dumb waiter, landing on the shopping center floor with both feet inside an empty box. Several large boxes tower over him, so he can't see the store's displays.

Taking a deep breath through his nose, he notices the unique fragrance especially pine scent. He determines that this smell is from the outdoor equipment store in the west hexagon of the shopping center. He smiles remembering the last time he was here with his friend from school.

Boy did they ever have an escapade before the Police Chief found them in the shopping center.

After moving several empty boxes out of the way, he heads down the narrow corridor to the store's entrance. He passes many displays of backpacks, tents, sleeping bags and dehydrated packaged food. Climbing equipment, ropes, spelunkers, carbines and other assorted stuff comes next with a display of portable potties and TV's right near the entrance.

When he gets close enough, he looks at the monitor in the main corridor.

The west corridor's monitor displays, "Wednesday, June 9, 2483 3:20 P.M. Bridget, Diversity."

As he arrives, he hears the sound of footsteps marching through the main corridor. He immediately falls to the floor, rolling under one of the TV display units. After the sound retreats into the distance, Cliff rolls out from under the display units, stands and opens the doorway to the west corridor. He listens for only a half-minute before he dashes across the wide corridor into a food store.

Upon opening the door, he is assailed with the scents of fruits, flowers, deli meats, floor polish and ice cream although he doesn't actually smell all of those items, his mind reminds him of the scents that he usually is around. Heading for the fruits displayed on several aisles, he is not sure which to start with nor how many of each he wants.

After getting several different fruits and eating half of them, he finds the closest restroom and hurries in. After coming out of the restroom, he heads back into the food store for the milk boxes and water boxes. He has a fondness for chocolate milk and marshmallows.

His mother makes his hot chocolate with tiny marshmallows on Friday nights when he is home. Before long is has a chocolate mustache and he is heading for the restroom again.

Getting full of bites of cupcakes, apples, bananas, grapes and pears, he walks towards the deli area where he procures a couple turkey sandwiches and a small tray of vegetable sticks along with his usual assortment of candy bars. Sitting at one of the few black metal tables, he munches away on one of the sandwiches and half of the vegetable sticks, finishing with a single chocolate bar. He takes a couple of gulps of apple juice and wipes his face with one of the napkins on the table. He stops for a moment when he hears a noise of a door opening and then closing. Remaining quiet, he waits before continuing eating. After the door closed, no other noises were heard. He returned to his munching until he was satisfied. Gathering the garbage, he tosses it in the recycler.

* * *

After searching the central hexagon, the eight guards begin searching the northwest hexagon composed of specialty stores displaying arts and crafts, beads, threads, fabric, chocolate and toys for toddlers to adults.

They divide into twos, each taking one of the four stores. The first guard and another investigate the fourth store and the music/movie store, closing the door behind them after they enter.

The store is divided by several cubes delineated by movies and music into various categories. Banners, flying from the ceiling rafters every two meters, proclaim the latest or upcoming movie as well as the newest, youngest and latest musician's and band's cubes. On top of each cubic display, a holographic representation of a movie trailer or a performing musician rotates after the performance ninety degrees.

The first guard takes the outer music aisle while the other takes the outer movie aisle leaving the central till last. The first thing they notice is the noise and the second is the constantly flashing media.

The noise is rampant from either side of the music/movie store making it hard for the two guards to hear any other sounds. The first guard believes he sees a shadow coming out of one of the cubic structures. He signals the other guard to back him up as he investigates. The other guard watches the first guard and everything else around him.

The first guard moves quickly to the cube and discovers that the shadow comes from one of the holographic images on top of one of the cubes. Allowing the other guard to resume his search of the movie aisle, the first guard backs up to where he was and continues trying to find the boy. He soon finishes exploring the music side and meets up with the other guard at the far end of the store. The other guard comes empty handed.

The first guard says, "I hope the other teams are having better success."

The other guard responds, "We better find him soon.

"This place is spooky without any people in it. I get the shivers every time I hear something unusual."

The first guard says, "You'll get used to it. These mechanized machines were prized by the older civilization."

The first guard looks at his pilo.

The first guard's pilo displays, "Wednesday, June 9, 2483 3:30 P.M. Bridget, Diversity."

The two guards walk down the main aisle towards the store's entrance. The other guard opens the door to the west corridor. They meet with the other six guards and the first guard decides to check the southwest hexagon across the corridor, when one of the guards excitedly points to the one of the stores in the southwestern hexagon across the corridor. The first guard and every other guard look up toward where the guard points. They all act as one when they see what the other guard was pointing.

A black helmet bobs in the lower part of the display windows heading west and then quickly disappears leaving all of the guards gaping except for the first guard.

The other guard says, "I saw him through the window, just the top of the black helmet bobbing up and down."

The first guard asks, "Which way was he going?"

"Towards the west," responds the other guard.

"Be watchful! Don't let the boy across.

"There's a short corridor with only two exits into each hexagon. Watch those doors," says the first guard, before sending two other guards to the small corridor separating the southwest hexagon and the western hexagon.

Both guards nod and head off down the main west corridor at a run. The first and the rest of the guards keep watching the appliance store in case the helmet bobs again. When the two guards arrive, the first guard starts running first.

The other five guards run to the southwest hexagon's entrance. The first guard arrives and opens the door, looking first towards the west and then the east. Rows of appliances fill the floor from wall to wall. Each is labeled as a demo model (Not For Sale). Refrigerators, freezers (upright and locker), ranges, ovens, washing machines, dryers, microwaves, toaster ovens and dishwashers are displayed along major aisles and between each group an area set aside to display kitchens, bathrooms and wine cellars. About every thirty meters, an automatic payment counter appears nestled between appliances with shipping from a choice of various carriers.

The boy with the black helmet is nowhere in sight. The first guard sends each of the others down an aisle between appliances to the west. While they don't bother checking inside the appliances, they watch for any movement among the appliances or in the cross aisles between groups.

They check behind and between every appliance that has room for a small boy as well as the many shipping boxes where a boy would love to play for hours at a time. Occasionally, a guard will check twice just to be sure. They continue along all of the major aisles and minor aisles.

By the time they reach the small corridor, none of the guards including the first has seen the boy.

The first guard sends pairs of guards to the other three stores in the southwest hexagon and by the time their search is over and they have met up with the guards in the small corridor, none of them have seen the boy.

* * *

Sitting on one of the benches in the main east corridor, Karl and Robert munch on protein bars while taking several gulps of water. Robert wipes his forehead removing the sweat about to fall off his eyebrows. He can't remember having to walk this far ever in his entire life. He feels much older than he really is. He may have to adjust his exercise routine.

"Well that was very disappointing. I feel that we're missing something, but I can put my finger on it. Most of the activities that a boy would be interested in are situated within the eastern hexagons," says Robert.

"This particular boy is probably more interested in the major food stores in the western hexagons rather than the music, movies or toys that are in the other two west hexagons. I can't be sure he has had any food since yesterday. Since you have mentioned it previously, he has visited the shopping center before," responds Karl.

"We'll search the next two hexagons west of the central hexagon, since the boy can't get into the central hexagon.

"But we have to play our cards correctly." says Karl.

"I agree to that for the time being, unless I'm forgetting something," responds Robert.

He puts his left hand up against his forehead. After rubbing his forehead, he drops his hand to his side.

"After those two sets of stores, we'll concentrate on the western hexagon in the morning, after we have had some rest," says Karl.

Remembering what he wanted to say, Robert says, "The barricades will start coming down about seven thirty this evening all over the shopping center. We either have to be out of the building or we'll be trapped inside. There aren't any other exits that we can get to once the barricades are down. Good thing we brought camping equipment."

After shaking his head in agreement, Karl looks out over the inside of the store. Remembering to check his messages, he brings out his pilo from his pants pocket.

Karl's pilo displays, "Wednesday, June 9, 2483 4:00 P.M. Bridget, Diversity."

Robert says, "These next stores have more displays because we're getting into appliances, sporting goods, outdoor clothing and equipment, men's and women's apparel, specialty goods, and last but not least, food stores and delis on their western edges. Now that I'm thinking of food, I'll bet the boy is too."

They throw their protein bar wrappers in the nearest waste bin and proceed out of the east corridor to the outer covered walkway around the north and south sides of the central hexagon. They decide to walk around the northern side.

After going through a smaller corridor between the central and northwestern hexagons, Karl and Robert quickly arrive in the main west corridor.

They carefully look up the corridor to the main west entrance without seeing the boy or any guards coming or going although the distance is deceiving and is much longer than perceived. Carefully watching the doors along the corridor walls, they walk up the main west corridor and enter the music/movie store on their right. They walk through the door and are blasted by the noise in the room.

The main west corridor's monitor displays, "Wednesday, June 9, 2483 4:00 P.M. Bridget, Diversity."

Through the noise of the movie trailers and the music videos, Karl and Robert walk around the cubic displays along the central aisle looking for any sign of the boy. By the time they reach the other end of the store, they look at each other exhausted. Robert could not imagine anyone being civilized with so many video trailers on display throughout the store. He feels assaulted.

They take another swig of their water boxes and head through the central aisle of the store for the main west corridor. When they exit the music/movie store, Karl decides he wants to take a look through the appliance store before investigating the food court, but Robert's stomach growls, so they head directly for the food court.

After eating, they consider other options before going back to the appliance store as the most possible location for the boy. They only hope the guards didn't find him there.

Evening

One of the corridors monitor's displays, "Wednesday, June 9, 2483 6:00 P.M. Bridget, Diversity."

Cliff quietly walks through the main west corridor, listening for any unusual sounds like other footsteps or voices. He arrives at a cross corridor into the south part of the west hexagon. He walks into the smaller corridor where lights are more numerous.

The advertising flashes momentary snatches of sale items on every surface except the lighted ceiling. The noise is actually quite pleasant with only momentary spasms of unpleasant noise which serves to irritate his ears and the glare of the garish advertising assaults his eyes. Arriving at a convenience store, Cliff walks in to stock up on supplies for the next day, not wanting to carry too much, and to grab several snacks that his mother wouldn't usually let him have.

He finds a small table and chair where he can finally sit down and rest. He takes a gulp from the water box in his bag of goodies which he places on the floor. He's thankful for the quiet ever since the southwestern hexagon where he almost got caught by the six guards, but hiding in a washer wasn't such a bad idea. He could see them, but they didn't see him even when they were looking right at him. He was glad for the filters on the glass face of the washer.

He's beginning to think that the guards do not know about the dumb waiters because they only searched the full and empty boxes around the central tower of the store. At least, he's never seen them using the dumb waiters to transfer to the maze. *Maybe they don't know the maze that well either. They can't all be that dumb to miss me even when they walk right by me.*

After a couple of cupcakes, cookies and several assorted candy bars, Cliff throws all the refuse in the closest waste disposal and walks out of store into the small corridor which luckily is empty although he thought he had heard two guards in the corridor. He's glad they decided to go somewhere else. Instead of turning back to the main west corridor, he decides to head the other way to the closest restroom, realizing that he needs to empty something.

He arrives at the men's restroom and walks in.

Two guards come out of a small tailor shop into the small corridor meters from the men's restroom, but the restroom door is already closed. They look over at it, but shake their heads realizing that they had already checked it out before searching the tailor shop. They do a cursory visual check of all of the other doors in the corridor.

One of the guards says, "Which one do we search next? This is becoming alarmingly aggravating."

The other guard responds, "We're to search the other outer deli next and then the big supermarket next to the main west corridor. From there we report to the main west entrance. So, we only have about an hour or two more."

The two guards walk past the restroom and enter the door to the outer deli across from it. Deciding it was past time to grab something to eat, they made the most of their search eating deli sandwiches and fruit drinks. After a brief conversation about their fruitless search, they sit for a moment to catch their breath and finish their fruit drinks

* * *

Coming out of a hardware store into the main west corridor, Karl and Robert carefully survey the corridor before proceeding. It remains empty for some time.

Karl looks at Robert who shrugs his shoulders not knowing what to say. Karl opens his mouth to speak but decides not to and closes it. He gets antsy and pulls his pilo out of his pants pocket.

Karl checks his pilo pushing several buttons, looking over the display trying to decide their next best site, while Robert keeps watch. During this time no doors open onto the main west corridor and only the humming of the machinery providing the air conditioning can be heard.

Karl's pilo displays, "Wednesday, June 9, 2483 6:30 P.M. Bridget, Diversity."

"The coast looks clear; I can barely see the main west entrance at the far end.

"We're still too close to the central cone," says Robert, "He could have gotten past us heading the other way. The major inner corridors also exit to the outer walkways around the perimeter. This is almost hopeless."

Karl responds, "I'm not surprised that we haven't run into any of the guards. They have to be somewhere in this center doing the same thing we're doing. I am hopeful they are ahead of us. Cliff is more likely to be ahead of the guards. It will take more than persuasion to extract the boy from those guards."

"Let's search the south side, while we're here, and then come back for the rest of the north. It's going to be tight if we don't find him soon. The barriers start coming down around 7:30 P.M.," says Robert.

"Well, then let's get moving. The more we stay in the main west corridor, the more likely we will be caught by the guards," says Karl.

They quickly walk across the corridor to the door on the opposite side which puts them in the mega appliance store.

As they enter, they hear doors closing and opening west of their position. They wait until the noise dissipates and then start searching for Cliff, always keeping an eye and ear open for the guards as well although they have about the same amount of indecision about them as they do about the boy.

When they have finished searching through the appliance store finding no sign of Cliff, they both head through the smaller corridor west of the store and walk to the outer deli. After grabbing a late supper and taking a needed break, they both feel energized for the next round of searching

The department store is the largest in the south part of the western hexagon. Shoes, deli, electronics, food, furniture, bedding and household sections make up the largest floor areas in the store. Kiosks scattered throughout the store proclaim anything it doesn't have can be ordered with payment counters on every corner.

Karl and Robert think the same thing about a child in this environment. He could be hiding anywhere. They decide to divide the store up into departments with each of them taking a different aisle. After deciding on which departments to take Karl looks over at Robert.

"Remember to look in the washers and dryers," says Karl to Robert, "Boys love to hide out in the strangest places. I speak from personal experience. I had many an adventure within the confines of the washer's basin before I got too big."

* * *

The shopping center's main west corridor monitor displays, "Wednesday, June 9, 2483 7:00 P.M. Bridget, Diversity."

Worn out from walking, Cliff stumbles into the northern wall of the corridor.

He slides down to the floor, completely exhausted. Motionless and tense, he sits quietly as if he is waiting for the inevitable. He feels he could not walk another step without some rest. His arms are limp at his sides and he finds it hard to keep his head up with the weight of the helmet always bearing down forcing him forward and out of balance. He forces his head backwards against the wall.

Finally, he relaxes, not hearing any other sounds which make him feel much better. The various noises are dying down leaving a level of thankful quiet. He's grown to like the shopping center for all its hide-a-ways and neat places to play and have fun.

He opens the designer label bag. He searches through it until he feels the item he wants. He pulls out cookies individually wrapped in plastic.

Unwrapping one of the cookies, he tears at one corner without success. He tries another and the package splits open, causing cookie crumbs to scatter around him.

After eating a couple cookies, he pulls the water box out of the bag and takes a long drink. He replaces the rest of the cookies and the water box back in the bag. He's not sure of the time, but he knows he needs some rest before continuing on. Given the opportunity, he can keep evading the guards and reach the outer perimeter of the hexagon. Then he remembers the guards at the main entrances. He would have to duck into and out smaller corridors to evade the main entrances. The more he thinks about escape the more tired he becomes. Lying down, he falls fast asleep, within minutes.

Guards finish searching the southwestern section of the west hexagon and meet at the main west entrance to decide on their next search area. After several moments of discussion, the first guard decides to keep searching for as long as they can regardless of the night which is fast approaching. Being well aware of the barricades coming down, he begins to rearrange his crew.

At that moment, he hears the barricades coming down as the same moment that he thinks he sees the boy sleeping on the floor three barricades away.

Quickly running, he hurries his men back into the main west corridor. They make it past the first two barricades, but with the group spreading apart, the last two guards slide under the second barricade before they are all stopped as the third closed barricade reaches the floor of the corridor. The first guard pounds his fist against the barricade, resulting in a sound that reverberates several seconds, and stamps his left foot on the floor and then as quickly makes his decision for his own next action.

He must act quickly before his men can grumble although there isn't much else they can do for the time being. He realizes his men are already weary and they need their rest; tomorrow he will have the boy.

The first guard starts taking off his backpack and setting up camp for the night. The rest of the guards watch him closely, but he gives no command while some feel the same way, they know they have no other course of action.

The rest of the guards decide to do the same and follow their leader's actions. Soon, three tents are installed on the floor; mats, sleeping bags and backpacks now almost empty are placed inside, and arrangements for guard rotation are decided until six guards are sound asleep in tents. The other two stand guard one at each barricade walking back and forth from one side of the corridor to the other.

At first, they hear each other's footsteps and that does not bode well for their sleeping companions, so they synchronize their marching from end to end. They match their turns and with that their duty time is almost over as two guards in one tent get up and dressed for their oncoming duty.

The tents are parallel with their openings facing the third barricade, because the first guard is almost certain he saw the boy lying down in the corridor beyond the third barricade. Now he has to wait until the morning, but he intends to be ready no matter what may be on the other side of the barricade.

* * *

The shopping center while minimally maintained with automation runs into night mode. The lights dim with several stores going dark. Stars shine in through the transparencies in the roof. The clouds are high and fast moving across the sky from the southwest to the northeast.

Barricades close off certain parts of the center. Small round and flat automated cleaners start cleaning the floor and ten centimeter spheres do the windows and glass displays both within the stores and corridors. Oval spiders clean the walls moving deftly up and down. The light panels use a minimal amount of water while the soap clings to the surface until it is swiped off and the encapsulated dirt sent to the recyclers where the grime is separated from the soap.

Karl and Robert arrive at a barricade blocking them from going further. They both turn and look behind them as barricades all along the corridor come down. Quiet as they are it still takes time for all the barricades to fall and then the sound of cleaning equipment takes over. Karl checks his pilo.

Karl's pilo displays, "Wednesday, June 9, 2483 7:30 P.M. Bridget, Diversity."

Robert says, "Looks like a good safe place to stop and get some sleep."

After looking around, Karl says, "I agree with you. We need some rest and some food."

Taking off their backpacks and setting them on the floor, Karl and Robert set up camp while munching granola bars.

They bring out folding chairs first and sit in them as they finish eating. Robert thinks about what is happening back in his region although he is certain enough qualified officers were left at the station. Karl knows he needs this rest. He has his suspicions about what is on the other side of the barricade, but that will have to be left to the morning when he is fully rested.

After finishing his granola bar, Karl sets up the tent laying it out flat on the floor right side up a couple meters from the barricade. Getting the poles from his backpack, he pulls the folding poles apart until both are at their maximum length. Inserting the first pole, he puts one end through the middle strap and on through the rest of the loops until it is past the pocket at the other end. He has to bend the pole to get it into the end pocket.

He pushes the pole further through the loops until he can start pulling the other end through the closer loops and into the pocket closest to him. After popping the pole into the far pocket, the tent puffs up vertically with the tent floor remaining flat except for the two ends curling up. The tent opening faces away from the nearest barricade.

He does the same for the second pole and soon the large tent is in place with all the poles taut. Robert puts his mat and sleeping bag in the tent as Karl gets his mat and sleeping bag out of his backpack. Soon, both Karl and Robert are in their sleeping bags fast asleep.

The cleaning equipped robots sweeping and mopping the floor go around the tent and two chairs not calling for cleanup because their analysis reveals human occupation which overrides all other prerogatives. When they have finished mopping the floor of the corridor, they move to the inside middle wall between the two barricades. A small wide door opens in the wall matching their height and width. With one behind the other they zip off the floor into the doorway and the door closes without a seam.

On the other side of the barricade, Cliff sleeps several meters from Karl and Robert. On the opposite side, behind the other barricade six guards sleep on the floor with one guard standing watch at the barricade between the guards and Cliff.

Likewise for Cliff and the guards, the sweeping and mopping robots do not bother with the humans per their instructions. After going about their duties, they return to the inside wall as the other two did with the door closing behind them. The noise of the cleaning bots becomes silent.

Inside an elaborate system of conveyer belts and lifts, the various robots are emptied of their waste products and refurbished while those suffering various system defaults are set aside for repair. New robots are brought on line as old ones die off and are sent to waste control which recycles much of the material.

The new machines receive additional programming based on the track records of their peers.

THURSDAY

Morning

The guards begin to stir as they get out of their sleeping bags. The shopping center's corridor monitor displays, "Thursday, June 10, 2483 8:30 A.M. Bridget, Diversity."

Cliff awakens to the sound of barricades lifting. He lies still for a moment and then stands smoothing his uniform and thankful for the many restrooms along the corridors where he could clean up from his adventures in the maze until the sound of other people interrupts his thoughts. By the sounds of the voices and the activity, guards are on his right side and someone being very quiet without speaking is on his left. Obviously, his supposed rescuers are out numbered leaving him little choice.

The guards are wrapping up their camping area, putting on their backpacks as the single guard without a backpack spots Cliff twenty meters away near the north wall of the corridor. He yells, "There he is." The rest of the guards react immediately, leaving the last guard to put his backpack on while running towards the boy trying desperately to catch up.

Already prepared, the first guard and the second immediately start running towards Cliff leading the other five with the sixth still trailing. The rest of the guards had gathered their last few unpacked items and followed. The five guards stay behind the two lead guards by a good two meters with many of the guards still trying to get the rest of the items in their backpacks while the six still struggles to even put on his backpack.

Karl comes out of the tent with his shoes on and sets his backpack outside the tent. He starts to go back into the tent to retrieve his sleeping bag and mat when he spots Cliff as the barricade rises a meter from the floor.

Karl runs for him, but he stops when he sees the eight guards running faster; they are all most on top of Cliff with two guards way in front of the other guards. Karl weighs his options, but it doesn't look good.

Robert hears the barricade rising and notices that Karl is already out. He quickly puts on his shoes and tucks in his shirt. He comes out of the tent and looks over it finding Karl standing several meters from the tent, Cliff in the middle and eight guards running towards them. Running around the tent, Robert catches up with Karl.

Cliff recognizes the sounds of both sets of footprints and realizes that the guards will arrive first. He makes a quick decision even though he already knows what is about to happen.

He yells out to the two people on the other side who have stopped, "Don't worry, I'll be alright."

The two lead guards arrive at Cliff's position, but don't stop realizing that they have arrived before the two opponents have had time to get to the boy.

Looking back over his shoulder, while still running, the first guard says, "You six surround the boy. If they get away from us, send a message to the chief for reinforcements." The second guard keeps pace with the first as they get near Cliff.

The two lead guards run past Cliff while the other five surround him. The sixth guard arrives with his backpack finally on. The two lead guards stop about a meter from Karl and Robert who are smiling. The two lead guards are taller and more muscular than either Karl or Robert, but Karl is not easily intimidated while Robert wishes he had more men with him.

Deciding to give it a try, Karl says, "We really can't let you have the boy. We'll take him back to his mother and you can return to Ingrider empty handed."

Catching his breath, the first guard asks, "You think you can get past us and my other guards?"

Karl says, "No, but you will release him into our custody."

The first guard says, "Love to do that old chap, but your rules don't apply here.

"Your Chief of Police of Bridget can't do anything in this particular region. It is out of his jurisdiction."

Karl says, "True, but not out of mine."

The first guard says, "My master does not recognize your jurisdiction either.

"Take off your backpacks very slowly and place them on the floor."

Karl and Robert willingly comply, but Robert catches Karl's wink and remembers what he said about being captured. Robert relaxes but still has questions. Robert tries to talk, but Karl motions him to be silent for the moment. Robert hangs his head and waits for the lead guard to say something.

The first guard says, "Place your hands behind your back. My second will tie up your hands and then we will go someplace nice and quiet."

The second guard smiles and removes a couple of clear plastic ties from his right pants pocket.

He walks around the two men and ties Robert's hands together with one of the plastic ties zipping it tightly around his wrists. He does the same for Karl and then walks back to the first guard. Unknown to the guard, both of Karl's and Robert's hands were twisted, leaving some room for movement. As they relax their arms, the tight plastic ties become loose around their wrists. Robert nods slightly to Karl and Karl does the same so they both know they are okay.

The first guard turns around to the other guards surrounding Cliff. They in turn have one eye on the boy and another on their leaders waiting for their leader to tell them what to do next. A couple of the guards smile at Cliff but luckily he cannot see their leering smiles.

The first guard says loudly, "Take the boy to the locker behind the stairs under the central area. I will come and get him after we're through with these two guys."

The first guard turns back towards Karl and Robert.

Returning to his normal voice, the first guard says, "I only wish Ingrider could be here to see this.

"Okay, turn around and let's march to the next small corridor on your right. I know of this quiet little place that you will be delighted to see."

Keeping their arms twisted to keep the plastic ties tight in case the guard's look, Karl and Robert turn around and walk through the corridor to the east. The two guards follow Karl and Robert as they walk away from Cliff. The other six guards surrounding Cliff march the other way at a higher rate making Cliff run between two guards each of which have one of his hands.

When they arrive at the main west entrance, they walk to the two flighters in the small clearing outside the entrance. The two smallest guards take Cliff and with some dexterity squeeze themselves and Cliff into the storage locker of one of the flighters. Two other guards climb in the other storage locker and the two lead guards climb into their respective cockpits.

Soon the turbo fans are spinning up and the flighters jump into the air, turn to the east and engage the dual props pitching them forward towards the central cone.

* * *

The two guards shove Karl and Robert though the smaller corridor, trying to keep them stumbling which seems to work. Robert stubbles when he is caught off guard. Karl catches him before he falls to the floor. Robert stays far enough in front of the second guard to avoid being shoved. The shopping center's corridor monitor displays, "Thursday, June 10, 2483 9:00 A.M. Bridget, Diversity."

After walking through a smaller corridor, an exit door, the perimeter around the shopping center and the surrounding forest into a short grass meadow, the two guards with Karl and Robert arrive south of the west hexagon where they stop outside a meter and a half diameter hole in the ground fifteen meters deep.

The sky above them remains clear with only a few high clouds moving to the north faster than a flighter could move over the ground. The sun casts long shadows putting half the large clearing in sunshine. Animals with their tongues out panting rest in the shadow on the cool grass while others enjoying the warmth bask in the sunshine.

Karl and Robert stand next to the two guards waiting for the guards to give them their next set of orders which look pretty obvious. Karl looks in the hole and sees something which puts a smile on his face while Robert only sees a deep dark hole with an even darker bottom.

The first guard says, "I don't have time to do more than this, but I will be back later today to fill in this hole. So jump in."

Robert says, "You can't do this.

"You're under some control that's making you so mean, intimidating and thoughtless."

Karl says, "It's all right, Robert. We'll play his little game."

Karl jumps in and the second guard pushes Robert in feet first as Karl disappears into the hole.

"They'll be down there all afternoon and most of the evening before we ever get back," says the second guard.

"I'll pilo the city and get another two flighters out here. After I have the boy in a more secure area, I'll return, but since we don't know exactly what Ingrider's intentions are we'll have to wait before coming back out here. They should be well rested by then," says the first guard.

After landing on his feet with his legs well spread, Karl quickly backs into the wall of the hole as Robert lands beside him, bending both knees and falling backward to the wall. Struggling to get up, he straightens out his right leg, holding his foot above the ground. Grimacing and bending forward on his left leg, Robert says, "Ouch. I think I broke my right ankle."

Karl says, "Take your weight off of it until the nanos have time to reconstruct your ankle bones which will only take a moment or two."

Robert lifts his right foot and leans against the wall of the hole which is on his left to take as much weight as possible off of it. Although he senses the throbbing, he feels little else which initially puzzles him until he realizes the biologic nanos are at work stemming the pain and healing the wound as good as they can. He remembers this from a long time ago when he was a teenager in a high school biology class. He also remembers why he didn't like the class: the teacher.

Never in his entire lifetime has he ever been injured since he was a youngster until now.

Robert says, "I can feel it getting better with every movement. I can even wiggle my ankle without any pain."

Karl says, "Try putting some pressure on it."

Robert sets his right foot tenderly on the dirt floor and puts a little weight on it, waiting for the pain to hit, but as he puts more weight on it, he's pleasantly surprised by the lack of pain and the throbbing has gone away as well. However, with his full weight on his right leg, he notices something else. His right leg is bowed out like he had been riding on a horse.

Robert says, "It feels a little awkward, as the bones aren't in the right place. I'm going to have to walk with a limp for some time, probably whenever I get to a doctor to reset my ankle."

Karl says, "That probably means the nanos took the fast route to workability.

"It will be like that for a long time until something else happens to your foot to cause it to be realigned."

Robert asks, "Why did you agree so readily?"

Karl says, "The inside wall is made of brick that only serve to keep the dirt from caving in filling the hole. If you look closely, they are quite loose and only keep their position by sheer weight."

Robert remarks, "Why didn't I notice that?"

Karl says, "Besides, it gets the guards out of our way for a long time. They won't be back until later this afternoon, just to give us time to mellow. So we have time to get out of here.

"This is what I have in mind."

Robert listens intently.

"They are going to be mighty ticked off when they come back and find that we are gone. I almost wish we could hide out in the forest and watch their faces," says Karl.

"We'll be able to have an edge next time," responds Robert.

Back to back, Karl tries to break Robert's plastic tie, but is unsuccessful. He turns around putting his back against the wall. Karl slides down until he sits on the ground. Bending slightly forward, he rolls to his right and then left as he pulls his arms out from under his legs. Once he has his arms in front, he pulls off his belt and opens the clasp taping it onto the plastic straps around his wrist. The plastic ties separate and fall to the dirt floor. Karl rubs his fingers around each wrist even though the ties weren't that tight. Feeling for Robert's wrists, he does the same with the ties on the dirt floor.

Karl and Robert, unbound, with their backs together remove bricks as they climb up the hole step by step with the top getting closer with each step. Before long, they are out of the hole and on their way back into the shopping center to retrieve their backpacks and water boxes because they are both thirsty.

* * *

The garden outside the kitchen shows recent activity with various gardening tools lying about. Inside, Tarcey's kitchen console monitor displays, "Thursday, June 10, 2483 10:30 A.M. Bridget, Diversity."

Pacing around the kitchen center console first clockwise and then abruptly counterclockwise, Tarcey stops facing the kitchen and heads right for the kitchen' double sink. She opens the cabinet door to the left of the sink. Removing a box of cereal, she places it on the counter with a questioning look on her face, trying to remember why she is doing this.

A moment later she does something else to ponder for the rest of her life.

She goes right to the end of the kitchen counter and opens another cabinet door filled with glassware on the bottom, stemware in the middle and cups hanging from the top of the cabinet. After looking over the glasses, she selects one in the front. Removing a small glass, she returns to the double sink.

She reaches for the faucet handle and stops short holding her position with the small glass under the faucet. Her hand is mere centimeters from the handle and the glass is centered under the faucet nozzle.

After several seconds, she returns the small glass and the cereal to their places in the cabinets, placing her hips back against the counter as she looks out the bay window on the other side of the dining room. She ponders her moves trying to figure on some semblance of meaning.

Tarcey says, "This is too weird. The last time I had this feeling, I thought he was lost in the river. I better message Robert. I haven't heard a thing so far. They have to keep me up to date or else I have to join them."

She heads for the dining table, sits down in one of the chairs, and removes the pilo from her purse which is on the table. After turning it on, she writes:

Tarcey's pilo displays, "Robert, where are you and have you found Cliff yet? His birthday will be Saturday and I have special plans. Although I suppose I could cancel them, but that would make Cliff very unhappy. He's been looking forward to this event."

She pushes the send button and returns the pilo to her purse. She decides to finish her planning for Cliff's birthday party. There are still many people to call.

She realizes that many of the calls she has received are from Cliff's student mothers and fathers offering their help and concerns. Realizing, she hasn't even replied to all of them at this time, she begins to wonder at how it will all get done.

Maybe, she can enlist their help, at least some of them. She takes out her pilo again and starts going through the checklist adding, changing and deleting items as necessary. Staying focused with a grim look on her face as she makes several critical decisions. Only when she has the list filled does she smile. With her list in order of confirmed, possibilities, part-time, travel only and not available, she stops.

Moments later, she is using her pilo to call one of the student mothers who had already offered to help with decorations, meal planning and preparation. After the pleasantries, Tarcey gets directly to the point with the other party agreeing whole heartedly.

A half hour later, she is talking with another student mother about getting barbeques delivered in time with contingency alternates. They spend the rest of their time talking about how much faster they grow older attempting to bring up children.

After two more calls, she checks the time and finds an hour has gone by without a word from Robert. She's not too concerned since he's done this before, making her wait much longer than necessary. Not liking it a bit, after putting up with it, hoping he would change, she decided that it grated her nerves so much that she could no longer stand to be near him without breaking out in hives. But, of course, that is not her true reaction.

Much more sensibly, she can put up with his attitude at a distance and she still remains awed by his unwillingness to change. When she is near him, she tries very hard to remain complacent and not be goaded by his off-handed remarks and insinuations.

* * *

The shopping center buzzes with activity. Displays are changing, new merchandise arrives at the outer doors, small robots remove packing material and left over packing. Parcels are being delivered to each of the stores. The shopping center's corridor monitor displays, "Thursday, June 10, 2483 11:30 A.M. Bridget, Diversity."

The weather outside has turned nasty with rain showers, high winds and an occasional lightning strike. Many animals dash into the forest to get out of the rain. Rivulets form between the cones sending gushes of water through the downspouts out onto the perimeter down through pebble covered drains.

Karl and Robert have their backpacks on walking out of the shopping center along the smaller corridor to the northwestern exit. They barely get out into the rain showers when a bolt of lightning strikes only moments away. Both return back into the corridor shaking the rain off of their backpacks and their clothes. They each watch the display of lightning and thunder interspersed with waves of heavy rain as the trees bend.

The perimeter around the shopping center fills with water that can't drain into the ground fast enough with the rain gushing out of gutters and pelting the perimeter. The bark, that makes up most of the ground cover, floats. Even the forest fills with rainwater and spills wide waterfalls of leaves and small branches into the prairie beyond. Animals are curled up under and around the largest trees with the younger animals closer to the trunks and the larger animals which get some rain on them farther away.

Karl asks, "Having toured this amazing conglomerate of shopping stores, I am completely amazed. Even a child would have a time in here with all the variety and yet, it's not used by anyone. The goods seem to rotate by age with the oldest products being recycled and the newest brought forward. So, the only reason you call this a derelict shopping center is to keep people out?"

Robert says, "This one is too mechanized for most people. They want a face to face relationship when they buy something.

"At least, that is what I hear most.

"Tarcey is quite vocal about her shopping needs."

Karl says, "I don't have many reports on Tarcey.

· "She was a member of Ingrider's original church in Bridget. She quit a week before Cliff was born, never returning."

Robert says, "She was a little mixed up then. She was one of the principles translating the library information.

"She quit to care for the child and has been out of work ever since."

Karl asks, "And you had a relationship with her several years before Cliff?"

Robert says, "We're two peas all right, but clearly not of the same pod.

"I work too many hours away from home.

"That is one of the reasons for thinking about being a District Councilman."

Karl asks, "So you're not the father of Cliff?"

Robert says, "Hardly, we broke it off, before getting to that stage or even discussing it.

"She wanted a child very much and decided on in vitro as the preferred way."

Robert's pilo beeps.

Robert says, "It's from Tarcey."

Karl says, "Don't give away anything about our recent engagement. It will only raise her concerns. She has enough on her mind with her child missing.

"Let her know where we searched and what we ran into. Mention that we saw Cliff was in good health when he was recaptured by the guards."

Robert says, "Yep, this calls for a little dexterity and tact which I have had to do too many times."

The weather begins to subside with the wind decreasing and the rain turning into light showers.

The dark clouds above turn lighter and begin to dissipate. Soon Karl and Robert are walking through the perimeter and into the forest.

Afternoon

Karl and Robert sit in their flighters in the clearing finishing a protein bar and bran muffin respectively. Their water bottles are on within their cockpits on the shelf below the short windbreaker window.

Raindrops hang off the top leaves of short grass glistening in the sunshine. The entire clearing literally sparkles, casting several tiny rainbows across the middle. The tall grass beyond waves as the wind gently blows through to the prairie on the other side. High clouds move swiftly across the bright blue sky.

Karl's cockpit monitor says, "Thursday, June 10, 2483 12:00 P.M. Bridget, Diversity."

Karl says, "I'll fly over the old city to investigate the six gate exits including the lower terrace's stairwell to the maze. You said there were six guards assigned to each gate. You didn't indicate how many are assigned to each terrace level, but you believe the red sashes seem to have the top terrace. I will spend more time around the shopping center especially the central cone. That circular room in the center of the complex mystifies me. You head back to Bridget and organize a worldwide search at all of Ingrider's past visitations.

"I'll meet you in Bridget in about an hour."

Robert says, "That circular room happens to be over a geothermal steam vent rising through the ground. It is the most common power source all over the planet. Wind turbines come in a close second, but only between two latitudes around the north and south hemispheres. Solar panels take what's left providing electricity for most of the homes in each region.

"It is used to provide electrical power and steam heating for the entire shopping center. Be careful, he knows we fly over and that our only weapon is common sense.

"There are other exits other than the regular small and large corridors. They once were used as employee entrances and exits for smoking breaks. The large doors are no longer used. They had been used to convey goods to the stores from trucks with a large capacity for cargo. That was before the entire center became automated."

After starting their respective engines and warming up the turbo props in the wings, they take off vertically and then engage their dual props for normal flight.

They fly away from the clearing with Robert flying north towards Bridget and Karl flying southeast towards the old city.

*   *   *

Karl watches the old city come into view with the individual levels becoming clearer. His cockpit monitor displays, "Thursday, June 10, 2483 12:30 P.M. Bridget, Diversity."

Karl reaches the outskirts of the old city and watches from above. White habited acolytes scurry all over the old city moving tables and chairs into position. On the three lower terraces, acolytes form groups by ages around taller and older acolytes, some sitting on the ground while others have chairs to sit in. E-books are passed out along with small pilos. The upper terrace buzzes with red sash acolytes obviously preparing for something, cleaning the gardens, walkways, benches and floors, leaving a glistening shine on all the flat surfaces.

The wind twirls through the flags and banners with down drafts and up drafts throughout the top of the circular hub. Birds sing as they clean their wings while grasping tree branches in the nearby forest.

On the perimeter, other small mammals cavort and rest in the midday sun while their parents keep their eyes and ears watchful for any danger.

Several guards safeguard the base of the hub at the entrance and no one exits or enters the hub. Karl circles the old city.

Two guards fortify each of the six gates standing guard on either side of the large double doors. Four other guards mill about on the lower terrace. One checks the time, pulls the sleeve of the closest guard.

Those two guards march out the open gate to relieve the other guards.

The other two head into habitats near each set of terrace steps to the gates. The habitats are as tall as each of the terraces and extend fifteen meters under the terrace except for the habitats on the upper terrace which are only ten meters long extending out over the lower habitat.

As Karl reaches the east end, he turns sharply and heads directly over the center of the old city to the western side of the old city. Similar activity occurs on the west side of the city. After he reaches the western side, he heads north across the perimeter and the surrounding forest of mostly evergreens interspersed with lighter green deciduous. He continues flying across alternating short or long grasslands over an ever widening plain of isolated sand dunes, dust bowls, twisted trees, tall dark grass clusters and spotted watering holes.

When he can no longer see the old city behind him except for the tall tower, he executes a shallow turn southwest towards the derelict shopping center.

* * *

Karl's flighter nears the shopping center. The central tower comes into view first with the outer smaller towers appearing right after. His cockpit monitor displays, "Thursday, June 10, 2483 1:00 P.M. Bridget, Diversity."

Over the shopping center, Karl flies around the periphery noticing entrances and exits which he transfers to his pilo.

He flies low over the short grass clearing and the entrance to the maze.

Evergreens, brambles, bushes and vines hide most of the shopping center up to several meters from the perimeter while the inside covered corridors remain clear

Transparencies, in the bottom third of all the cones, allow daylight to reach into each section, providing most of the light.

The shopping center contains six sections surrounding a central section, all hexagons. A short six-sided cone caps each outer section. Capped with a tall six sided cone, the central section has a circular room beneath the cone whose wall is free standing. Within the circular room, piping, framework and machinery are partially masked by steam. Inside the circular room is an enclosed rectangular room with a roof.

The walls are five meters tall with each wall hundred meters long. The walls are basic tan background stucco with large white hexagon relieves. Broad black bands five centimeters wide surround the large hexagon at the top and bottom of each wall. Each hexagon contains a single color square, triangle or circle with no two adjoining having the same color.

Brightly colorful banners undulate in the light wind from the central tall cone to the smaller cones. Each banner is completely different than the others with symbols used like letters, probably to indicate the type of stores in each hexagon.

As he flies past several of the transparencies of the outer hexagons, displays are updated; old material is replaced with new; advertising changes moods with different colors intertwined.

Stores completely rearrange some of their goods, display and advertising, including new aisle arrangements with everything happening in a coordinated rush. Sometimes two actions would lead to a disaster, while a single action comes to a complete stop.

After the disaster is eliminated, the action continues at an alarming rate. Entire displays are uprooted and carried away as new displays take their place with even the aisle's flooring changing color and texture to an abstract variation. The outdoor equipment has completely rearranged the store for the summer season with water and hiking emphasized in all the displays and advertising.

Displays near the entrances are swapped out with upcoming seasonal merchandise, items for sale and discounted or discontinued merchandise. Empty boxes, wrapping, filling, straps and any other extraneous materials are gathered and taken away to be recycled.

Wishing he could spend more time, even though the search for the boy was daunting, he continues to fly around the west hexagon marveling at all the activity that very few will ever see. He's also beginning to see Robert's reasons for calling it a derelict shopping center. The mechanisms of all the displays and advertising would dull people's senses causing all type of catastrophes. Completing his survey, Karl turns in a wide arc and flies north towards Bridget.

* * *

Karl lands in front of the police station not far from Robert's distinctive flighter. He shuts off the turbo props in the wings and waits for them to quit spinning. He secures the dual props in the rear and turns off the engine. He goes through the checklist marking all the faults, if any.

He signs his name and places the folder back in its pocket on back of the seat cushion where the information is transferred to the central processing center in the city for updating records of repair and recycle. When finished and verified, the checklist is wiped clean.

The sun hides more often as cloud formations increase over the southern mountains. Dark clouds begin building at a quickening pace with rain showers darkening the lower mountains. The winds have not yet reached the city, but it won't be long before the winds bring showers and gusts.

As he climbs out of the cockpit, he watches officers stream out of the Police Station down the steps running for their respective flighters. After they have climbed into the aircraft, they take off vertically almost in unison. Arriving at slightly different altitudes, they engage their dual props and take off in all the major and minor compass directions.

Karl walks into the Police Station as more officers rush out into their flighters now wearing flight suits, gloves, boots and helmets. He barely squeezes into the double doors when he is jostled every which way by the onrushing officers. He loses sight of where he is with all the spinning and it isn't until all the officers have passed by him that he can return to his senses.

He looks out the two doors as the officers get to their respective flighters and begin taking off. As the last of the aircraft takes off, the skies over the city become dark and foreboding. In the distance, lightning strikes and the thunder quickly follows. Unfortunately, the lightning strikes continue getting closer.

As he watches out the glass windows, the last of the officers walk calmly by him staying out of his way.

After going through the front doors and down the stairs, they spread out for the sidewalks branching to each grid of the city that Ingrider had visited.

Lightening and the resulting thunderous boom strikes the high flag pole above the Police Station raining sparks all over the grounds and flighters.

The bright flash briefly highlights the entire area.

Now the previously full field of aircraft is practically empty with all three rows having ten or fewer flighters spread out over the field. A couple more officers quickly pass Karl going out the front doors down the steps to their aircraft. Soon even fewer flighters dot the field.

The thunder from multiple lightning strikes reverberates across the Police Station, undulating the windows causing them to repeat the sounds inside. The rain comes down in torrents of water for brief times, returning to a steady drizzle. Water accumulates in the gullies along the many streets, emptying into underground sewers at one corner of each intersection with leaves building diversions along the way. Road nanos remove blockades as soon as they are formed allowing the water to flow freely into the sewers. The leaves are picked up in recyclers on single wheels, which are in turn dumped into larger vehicles with four wheels although some use only three.

* * *

Robert's office empties from a meeting with top officers. His monitor displays, "Thursday, June 10, 2483 2:30 P.M. Bridget, Diversity."

Robert sits at his office desk as Karl walks in. Only a few officers' desks have people frantically pushing buttons on their pilos. The rest of the desks are empty, some looking like they had left leaving coffee cups amid a confused desktop.

Robert pushes buttons with a serious look on his face like the half dozen officers still manning their desks. Karl marvels at all the activity. Some would say the police station was overwhelmed with some kind of project.

Most of the desks are empty with only a select few of the returning officers filling out reports, sending and receiving messages on their pilos. Doing research, one of the officers studies the results making notes on a paper pad.

Each cubicle has four desks butted together with some cubicles in better shape than others although there isn't a new metal desk in the entire station and that probably includes every northern region. Funds are at a premium at every police station especially at the northern provinces. The southern half of the globe got more of the money, that is, more funds committed.

Very few cubicles have candy wrappers, paper lunch bags, food scraps and assorted paraphernalia not only covering the desks but all around the floor of one or all the nearby desks.

A few officers come in through the front double doors stopping off at their desks, checking their pilos for new messages or assignments. One, especially, pulls a candy bar out of one of the drawers and after tearing the wrapper sits down with his feet on the desk, leaning back in the chair until he is comfortable. He munches on the candy bar, savoring the taste.

Most desks are decorated with, at least, some flowers in pots or containers with the usual family or loved one's pictures. Along the walls, calendars and wanted posters are pasted between the desks while the central desks have calendars and posters on the outside of their desks In the northwest corner a long tall cactus occupies a green pot while the other corners contain various short evergreen trees probably transported from the nearby forest. They are, of course, the most likely to be decorated during Christmas.

Most of the returning officers, after checking for messages, head right back out, through the hallway to the front doors and back out to their flighters where they once more take off and head to their next destination.

Others not quite sure check their own results or ask for their fellow officers opinions. Four officers joke around, telling each of their exploits, during the last few days. The laughter gets to its raunchiest when a sergeant comes between all of them and puts a quick stop to the reveling. The shamed officers return to their duties alerting other regions and trying to get the location of Ingrider's previous conferences, meetings and impromptu meetings with the press within the city of Bridget.

Some seek new assignments from their commanding officers usually through inquiries over their pilos or face to face with some bickering or down right refusing to obey their commanding officer until with the right reasoning the officers are convinced enough to follow orders.

After looking around at all the activity, Karl says, "You certainly move fast. Some people are going to think you're understaffed for this operation."

Looking up after Karl makes his comment, Robert says, "I've got dozens of officers locating and searching every place that Ingrider lived, visited or staged a conference in within the region of Bridget. It's going to be awhile with the large area to cover. I don't expect any results soon.

"Extending our reach even further, my office is contacting every city on Diversity that Ingrider has been to and each region is doing the same when they have additional information. Some of the smaller regions have reported back and I'm expecting some others later this afternoon.

"No sign of Cliff, yet, but we haven't had enough reports coming back. The other regions are aware of our timeline and are pressing forward with all the information they can gather.

"Tarcey called earlier about the boy.

"She is coming in a half hour. She wants to talk with you."

Karl asks, "Do you have a private office we could use?"

Robert says, "Use the small conference room at the end of the hall."

* * *

The hallway to the conference room has high windows on the outer side. It's painted in a neutral grey. The conference room's monitor displays, "Thursday, June 10, 2483 3:15 P.M. Bridget, Diversity."

The conference room's walls are painted light green with an oak wood floor. Two high windows on the outer side keep sunshine from ever casting shadows. Three rows of panel lights cover the ceiling with only the central row lit. Near the door, a ceiling vent pulls air out of the room while at the other end two vents bring warmer air into the room as necessary keeping the air temperature in the conference room slightly lower than twenty-one degrees centigrade.

A small table against the wall contains a coffee pot with paper dispenser, ceramic and paper coffee cups and several unopened water boxes. A blank white board hangs from the center of the wall with several colors of pens in the tray along the bottom edge along with a red laser pointer. The meter white board has several figures and drawings along with street maps, photographic and artist depicted pictures and several colors of pointers around various objects.

Karl sits at one end of a small conference table with his hands in his lap as he swings his left leg over his right and absent mindedly moves it back and forth or around in a circle. While he sees a beautiful woman at the other end, he isn't quite sure what she wants, but he is hopeful for a common agreement which he hopes won't take too long. This one is going to be tricky; she's very smart with a quick comeback.

Tarcey, at the other end, stands, gripping the top of the chair with white knuckles. Her mood is dourer, if not outright defensive. She is not certain that this man can do anything to get her son back. If they come to a reasonable agreement, it will be on her terms for sure.

Karl says, "This is a kidnapping case, not a lost child.

"It involves some nasty people who are under some influence. People using the GHD would not react like this."

Relaxing her hold on the chair and rethinking her attitude, Tarcey says, "The old civilization was also under some influence, but was unable to destroy it.

"They left no record of their reason for leaving. Leaving was one way to escape.

"The General Health Device works in conjunction with our immune system and augments our biologic nanos. Safe guards are in place to prevent catastrophes."

Karl says, "Right now, we are concentrating our search patterns wherever Ingrider has been.

"We will find Cliff, before anything happens."

Tarcey asks, "You think something is going to happen?"

Karl says, "An offering is in preparation in the old city and Cliff is the sacrifice.

"I will not let anything happen to that boy. You will have him back. However, I can't make any promises that I will be able to get your son out before his birthday this coming Saturday. I'm working against too many people. They have him well guarded."

Tarcey says, "Ingrider was not a merciless man when I knew him. He has certainly changed. He was so kind and gentle around everyone no matter where he was. What could have changed him so?"

* * *

Karl sits in the cockpit of his flighter with Robert standing by. The clouds above him are in turmoil shifting one way and then the other. Waves of black clouds are interspersed with white and gray before they in turn become black.

Karl's cockpit monitor displays, "Thursday, June 10, 2483 5:30 P.M. Bridget, Diversity."

The wind blows gustily clearing the field of anything loose. Karl keeps his eyes inside the cockpit until he hears something pop against the fuselage. He looks up to see the wind blowing everything loose from the ground into the air.

Robert hangs on to Karl's fuselage as he says something. Noticing Karl's lack of response, Robert attempts to move closer.

Robert pulls through the steady wind between gusts, keeping his right hand on the fuselage as he gets closer to Karl's cockpit and both feet flat on the ground.

Reaching the cockpit, Robert says loudly, "Be careful. The reports are negative so far but only a quarter of the world has reported in.

"I don't expect any more reports until tomorrow."

Karl replies equally loudly, "I'll camp near the shopping center. There are certain places I want to visit. If I find what I am looking for, I might be able to achieve Cliff's release way before the sacrifice, but don't hold your breath. There have been other cases where I have been thwarted from achieving an early success.

"A six sided cone covers the shopping center central core. A circular room occupies the inside of the central hexagon with piping, turbines and generators giving off vast amounts of steam. The geothermal vent provides all of the heat for the complex."

Robert says loudly, "That's probably the heating and electrical room for the shopping center and the maze below.

"The cone vents the excess heat, usually in the form of steam, from the geothermal process which also provides electricity and drives most of the larger stationary machines."

Karl says, "You also mentioned tunnels. I'm sure I heard you say you don't have subways and I haven't seen any indicators for subway access or maps and my resources could not find any on this planet. Apparently, you weren't lying when you said you use flighters for basic transportation."

Robert says, "First off, they were here long before my grandparents colonized this planet. My ancestors didn't find them for twenty-five years. They're for the farming equipment according to the library.

"We think that the computers down there also could make harvesters and transporters for the grains and produce. For some reason they only plant and cultivate. If we don't harvest, the plants are plowed right back into the ground."

Karl says, "I'll fly over the farm that Bridget surrounds if you don't mind. I'm not sure we'll be able to use the tunnels, but one never knows."

Robert says, "I'll bring the key you will need to get into the tunnels. We try to keep people out, but occasionally someone goes missing ignoring the signs.

"That's when we find them in the tunnels, although I haven't the foggiest idea how they got there."

Robert backs away from Karl's flighter keeping his hand on the top edge of the fuselage. He uses one of the tail fins next and practically flies into the stair railing behind him. Karl takes off vertically using the turbo fans, but has to quickly engage the dual props to keep from being blown into the Police Station.

He finally gains more control as he increases his altitude, until he is flying south into the wind.

Evening

The shopping center slips into shutdown mode as the cleaning bots begin moving into the stores. Its main western corridor monitor displays, "Thursday, June 10, 2483 6:30 P.M. Bridget, Diversity."

Karl walks along the long wide main western corridor towards a "T" intersection ahead mere meters away. The corridor looks curved and has intersections to the north, south, east and west. The outer corridor, surrounding the inner, provides access to each of the six hexagons that make up the shopping center. The floor has become nothing more than polished concrete with the gray varying in tint. The lighting remains primarily from the transparencies in the outer cone with additional light panels behind valances around the tops of each wall of the circular corridor. The inner corridor wall is free-standing.

He turns right into the inner curved corridor and walks till he comes to a door on the left wall. All along the right side curved wall of the corridor, several shops close down. A solid wall free standing with tapered columns every few meters occupies his left. With no windows or decoration, the wall seems entirely plain except for columns. Karl takes that this corridor is also wider than the rest with plenty of room for a flighter's wingspan.

The sign on the door says: "For Authorized Personnel ONLY". It doesn't have a window allowing Karl to see into the circular room. Karl tries to open the door, but the lever doesn't budge. Karl removes his backpack and sets it on the floor. After taking one box out of a side pocket of the backpack, he opens it. On the side of the box are the following words, "lock nanos 100".

After opening the corner of the box with his right hand, Karl taps the box into his left palm.

Several small round black objects, smaller than the head of a pin, fall into Karl's left palm. Needing less, he puts half of them back in the box. Resealing the box with his right hand, he places his left hand over the door's lock, holding for less than a minute and then releasing his hold over the door's handle.

The lock clicks open with the door swinging freely into the circular room. The sounds of steam escaping, turbines whining and generators spinning at various frequencies impact on Karl's ears. Putting the box back into the side pocket, he zips the pocket closed. After putting on his backpack, Karl walks in, closing the door behind him and locking it from the inside.

Light panels behind valences around the circular wall light the wall with a soft glow leaving minimal shadows. Additional light panels throughout the framework light the walkways, the ladders, the instrument clusters, the compressors and major piping outlets of the geothermal facility.

The circular room's three stories of framework are filled with piping and vents hissing, moaning and cracking. On his right, two electrical conduits exit the middle of the back wall of a rectangular room, curving ninety degrees into the floor. The main turbine generators have conduits running along parallel to the floor for a meter before curving with two forty five degree turns to go under the floor.

A small dome encloses the geothermal vent on the left with puffs of steam exiting from random places around the edge of the dome. The floor rumbles from the release of gases by the geothermal vent. The framework of the facility counter balances the rumbling from the floor keeping the entire process running smoothly and efficiently, reducing the amount of maintenance.

Four large turbo generators turn with a low hum between the dome and the room. Feeling the increased heat and the vibration from the generators, Karl removes his backpack, setting it on the floor of the circular room. The conduit coming out of the generators are almost eight centimeters in diameter supplying over six hundred amps of current to the shopping center.

He removes his coat as he starts to sweat tying the arms of the coat around his waist as drops of sweat fall off his forehead and his hair becomes damp as it tries to dissipate the excess heat. Already, he feels relief from the heat within the room. Grabbing his water box from his backpack, Karl takes a large gulp, washing his face and hair with some of the water. He replaces the water box on the backpack as he surveys the framework and ladders.

Karl puts on the backpack and walks over to the plastisteel framework holding the piping, vents and gages as well as providing access and walkways. After climbing the first ladder, he walks on a walkway above the turbo generators as they hum pushing all that steam through the turbines which in turn spin the generators with excess steam venting at higher pressure points giving a definite sense of heat throughout the complex.

Steam rises from the generators making the rails hot as the generators are cooled by spring water which turns to steam on the hot generators. Karl refrains from touching them until he walks past the generators. On the other side, more piping and vents come into view. Nearby around the corner, the ladder goes up.

Karl climbs up the second ladder. Before he is even on the second step, a metallic sound startles him. He's not sure if it came from the level below him or above him. Halfway up the ladder, he stops climbing and looks around below him trying to see anything amiss on the lower level. Cautiously, he continues to climb up the ladder.

He stops as his head reaches the next level walkway. Suspicious, he looks above the walkway from the outside corner trying to get a glimpse of anything suspicious on the walkway, but it is empty as he had feared.

Wisps of steam cross over the otherwise clear walkway rising above and along the framework. Continuing up to the walkway, he steps onto it. A shadow moves at the end of the walkway which Karl catch's out of the corner of his eye because he was watching the gauge panel to his left.

Karl walks slowly towards the end of the walkway noticing where the piping and vents direct steam, keeping the streams small. Most of the piping is within reach of the walkway probably for maintenance. He gets to the corner of the walkway, looks around and starts walking to the next corner, carefully watching for any movement above or below him.

Startling Karl, the second guard from the walkway above, says, "Thought you could get away, huh. But I found you first.

"The other guard was sure you would land in the city. But you are more daring."

Karl stops and looks around trying to get an angle on the guard's location, but the guard is enveloped in steam making it hard to gauge his whereabouts. As he turns back, something rams into his shoulders from above and pushes his chest to the inner rail of the walkway. Falling off the top rail and bouncing off the second lower rail onto the walkway, Karl shakes his head to clear his senses, turns over and sees the second guard standing over him.

The second guard says, "Thought we wouldn't find you. This time I will make sure you die."

Karl asks, "How can you be so sure?"

The second guard says, "When I get through with you, you're going to love your steam bath. Over a hundred degrees Celsius will definitely cook you."

The guard lifts Karl up and shoves his back over the rail above the main piping. Karl grabs the rail with both hands and twists the guard around with his hips and legs on the lower rail. The guard releases him and Karl swings landing a left upper cut to the guard's chin. The guard returns with a left hook catching Karl with his back against the rail again. Karl reels back against the hot rail protected by the clothes he wears. But he still feels the heat.

The guard continues to push Karl backwards over the rail, edging closer and closer to the top rail where Karl's waist is for the moment. He tries to push the guard's arms down, but it only results in him being lifted closer to the rail. Deciding to try a different tactic, Karl grabs the rail with both hands pulling upwards which stops his upward progress, but the exertion is overcome by the guard's brawny endeavor. Beginning to realize he will have to do something else, he spots the piping surrounding their heads.

Karl strains to hold onto the rail with his left hand as he releases his right. Copious amounts of sweat fall off Karl's forehead sometimes falling into his eyes temporarily blinding him for a moment. Squinting, Karl spies a three centimeter pipe within reach and pulls it back and forth with his right hand straining against the heat and sweat realizing that if this effort fails, he will be falling two levels down. The pipe breaks at the junction and sprays super-saturated steam into the guard's face.

The guard releases Karl and covers his face yelling and then muffling foul words walking backwards towards the ladder to the lower level. Karl recovers from the rail and pushes the guard backwards along the walkway moving him closer to the ladder.

Steam rises from below.

Karl says, "Not as easy as you thought."

Before they get to the gauge panel, the guard reaches out and grabs Karl's right hand, placing it on the rail where steam jets hit it. As Karl's hand against the rail sizzles from the high pressure steam, he wrenches the guard's hand off of his right hand, using his left shoulder. The guard is thrown back another step closer to the ladder.

Ignoring the pain, but unable to make a fist with his right, Karl lands a left hook into the guard's red deformed face, making the guard walk drunkenly backward another two steps where he is only a step before the ladder.

The guard takes another step backwards, but he's on the edge of the walkway at the descending ladder with only the ball of his right foot on the edge of the walkway. He struggles to regain his balance with his weight past the edge of the walkway.

The guard's face begins to change, his cheeks become smooth, his mouth returns to its place, his nose straightens and his eyes clear with new eyelids and eyebrows. He takes a deep breath and exhales slowly through his nose.

The second guard yells, "I can see!"

Reaching for the rail and missing it with his fingertips, the guard falls off the walkway at the ladder backwards. He lands on the next level with his neck broken on the rail and his legs twisted underneath awkwardly. His right arm hangs loosely over the rail while his left arm drapes across his chest.

Karl looks at the palm of his right hand. The black impression of the rail disappears. The ridges and new pink skin replace the blackened line which gets absorbed beneath the skin.

As he opens his fingers, stretching his skin over his palm, more guards enter the circular room. Not feeling any pain, he intentionally keeps that palm away from surfaces.

One of the guards below says, "He's up on the second level. You go that way and we'll go this way."

Karl runs to the other end of the walkway and turns the corner, climbing up the ladder to the third level. The bottom step of the central ladder going up to the conical top rests on the fourth level. The conical tower opening is hidden in steam.

Another guard below says, "He's killed the second in command. We've got him now. Hurry, he can only get away through the tower."

Karl runs down the walkway and turns the corner to the final ladder to the fourth walkway. He climbs the ladder to the fourth walkway and takes a few steps to the central ladder going up the inner cone which is tighter than the outer cone. The top of the cone shines with the lights within the cone's very top.

As a guard climbs onto the last level, he points to Karl getting on the ladder to the conical tower and says, "He's on the top level, hurry."

Karl climbs the ladder as two guards appear below him arriving at the ladder. One starts climbing after him, moving faster than Karl does. The other guard stays at the bottom of the ladder pulling out his pilo and sending messages to other guards to gather on the upper level near the conical ladder. Karl gets about halfway up when the other guard catches his right foot.

Karl releases his hands and falls on the guard's shoulders, making the guard grunt. Karl keeps his weight on the guard and waits with his left hand tightly on a rung. He jumps causing the guard to lose his grip on the ladder with the right hand. The guard tires from the exertion.

Finally, the guard can't bear his weight any longer and falls down to the walkway on top of the other guard. Straining, Karl bears all his weight with his left hand until he gets his feet in the rungs. Karl continues up the ladder.

* * *

Climbing out the top of the cone through the steam, Karl catches his feet on the bolts and nuts holding the seam together. He tries hard not to use his sensitive right hand on the hot seam as he moves down outside the cone, although the pain has long since disappeared. About halfway down, the feeling of pain in his right hand dissipates and he begins using his right hands which allows him to make a faster transition to the seams between the cones.

Landing on the roof at the base of the conical tower of the shopping center, he gets his bearings looking out over one half of the cones making up the shopping center. Removing his backpack and his shirt, he wraps his right hand in his shirt sleeve to protect it until he has time for a bandage. He runs across the top of the shopping center using the seams, until he gets to the west perimeter.

Karl gets down on his stomach as he nears the west perimeter. Below, his flighter sits right where he left it, unguarded. Karl finds a nearby deciduous tree with long branches close enough. He takes several steps back along the seam between two cones in line with the branch. He runs as fast as he can and lands his hands on the branch. Using hand over hand, he follows the branch inward until he is standing over another. Soon enough, he's on the ground walking out of the forest.

He cautiously approaches the flighter without incident keeping a watchful eye out for any guards patrolling the perimeter or coming out of the main west corridor.

After securing his backpack in the storage locker inside the nose cone of the flighter, he climbs into the cockpit and spins up the turbine fans, punching in his destination. When he finishes with the final checkout, he fastens his straps around his midsection tightening each. He looks out over the plains and watches the clouds high above.

Clouds are racing across the sky leaving patches of open sky with updrafts and downdrafts amongst the tree tops.

Pushing the throttle forward, he braces himself as the flighter leaps into the sky. When he reaches the desired altitude buffeted from the whirling winds, the dual props in the rear come up to speed quickly. Titling the wings horizontal, he changes course. He flies northwest towards Bridget's farm.

* * *

Karl's flighter climbs into the sky above the shopping center heading over primarily deep green forest. The tops of the trees dance in the wind. His cockpit monitor displays, "Thursday, June 10, 2483 8:30 P.M. Bridget, Diversity."

Noticing the time and feeling the loss in energy, Karl spots a small clearing north of the shopping center and lands his flighter there, breathing a sigh of delight as he lands vertical orienting his flighter into the main course of the wind. After powering down and securing the check off list, he gets his backpack out of the storage locker and walks around the left wing back to the fuselage.

The weather is improving to a star filled black sky with the two moons high above the horizon, providing most of the light in the meadow. A few dark clouds to the north hover over the northern range of mountains. The wind is calm below four knots, but shifty with sporadic gust to fifteen knots.

This clearing isn't much wider than the flighter, but the wall of fog growing up around him makes the space seem even smaller. He sets up the tent next to the fuselage between the left wing and the tail assembly. He orients the tent between two eyes on the top edge of the fuselage normally used for lifting the craft. After putting the two rods through the top of the tent, he puts the tent into place.

Taking his mat and sleeping bag out of his backpack, Karl places both inside the tent. He takes his backpack into the tent as he looks to the west. Dark clouds fill the horizon all the way to the mountains to the south obscuring stars along the horizon, looking broad and deep. The rest of the sky is cool and clear giving him a good look at the Milky Way and several galaxies and clusters.

He decides to set the rain guard in place and dig a trench, because those clouds look awfully dark and menacing. Tying two ends to the two eyes on the fuselage, he ties the other two ends one to the left wing strut and the other to the tail strut. Pulling the last of the ropes, he ties off a quick knot which he will be able to pull apart as necessary.

Taking the folded shovel off the side of his backpack from inside the tent, he quickly digs a trench around the outer part of the tent close enough to the sides to catch any runoff. He has to bend under the fuselage, but that's only one side. He leaves the grass turf beside the trench so that he will be able to restore the trench back to level grass in the morning.

He puts another pole in the center to raise the center of rain guard using the side of the fuselage to hold the other side. Taking a walk around the flighter, he makes sure all the hold downs are secure and won't come loose unless the aircraft disintegrates. He checks the trench, the tent tie downs and the rain guard last.

Satisfied that the rain will be directed to the trench below and the trench hasn't fallen in somewhere around the perimeter, Karl finally climbs into the tent pulling his backpack behind him.

After sealing the outer door and the inner seal of the tent opening, he removes his shoes, tossing any accumulated dirt outside, and climbs into his sleeping bag. He runs through a quick checkout of everything he wants to accomplish in the morning and starts to lie down, but sits right back up with a start. He remembers the guard's face and his right hand.

Before closing his sleeping bag up, he opens one of the side pockets on his backpack and removes some salve, gauze and cotton wrapping laying them on the mat beside his sleeping bag.

He rubs the salve into the palm of his hand over the burned skin area. He places the gauze on top and wraps his hands several times tightening it with Velcro. After exercising his fingers to make sure they still work, he gathers the remaining items.

After putting everything back into his backpack, Karl zips the sleeping bag closed and lies down. He closes his eyes and thinks over all that has happened in one day. As he begins to drift off to sleep, he hears the first drops of rain on the rain guard. Before long, he is fast asleep as the rain drops practically drench the rain guard, pushing it down onto the tent. The trench around the tent gushes with water, but doesn't overflow keeping the rushing water within its boundaries.

* * *

The passageway lights are dimmed with shadows in abundance. The cell's monitor displays, "Thursday, June 10, 2483 9:00 P.M. Bridget, Diversity."

Opening his eyes and realizing he won't be seeing anything, Cliff closes them.

Cliff senses the darkness around him even though the passageway light still shines dimly. He remembers being fed and now realizes he doesn't have a chance of escaping by himself.

Guards patrol the passageway every half hour. He can't even pull the same trick because all the guards are now aware. If he heard right, they would be turning him over to the red sashes pretty soon. At least, they have stopped moving him, removing the helmet and then replacing it, leaving him in a different cell.

One thing is different about this cell. It has a lavatory in one corner with a sink in the opposite along the same wall. He wouldn't have to call the guards and wait for them to get there which hasn't been easy. As long as he is awake, he decides to make the most of it and carefully avoiding the uncovered stones, he jogs around the cell by memory, until he finally begins to tire. When he can no longer keep his pace, he stops, slowing his breathing until he is relaxed.

He cools off by walking around two more times and then he heads for his usual darkest corner away from the light panel. He turns around and watches the bars of his cell. Listening for any unusual sounds, he decides to get some rest before the sound of footsteps come near.

Shaking off the initial chill of the colder air, he curls up after lying down on the dirt covered floor and tries to get some sleep, but initially restless, he turns over trying to get comfortable on the hard surface. After only a few seconds, he turns over again still not quite as relaxed as he wanted to be.

His thoughts are rampant as he relives each and every scenario from his earlier escape from a cell to his second capture in the shopping center. He attempts to change the events, but each time he gets the same result as if he is caught in a loop. He wonders who the two men were that tried to rescue him, but the guards wouldn't let them.

He wonders what happened to them and if he will ever see his mother or the two men again. He has other thoughts of good times and bad times. The time he and his mother went river rafting now that was fun. He remembers starting school and all the aggravation that caused for both his teachers and his mother.

His body finally relaxes as the thoughts eventually disengage his mind and he falls into a peaceful sleep, until the next set of guards march by, waking him from a peaceful sleep. Soon he is in a deeper sleep completely unaware of his surroundings.

Occasionally, two or more guards would march past the cell talking about wives and girlfriends, but Cliff doesn't notice. Neither did he notice when the door above him was opened several guards came down the stairs. They close the door and walk under the staircase to the locker. Standing outside the door, they converse about the boy's eventual sacrifice upon the stone and the ceremony leading up to it.

He awakens suddenly when the guards talk louder. Cliff listens closely trying to understand what the ceremony is all about. He only hears bits and pieces and some of the words don't make any sense. He can't understand what this is all about. Why does he have to be involved; why not use an animal sacrifice? It doesn't make sense from his point of view. He's gotten into trouble before, but he can't imagine what he has done this time.

Soon the guards leave, but that doesn't stop the traffic of more guards or acolytes. It must be a heavily used intersection.

* * *

Hanging the wet rag on the inner rack of one of the doors under the sink, Tarcey wipes her hands on her apron and removes it, hanging it on a hook under the kitchen console. She looks at the console monitor where the counter is clean and smooth, recently polished to a high shine. Above the console, the console monitor in its reduced configuration displays the date, time and location.

Beyond the central console, a large dining room table with six chairs where the two end chairs are high tops. Out the bay window, the deck surrounds three fourths of the house. The birds frolic and feast on worms coming out of the wet grass and ground.

Tarcey's kitchen console monitor displays, "Thursday, June 10, 2483 9:30 P.M. Bridget, Diversity."

"My, my, how this day has gone. The week is almost over. I don't like being left in the dark. Those two are not telling me something important.

"One of these days they'll tell me everything that has happened and then I'll understand, but that doesn't make it any easier right now," says Tarcey.

She walks out of the kitchen, past the breakfast table, down the stairs, to her bedroom as clouds come over Bridget with a light rain at first increasing to a full downpour. From the back bay window, the garden vanishes as the rain pounds the grass until only a few individual leaves are above a large pond. The rain tries to slice into the outer siding and windows, but they are always opposed. Soon the wind diminishes and the rain turns to a soft shower. Slowly, the pond in the back yard retreats into the ground and the green grass returns along with the garden.

FRIDAY

Morning

With his eyes not open and the smell of a meadow after a rain easing into his senses, Karl remembers the hard rain last night and he smiles as he also remembers the rain guard in place. He opens his eyes to sunshine and a clearing sky. The light wind still blows water off the taller trees into the clearing and he can hear water running through the trench outside the tent perimeter as it continues to drip off of the rain guard.

He gets out of the sleeping bag, puts on his shoes and checks the bandage on his hand while he is still sitting down. He opens the Velcro and unwraps the cotton wrap. The gauze falls off and the palm of his hand glistens with pink skin. Getting more salve from his backpack, he works it into his palm. Karl gets another piece of gauze and rewraps his hand, closing the Velcro fastener tightly.

After putting everything back in place and zipping the outside pocket, he places the backpack outside of the tent, opening the main compartment. He slides back into the tent, rolling up his sleeping bag and mat. He places each in his open backpack. Removing the rain guard next, he lets the water run off under the wing of the flighter until it is dry. After cleaning out the inside of the tent, he puts all the garbage into a separate plastic bag. He folds the now dry rain guard and places it in the backpack.

Soon the tent is down and folded along with the poles which are in turn placed in the backpack. Next, using the shovel, Karl returns the grass turf to the trench patting them into place. Lastly, Karl places the closed backpack in the nosecone, securing it for flight. He pulls out his pilo from his right pocket.

Karl's pilo displays, "Friday, June 11, 2483 7:00 A.M. Bridget, Diversity."

Not seeing any messages, he sends a message to Robert ending with:

Karl's pilo displays, "Bring the key and we'll tour the tunnels together.

"I'll see you about eight-thirty in the northeast corner of Bridget's farm."

Karl climbs into his flighter, fastens himself in, engages the fuel cells, warms up the turbo fans and takes off vertically into the clouds before heading northwest, using the dual props in the rear. The city of Bridget comes into view with the farm in the center. He checks his time and figures he will make it with time to spare.

* * *

Karl's watches the trees become taller and not as close as they seem to be at a distance. His cockpit monitor displays, "Friday, June 11, 2483 8:30 A.M. Bridget, Diversity."

Karl flies over the four rows of trees surrounding the farm. A few acres lie fallow, while many others show mid-growth. A very few late bloomers have tall spindly stems. Corn, wheat, peas, carrots, beets and potatoes prominently fill alternating rows. The farm has several hundred acres. The farm's far corner lies blanketed in fog hiding even the tallest evergreens. A few evergreens show their tops through the edge of the fog on both sides making the trees look disconnected.

Karl flies in a sharp forty-five degree turn until he's flying back in the opposite direction towards the northeast corner. Several machines are weeding and a plow turns rows of dirt in one section of the field. Rows of corn fields are directly below him. Robert stands on the ground near his distinctive flighter.

Karl lands several meters to the west of Robert. After securing the turbo fans and the dual props, he gets out of his flighter. He stands for a moment surveying the farm. Seeing wheat fields off to his left, he watches as underground pipes thrust up through the ground. He laughs as the sprinklers water the wheat. After taking several steps, he stands next to Robert who's looking out over the farm to the southwest.

Karl says, "Thanks for coming."

Breaking his concentration, Robert turns his head towards Karl with a smile from ear to ear turning into a passive face.

Robert asks, "After what you went through last night, how are we going to make it through today?

"Three-quarters of Diversity's population have reported no sign of the child. The rest of the reports will trickle in throughout today and tonight. We should have all the figures in the morning.

"I've sent people to investigate the shopping centers based on your findings."

Replying without hesitation, Karl says, "It was only a hunch. While there are more than enough hiding places, I seriously doubt Ingrider would hide the kid in the shopping center, while the maze remains the only other possibility. The shopping center would be stretching the guards too thin."

Robert asks, "We have to check all possibilities, including the tunnels. How else will we know?"

Karl says, "Oh, we'll make it. This time I'll have you with me, not only, for guidance, but also in case we run into trouble."

Robert says, "But I'm a desk jockey. I wouldn't know how to hit someone. I've never hit anyone in my entire life. Not even my children when they have been their most troublesome, although at the time I certainly considered it."

Karl asks, "What's the long knife on the back of your backpack for?"

Robert says, "I figured we're going to be camping, so it's protection from the animals calling the forests their home. Some have been known to climb onto the farming equipment as it moves into the tunnels from the farm. Most of those are really big and quite dangerous, especially the great bears. They resemble the grisly bears native to Earth in the northern continents and they are just as ferocious."

Karl asks, "Well, let's get over to the tunnel. You brought the key?"

Robert says, "I hate to say this, but I did not. I guess I have too much on my mind with the entire worldwide hunt for the child and the request for more troops."

Karl says, "That's okay. I brought a few things that will probably work."

Karl and Robert walk south along the inside of the tree line, snapping twigs along their path until Robert stops, kneels and brushes the dirt off the top and around the edges of a meter wide circular lid.

Robert shakes dirt off of the lock. Robert stands and moves away from the lock allowing Karl to step into position beside the lock. Karl kneels and takes off his backpack. He removes a small box from an outside pocket. Opening the small box, he taps it once in his left hand. He puts his left palm next to the lock and waits. Within seconds, the lock snaps open.

The lock drops into Karl's hand. After replacing the small box and sealing the outside pocket, Karl removes the lock, setting it on the concrete flange around the opening, lifting the lid. Inside the hole, ladder rungs, spaced every thirty centimeters, are attached to the concrete side of the hole opposite the lid's hinge with small horizontal light panels providing more than enough light, but not enough to determine the depth.

Transfixed, Robert surveys the farm, watching several machines, tilling, planting and plowing, throwing mounds of dirt into the air. Dust clouds mask most of the machines especially the ones doing the plowing since they bring up the drier dirt below the one to two inches of rain soaked soil. Breaking from his reverie, Robert looks into the vertical hole.

Robert goes in first with his right foot and then his left. Lights behind the ladder brighten the shaft. After Robert has passed the top edge of the flange, Karl follows bringing the lid over the top allowing it to drop onto the flanges with a resounding thud which echoes through the cavity for some time.

* * *

The tunnel ends at an intersection with two other tunnels with some sort of hexagonal shape in the middle of the intersection. As they get nearer, the object's massive height and girth come into view. The nodal's monitor displays, "Friday, June 11, 2483 9:00 A.M. Bridget, Diversity."

Karl and Robert stand next to a slightly tapered hexagonal computer console in the center of a hexagonal room with three exit tunnels at one hundred and twenty degrees apart. The tunnel they entered is behind them.

Each of the tunnels is circular with a diameter of twenty meters. The floor consists of primarily dirt over flat stones with a width of about six meters. The walls of the tunnels look like tiny tiles of ceramic, glistening with miniature rainbows of color. Light panels every one hundred meters provide the only light, leaving long periods of semi-darkness between them. Where the lights do shine, the walls glisten with the colors in a range of green.

The two and a half meters high conical console has a cap like an inverted hexagon cone, making its overall height at two and three-quarter meters. About waist high or lower, the center holds a rectangular screen above a keyboard with many odd shaped brush strokes, one per key, and a mouse pad below the middle of the keyboard. The keyboard is repeated on the screen with smaller keys leaving the impression that it is a touch screen like the pilos.

The screen displays several lines of character strokes overlapped with a blinking underscore as if the computer was awaiting a command. As he keeps looking, command characters appear after the prompt and more lines of characters are displayed on the thirty centimeter diagonal screen.

Karl looks closely at the characters displayed, noting the multiple overlapping brush strokes.

Robert says, "This is Bridget's nodal, using the name the originals used. They are all identical in every city surrounding a farm complex. At every intersection, a nodal and a farm exist along a hexagon with one hundred and twenty kilometer sides. Not every intersection has a city because we are not that populous.

"The nodal controls the farm equipment which it also maintains. It is capable of completely rebuilding, updating or reconfiguring itself or any of the other equipment even to the utter destruction of one of the nodals. The nodals are completely automatic operating the farms as long as the products are harvested and used. We have had cases where cities have wasted products dumped back into the farms cultivated fields with the resulting shutdown and plowing under of all the crops including ones ready to harvest."

Pointing at the nodal's screen, Karl says, "It certainly looks almost normal.

"A screen and keyboard with fingertip mouse pad like the ones in the twenty-first century. Only the characters are different on the screen and the keys. Each brush stroke glistens like fresh paint even when overlapped."

Robert says, "Yes, primitive compared to our own monitors, but still working. And each one can be rebuilt as long as one of the nodals works.

"We changed the clock to our configuration, but we haven't changed the programming code.

"Sometimes a nodal is shut down, because of a virus or mutation gone wrong. All programming is removed and the system is purged. After reloading with original programming, it is retested until operational."

Karl asks, "Do you know how to operate one of these?"

Robert says, "Sorry, it has never been on my agenda.

"I believe anyone who worked on the translation can work the keyboard and read the screen. Tarcey could."

Karl asks, "That's what I thought you were going to say. Based on the information I have, she has other skills too. How far do these tunnels go?"

Robert says, "All around the world except for the oceans and larger lakes. Narrow fjords use the nearest nodal for their sustenance. Small islands will use the closest larger island nodal or mainland nodal."

Karl looks up at the top of the tunnel above the nodal. Hundreds of iridescent, ten centimeter long rods, with a diameter of a single centimeter having three transparent, overlapping, flapping wings on each side, head in and out of the tunnels, going in all three directions at an unbelievable pace.

Pointing upward with his right hand, Karl asks, "That puts a damper on searching the tunnels. What are those?"

Looking up along Karl's arm, Robert says, "We call them dragonflies because of their peculiar assembly.

"That is the only similar classification we could come up with at the time, but it has stuck."

Startled by a sound coming from a tunnel, Karl and Robert look over at the right tunnel. A bright red tractor, pulling a brown and yellow tiller with four tines on each plow and yellow funnels which normally carry seed or fertilizer, having bright yellow flags on top of the corners and each yellow funnel, comes out of the right tunnel around the backside of the nodal and out the left tunnel.

Sufficiently informed, Karl and Robert turn around and start walking back to the shaft, discussing various uses for the byproducts of the harvest, especially corn husks, pea or bean vines and asparagus stalks.

They get about halfway when Karl suddenly stops. Robert brings up the rear walking with a slight limp.

Robert asks, "What's up?"

Karl says, "Thought I saw something move ahead of us into the shadows beyond the next light."

Lights in the tunnel shine on the path every one hundred meters casting a tight beam with long dark shadows between. Only the radiance of the walls of the tunnel keeps it from getting too dark. It makes it equally hard to see beyond each light panel ahead of them though.

Karl starts walking cautiously forward, while Robert stays right behind. As they walk under the next set of lights, four guards step into the far set of lights, two from each side. Noticing their stance, Robert quickly steps in front of Karl. He brings his left hand behind him and taps the knife sheath. Without looking backward, Robert gauges the four guards, looking at their lack of weapons and muscular strength.

Robert asks, "Is there something we can help you with?"

The lead guard says, "If you come peaceably we'll take you back to our Chief."

Robert brings both hands into play as he talks.

Robert asks, "And if not peaceably?"

The lead guard says, "We'll have to kill you."

Robert says, "Or we'll have to kill you."

Karl steps out from behind Robert and throws the knife. The lead guard caught not looking, stumbles forward. It enters the guard's chest, cutting through the aorta. The guard looks down at the knife. He tries to remove it with both hands but before he can pull it out, he looks up incredulous as his eyes turn upward.

He falls forward to the ground with blood pumping out of his body onto the dirt covered stones soaking into the dirt between the stones. Taking one glance at their leader, the other three guards rush Karl and Robert with one leading and the other two about four meters back.

Gauging the guard's progress, Karl moves forward, running towards the curved wall and grabbing the first arriving guard's shoulder, swinging around and flying through the air horizontally into the other two. The two rear guards are caught not anticipating this move and come to a stop which is what Karl expected.

The twisting guard's momentum brings him into Robert's arms. With Robert's arms fully wrapped around him, the guard struggles to get free, but Robert tightens his hold making it harder for the guard to breath.

The two rear guards go down as one is pounded with Karl's head and arms and the other is hit by Karl's lower legs and feet to the guard's head.

Karl quickly recovers and hammers his right foot into the chest of the closest guard lying down in the dirt moaning. The guard grunts as air flows out of his lungs and the sharp sound of a rib fracturing punctuates the air.

The other guard rolls away and stands up, shaking his head with a small laceration above his right eye, bleeding into his eyebrow and down his cheek. Karl and the guard circle each other, arms forward as wrestlers with the other guard, lying on the ground, moaning and clutching his chest. The other guard lunges forward.

But Karl is ready for that move.

Karl spins to his right, stepping out of the way. The guard misses and Karl pounds both hands into the back of the guard as he goes by.

With his momentum, the guard hits his head hard against the tunnel wall with a resulting crack as one of the guard's ribs takes the brunt of the hit, arching his lower back. He collapses to the ground.

Karl watches Robert hold the first arriving guard in a bear hug until the guard no longer struggles, his face turns blue and he goes limp in Robert's arms.

Robert drops him to the ground and points to the other guard now rising, clutching his right side, breathing heavily.

Karl wasn't expecting him to recover quite that fast.

Karl turns as the guard slams into him. He relaxes and lets the guard carry him to the tunnel wall. Exhaling as he hits the wall, Karl waits until his back braces against the tunnel wall as he slams his two hands on the guard's back near the broken rib.

The guard grimaces and tries to raise Karl above him, but Robert slides into place behind the guard and grabs hold of the guard's upper waist causing the guard to try to scream, but he can't breath. He squeezes until he can feel the ribs bend. The guard lets loose of Karl when the pain is too much and starts squirming in Robert's arms to no avail. The guard goes limp and Robert releases him. He tumbles to the ground with blood coming out of his mouth.

Karl says, "You don't fight, huh? That was pretty good."

Robert responds, "I was one of those kids who broke up fights when I was in elementary school. I found the best way was to hold tightly until they were out of breath.

"My escapades preceded me into high school and college, keeping me out of fights. No one dared to fight me which made me quite happy."

Karl says, "Thank you, anyway. I wasn't too sure I could have handled all three."

Robert asks, "Should we leave them or tie them up and bring them with us? I can call for another flighter to come and get them. Take them back to the station."

Karl says, "We'll leave them.

"They'll have more to worry about empty handed. Let's return to Bridget and think about what's next."

* * *

The Police Station fills with officers manning every desk. Some have doubled up making for tight corridor's. Robert clears the way into the conference room. It's monitor displays, "Friday, June 11, 2483 10:30 A.M. Bridget, Diversity."

Karl and Robert walk into the small conference room. Robert sits at the head of the table and Karl sits to his left. Several other officers take places around the table with only one chair empty. Everyone has a pilo, Robert and Karl read from theirs while the other officers take notes.

Robert says, "All stations have reported. No sign of Cliff. Ingrider hasn't moved from the old city's upper level. He has sufficient guards and red sash acolytes to handle anything we can throw his way from my regional offices. I wouldn't be able to lay a hand on the man's shoulders without being accosted myself."

Karl says, "We can rule out the tunnels since we don't have the manpower to search them anyway."

Robert says, "It's a late Friday morning. The offering goes off at twilight Saturday evening.

"The ceremony is elaborate enough for us to achieve our goal. We're about out of time to do anything else."

Karl says, "I'm beginning to think that something is wrong with my GHD. Since the maze gassing, I've been more aggressive. And I'm getting to like it, even though, it doesn't seem to interfere with my thinking processes.

"I've killed two men now. Any other deaths in my entire life have been accidental, beyond my control. Luckily most have been suicides.

"It was as if I wanted those men dead. I've never experienced that feeling, before in my life."

Robert says, "My GHD is shielded with protocols. You may not have been high enough to require that sophistication.

"Tarcey has the same protection for herself because of her involvement in the library translation, but I'm not so sure about Cliff. Tarcey mentioned something, but I missed it."

Karl says, "It wasn't the gas. Something is interfering."

Robert says, "Well you seem all right now. You're not trying to kill me."

Karl says, "That brings up something else. How does Ingrider know where we are and what we are planning? He has been ahead of us at every juncture."

* * *

R obert sits behind his office desk punches at his pilo looking concerned. Karl walks in and sits down in a side chair wearing a smile.

Robert's monitor displays, "Friday, June 11, 2483 11:30 A.M. Bridget, Diversity."

After looking up from his pilo and turning his head towards Karl, Robert asks, "I can't talk you out of it?"

Becoming serious, Karl says, "We have to take the chance.

"If I do anything to protect myself, he'll know. Nothing is very secure around Diversity. That may be part of the problem."

Robert asks, "How will I know you're going to be there? You won't be using your pilo, because you think Ingrider has tapped into our communication."

Karl says, "I'll be there and thanks for showing me the silent method of using the flighter. It will come in handy if plan A doesn't work. I'm hoping that I don't have to go through too much, but this is not going to be an easy process. He is well guarded. By going in by myself, I'm reducing his options."

As Karl rises from his seat, so does Robert who shakes his hand across the desk as they look each other in the eye not sure if they will ever see each other again.

Robert says, "Then, I'll see you Saturday evening. Be careful, the maze goes under the hub, too. Believe me, he'll try to escape. He still has several outstanding warrants in all most every continent and region."

Karl turns to leave and abruptly turns back, facing Robert who still stands behind his desk.

Karl says, "If you do your part, I'll do mine. Ingrider doesn't stand a chance. And I don't believe I said that."

Karl turns around and walks out of Robert's office. Robert wishes him well as he says a silent prayer before his sits back down in his seat. He takes out his pilo from the top right side drawer, turns it on and starts compiling a list of leaders and officers he can trust, including the new ones that will be coming to their aid.

He'll have to work this out with some other reason for its existence. Perhaps a conference or maybe several that would attract a sufficient number of people that would not be out of the ordinary. *It's a good thing I got the other regions earlier this week, so it wouldn't be as obvious. That's what I will have to do.*

Checking for lodging and officers with additional space available within their homes, he compiles a list of every available hotel, motel and hostel. The officers' homes fill out the rest. He compiles a list of available rooms for the time period, hoping that this won't take more than two or three days not counting the staging operations.

With that, he remembers to get the necessary equipment.

He considers several weapons, but dismisses them all as too unwieldy and not enough training time. He thinks about other devices that would work in crowded situations like this.

Karl's flighter flies toward the shopping center with the central tower slightly to the left. He checks his altitude and begins the descent over his chosen landing sight. His cockpit monitor displays, "Friday, June 11, 2483 12:10 P.M. Bridget, Diversity."

Karl lands his flighter vertically in a clearing near the entrance to the maze on the north side of the shopping center. He exits the aircraft, walks around the left wing, past the canard to the nose cone which he opens to get to the storage area. Two identical backpacks, side by side, almost fill the area. Karl takes one and opens the main compartment which is empty.

He carries that backpack over to the high grasses and shovels handfuls of grass into both sides of the main compartment of the backpack. When both sides are sufficiently full, he zips the two sides together. He pulls an old scratched pilo from a side pocket and puts it in his vest pocket. He puts the backpack on over his light vest and his usual uniform, fastening the straps around his chest and abdomen. He closes the nose cone of his flighter and heads for the stairwell, near the edge of the forest which surrounds the shopping center, leading to the maze.

He opens the sliding door by pushing the stone. Gears below grind through their turns. The door slides open revealing the stairway. He looks around the meadow and the sky above to make sure he is not being followed or watched. He heads down into the maze. The door slides close behind him when he reaches the bottom step.

* * *

Karl walks along the maze, glancing at his pilo occasionally. He walks, casually whistling as if trying to attract attention rather than be quiet in order to surprise a guard he might meet along the way. Karl checks his pilo.

Karl's pilo displays, "Friday, June 11, 2483 2:00 P.M. Bridget, Diversity."

On his pilo, he sees four guards waiting around the broad right curve of the passageway, two on each side facing towards him. They carry night sticks as their only weapon and seem ready to pounce as soon as Karl rounds the corner.

As he nears the corner, he starts making even more noise, scraping his finger nails across the stones imbedded in the wall of the passageway while stamping his right foot firmly on one of the loose stones. He hopes this will heighten their anxiety and by the readings on his pilo, it has.

As he nears their position, he increases the noise level and the frequency of stomping, being overly obnoxious. He can only imagine what the guards must be thinking as he nears their position. The guard's begin to get overly aggressive as Karl taunts them. They want to run and tackle him, but they hold back for the time being as they were instructed.

Around the slight bend, the four guards are ready for Karl's appearance. As Karl comes into view, the first two grab him and force him to the ground very unkindly. Karl acts completely surprised and bewildered. He offers minimal resistance as if in total shock.

They force him to his knees bringing his arms backward and upward forcing him to bend forward. A guard holds Karl's head down as the other fastens plastic straps around Karl's wrists. One guard unfastens the backpack straps and removes it over Karl's head, handing it off to another guard who puts on the backpack. Another guard checks the straps around Karl's wrists. Karl keeps the strap tight by rotating his lower arms outward ever so slightly

A brown collar is placed around his neck with a yellow propylene rope attached. Heavy iron shackles are snapped around each ankle, restricting his forward movement, injuring the skin of his ankles with every movement. They lift him up onto his feet with the shackling grating against his ankles. They march slowly further into the maze with one of the lead guards holding the yellow rope, leading Karl through the passageway. With each step, Karl watches the blood flow from his ankles onto the dirt path.

Two guards lead and the other two guards follow with Karl between. With his hands tied together behind him and shackles around his feet, Karl is hoping that he gets to meet Ingrider next. *Whatever transpires next had better be quick, so that I can begin the rest of my plan. After that whatever happens, as long as I have my clothes, I can escape Ingrider's clutches and the guards using the maze. If my timing is right, Ingrider won't even suspect my intentions. I'll be long gone before the guards react.*

The guard, holding the yellow rope, leading back to the collar around Karl, tugs whenever he feels like it, pulling Karl off his feet for a moment, throwing him off balance. Karl stumbles for several steps until he recovers dragging the chain behind him with the shackles grating against his ankles.

More guards are encountered at every intersection. Congratulations are given to the four guards with lots of handshaking and back patting and then its back to marching through the passageway. The guards remain resolute while Karl keeps thinking of options which don't look to promising at this juncture. With the increased activity of the guards, he's pretty sure the boy is back in the maze which solves one of his problems.

After a while, the guards arrive at a "T" intersection with a protuberance. One of the guards takes something out of his pocket and hands it to another guard who walks over to the right of the protuberance, placing the object into a depression about eye level. He turns the object clockwise a quarter turn. The other three guards keep their eyes on Karl until they hear the door opening.

A door opens in the wall, revealing a rising stairwell. The four guards and Karl march up the stairs and turn right to the terrace steps on the lower terrace. Karl squints in the bright light. Activity abounds on the lower level with children playing and older acolytes watching.

As the four guards and Karl continue up the other terrace steps, Karl notices the bright day with the sun high in the sky to the west. The heat rising from the stone face of the terraces makes the entire complex look artificially shimmering, making everything look as if he were on a different planet.

* * *

Wearing white habits and red sashes, acolytes mill about on the upper terrace memorizing verses and chants and reciting to each other. Quietly, they watch as the guards and Karl come up the last terrace steps. A few recognize his face and are unable to hold back their surprise. Some look back at Ingrider on his throne deep in thought as if he didn't know his greatest enemy was coming up the steps. The rest continue with their duties oblivious to Karl's entrance.

When the guards and Karl reach the top step of the top terrace, the guards immediately lower their heads.

The red sash acolytes begin to separate leaving a wide path to the throne. The guards march Karl up to where Ingrider sits in his great chair. All four guards kneel on their right leg, a meter from his throne, and they force Karl to do the same, but Karl does not bow his head. He stares at Ingrider waiting from him to decide what to do with him. Ingrider stands looking out over the terrace watching every acolyte and guard bowed waiting to see what he will do. He consults his pilo.

Ingrider's pilo displays, "Friday, June 11, 2483 3:00 P.M. Bridget, Diversity."

Ingrider looks up and smiles. Karl smiles back looking deeply into Ingrider's eyes. Ingrider is initially confused, but soon recovers. Ingrider has to break eye contact, the man is some kind of devil. He looks over Karl's head for the rest of the conversation.

Ingrider says, "Finally, at last, the great Karl P. Perkins, rescuer of lost children whether accidental or coerced. Without a doubt the best of the best.

"I've read all your books and I've had agents attend several of your seminars.

"I have to apologize that I haven't had the time to attend your seminars myself, but we have learned enough of your techniques through your books, video presentations and audio instruction at all levels from the beginning to the advanced.

"Using them, we have kept you out of our sight now for four days and nights. At the moment, I have you; you won't be any more trouble; we will be able to continue our ceremony unimpeded. Not even your companion, the Police Chief, will be able to get you out of here.

"You are very good, but not good enough. Even though you bested my second guard, you will never get by my first or me. Myself, the red sashes and the guards are more powerful than you will ever know.

"Take him into the lower chamber. Following the usual procedure, place him on the stone and strap him to it. Keep two guards on duty at the top of the stairs, two at the maze entrance and don't allow anyone access. He will be all mine and I can hardly wait to begin our fun."

The guards march Karl past Ingrider into the hub entrance.

* * *

They head down a spiral staircase lit by candle every few meters. The air is very still and the sounds are muffled except for their own feet on the loose stones. Karl marvels at the darkness around him. He can't even see the other side of the hub even though he is certain there are steps and candles on the other side or perhaps hidden rooms that only a few know about. It's almost as if the steps appear before them and disappear behind.

The very center of the hub looks so dark that you can't see the other side. After going around several times, the light of three candles can be seen below them.

When they reach the bottom of an illuminated round room, a large ellipsoidal stone occupies the center with many types of cutting tools hanging from a rack above the stone ringing like chimes as the air moves around the room. Flat light panels in circular form around the rack provide all the light leaving no shadows within the room.

Without a word, as if they had repeated these steps routinely, the guards strip Karl to his shorts and place him on the ellipsoidal stone. His clothes are thrown into any empty box against the wall or on the counter. Not all of them land in a box. His pants get hung up on a corner of a box and they miss entirely with his shirt with it landing on the floor. They tie his hands and bare feet with leather straps whose ends go through round holes in the stone.

They place another strap of leather across his midsection with a broader strap across his kneecaps. He begins to think that this will be a very interesting procedure, but he is ready for it because the next step allows him an opportunity to escape. He hopes Robert's fly over is recording. It will be interesting to see the look on Ingrider's face when he finds out.

Two guards leave through the maze exit as another two arrive from the maze to stand guard at the entrance. The other two head up the stairs stopping as they reach the next level. They both stand at attention with their backs to the room effectively blocking the stairs to the lower chamber.

Karl looks around the room, noticing counters and cabinets, the entrance to the maze, the two guards at the maze entrance, the stairs, the two guards on the stairs and the rack of knives above his head still chiming with the occasional puff of air. There are plenty of empty cardboard boxes, some on the counter and a few scattered on the floor.

He remembers seeing a drain around the base of the stone and shivers at the prospect of what is probably going to happen.

People, talking in the maze, arrive at the closest intersection, but Karl can't quite make out what is being said.

Otherwise, his own breathing is the only sound that comes to his ears and the occasional rattling of the knives over his head. He counts the number of cabinets above the counter for about the umpteenth time.

The hub's chamber monitor displays, "Friday, June 11, 2483 3:10 P.M. Bridget, Diversity."

* * *

The sound of running water wakens Karl from his nap. Moving his head as much as he can, he sees the guards are still there. The hub's chamber monitor displays, "Friday, June 11, 2483 5:30 P.M. Bridget, Diversity."

Karl waits and waits.

Sweat soaks Karl's body as he is not quite sure where he is feeling slightly delirious. A door opens above him and footsteps rock the stone on the spiral staircase. Ingrider enters the chamber.

He says, "I was so happy when I first entered this room and saw the knives above you. Lasers are too clean.

"These knives actually open the wound. I won't go too deep, I promise."

Karl says, "No matter what you do, you can't hurt me.

"When I escape from here, I'm taking you to Bridget's Police Station. I'm sure you'll love the facilities."

Ingrider says, "Oh, you little man. I know the GHD protects you. When it works. Those little nanos aren't going to do anything this time. They work fine for minor scrapes and cuts, but what I have for you will overwhelm them.

"You'll feel all the pain and it will take a month of Sundays before you'll be able to move as well as before."

Karl says, "You will be punished, you know, and it won't be anything as what you may have planned for me. The rehabilitation doctors will put you through more hoops than you ever thought possible. They are very good with their tools, but unfortunately you might go crazy."

Ingrider says, "After tonight's rehearsal, you won't matter. When I get done here, you won't be able to move any part of your body anywhere.

"You've given me and my guards more than enough trouble. The rehearsals and the child's ultimate sacrifice will continue without your interference. Your Police Chief and his officers are no match for my red sashes and my one hundred elite guards. My guards have repeatedly put his officers to shame more than once.

"The ceremony cannot be stopped by you or Robert's minimal officers. Once the boy is on the alter it will be all over. It will be over in seconds. His blood will flow throughout the hub and down through the terraces refreshing the bodies of the chosen."

Evening

Ingrider finally raises the long knife after Karl has passed out for the fourth time. He rinses it and the rest of the knives in the sink in the middle of the counter and places them over Karl's limp body hooking them onto the rack above him. The knives continue to rattle and chime for some time.

The chamber monitor displays, "Friday, June 11, 2483 7:10 P.M. Bridget, Diversity."

He smiles at his work of art. He knows for sure that this man will not be going anywhere for a long time. The cuts were precise, keeping him in pain with every move as possibility that some part of his skin will tear leaving a nasty scar.

Karl is covered in red blood, turning from bright red to dark red, from the top of his forehead to end of his toes. His eyes are closed with a laceration of his left eye and his breathing is regular. If someone were to check his blood pressure and pulse, they would find them normal.

Lacerations are everywhere along the major lines of his skeleton. The blood continues to drop from every part of his body onto the top stone traveling along rivulets etched into the stone to the edge where it drops through six holes equally spaced around the edge of the stone further dropping to the grid below where globs of dried blood are already attached.

Ingrider calls the two guards on the stairs to come down. They quickly stop watching activity on the stairs above them.

They turn around and walk in step to the floor of the chamber. They walk over to each on one side of the stone. Neither expresses any signs of emotion keeping pensive faces throughout their next routine.

They unfasten the straps around Karl and place the straps in the sink to drain. They gather Karl's clothes and put them on him. One of the guards pulls out a pilo and requests two more guards from the upper terrace.

Ingrider leaves the room, climbing the stairs with more important tasks to perform. Rehearsals, planning, cleaning and advanced preparation for the coming ceremony are only the top few that come to mind.

Coming down the stairs from the hub entrance, the other two guards arrive and the four use white towels from beneath the top stone on racks, each taking a towel, to take Karl's bloody body off the stone.

They carry him into the maze while the two guards at the maze entrance watch them go. Arriving at a cell which is already open, they lay his body on the dirt floor of the cell and walk out. One of the guards walks over to the control panel and lowers the bars, sealing the cell.

Several moments later, the four guards return with the bloody towels still in their hands. They stop when they reach the stone, talking adamantly about their roles in capturing and putting him in the cell. All are proud of their service to their lord and master. After gathering the bloody towels from the other guards, one guard walks over to the sink and drops the towels into the basin where the blood leaches out into the drain.

After each has washed their hands in the sink getting all of the blood off their hands, the one guard stays to wash the towels and return them to the rack below the top stone. The other three walk over to the bottom of the stairs and wait, talking with the two guards at the entrance to the maze.

When the towels are clean, the guard returns to the stairs. All walk up the stairs disappearing beyond the candle lights into darkness leaving only the sound of their footsteps.

Their footsteps soon diminish to nothing leaving the room completely silent except for the breathing of the two guards and the occasional chiming of the knives.

* * *

Walking out of the hub entrance, Ingrider survey's the night sky empty of the two moons which will be rising within a half hour, but still bright with more stars coming out as the night gets darker. He returns to his throne and calls the red sashes to gather around him with a whistle signal, using one long note and two short notes. Every red sash no matter what level they may be on hears this signal and know that their response must be immediate and absolute.

The red sashes begin coming from all over the upper terrace forming a semicircle around his throne in two rows with the tallest in the back. When they have all gathered, they assume a yoga stance sitting down with their heads bowed. No sounds are uttered except the synchronized sounds of their breathing.

Ingrider pulls a pilo from under the throne's seat and brings up the ceremonial chant. Going to the last page, Ingrider calls up the sound system and plays the chant's music as the red sashes listen, keeping their attention focused on the pitch and tempo from the music.

Noticing the red sashes are in order and well spaced, Ingrider checks his pilo.

Ingrider's pilo displays, "Friday, June 11, 2483 7:20 P.M. Bridget, Diversity."

"I would like you all to turn to the last page. Please note the quick rise in volume from the beginning of the page to the last stanza," explains Ingrider.

"Too many of you are missing several key notes which in turn throws several others off key as well. I suggest we need to work on this perhaps in groups by age.

"Divide up into four groups by voice range, i.e. soprano, alto, tenor and bass. Put the ones whose voices are changing into the next lower range.

"One experienced red sash should lead each group and you know who you are since you did the same a week ago when I wasn't here. Practice until you all know each and every part of the chant including the pauses and inflections. You should not have to refer to your notes after this practice.

"Don't be afraid to bring up other stanzas that you are having trouble with. Others may be having the same problems. No one is perfect all the time, but if we work together, we will succeed.

"Your leaders will more than gladly work on anything you might bring up. The more work we get done in the next hour the better your performance as an entire group will be.

"Take a five minute break and form your groups on the upper terrace within the habitats near the major compass points to keep interference to a minimum. Return at eight thirty and we will practice as a complete group until nine. After that, I hope you would dream of the chant while you sleep."

The red sashes break up into four groups of five with the four most experienced red sashes leading the others separating to different areas of the upper terrace. White habited acolytes dutifully remove themselves from the upper terrace so that the red sashes will not be disturbed. With some of the white habited acolytes exiting at the cardinal points, they hurry to get past the habitat and down the stairs before the red sashes arrive.

* * *

On the lower terraces, younger white habited acolytes question older acolytes about the ceremony and their place in it. A few younger acolytes fear for their lives from some of the stories they have been told by a few students who still like to play pranks.

They are consoled by older acolytes that the stories they have heard are erroneous or, at most, are exaggerated. The younger acolytes settle down in chairs, on ledges or on the terrace floor and listen to their older brethren. Some cry softly; others wait not knowing what is going to happen. As the older acolytes speak gently to them, they begin to improve and start smiling.

"No white habited acolyte will be punished at the top of the central hub. Only our well-chosen animal sacrifices take place up there. One day you will more than likely get the opportunity to be a significant part of that very important ceremony," says one older acolyte to a young boy acolyte. The younger acolyte runs off to the rest of his gang to tell them the good news.

"But they are sacrificing a young boy tomorrow night. What's to stop Ingrider from sacrificing an acolyte who doesn't happen to fit in with this program? The boy happens to be my age," says another young acolyte.

"This is an especially reserved case arranged only for our most honored enemies.

"If this boy lives, all of our lives are threatened. Do you really want to go back into those cubicles for the rest of your life," explains the older acolyte.

"What can a five year old boy do to us? Most everyone here is bigger than I am."

"This boy will one day command an arsenal that even we won't be able to match. This is ordained by the prophets. Long ago, when the other civilization was here an oracle forecast that that population would evacuate the planet and another population would fill the planet with a child born who would utterly destroy our master and all those who believe."

"Wow, I have never had that in any of my classes. Now I'm beginning to wish I could be up there to see how it all happens."

"Like I said, I am sure that one day you will and you will be explaining it to someone like yourself," says the older acolyte.

"Thank you for the explanation; I will sleep much better tonight," replies the young acolyte as he leaves walking back to his habitat and his next session of learning. He joins with another group of kids his same age. Their teacher begins by asking each of them to write their new found knowledge in their pilos.

Each student picks up their individual pilos and begin.

* * *

Robert sits at his desk going over the itinerary for next evening on his pilo.

He looks up at his monitor which is completely blank except for the date and time in the upper right corner.

"It's time to look at the numbers again. They probably haven't changed but I need to review since they began on Monday," commands Robert.

"Bring up the numbers for the red sash acolytes, the guards and the over twelve year old white habited acolytes. Give me summaries only."

Robert's monitor displays, "Friday, June 11, 2483 7:30 P.M.
Bridget, Diversity."

After a few moments, Robert's monitor changes from all
black to white letters on a black background and displays:

Red Sashes	Guards	White habits($\geq$12)
20	100	300
	(36 on guard duty)	

Robert looks over the numbers trying to figure out how
many officers he will need. He looks back over his pilo while he
checks some figures pressing several buttons until he is satisfied.
He leans back in his upholstered chair with the high back and takes
in a deep breath releasing it slowly.

"Ok, now I have about six hundred officers coming in to
supplement my own officers. All I have to do now is find housing
for all six hundred. Well, I'll get my officer's spouses on that one.
I have enough headaches getting all the foodstuffs, clothes and
batons for them.

"I'm going to need more jail space. I can probably farm
them out to the closest cities. I'll get the officers in the morning to
notify the closest cities, when to expect a load of prisoners.

"This will either be either a nightmare or a wonderful
dream. So far, it's been a work in progress, but that will soon come
to a head. I sure hope Karl is right about Ingrider's plans. I don't
know why I question his judgment. Right now, I'm just glad the

day is over and I can climb into my bed. I'm not that old but all of this work is beginning to weigh heavily.

"But before I do that, bring the old city up on the screen."

His monitor displays the city from the viewpoint of the fly over as it passed over the central hub. He asks for a freeze frame as he looks straight down the central hub to each of the nine terraces and the central wall surrounding the city.

After spending several moments reviewing the freeze frame, he points his pilo at the monitor until it beeps off leaving a black screen with only the date and time in the upper right corner. He makes a few notes in his pilo and places it in the central drawer of his desk.

He touches the remote on the desk and the monitor shuts off leaving a blinking red light in the lower right corner. He pushes the chair away from the desk and stands up. Walking around the desk to his office door, he opens it and walks through. Before locking the door, he surveys the main office making sure no one else is there. Reaching for the light switch, he turns off the office and main lights plunging the Police Station into darkness.

After walking through, he turns around and takes a key chain out of his right pocket. He selects the office key, putting it in the dead lock and turning in around until it clicks. He removes the key and puts the key chain back in his pocket.

Checking that the door handle doesn't move, he turns around one hundred and eighty degrees and walks down the short hallway to the double doors of the entrance.

SATURDAY

Morning

The passageway's lights get brighter until the shadows disappear. Outside a nearby cell, the monitor displays, "Saturday, June 12, 2483 7:00 A.M. Bridget, Diversity."

Karl lies in the dirt with his pants and shirt on, both drenched in blood. His feet swell in his shoes with dark red stains around the tops of his shoes and he breaths. While blotches of blood trail from the passageway to the cell bars through to the inside of the cell and over to Karl, no blood pools around his drenched form. His face and hands are puffy but not overly so. Even his hair has splotches of dried dark red blood.

Karl awakes barely opening a swollen lacerated left eye lid. His nose and jaw are bloody making him look grotesque. He struggles to get up. He looks at his blood-splattered enormous hands with serrations along each bone on both sides. He can barely move his oversize fingers.

Karl slowly opens his unbuttoned shirt, feeling only a slight spasm of pain with each movement and sees even larger serrations along each rib. As he watches, the serrations begin to close without a scar leaving the skin pinkish on either side of the serration and black along the serration.

Deftly closing his shirt, moving his fingers as little as possible, he looks back at his hands; the wounds close as well. His swollen eye while still discolored appears less swollen and the same for his nose and jaw.

Karl looks out through the bars at the stone face of the passage wall. He flexes his now enabled fingers, fastens the buttons on his shirt, and zips up his pants after tucking in his shirt.

He removes his belt with his right hand as the swelling goes down and his fingers are able to grip. He holds the clasp with his left and opens the clasp with his right. With the clasp open, the inside cavity holds a couple of milliliters of a black substance writhing within its container.

After walking up to the bars, he puts his left arm between two bars and places the clasp next to the LCD display and keys, holding it there for a moment. The sound of gears turning against each other almost startles him until he sees the bars go up.

The bars slide up. Removing his left arm from the control before the cross bar hit it, he closes the clasp and puts the belt on tightening it around his waist. His fingers and face have returned to normal with his movements being less painful.

He slowly walks out of the cell into the passageway and wishes he had his pilo to check on his overall health. He can't be sure of what Ingrider did after he passed out. The walking journey isn't long but he'll have to walk to his flighter through the maze and the shopping center.

Karl leaves the cell turning right and walking slowly picking up more speed with every step through the passage as the pain diminishes. He turns right again at the next intersection. At the next intersection, he turns left heading into a longer passage almost walking normally and beginning to whistle.

* * *

Walking up to his flighter in the short grass clearing, Karl opens the nosecone storage locker. Karl removes his bloody shirt, pants, socks and shoes. All of the bleeding has stopped and his left eye, while sore to touch, can be opened fully with red vines emanating from his iris.

From one of the backpack's outer pockets, he removes a small round container. Opening the end he takes out a sheet of wet disposable cloths. Starting with his face, he wipes the blood off until the cloth can't contain anymore. He places the dirty sheet in a waste container on the back of the locker. He gets another sheet and continues to clean himself down to his toes. He removes the backpack setting it on the short grass. He opens the major compartment and starts removing clean clothes.

After dressing, he removes a more substantial vest that was lying under the backpack in the locker and puts it on over his now clean clothes. Pressing the button under his left lapel of the vest, he watches the OLED turn from red to green on the underside of the left sleeve button.

After closing the backpack he lifts it up on his back and fastens the straps around his chest and midsection. He checks the tightness of the straps and retightens the lower left which had somehow worked loose. Satisfied with the straps, he adjusts his vest pulling in certain areas.

He pushes a button under the left lapel of the vest and watches the OLED light underneath the left sleeve button turn from soft red to soft green. He removes his other pilo from his pocket and checks it and himself. The internal diagnostic returns reporting full operational capability and Karl's health is confirmed as improving without any major complications, bruised, cracked or broken bones.

Karl's pilo displays, "Saturday, June 12, 2483 7:20 A.M. Bridget, Diversity."

He sends a brief message to Robert.

After putting the pilo back in his right pants pocket, he closes the nosecone securing it for flight and walks around the left wing. He looks up at the clear morning sky with the sun still low on the horizon. Clouds and blue openings share the sky.

Karl gets in the flighter's cockpit, fastens the crossover belt, tightens the straps, goes over his checklist, and starts the engine. After the turbo fans have warmed, the flighter practically jumps into the air, rises up to an appropriate height and takes off, using the dual props.

* * *

Karl's flighter circles the shopping center before turning towards the central tower. He looks up, down, left and right for the other pilot. His cockpit monitor displays, "Saturday, June 12, 2483 7:15 A.M. Bridget, Diversity."

As he approaches the central tower of the shopping center, he sees another flighter coming towards him. As the other aircraft gets close, Karl looks in the face of the first guard. Karl lowers the nose down pushing the throttle all the way forward. He initiates a forty-five degree turn to the left, coming out under the first guard's former position.

The first guard also avoided Karl's flighter by pointing his nose upward and turning forty-five degrees left. They face each other as they get closer and closer with only a few meters between them when they intersect. Karl almost feels he could reach out and touch the first guard.

As they pass by each other, the first guard mutters something, but Karl only waves as the two flighters fly in opposite directions. Karl shoves his throttle forward and pulls up into the air. The first guard continues to look for Karl's aircraft below him. The flighters are so quiet except for the whirl of the dual props and the thrust of the turbo fans as they reduce the loads on the wings.

Once past the tall cone, Karl climbs vertically leaving the first guard trying to find out where he went. Finally, the first guard looks up as Karl's flighter heads into the clouds twisting clockwise.

The first guard pursues pushing his throttle all the way forward. He heads up into the sky through the clouds turning counter-clockwise. He suspects Karl will be waiting for him when he breaks through the clouds, so he widens his flying path hoping to catch Karl unaware. At least, that is what he hopes to accomplish with this little maneuver.

Karl levels out above the clouds, circling around the middle of the cloud, waiting and hoping to spot the first guard before the first guard spots him. Having anticipated the guard's widening circle, Karl keeps his path as wide as possible while staying hidden in the clouds.

When the first guard's flighter punches through the cloud, Karl quickly matches speed as he comes in along the underside of the first guard's aircraft while the first guard searches for Karl above the clouds, thinking that Karl has escaped him again, until he hears the roar of Karl's turbo fans below him.

Karl gets his fingers on the flighter's disconnect rod, but the first guard peels off into a spin back towards the ground. Karl does likewise with the opposite spin, but he can't quite get in position as the first guard evades his every move. The first guard stays right in front of him trying to piss him off and get Karl to make a mistake.

Karl gets ahead of the first guard, punches through the clouds, and spins down to the very top of the central cone, where he comes out of the spin barely above the cone, heading back up into the sky continuing the spin of the flighter clockwise. Watching Karl climb back into the sky, the first guard tries to match Karl's efforts with an opposite spin, but his left wingtip comes into contact tearing the fabric five centimeters from the tip of the Karl's wing. The fabric tears further before stopping under the wing.

The flighter's maintenance routine immediately begins an automatic fix to return to optimum flight status. The status screen on his window vanishes to be replaced by the maintenance routine. The routine waits for his approval before beginning the repair. Karl waits for his console monitor to display additional information.

The diagnostic screen appears on his console monitor describing the fault, the ability to repair and how long it will take. In this case, the repair time is short and it will give him optimum flight status. He slows for a moment to regain control and initiate repairs. Once the fabric is repaired, he pushes the nose of his flighter back up, following his enemy.

On the second spin up into the sky, Karl is ahead and the first guard cannot even get close to Karl's disconnect because Karl changes his spin with the turbo fans randomly. On the way down, the first guard almost gets in the same rhythm, but still doesn't get under Karl without Karl's flighter literally jumping sideways out of close contact.

The first guard gets ahead of Karl on the next way up when Karl suddenly slows catching the first guard with nothing to lead. Karl gets under the first guard's flighter before he can recover and gets his hand almost around the red rod when the first guard twists away. The first guard stays in front on the way down, but Karl is not able to catch him this time, either.

Karl begins the trip up with the first guard behind him slowly catching up and as he gets under Karl, Karl twists away before the first guard can get to Karl's disconnect bar. Staying ahead Karl continues spinning downward with the first guard trying to ram him with his nosecone or hitting his left wing with the first guard's right wing, but Karl evades each time as if he could read the first guard's mind.

The first guard is so mad, he decides to ram his nose cone into Karl's tail fins, but they both drop into the clouds and when the first guard comes out, Karl is nowhere in sight. Breaking off his spin and forward thrust, he levels out and climbs to below the cloud cover and circles above the central cone's tower.

* * *

The morning sun hangs above the horizon while several clouds move across the sky. The city of Bridget begins to move a major portion of the cities population from their homes into their work places. At the same time, officers arrive at the police station to begin their duties. Inside the Police Station, Robert's monitor displays, "Saturday, June 12, 2483 7:35 A.M. Bridget, Diversity."

Robert sits behind his desk, worried about several things and not thinking too straight this early in the morning. Coming in early, he has finished with most of the work he began yesterday and he only has to wait for some particulars to fall into place. He has contingencies, but he hopes he doesn't have to use them.

He talks to Tarcey, using the monitor on the wall opposite his desk, but his mind is on other things even as he tries to reassure her of their preparation. He tries to focus, because he doesn't want to upset her. He wants only to reassure her that they are doing everything possible to get Cliff back. He'll still have to be cautious not to get her upset.

She wears a white blouse and grey skirt. She stands with her back to the kitchen counter facing the central console. She's concerned with what she feels is a lack of evidence or progress.

Robert says, "I've gathered enough men and women. We have to get in position and then wait for Karl's signal. Some of my officers are setting up the staging areas on the other side of the forest surrounding the old city."

Tarcey asks, "And where is Karl?"

Robert says, "He's running a diversion for our benefit. It was the only way to keep Ingrider focused on Karl instead of us.

"We have one more planned meeting and then everything will be in place. I still don't understand how he is going to get Cliff out during the ceremony, but he knows what he is doing. I wouldn't want to be in his position."

Tarcey asks, "Is he going to be all right? He's not injured or being held where he can't escape? The more I read about this man, he makes some magician's furious."

Robert says, "This is a difficult experience for all of us. He had a rough day yesterday and last night, but I got a brief message this morning saying he was alright.

"I don't know about Karl, but I will not be the same until this is resolved. I'm trying to juggle about 1,000 officers from various northern regions."

"There must be some way you can find out if he is alright," says Tarcey, "He could be lying in one of the clearings someplace waiting to recover. Could you at least fly over the old city and check on his whereabouts?"

"I'll give it my best shot, but I can't guarantee the outcome. We're dealing with some nasty and rotten people. And don't blame me if I can't find him. I'm only the messenger here. He left explicit instructions not to be disturbed with the usual allowances for emergencies."

* * *

Ingrider sits on his throne with a disabling look on his face. Not without a loss for words, Ingrider decides to cool his jets and be somewhat reasonable, even though, he is sure that is enemy could not possibly escape. The cuts alone would keep the man lying down for at least two days and that is only if he didn't get some infection lying in that cell with rats and vermin all around spreading germs everywhere. He consults his pilo.

Ingrider's pilo displays, "Saturday, June 12, 2483 7:45 A.M. Bridget, Diversity."

He puts his pilo away and claps his hands together surprising the white habited acolytes on the upper terrace as they try not to look. They momentarily stop their duties or conversations and then begin their tasks and talk again. They are much quieter though.

A guard kneels with his head bowed a meter from Ingrider's throne. Ingrider rises from his seat and stares at the guard in front of him.

Ingrider says, "He what? He was in no condition to even move. Is every one of my guards incompetent? He couldn't lift a single finger let alone walk out of that cell.

"Did they leave the cell bars up? Do I have traitors amongst us? But wait, we have his backpack.

"Bring me that backpack!"

The guard bows lower and retreats down the terrace steps. He stops at the next habitat along the east steps, goes inside and comes out with a backpack over his shoulder. He walks back up the terrace steps.

He returns to the upper terrace a few moments later with the backpack. Bowing and kneeling, he hands it to Ingrider, thankful to get it out of his hands, hoping that it will be enough to keep his head on his shoulders.

Ingrider opens the main compartment and grabs bunches of grass which he brings out for all to see. The guard, the red sashes watching Ingrider and the whiter habited acolytes all gasp quickly averting their eyes. He throws one bunch after another to the floor until the backpack is empty.

The red sash acolytes milling about on the upper terrace let out a group exclamation. They feel Ingrider's angst with each coming up with solutions. In disgust, Ingrider throws the backpack to the terrace floor, scattering grass over a wide area. In a rage, he jumps on the backpack again and again, until the backpack is broken into several pieces among the grasses.

"Find that man. He couldn't have gone far and he will be leaving a very bloody trail which you won't be able to miss," admonishes Ingrider.

The guard stands keeping his head bowed and walks backward to the terrace steps. He turns around and walks down the steps, raising his head when he gets to the second step. He gathers other guards using his pilo as he continues walking down the steps to the lower level.

He walks down the secret stairs on the lower terrace into the maze followed by several guards. The white habited acolytes gather together in groups on the lower three terraces to discuss among themselves what will happen next. Some are worried that the ceremony will be canceled and they will have to move away from here to another place far away.

In an entirely different way, the red sashes react as quickly, gathering the pieces of the backpack and the loose grass, bringing out brooms and dustpans. Within minutes all traces of the backpack and grass are gone. The red sashes quickly fade into the background staying out of sight of Ingrider.

Sitting on his throne, Ingrider, now composed, still rages inside about how incompetent guards can be at times. He is thankful for his red sashes devotion to duty and feels he must find some way to reward them. As soon as all of this is finally finished, he will be able to give them his thankfulness. But for the meantime, he will have to be careful how he reacts so as not to upset the younger white acolytes.

* * *

Karl's flighter continues to engage with the other flighter neither one gaining an upper hand. Karl's cockpit monitor displays, "Saturday, June 12, 2483 8:00 A.M. Bridget, Diversity."

During the last spin downward, as he comes out of the clouds, he continues further downward towards the cone at a higher rate of speed because he noticed the first guard was trying to ram him. When he gets to the cone instead of breaking off back upwards, he slows his descent and slides along the tall cone's surface leveling out until he is above the lower cones heading south. He flies towards the perimeter of the shopping center, easing between the forest and the outer walls of the shopping center.

He flies clockwise around the perimeter staying below the walls and flying slowly to reduce his noise signature using the turbo fans for ground effect and slowing the dual props to whisper speed keeping his forward momentum.

Occasionally, Karl brushes one wingtip against the trees or against the outer wall of the shopping center without encountering any damage. Thinking Karl is pulling another stunt; the first guard continues flying up into the sky until he realizes Karl isn't below him or in the clouds. He looks all around but doesn't see the flighter anywhere above or below him.

The first guard's flighter quickly turns around almost falling into a downward spin as he spots Karl's left wing on the edge of the perimeter. The first guard uses his downward speed to get to a position in front of Karl's flighter as Karl's flighter nears the main west entrance. Karl's flighter turns away from the entrance before getting there and then disappears.

Karl watches the first guard's flighter fly towards him to cut him off and force him out of the perimeter. So Karl turns very slightly away from the shopping center wall, raising the right wing and then flips back and turns through a broader roll into the main west entrance. The sound of the dual props spinning increases in the confines of the main west corridor as Karl tries to put as much space between his and the guard's flighters.

The first guard loses sight of Karl's aircraft in the perimeter and looks to see which direction he could have gone in. The forest and grass clearing show no sign of any flighters which would be very obvious. For a moment, the first guard is dumbfounded. Not seeing the flighter outside of the perimeter, the first guard decides to follow his only course of action. He slows his descent, drops into the perimeter deftly and turns into the main west entrance.

He lets out a yell as he enters the confined space pushing his throttle forward as he catches a glimpse of Karl's flighter far into the corridor. Realizing how far behind he is, he shoves his throttle forward, cursing the day and the shopping center.

Karl hears the yell as he reaches the midpoint of the main west corridor. He formulates a plan as the central room looms ahead that might buy him some time. For now, he keeps the throttle forward knowing the guard can't catch him before he reaches the room.

* * *

Ingrider struts around in front of his throne, mouthing words that only a few have ever heard. Every white habited acolyte and red sash acolyte keep a fair distance, hoping not to be called. The guards, facing outwards, do not even think of any reason to approach, knowing that for whatever reason Ingrider could kill them all. They know full well not to approach him when he is in this kind of mood. Ingrider stops in front of his throne and consults his pilo.

Ingrider's pilo displays, "Saturday, June 12, 2483 8:30 A.M. Bridget, Diversity."

He looks up directly at the guard on the east edge of the top terrace looking at his bowed head. The guard faces to the east away from Ingrider.

Ingrider yells, "Bring the first guard!"

Regretting the day he was born, the guard near the east terrace steps turns around and walks forward, immediately kneeling a meter from Ingrider. Waiting for Ingrider to acknowledge him, he waits. Finally Ingrider steps away from the throne towards the guard. Recognizing, that this is not his first guard, Ingrider wonders briefly where he might be.

The guard says, "He's over at the shopping center in his flighter trying to bring down Karl."

Ingrider asks, "And where is he exactly? And don't tell me he's flying his flighter within the wide corridors of the shopping center. How does he expect to turn around?"

Gulping, the guard says, "Last reports imply they were flying through the main west corridor in the shopping center heading for the circular room."

Gasping before recovering, Ingrider asks, "Flying flighters inside the shopping center. Where do these people come from? If they crash, they will destroy the shopping center's electrical and heating units along with the geothermal vent. It would take months to rebuild. Our food and clothing would be unavailable for several weeks or longer. He's trying to kill us through starvation."

Having no pertinent explanation, the guard does not answer and backs up slowly, keeping his head down, hoping that Ingrider will not call him back anytime in the near future. He returns to his station near the habitat hoping that Ingrider doesn't push him down the terrace steps.

The sun rises farther into the clear cloudless sky with only a few clouds on the eastern horizon.

It casts medium hazy shadows in and around the old city with the heat baking the city even the shadows wiggle.

The sun's warmth heats the stonework bringing all of the white habited acolytes out to begin breakfast. First tables, then chairs alongside the habitats come out followed by white table cloths, red bowls and plates with the same color glasses. Platters of pancakes, waffles and French toast are set in the middle of each table. An assortment of syrups and sliced fruit arrive on the ends of each of the tables. Milk, orange juice and apple juice pitchers come next. Lastly white napkins and white handle silverware are set by each place setting. The lead acolyte of each habitat walks around the tables surveying the handiwork of his/her peers.

Soon hundreds of children in white habits walk gracefully and gleefully to their respective tables. The meal is readily consumed with the cleanup in reverse order taking several minutes as the children rush away to play.

The southern mountains show only a hint of purple in the far distance with a deep green near the prairie. Herds of buffalo, cattle, antelope and all their predators find shade in the tall grasses or soak up the sun's rays on the short grass. Birds land on the backs of horses, cattle and buffalo picking off the bugs and insects hiding in their furs

* * *

The shopping center's quiet is interrupted by the sound of the two flighters through the corridor. The corridor's monitor displays, "Saturday, June 12, 2483 9:00 A.M. Bridget, Diversity."

The first guard hears the dual props sound from ahead of him before he spots Karl's flighter as it heads ever closer to the circular room. The first guard tries to figure out why Karl would be heading for the circular room. *Does he intend to destroy the power system and shut down the shopping center?*

Karl's flighter weaves back and worth through the corridor as the first guard's aircraft finally catches up to him. The first guard tries, but can't quite get into a position under or on top of Karl's flighter, even though he tries several times in the short seconds before they both have to make a decision or crash their aircraft into the circular wall.

They get closer to the circular room's wall as Karl's flighter almost comes to a stop and flies up to the top of the circular room's wall and as quickly comes down with the wings turning and the turbo fans acting as brakes. After the guard's eyes blink, Karl's aircraft stops only for a millisecond in front of him and hops over the circular room's wall. The first guard's flighter has to reverse his dual props, engage his turbo fans, tilt the wings up and come to a complete stop.

His left wing barely touches the circular room's outer wall. He breathes again finally relaxing against the back of the seat.

He unfastens the straps to breathe easier and looks above as if trying to figure out what went wrong. He goes through several scenarios, until he hears turbo fans and dual props straining to maintain flight in these tight quarters.

The first guard recovers and after engaging his turbo props, the flighter hops up to the top of the circular room's wall. Karl's aircraft comes out from behind the inner tower of steam piping circling the tower climbing towards the top. Karl's flighter glistens from the steam cleaning as droplets form before descending, creating rivulets on the pavement far below.

Before dropping to the floor of the circular room, the first guard's flighter zooms forward as the dual props engage. He uses the turbo fans in the wings and the dual props to maintain some semblance of flight

The first guard catches up with Karl as he nears the top of the cone. Karl falls off the inside of the cone keeping his flighter near the wall of the cone.

The first guard comes right behind him afraid to try anything in these confining spaces, matching Karl's moves, too afraid to try his own. Somehow, he must gain the advantage, but Karl is a very gifted flighter.

Karl jumps over the circular wall using the turbo fans and heads straight out the main west corridor, turning the flighter ninety-degrees in seconds with the deft use of wing control and reverse turbo on the one wing. The first guard is astounded again, but recovers much more quickly executing the same maneuver only more awkwardly. Karl continues to randomly slip from side to side and top to bottom along the main west corridor and the first guard is unable to get anywhere near to Karl's disconnect.

Finally, Karl keeps the first guard's flighter away from getting under or over him, heading out of the shopping center and high into the sky. Reaching his highest elevation, Karl continues his spin downward. Karl fades each time into a new direction. His heads up display shows that only two minutes of fuel remain.

Karl comes out of the downward spin several meters above the forest which surrounds the shopping center on the south side and heads back to the west side of the shopping center.

Karl lands his flighter vertically in the small clearing near the main west entrance. He hops out of his aircraft as the dual props and turbo fans wind down and runs inside the shopping center. Finally locating Karl's flighter in the west perimeter, heading for the main west entrance again, the first guard lands after spotting Karl's aircraft in the small grass meadow. He climbs out, after the turbo fans and dual props have spun down. He runs inside following Karl.

The sounds of the surrounding forest return once the animals find out they're not going to be killed. A few chirps from a couple birds and a brook running over small rocks and larger tree branches along with a few scurry animals become the background sound throughout the perimeter of the shopping center.

* * *

The shopping center returns to a quieter sound of operation as the stores change displays for the noon customers. The corridor's monitor displays, "Saturday, June 12, 2483 10:00 A.M. Bridget, Diversity."

Karl passes several shops along the corridor until he spots a men's clothing store which he happens to remember has a rear entrance to another corridor. He turns his head to look behind towards the main west entrance. The first guard enters the corridor a hundred meters behind Karl coming fast.

The guard runs toward Karl when his spots him, closing fast. He watches as Karl ducks into a nearby store. The guard looks up and sees the sign for the men's clothing as he passes several doors closing in on Karl.

Karl dashes into the store, closing the door behind him. Grabbing a nearby chair, he wedges the chair under the door handle effectively blocking the door. Quickly pulling out his pilo, he checks for exits in this particular store. After putting the pilo back in his pocket, he heads for the back, weaving in and out of racks of pants, shirts, suits and coats. After meandering through the suits and pants section, he arrives at the back.

At the back rear wall, he finds an exit door and opens it into one of the smaller corridor between stores. He silently closes the door, feeling the catch latch smoothly without making any noise. He hears the noise of the guard at the front entrance, trying to get by the door.

The guard pushes the handle, but the door doesn't open. He puts his shoulder into the door with a gentle shove and feels the door give slightly. He decides to use more force and steps back away from the door. He swings his right leg up, moving forward on his left, hitting the door with a crashing sound as the chair's back splinters and the door flies open. Looking at the several pieces of broken chair, he looks around the door frame for any more surprises, but it appears clear.

The guard cautiously looks throughout the store as far as he can see for any traps, but the store looks normal except for the row of clothes that Karl had gone through.

Karl waits by the side of the door in the smaller corridor. The first guard follows through the aisles, continuing through the rack of clothes, and finds the exit on the back wall. He opens the door out into the corridor.

Karl shoves his left elbow into the guard's throat and punches the guard's face into the door with his right hand. The guard collapses to the floor with the door closing, leaving the guard lying on his left side inside the men's store.

Karl runs through the smaller corridor past several smaller stores. The small corridor links up with the main west corridor. He stops and looks up and down the corridor. He spots an outdoors equipment store and heads for it.

The guard finally recovers, opens the exit door staying low, staying out of the way of anyone kicking, until he is sure no one else is there. He tries to follow Karl. When the guard gets into the smaller corridor, all the nearby shops have closed doors.

He looks and listens, but doesn't see or hear anything out of the ordinary. Advertisements in the windows blanket the windows and doors, keeping him from seeing too much inside the stores. Deciding that it would be too much to do all by himself, he would rather be chasing rabbits. Since he left his pilo in his flighter, he'll spend some time looking through the doors, but he doesn't expect to find anything. Karl has escaped with plenty of lead time.

He walks all the way to the main west corridor, acting dejected, but knowing at the same time more guards will be able to do the job and they would have Karl eventually. His thoughts return to his own failure at not being able to capture Karl.

After opening several doors and listening at each, including the outdoors equipment store, the first guard walks out through the main west corridor to his flighter, looking glum and confused.

* * *

Twenty red sash acolytes sit in various positions in two rows semicircular around Ingrider's throne, chanting a lament.

Listening to his red sashes chanting, Ingrider stops them when they hit the wrong note and mangle the chant. He critiques their technique; they continue with the chant. All of the red sashes perform beyond measure which makes him very glad. He consults his pilo.

Ingrider's pilo displays, "Saturday, June 12, 2483 11:00 A.M. Bridget, Diversity."

A guard approaches and waits for a moment of silence. He approaches with his head bowed and kneels a meter from Ingrider. He whispers a few words.

The red sashes continue with their chant not exactly knowing what else to do. Only the leaders realize they should probably stop and get out of his way, but it is best not to second guess their master.

Not catching the words at first, Ingrider leans over towards the guard as he repeats his statement. Ingrider stands up, dismisses the class and says, "Where have I gone wrong. He was my favorite pupil, so fast to teach and eager to learn." The red sashes immediately stop the chant and leave orderly, returning to their assigned habitats at the four cardinals on the upper terrace.

He calls all the guards up to the hub base. The call is repeated on every lower terrace until all the guards have acknowledged the command including those guards currently asleep. Guards gather towards the east steps with more coming from the lower levels, leaving the other thirty-six at the gates and the lower level habitats. A few only have to walk around the upper terrace from the other side to assemble around Ingrider's throne. When all sixty-three guards have assembled around him, bowing their heads and kneeling, Ingrider speaks.

He says, "The first guard has lost our enemy, Karl, in the shopping center. Leave the six guards at each of the gates. Send the rest to the shopping center and follow the first guard's instructions."

All sixty-three guards nod as one and group by twos down the terrace steps. Ingrider seems lost in his own thoughts as he returns to his central seat. The red sashes return with fresh fruit, garlands of flowers and a large feathered fan carried by the leaders with the rest of the red sashes forming into two semicircular rows around the throne.

Switching positions, Ingrider can't seem to find a comfortable position until he stands and lifts up the seat pad.

Several loose pebbles are scattered across the seat of the throne. He looks at the stones for only a moment before acting.

With his left hand, he picks up each pebble placing them in his right hand. When the seat is clear, he replaces the pad and sits down, ending with a sigh. The red sashes gather around the throne with several depositing the fresh fruit beside it and fastening the garlands of flowers around it and up the back side. Two red sashes move the fan up and down stirring the air around Ingrider and the rest of the red sashes, causing habits to flutter, quietly humming one of Ingrider's favorite tunes.

A red sash acolyte comes forward and removes the pebbles from Ingrider's right hand, apologizing profusely for some of the younger white habited acolytes who were playing around his throne earlier in the morning. Ingrider continues to look at his hand that no longer has any pebbles in it for quite a while as he remains lost in thought. The red sashes continue the fanning and the humming of a happy chant as they continue to decorate the throne and the immediate surrounding area. They gather in a semicircle around his throne in two rows, keeping their heads bowed and humming softly. Once in a while a particular red sash will casually look up towards the throne, trying to catch a glimpse of Ingrider's current attitude. For several more moments, Ingrider continues to stare at the palm of his hand before finally closing his grip and sitting back on his throne.

The red sashes end their humming immediately and open their individual pilos to rehearse their positions and the lyrics of the chant they will be singing as they process up the outer steps of the hub. Several try to trade for better positions.

Afternoon

The sixty-three guards return to their respective habitats for mere moments as they retrieve backpacks stuffed with everything they thought they would need for the next four to six hours. Soon, after streaming through the east gate into the east field, the designated pilots quickly walk to their assigned flighters.

Two other guards travel in the storage locker inside each nose cone. Two rows of aircraft are parked and tied down in the east field. The wind blows lightly moving some of the tail rudders randomly back and forth. The ailerons and elevators move up and down with push and pull of the wind, while the flighters themselves rock with the rush of wind that moves through the field.

Eight pilots climb into their cockpits as two guards in each of the storage lockers close and lock the nose cone for flight. The flighters take off vertically rising into the air to an appropriate altitude above the old city. They engage their dual props and fly west towards the shopping center.

When the eight flighters return, they each take another two passengers in the storage locker and are back into to the sky heading west. After the eight return a third time, they get two more passengers, leaving seven guards waiting for transportation.

The eight flighters return shutting down three of the aircraft and fastening them to hooks driven into the clay soil. Five flighters take off with no one waiting for aircraft to return. Every aircraft has two guards in their nose cone's storage locker. They take off vertically, switch directions until they are pointing west. They engage their dual props disappearing over the hub.

Returning to the shopping centers west entrance for a fourth time, one of the guard's looks at his pilo as the five flighters begin their vertical descent to the short grass field west of the west entrance.

The guard's pilo displays, "Saturday, June 12, 2483 12:00 P.M., Bridget, Diversity."

After discharging their passengers, the five fligthers return to the sky, flying east towards the old city. When they get back to the old city field east of the main east gate, they shut down three of the aircraft. The three pilots climb into the other two flighters with only one passenger in one of the aircraft

Fifteen minutes later, the two pilots start their vertical descent after passing over the central tower of the shopping center.

The two flighters land in the short grass field, directly beyond the perimeter west of the shopping center, shutting down their turbo fans and dual props, climbing out of the cockpits, and after pounding in hooks for their ground tackle, secure their flighters. Their passengers open the nose cones and climb out of the storage lockers.

* * *

The shopping center remains quiet after the cleaning and display changing have finished. All the various machines have returned to their lockers. The corridor's monitor displays, "Saturday, June 12, 2483 12:00 P.M. Bridget, Diversity."

Lying on a cot, Karl wakes up slightly disoriented.

Bringing his feet to the floor in one motion, he sits up. After orienting himself to his new surroundings, he listens to the sounds around him.

Robotic sweepers and vacuums swish by in the corridor outside the store. A sweeper moves by his cot, heading to his right down the aisle. Five centimeter metallic spheres move about the windows and displays, cleaning with sprays, wiping with cloths and drying with blowers as they spin around or up and down to the next tool. The spheres have several other attachments for cleaning virtually everything that needs to be cleaned in place without having to return to a locker for more tools.

Karl walks to the store's entrance and barely opens the door into the main west corridor, watching outside in case someone was walking by. He puts his ear to the opening to listen for any sounds in the corridor.

He bends low and sticks his head out, getting on his knees. After looking both ways at an empty corridor, he stands. After opening the door and walking out into the corridor, he walks down the main west corridor to the next smaller corridor on his left constantly keeping cognizant of his surroundings.

He's decided it would be expedient to use the main west corridor, but he could be easily caught in that situation. He decides the more prudent path is through the smaller corridors. Using his pilo, he plots a course through the smaller corridors ending back at the main west corridor near the circular room. He activates the GPS and walks through the smaller corridor

Walking through several smaller corridors, he heads into the northwestern hexagon. As he nears the main corridor intersection, he comes to a stop before the corner and listens. He carefully looks both ways up and down each corridor on his knees with his head barely around the corner.

The main northwest corridor looks empty and so does the smaller corridor.

As he turns to head along the large corridor, he spots a shadow on the floor of the corridor at the other end near the intersection to the circular room. Thinking it may have been a bird flying past the transparencies in the cones overhead. He looks back for a moment, but nothing else happens and he writes it off to imagination.

He continues to walk through the main northwest corridor towards the center of the shopping center carefully not making a more noises than are necessary since the corridor has excellent echoing effects. When he cautiously gets to the circular wall, he turns right walking towards the circular room's entrance on the other side of the main west corridor. Looking around the corner, it remains as empty as the main west corridor which means his luck is still holding.

As he walks along the circular wall keeping from making too much noise and getting near the circular room's entrance, he

hears odd noises coming from the east and heading west, like
flighters with a large contingent of guards massing at the entrance.
The voices get boisterous and loud.

He can only imagine how many guards he will be dealing
with this time, so he will have to be very diligent in every move he
makes if he expects to get out of here alive. Luckily for him, they
are too far away for the time being.

As he hears the flighters land in the west fields, he hears
the voices of many guards echoing through the main west corridor.

He estimates from the different voices that fifty or more
guards will soon be looking for him. He smiles. *In a way it's
always nice to be wanted.*

* * *

The small group of guards march through the last of the main
west corridor with the first guard bringing up the rear all with
dejected looks on each of their faces. Other guards arriving via
flighter having recently arrived gather at the main west entrance.
The smaller group joins the larger group where they exchange
greetings. The shopping center corridor's monitor displays,
"Saturday, June 12, 2483 12:00 P.M. Bridget, Diversity."

Sixty-three guards gather at the main west entrance leaving
two flighters nearby in a short grass clearing beyond the entrance.
The larger group mills about trying to decide what their leaders
will want them to do. They have divided into several groups with

differing opinions. The leaders confer among themselves as how best to precede and catch their elusive opponent.

The first guard finishes walking through the main west corridor in-step but not very spirited. He spots the last of the flighters landing and watches the guards gather outside the main west entrance. He wonders if they know what they are here for. As he reaches the entrance, he picks four guards for each of the six main entrances to the shopping center. Before he sends four guards to the six main entrances, the first guard pinpoints their locations on his pilo to their six leaders who have gathered around him. He instructs them to guard the main entrances for each of the hexagons and the small side doors usually to the right of their main corridor.

The twenty-four guards divide up into two groups, one heading south and the other north around the outer perimeter to their designated main entrances. Four of those guards stay at the main west entrance.

The first guard selects another four guards for each of the six main corridors and stores within the hexagons. He motions for the six leaders of those twenty-four to come forward and gather around him. As they come forward, the first guard remembers something he wanted to note in his pilo. He brings it out of his pants pocket, turns it on and chooses the application he wants. Making his notation, he returns to the guards.

The first guard says, "Work in teams on either side of the corridor. Search each and every store thoroughly including every aisle, closet, restroom and changing room. Do not disregard any potential hiding place.

"Three men, at a time, search one store while the remaining guard stands watching for other doors opening or closing along either the main or between stores' corridors. Please coordinate with the entrance side of the main corridor when possible, that way you'll have three guards watching the corridor at the same time and we'll get through this much faster."

The leaders enthusiastically nod taking their men to the selected main corridors. After conferring with the four guards at the main western entrance, two teams of four walk through the main western corridor to the first store on either side. The north team takes the door that is closer while the south team has to walk several meters further to their first door. The other four teams divide into two and walk outside along the perimeter until they come to the outside west entrances of the main corridors, coordinating with the entrance teams already there.

The other sixteen guards with the first guard leading, head into the main western entrance marching by twos along the corridor, until they reach the other end near the circular room.

* * *

The central room of the shopping center has no monitor displays since it is primarily the maintenance center for the shopping center. The public was never meant to be in the central area. Outside, one of the shopping center corridor's monitor displays, "Saturday, June 12, 2483 12:00 P.M. Bridget, Diversity."

Karl walks around the rectangular room in the central room to the front of the room. It has several large insulated cables coming out the sides and back arching over into the floor.

Piping enters on the back side. The sounds of turbines whining, pipes cracking and steam venting fills the air around him. He feels the vibration through his feet and smells the ozone in the air along with fragrances of oil and grease.

On the front of the rectangular room only one door exists, to Karl's right about a meter from the corner. Karl walks to the door and stops in front of it, looking at the long handle which he hasn't seen in quite a while.

Karl checks the door. It is locked.

He unfastens his backpack, swinging it on the concrete floor of the circular room and removes a box from one of the outside pockets. Opening the round pill box from inside, he taps it in his left hand. He places his left hand over the key lock of the door handle and grabs slightly. The lock clicks open. Karl turns the handle and walks in, taking a step down to a dirt and stone floor. A single centered light panel in the ceiling provides minimal light. He blinks trying to adapt to the lesser light, but it still takes him a few minutes for his eyes to adapt.

Six small turbine generators arranged in two pyramids rumble the dirt floor in front of Karl. Piping enters and exits each of the generators. Large insulated cables exit the top of each generator towards the back wall. Steam exits the smaller piping around the generators heading below through meter wide screens in the base. Humming fans underneath the generators draw the excess steam downward.

To Karl's left, a stairway leads down into the maze. The single light panel is not bright enough to bring out any details at the bottom of the stairs.

Karl says, "There you are finally. I was wondering if you would be in this particular room. I was fairly sure that this entrance would exist.

"However, they're many others, I am quite sure. It's going to take a while to find them all. Thankfully I have the time to spare which will hopefully come to good use. The pilo is already programmed with the layout of the shopping center. I just have to match the maze with the shopping center."

Karl turns on his pilo's light and shines it into the darkness below. Karl walks down the stairs guided by the light of his pilo. At the bottom, he notes the location of the intersection and the stairs in his pilo.

* * *

The red sashes hum as they sit in front of Ingrider on the floor. Two red sashes pull up and down on a large multi-leaf fan stirring Ingrider's habit and some acolyte's habits. Heat rises from the surfaces of stone and the gardens in the old city. Water cascades out of a twenty centimeter pipe from the above upper terrace, falling to troughs beside the terrace steps, branching out to the gardens and outer rim of each terrace all around the perimeter, providing needed potable water for the plants.

Ingrider rests comfortably on his throne with his eyes closed and his hood off his head. Opening his eyes and turning his head east, he sees a guard walking up the east terrace steps. The guard's head bobbles up and down with each step on the terrace. Ingrider consults his pilo.

Ingrider's pilo displays, "Saturday, June 12, 2483 12:30 P.M. Bridget, Diversity."

He tenses and dismisses the fan and all the red sashes. The guard approaches with his head bowed; he stops one meter from the throne and kneels. Words exchange with vigor and much hand ringing on the part of Ingrider. The guard nods and retreats to the lower terrace where the water pools surround the city inside the outer wall.

Ingrider sits back in his throne. The red sashes start to return, but Ingrider waves them off. He broods with his hand on his right palm with the elbow on the arm rest and the hood pulled over his head. The red sash leaders gather their practice teams and head over to the west side of the hub where they can practice without bothering Ingrider.

The two leaders of the guards confer after watching Ingrider. They instruct the others to find duties elsewhere than on the upper level. The guards move off the upper terrace scattering to the six compass headings until the upper terrace is completely clear without a red sash or guard anywhere to be seen.

Ingrider doesn't even notice as he fidget's as if there were still pebbles underneath his seat pad. He gets so upset, that he stands, turns around and throws the seat pad off of the throne. The seat is smooth without any pebbles on its surface.

Ingrider calms down and retrieves the seat pad placing it back on the seat of the throne. He sits down carefully looking out over the upper terrace to make sure no one saw what he had done. He checks the entrance to the hub as well, but is relieved to find no one on the upper terrace or in the hub entrance as far as he can see. He can hear bits of the chants when the wind is blowing in the right direction and he imagines the guards have retreated to the coolness of the habitats.

* * *

Robert's office is occupied by him alone even though he is talking with someone on his large monitor. The monitor displays, "Saturday, June 12, 2483 1:00 P.M. Bridget, Diversity."

Robert sits at his desk talking with Tarcey on the monitor. Robert wears his usual uniform while Tarcey wearing a yellow apron over a white blouse with tan shorts stands before the kitchen console tying the last knot around a second roast beef roll in an aluminum pan. The first already tied roast beef roll sets within its pan on the console a pan length away.

Tarcey asks, "Is Karl available to talk? Has he rescued Cliff yet? Do you have a time when he will?"

Robert says, "No, he hasn't reported in and he won't. He left strict orders not to be disturbed. He's buying us time to get our act together.

"I don't believe he will until sometime later this afternoon or tonight. If this is about Cliff's birthday party, you'll have to postpone it to Sunday. There's nothing I can do to improve on Karl's abilities."

Tarcey says, "But you're leaving him out there alone. If everything is in place, shouldn't you be able to help him.

"From what I have heard, you've placed both my son and Karl in jeopardy.

"They may have killed him already and then who will rescue my boy?

"How can you be so complacent with all that's going on?

"Are you just going to sit there and twiddle you thumbs?"

Robert says, "Now wait a second. Let's not place any blame here until everything is settled."

Robert looks down to his hands on the desk and sure enough that's what he is doing. Smiling he looks back at Tarcey's image on his office monitor. He moves his hands to under the desk outside of Tarcey's view.

Tarcey says, "I didn't mean to say that Robert. I know you're trying your best under the situation. But I am under a strain too. I would be much better, if I was more informed.

"But Ingrider has hundreds of followers waiting to heed his commands. He has twenty red sashes which are his closest followers and his protectors."

Robert says, "That's exactly the words I used with Karl, but he insisted."

Tarcey says, "Would you at least consider flying over the shopping center and the old city? For me it would be reassuring if you didn't find anything. That would reassure me that they haven't found him."

Robert says, "I can pinpoint him with my pilo, but I am not doing it for security reasons. Whatever Ingrider is monitoring us with, we have to watch what we do and say. For you, I will consider finding him and helping him, but I already know I will either be captured myself or Karl will tell me to get back to my office. But if the report is negative don't blame me."

* * *

The guards mill about outside the door to the generator room. The first guard is inside behind the closed door. On one of the shopping center corridor monitors is the display, "Saturday, June 12, 2483 1:00 P.M. Bridget, Diversity."

The first guard, standing in the generator room, looks down the stairs. It looks like someone has walked down them recently, but he can't be too sure it wasn't one of his guards earlier in the day. Some of the stone steps are missing their usual covering of dirt with the imprint of a boot heel on one of the steps where the dirt was thicker. Some of the footprints are twisted as if someone turned as they were going up or down the steps.

The turbines next to him hum, moan and whine with high pressure steam whistling through the smaller piping. The squeal of a mouse punctuates the air as it runs across the top of the stairwell ridge disappearing under the wall of the room, steam trailing from its tail.

Excess steam exits the turbines and the piping. It is pulled downward by large fans below the base every so often with a definite reduction in light from the light panel as the fans take energy from the generators.

He walks out the rectangular room's door, taking a step up and closing it behind him. Fifteen guards gather around the circular wall talking amongst themselves about wives, children and significant others. A few discuss their last or upcoming vacation plans leaving out many details.

The noise level increases dramatically with the door open. After the door closes, the bigger turbines from the geothermal vent compress the steam into a higher pressure forcing it though compressors for even more pressure until it becomes super saturated steam. After generating electricity and transferring heat, the spent high pressure steam flows around the piping and gangways from the floor to the cone exit high above until it has cooled enough to return to the geothermal base to be reheated, compressed and sent to generators and heat controllers.

The first guard, "I want you four guards to search the stores in the west hexagon again. If you don't find him, gather all the other guards at each of the entrances and return to the main west entrance where you are to wait for further orders. The rest of you are coming with me. We have got to get to the maze. Do you have the maze on your pilos?"

Four guards immediately head for the west hexagon.

The other eleven guards all nod in agreement, bringing out from their individual pockets, their pilos.

The first guard says, "Good. When we get to the maze, we'll split it into thirds."

The first guard reopens the door and heads down the stairs. The rest of the guards follow with four guards marching out of the circular room.

Inside the rectangular room, the noise level subsides to less than a roar as the load decreases on the generators because the fans below are no longer turning.

Less steam escapes and when it does, it almost always, evaporates. The turbines rumble becomes smoother with all six units acting in conjunction. The generators hum subsides as well making the mouse come back out of the hole in the wall and run across the stairwell ridge under the turbine/generators.

A mouse scurries out from under the base, across the top of the header around the stairwell, and disappears below the wall and under the circular room's inside perimeter. It comes back out of the wall and smells the air in the room before returning to its' hideout.

The generators start another cycle, generating additional electricity and sending the rest of the unused steam for heat production throughout the shopping center.

* * *

After turning to the right for about the sixth time, Karl runs into a dead end. Looking all around with his pilo light, he looks at all the walls for anything that might give him a clue. Frustrated with his lack of finding anything on the walls, he turns to go back when his pilo light happens to catch something shiny on the stone wall. He looks closer at the stonework especially between the stones. At waist level, between two stones, he finds a shiny metallic lever hidden in several layers of dirt, caked on like it was cement. As he touches it, the dirt falls away. He pulls the lever and the dead end opens into another maze passage.

Karl walks through the opening in the wall. The dead end closes as soon as he exits to the next passageway that crosses the otherwise hidden passageway. He finds a similar lever with several layers of dirt on the inside wall of the passageway. He pulls the inside level and the dead end opens in the otherwise blank wall. He walks through to return to his original position at the end of the passageway, near a supposed dead end. He checks his pilo.

Karl's pilo displays, "Saturday, June 12, 2483 2:30 P.M. Bridget, Diversity." He waits for any new messages to appear, but none arrive.

He makes a note in his pilo and returns to walking through the maze, passing several intersections being careful to note each one in his pilo and watch out for guards or acolytes walking through the maze. After making several left turns, he finds himself back at his original starting place, in the passageway leading to the rectangular room's stairway. He hears the sound of voices and footsteps above him within the circular room. The door opens on the rectangular room. Muffled voices come from the stairs. The rectangular room's door slams closed.

Thinking of the quickest way to exit this passageway, Karl runs through the maze turning right at every intersection heading for the secret passageway, watching his pilo closely as it guides him through the maze. Keep his wits about him, he stops every so often and listens for movement and/or voices.

He hears voices behind him so he decides to slow down to a quiet walk and not make too much noise to attract unwanted attention. The sound of footsteps and voices behind him recedes into the background. As he nears the dead end, he stops for a moment just to make sure he isn't hearing anything.

Arriving at the dead end, Karl waits and listens until he is sure that the guards are not following him and are far away for the time being. He decides it's time to investigate the other side of the dead end. He takes a deep breath to recover from his last few endeavors before settling down. He listens again to make sure he is not being followed. With the coast clear, he makes his decision on his next few moments. But just to make sure, he goes through several scenarios in case his first decision doesn't work out as planned. Finally he decides to keep his initial decision.

* * *

Ingrider sits on his throne with his eyes darting wildly. A bowing and kneeling guard is nearby waiting patiently. He has passed on his message and is awaiting a reply. He's been waiting for the last ten minutes, he has waited even longer during some of Ingrider's worst moments. Ingrider consults his pilo.

Ingrider's pilo displays, "Saturday, June 12, 2483 2:30 P.M. Bridget, Diversity."

Jumping from his throne, Ingrider walks quickly to the edge of the terrace, looking down to the lower terrace. At the east gate two guards are relieving the two guards at the gate while two other guards are munching on something outside of the east habitat. White habited acolytes on the lower level are conducting classes for the younger students. His eyes dart downward to the secret stairway on the lower level near the east gate. He looks back at the guard near his throne.

After he returns to his throne, Ingrider says, "Have the first guard get the child moved to the locker under the stairway on the lower terrace. Later the guards will hand him over to the red sashes. He will be their responsibility. Hopefully, it will be better than the guards. They have practically lost him more than once. I cannot allow that to continue all the way to the beginning of the ceremony.

"Keep the majority of the guards on duty at the shopping center until 7:00 P.M. That will give them more than enough time to return to the city and reinforce the gates during the ceremony."

The guard rises keeping his head bowed. He walks past Ingrider to the east terrace steps, taking out his pilo from his pants pocket. By the time he has reached the second step down, he raises his head and sends a message to the leaders.

Still looking wildly at anything that catches his attention, Ingrider steps back to his throne, lowers his hood over his eyes and motions a white habited acolyte to come closer. Dutifully, but guardedly with trepidation, a female white habited acolyte comes forward to one meter from Ingrider where she kneels and bows her head. She waits for Ingrider to speak.

Ingrider says, "Send for one of the red sashes."

Thankful that is all he wanted, the acolyte rises, keeping her head bowed, and quickly enters the hub base through the entrance. After entering the hub, she raises her head and walks down the steps to the next room.

Ingrider sits on the throne and waits for only a few seconds.

The white habited acolyte returns with a red sash acolyte. The red sash acolyte walks to about a meter from Ingrider where he kneels with his head bowed.

The white habited acolyte continues on to her previous assignment near the habitat by the eastern terrace steps. She picks up the sprayer and continues watering the flower garden. Trying not to hit the leaves with the water, she aims for the ground.

Ingrider says, "You and one of your choosing will take over responsibility of the child at about 6:30 P.M.

"He will be very cold and easily managed, but not too cold no matter how much he complains. Feed him and wrap him in a warm blanket until he can move again. Don't feed him too much, but keep up his fluids. Check him over completely. No broken bones or fractures or concussions. I don't want any bruises, blotching or scratches anywhere it would show.

"He will have been in the cold locker for a little over three hours. He'll be feeling really cold. That will teach him to try to escape from me or the red sashes.

"Instead of the guards bringing him in the processional, it will be the duty of the red sashes right behind me. No one sees or knows the location of that boy until the processional starts. Keep him well guarded and make sure he is well fed and physically able to walk up those steps. He will not be carried nor must he be trussed. It must look like he is willingly walking to his death."

* * *

A group of four guards, patrolling the maze, stop at an intersection meeting the other group of four without the first guard. They each take out their pilos and compare notes about passages, intersections arguing about the number of cells and dead ends checked and counter checked with the voice level increasingly louder with each sentence.

The third guard says, "He wasn't in our area. We searched every cell and dead end along the way."

Another guard says, "He wasn't in our area either.

"We did the same, but didn't find even a trace."

"The rest of the guards in the shopping center aren't having any luck either," says the third guard.

"Like, he has vanished into thin air, but then we haven't heard from the first guard. Maybe he already has found our opponent. Good thing we left one guard from the main west entrance on his flighter, in case, he doubles back.

The third guard asks, "Do you get the idea that something is being left out? Something doesn't make sense."

Another guard asks, "Like what?"

The third guard says, "Like why do we have to find this guy? All we have to do is kill the kid. There's no way that can be stopped not with all of the red sashes and guards. He's in a secure location where no one would be able to get him out without notifying a number of guards or acolytes."

The other guard says, "But the big boss wants to make sure. You know how determined he can be when he wants to be. That's why we have to locate him and keep him out of it.

"Now, let's go meet up with our first in command."

They form up by twos and march through the maze passageway heading east past several intersections.

Pointing down one of the passageways at the next intersection, the third guard turns into the passage.

"We turn left at the next intersection," says the third guard. The rest of the guards follow down the passageway to the next intersection.

* * *

In another part of the maze, the first guard leads his group of three guards through the passages. He stops the group and listens. He thought he had heard something moving through the passageway at the next intersection, but listening now, he hears nothing come from the nearby intersection.

The three guards quit their idle chatter and wait for the first guard's instructions. They remain quiet even though each of them wants to keep moving in this spooky place where sounds travel for a long ways. He checks his pilo.

The first guard's pilo displays, "Saturday, June 12, 2483 2:40 P.M. Bridget, Diversity."

The first guard stops in front of Cliff's cell and opens it.

Pointing to two of the guards with both hands, the first guard asks, "You two take the boy out of this cell and put him in the cold locker near the stairway on the lower level at the east gate of the old city. We'll set up guards at that intersection later this afternoon. Is that clear?"

The two guards answer, "Yes, Sir."

The two guards take Cliff out of the cell and march through the passage. The other guard follows the first guard as he goes deeper into the maze. At the next intersection, footsteps come from the right passageway. The first guard keeps his man behind while he goes on alone.

The guard spots Karl ahead in the passageway running away from him and runs after him. Karl approaches the open dead end. After going through the opening, Karl stops, stepping to the side of the opening.

He turns around and watches the dead end close, leaving no trace of an opening in the passageway wall.

Having already caught the first guard at the shopping center, he has to make some other move.

After running through an intersection, the guard abruptly stops at a dead end. He looks up and then down on each wall running his fingers over each stone. Pushing several stones along either side, he walks back to the intersection. He keeps thinking that he is missing something about secret passages that his opponent somehow knows.

As he walks through, he unexpectedly gets hit from the right side and falls down into the dirt covered stones two meters from the intersection with the other person beside him.

The first guard looks over at who hit him. He can't believe his eyes and has to blink just to make sure.

The first guard asks, "What the? You! Aren't to supposed to be managing the Police Station?"

Recovering from the unexpected encounter, Robert says, "I didn't see you coming. But I am glad to have found you.

"By the way, I wasn't running that fast. I thought that it might be Karl and I was excited.

Both get up and brush the dirt off their clothes.

The first guard says, "You're glad. This is my lucky day."

Robert says, "That's why I came to see you.

"I would like you to take me to Karl's cell so I can see for myself he's in good health."

The first guard says, "Not a problem. Right this way."

The guard turns to go through the intersection again.

As he nears the midpoint of the intersection, he's hit from the right side again, losing his breath and pushed violently against the wall. His head hits the stone wall, knocking him out cold.

He collapses.

Karl gets back on his feet and brushes off the dirt.

Robert says, "I guess this is his lucky day."

Karl asks, "What are you doing here?

"I thought I made myself clear. You need to stay in your office and run the operation. If Ingrider even gets a hint that you're here helping me, then our entire plan is upset."

Robert asks, "What happened to your face and hands?"

Karl says, "Ingrider and his lovely tools. They're healing quite nicely.

"That's why I'm the diversion so Ingrider doesn't know what's happening.

"Whenever I have my next shower, the black stripes will wash away."

Robert says, "Yes, but you don't know Tarcey. She has been on my case all day. She's becoming as concerned about you as she is about Cliff."

Karl says, "We've wasted enough time chattering away. The guard will soon be awake and we don't want to be anywhere close when he does. He probably has more guards on the way.

"Thanks for the new vest. It has worked. I'm no longer over emotional. I even feel more confident.

"We'd better get moving if we don't want to get caught."

Robert smiles.

Karl heads back to the dead end.

Robert follows.

Karl pulls the lever; the dead end opens to a passage beyond. An amazed Robert watches as the wall opens. He's even more amazed when it starts to close as Karl goes through.

Robert follows quickly pulling his legs through before the opening closes down on his ankles. He stops to feel the edges that he cannot see, but the stones do not give away their secrets. He turns around. Karl is several meters away from Robert. Robert runs to catch up.

Robert checks his pilo to determine his location even though he has never been in this particular passageway of the maze. He updates his pilo's folder noting the doors location and operation characteristics. He marvels at the ingenuity of the older civilization and their secret passageways. There are obviously more passageways yet to be investigated. He realizes he will have even more work to do after this kidnapping business is out of the way. But that will have to wait.

* * *

Stirring from lying in the dirt, the first guard opens his eyes, sits up and rubs the back of his head. Luckily, he doesn't find any wetness behind his head or between his legs. He notices the dirt on his habit and pants and feels the pain in his ribs on both sides. He shakes his head, trying to remember. *Why am I lying in the dirt with my head hurting?*

Remembering how he got there and who hit him, he scowls and slams the butt of his right hand on the ground scattering dust all around him making him cough. When the dust subsides, he pulls his pilo from this right side pants pocket. He turns it on. He checks it looking at the time and for messages.

The first guard's pilo displays, "Saturday, June 12, 2483 3:00 P.M. Bridget, Diversity."

He writes on his pilo using the attached pointer.

The first guard's pilo displays, "Change of plans, bring all guards to maze. Get secret locations from Ingrider with diagrams.

"Meet at the attached location and time. Be prepared to search the maze through the night."

He attaches the picture of the location showing longitude and latitude. After pressing send to distribute the message to the guards in the shopping center and the eight guards in the maze, he puts the pilo away in his pants pocket. He rubs his head and feels the bump on top, but no blood appears on his hand.

The first guard gets to his feet and looks at the intersection, checking out both sides, before going through. Satisfied, he walks through quickly, constantly watching either side. When he arrives, the one guard he left behind barrages him with question after question. The other eight guards arrive at that time and add their voices to the discussion.

Ignoring their heated routine, he assigns routes for all the rest of the guards. After looking over his pilo's map of the maze to try to discover the secret passageway at the dead end, he decides he just as well wait for the locations from Ingrider.

He gives them a time to return to a certain location within the next hour. The other guards record in their own pilos the time and place with a note marking their current location in case they get lost.

The first guard says, "Head out with your group leaders and stick close together. Keep your eyes and ears open at all times. Cut the unnecessary jabber and keep communications to a minimum.

"Meet with the rest the guards coming from the shopping center at the appropriate time. We'll have the secret locations at that time and we'll make a decision on what to search and where."

The three head guards disperse with a few certain that the first guard is sending them on a wild goose chase with at least one concerned guard thinking the first guard has lost it. But like dutiful soldiers, they proceed to their duties without question.

The first guard heads back to the dead end to try again to find the secret passageway, carefully moving through each intersection so as not to be caught blindsided again. Activity remains high within this area of the maze as the few guards under his command quickly run through the passageways and intersections trying to find either Karl or Robert. Of course, they pass by the several secret passageways in their section of the maze, completely unaware of the passageways that are so close.

* * *

Robert stands by his flighter's open storage area, removing two twelve centimeter cubes, looking like blue cheese. He closes the nose cone and locks it in place for flight. He walks back to the edge of the open stairwell where they still have their backpacks on the ground.

Karl puts a granola wrapping in the dirt near the top of the stairwell, returning to stand beside Robert. Karl checks his pilo.

Karl's pilo displays, "Saturday, June 12, 2483 3:00 P.M. Bridget, Diversity."

Checking his messages, Karl asks, "So you knew I was here because I removed the foil wrapping you had left from our past excursion?"

Robert says, "I stopped by your flighter first. I checked your fuel level. You're too low on fuel to fly very far. Here are a couple fuel cubes."

He passes the two cubes to Karl.

"They'll bring you back up to full.

"When you stop by the Police Station later, we'll bring you back up to full," says Robert.

Karl takes the two cubes from Robert and places them in his backpack on the ground a few meters from the maze entrance. He puts the two cubes in the main compartment.

He puts his backpack on, connects the straps, tightens the straps, and starts down the stairs into the maze. He turns on his pilo light which eliminates the darkness in front of him to guide him through the passageway beyond.

Stopping about halfway down and turning around to look at Robert, Karl says, "I've drawn out as many of the guards as I can except for the ones at the gate. I have to keep them all busy. This maze has many secrets and I haven't found them all yet, but I'm starting to get an idea."

Robert says, "But you don't have enough time. In a few more hours the ceremony begins and it will be too late. Once he is on those steps or at the top, my men won't be able to rescue him. And right now we don't even know where they are holding him."

Karl says, "You do your part and Tarcey does hers, that's all I can ask at this time. Perhaps under different circumstances this could have been a vacation.

"I may find the boy through sheer luck, but knocking out that guard has been the only good luck so far. I have never relied on luck to get me out of any situation; intuition works for me.

"I wouldn't call Ingrider's intrusions or the second guard's death as good luck. Every life is valuable and with the right influences, everyone can have a good life full of challenges, defeats and opportunities."

Karl turns back, disappearing into the darkness of the maze. After donning his backpack, Robert climbs into his flighter and flies off vertically, changing direction to the northeast towards Bridget. The sliding door activates leaving nary a sign of the presence of the maze entrance.

A robin spots a wriggling worm and lands right on top of pulling it apart with it beak.

* * *

The fifth and sixth guards turn around towards the larger group of guards outside the west main entrance. The shopping center's corridor monitor displays, "Saturday, June 12, 2483 3:00 P.M. Bridget, Diversity."

All the shopping center guards gather in two orderly rows standing at attention half circling four other guards. They are all wearing crisply pressed uniforms.

Guards fifth and sixth face the large group, except for the two guards standing at attention behind the leaders about two meters. The larger group has resolved their differences. Behind the leaders are two flighters in the short grass clearing outside the perimeter of the shopping center.

The fifth guard says, "The first guard has changed his mind. We're to return to the maze. Somehow, Karl got by us and into the maze. He seems to know the secret locations to other passageways."

The fifth and sixth guards turn around and face the other two guards who look straight at them ready for their orders.

"I want you to head back to the old city," says the fifth, motioning to the sixth guard to continue with the instructions.

As the fifth guard turns back to face the larger group, the sixth guard says, "Get the secret locations with access codes or diagrams from Ingrider and meet us in the maze at this location and time."

The sixth guard points to a place on his pilo screen, showing it to the other two guards who copy it to their own pilos by pointing their pilos at the sixth guard's pilo.

After acknowledging the map location and time, the two guards run for their flighters and take off vertically heading east towards the old city.

As the sixth guard turns around to face the larger group, the fifth guard says, "Let's go!"

Before the two flighters reach their flying altitude, the other guards plus the two leaders march into the shopping center through the main west corridor entrance. They march by twos with the fifth guard in front leading and the sixth guard in the rear providing the rear guard.

The sound of footsteps echoing through the main west corridor diminishes to a lingering memory. Moments later, the west entrance is completely empty of guards and flighters nearby while the guards have entered the circular room and followed the stairs to the maze through the rectangular room.

Only the typical sounds of the shopping center echo through the corridors. Birds and small animals return to the short grass clearing mindful that the humans could return at any time.

* * *

Red sash acolytes process up the outside steps of the hub in a disorderly fashion with some hurrying and others dragging, leaving the two leading read sashes far up the stairs while the rest have caused a jamb only a few steps above the upper terrace. Ingrider stands on the edge of the upper terrace at the east edge of the terrace steps.

Ingrider yells, "You're moving too fast, slow down, this isn't a race. Spread out farther, you're grouping. NO! NO! Stop that this second. This will simply not work.

"Come back down and start over. We'll get this right eventually. Let's try to be reverent and courteous as we practice. Order up behind the hub and come back out at the proper pace and spacing. This isn't a competition or a race to see who can be the fastest or the slowest. I want you to take three deep breaths and let it out slowly until your lungs are screaming. Shake your hands and shoulders to release the tension. Say a prayer to our master and remember he is watching you."

The red sashes on the upper terrace return quickly behind the hub while the bunch on the stairs untangles themselves. The two leaders wait patiently for the group to clear the steps.

Ingrider watches the red sash acolytes untangle themselves. They march quietly down the steps until they reach the bottom where they continue on around the hub. Ingrider watches the last acolyte move around the base of the hub before consulting his pilo.

Ingrider's pilo displays, "Saturday, June 12, 2483 3:15 P.M. Bridget, Diversity."

A guard approaches up the terrace steps to the upper terrace. Along the way several white habited acolytes wonder what could be happening now. As he takes the last of the steps up the terrace steps, he stops on the third lower step, kneels and bows his head when he sees Ingrider at the top of the stairs on the edge of the upper terrace directing his red sashes as they march up the stairs.

At first Ingrider doesn't notice the guard at his back, his entire focus is on the red sashes on the stairs, marching as one while they sing the chant. However, he notices the white habited acolytes looking behind him at the upper East stairs. He turns and acknowledges the guard keeping his temper in check. The guard hands a paper message and writing pen to Ingrider. At first incredulous for using such a primitive method and then realizing the significance, Ingrider takes the note and pen from the guard, wondering why the message was so important as not to be messaged via his pilo. *I haven't used this form of writing since before I became their leader.*

Ingrider reads the message without arguing its need and turns around to watch as the red sash acolytes start back up the stairs in an orderly and properly spaced position. They remain in perfect formation as they all go up the stairs. The guard waits behind him, keeping his head bowed.

Any white habited acolytes watching Ingrider, the guard and the red sash acolytes would think that everything was in order and the ceremony would continue without interruption. They return to whatever they were doing on the upper terrace, ever mindful that Ingrider had everything in control.

Ingrider says, "Much better, keep the pace and your space," to the red sashes on the stairs. The continue up the stairs until the two leaders are on the south side and the rear end has just stepped onto the stairs from the upper terrace.

After scribing a reply message on the other side of the paper, he turns again and hands it back to the guard, dismissing him The guard turns, stands and walks back down the terrace steps. When he reaches two more steps down, he raises his head.

Turning around to face the red sashes, Ingrider returns his gaze and ear to the red sash acolytes as they march up the stairs, correctly timed and sufficiently spaced without any bunching or stumbling. However he can't even bring a smile to his face. *Time is getting shorter and nothing of any significance must interrupt the planning and preparation for the ceremony. I must not fail in any way. We are entering the final stages. The closer we get to the ceremony, the less chance for our enemies to intervene. We have the boy and they won't be able to rescue him in time. The ceremony will proceed.*

* * *

The cold locker's monitor displays the temperature as slightly above 0 degrees Centigrade and also displays , "Saturday, June 12, 2483 3:15 P.M. Bridget, Diversity."

Cliff sits in a darkened room with a single light above barely highlighting the bottom half of his clean almost white face. Every breath he exhales turns into a fog in front of him. A mouse or rat scurries around beyond the door. Water runs above him momentarily cycling and stops. No other sounds intrude upon his presence. He can almost feel the water vapor in the air.

The coldness makes the walls of his cell wet with moisture running off to a small drain field surrounding the outer wall except for the door. The door's threshold also has a channel which routes the water off the door around the sill to the outer drains in the wall. When the fan starts up again, it will pull the excess moisture out of the air and off the walls making the environment easier to handle.

Turning his head, Cliff stands for a moment waiting for the fan to start moving the air within the room and remove most of the moisture in the air.

The fan starts and settles down to a smooth rumble drowning out all other sounds. Cliff feels his black habit ruffle against his skin. He shakes off the cold air until he feels strangely warm as the moisture level in the air goes down. This is nothing like the other cells.

He walks over to the closed central opening, feeling the edges. He stops for a moment to listen for any noises outside the door. He doesn't want to be surprised when they come to take him for the last time. Hearing only the usual sounds, he inches forward.

As he nears the door, the sensation of bitter cold hits his front half causing him to pause in mid step. He shakes off the cold hearing flakes of ice fall from his black habit. After putting his hands on the door, he quickly pulls his hands off, because of the cold sensation; they almost stuck to the door. He blows on his hands until the coldness of his bones has waned.

Waiting, rubbing his hand together, he tries to warm up, stomping his feet to keep his legs moving, knowing he doesn't want to the sleep at this time. He blinks realizing that he was dreaming while standing in front of the door. After putting both hands up to his cheeks, he's sure their still cold, but warmer than when they first touched the door.

When they begin to feel warm again, he tries once more.

Cliff puts his fingers on the left edge again and continues searching upwards, touching lightly to keep the cold off his fingers. The door is a little taller than he can reach. He moves his fingers downward to the dirt floor which also feels cold to the touch. Feeling inside the edges, first, he then touches the outside edges, trying to find some kind of an opening.

He has to stop ever few seconds to warm his hands.

After touching the dirt below the opening, he follows bottom edge from the left to the right side and up along the two right edges until he cannot reach any further.

There wasn't a single break, pinched edge or tear along any of the edges he could reach. He's disappointed that he can't think straight enough to figure out of a way out of here. *I won't be able to bleed off this cold air that way and the door is way too thick.*

He walks back to his place in the darkest corner and lies down trying to find a comfortable position. His thoughts trouble him and he turns over several times. The fan continues to rumble pulling moisture out of the air. He can feel it through the ground as if he were on one of those walking rides. Dust falls from the walls regularly leaving a buildup along the edges of the cave

Water runs above him, cycling on and off randomly for some time and then suddenly abating. The fan stops suddenly, Cliff relaxes as the air becomes still again, and he falls into a deep restless sleep. Ice begins to form on his habit and his helmet as the excess water condenses. It quickly covers a thin layer over the top which continues to build as each moment passes. With each breath movement some of the ice on the edge breaks off falling to the ground, but it is the thinnest part until later when the large ice cap begins to break because of gravity. The ice disappears every time the fan comes on and reappears every time the fan goes off.

If it wasn't so cold and the cycle wasn't so loud, he could get some sleep, but he has learned repeatedly to stay awake when cold. Otherwise, he could easily die. He laughs out loud thinking about how that would rob Ingrider of his ceremony. Quickly, he stops laughing because it uses too much of his body heat.

* * *

The living room lights are dim. No fire burns in the fireplace and the large screen monitor is blank. Only the kitchen lights are at full brightness. The breakfast table monitor displays and beeps, "Saturday, June 12, 2483 3:15 P.M. Bridget, Diversity."

Wearing a black and white vertical striped dress with ruffles around the collar, the sleeves and the hem, Tarcey sits at her breakfast table hand sewing a few stitches at seams for reinforcement. The torso is approximately the same size as her son Cliff, but it doesn't move as much as he does.

She's sewing together an overstuffed child's torso with attached legs and arms. The outer cloth looks exactly like pink skin of a new born baby.

A plastic bag filled with a dark substance rests near the torso, jiggling like gelatin wiggles with every bump of either of the dogs as they turn over against the table legs. She sews with black thread the last of the long seams on the left side of the torso finishing with a flurry of knot tying.

After cutting the loose thread, she puts the scissors on the top of the torso. She pins the needle onto the chest of the torso below the neck. Moving the torso, she looks for her scissors which were on the table a second ago, but they fell off the torso after she laid them down after cutting the thread. After lifting the torso above the table, she finds the scissors where the torso's legs would be attached.

Using the pair of scissors, she cuts across the chest area through the outer pink garment, the inner white and the netting underneath. Doing two cuts ninety degrees to the other cut at its ends, she folds over the two flaps which open up over the heart area of the torso. She exposes feathers stuffed inside the body to build up an appearance of girth. Some of the feathers flip up into the air and fall down below the table.

After removing most of the feathers about where a heart would be, she places the feathers in a plastic container to her left on the edge of the table. More than one feather escapes out of the container and floats to the floor. The dogs snap at the feather as it floats by their noses.

Reaching across the torso, she picks up the filled plastic bag and places it in the torso's empty chest cavity. She stuffs more feathers from the container around the plastic bag until it holds its position which brings more feathers out of the container floating down by the dogs which are now trying to catch the feathers. Covering the rest of the plastic bag with the remaining feathers, she packs them in tight always applying pressure with one hand.

She brings the left half of the netting over the plastic bag and then the right half. Holding the seam together with a couple of pins, she grabs the needle from the torso and begins the needle work using common overhand stitching.

She sews the netting together with a couple of stitches lightly around the edges to keep it from unraveling. The pressed feathers keep the torso tight without breaking all of the stitches. Next the two halves of the inner white cloth flap are sewn over the netting. She tugs both sides of the stitches until she is satisfied they will hold for the time being. She finishes with the slightly pink outer covering sewing it even lighter so with the right force the stitches would break.

Over the chair next to her hangs a black habit with a white emblem over the heart area. At the other end of the table, a black stuffed helmeted head with a stuffed neck rolls back and forth like a metronome. Realizing she has to do the head and neck before the habit, she puts the scissors on the table in front of her and place the needle after attaching more black thread in the torso near where the neck would be.

She reaches across the table and pulls the helmeted head over to the torso. Turning the torso over, she attaches the back of the neck to the torso with a single stitch. On each side, she does the same. Carefully turning over the torso and head together, she sews a single straight stitch on the front edge carefully tucking the edge of the cloth under to keep a straight seam. She does the same for the left and right shoulders and the back turning the torso and head as she goes. After surveying her work, she carefully places the torso on its back.

Taking another needle from her bobbin, she starts sewing the neck to the torso with an overhand stitch turning the torso and head as she goes around. When finished, she changes direction and does the same stitch ending with a flourish of knot tying.

Tarcey says, "I sure hope it works. The hands and feet were tough to make. With the helmet, I don't have to worry about his face or hair. That would be stretching this dummy's impression way beyond my abilities.

"I'll be done soon enough. Looks like I'll make the 4:00 P.M. deadline at the Police Station."

She raises the torso to a sitting position holding the helmeted head like a baby with her right hand. With her free left hand, she places the black habit over the head and shoulders. She pulls it across the torso on to the waist. She reaches inside and routes each arm through the correct sleeve being very careful to not tear any of the seams in the torso of the black habit. She doesn't want to spoil the surprise.

* * *

Walking through the passageway, Karl stops meters before the bottom of the stairs up to the rectangular room within the circular room in the center of the shopping center. Dimly lit, the stairs stand without supports. He checks his pilo.

Karl's pilo displays, "Saturday, June 12, 2483 3:15 P.M. Bridget, Diversity."

Standing against the darkest wall, he waits for anything to appear on his pilo, hoping no contingent of guards are waiting for him at the top of the stairs or outside the door of the rectangular room above him.

His pilo reports no unwarranted sounds are evident either in the passageway or in the circular room above him. He listens for the sound of footsteps and voices in the maze or the circular room, but the noise of compressors, generators and escaping steam are all he hears. Karl decides based on the report of his pilo and his own judgment that the coast is clear, but walks cautiously forward toward the stairs, knowing he is most vulnerable at this time, ready to run the other way if necessary.

Walking back behind and under the stairs, Karl finds another dead end shining his pilo everywhere trying to highlight anything on the walls around him. Above him, the door opens on the circular room and guards enter marching towards the rectangular room.

Karl overhears their chatter and the sound of their boots on the floor. Too far from the passageway, he makes his decision. Turning off his pilo's light, he moves under the lower part of the stairs, sitting down until his knees are up to his chin. He waits hoping that none of the guards are predisposed to looking under the stairs.

The rectangular room door opens and several guards walk down the stairs into the passageway. The three lead guards shine their pilo lights on the path before them leading the rest. After the last of the guards disappear into the dark passageway and the sound of footsteps diminish to nothing, Karl turns on his pilo light and gets out from under the stairway. Something flashes back at him as he starts to stand up. He hunts for it again not quite finding it until he moves his pilo light back towards the stairway.

It sparkles more towards the stairwell than the door, almost on top of him.

The lever is painted a disguising color with some chips having long since fallen away exposing the inner chrome layer. After Karl pulls the lever; the wall opens as a door with a whooshing sound as the two different temperatures of air meet. A rush of cold air exits the storage locker creating a miniature fog outside the door. Looking in hesitatingly, he enters.

He shines the light around the inside of the room. Stone covers the walls with clay packed between the stones with signs of deterioration. A toilet and small sink are to his left in the far corner.

He moves the light to the dirt floor.

The bare outline of someone about Cliff's size shadows the dirt in the corner with small footprints around the edges. The rest of the dirt shows signs of movement in a circle around the perimeter of the locker. Ice flakes off some of the stones and falls to the floor where the heat of the floor melts the ice forming small puddles which drain off the edges of the locker.

The compressor above rotates until he can feel a breeze going through the cell removing the ice crystals from the walls, the door and the floor before they melt. He backs out and closes the door until he hears it latch with a gasping sound. He makes a notation in his pilo noting the location and type of room behind the stairs and the location of the lever. He checks the location again to confirm his entry.

Karl says, "Well, at one time you were here.

"If they keep moving you, my job will be much harder.

"We might have to go with plan B. And that will require some dexterity. Trying to extricate you from Ingrider and his guards is beginning to seem impossible. But then that hasn't stopped me before, so I doubt it will stop me this time. I can't let Ingrider enjoy his ceremony without spoiling it for him in a way he will not have thought about."

* * *

The first guard meets with the other groups of guards in the central part of the maze in the middle of an intersection with guards in each of the four passageways. The ones not too close to see the map use their pilos to follow the action or talk in hushed groups about what is going to happen next. The closest guards are gathered around the leaders who are bending over a holographic representation of the maze. The guard's standing around the map use their pilo lights to provide enough light to see the map. The first guard checks his pilo.

The first guard's pilo displays, "Saturday, June 12, 2483 3:30 P.M. Bridget, Diversity."

He has a 3D holographic two level diagram spread out on the dirt floor lit by several guard's pilo lights as the top three guards go over their three section assignments, the secret passageways and their return location. They argue among themselves trying to decide how best to proceed.

Green lines highlight the regular passageways through the maze closest to the floor. Exits to ground level in yellow which rise to the next level appear in the center of the shopping center, the small clearing outside the northwest perimeter and the east near the lower terrace of the old city. Nothing exists above the second level of white outlines delineating the old city and the shopping center showing both as two dimensional representations of the major areas.

Blue lines with dots indicate the cells or other storage rooms scattered around the maze with the majority in the central part. Letters in blue describe the type or use of cells, storage rooms or cold lockers.

The individual lines are detailed in the legend that happens to be closest to the first guard's position.

Red lines highlight the secret passageways through the maze none of which have normal exits or entrances and they float halfway from the floor to the next level. Some of the red lines only connect to one other passageway while others connect with two. Many orange lines outline cells within the maze usually along passageways.

The first guard says, "It would be best to seal off all the entrances/exits. Three guards at each will suffice while the rest of us are searching through the passageways. Don't act though if you see either one or both. Together they formidable and you won't be able to capture them yourselves.

"Send for the rest of us. We'll need everyone."

The first guard pushes a red dot on the edge of the holograph making the entire map suddenly disappear revealing a black box about two centimeters to a side and one centimeter tall. He picks the black box up as the rest of the guards take up their assigned positions. Several of the guards are jostled and they push back until finally everyone settles down.

Dividing into three equal groups, they go in three different directions at the next intersection leaving the south passageway empty. The first guard leads the last group marching by twos south through the south passageway. They travel through the passageway for some time before taking a left at the intersection.

* * *

Karl walks out of the southern section of the northwest hexagon of the shopping center. He heads through the corridor between sections to the southeast section. Stopping for a moment to catch his breath and take a break, he checks his pilo.

Karl's pilo displays, "Saturday, June 12, 2483 3:30 P.M. Bridget, Diversity."

Arriving in the center of the southeast section, Karl looks around a department store. A typical mix of men's, women's and children's clothing with a sign for toys pointing one way and a signs for electronics pointing the other way. Bed and bathroom signs point off to the south.

A vertical tower about two meters round comes into view near the middle of the store, surrounded by displays, including banners hung from the ceiling. Most of the banners fly from the center of the store to each of the departments. Each banner displays rotating animated advertisements for goods or services in their particular department of this store, loudly exclaiming the price reductions of a certain product or the clearance of a major brand from their shelves.

The vertical banners display odds and ends on sale or discounted disguising the tower and its height The banners are actually thin OLEDs which change colors and messages regularly. Each side of the banner displays a different message using the ability to display photographic pictures of people and things.

Walking over to the tower, he removes several empty boxes piled in front of a banner displaying household appliances. Most of the boxes are completely empty with many smaller boxes inside.

After throwing and tossing several boxes aside, he moves behind the banner to the central tower, brushing the banner aside out of his way. Before him is a tower reaching halfway to the ceiling well hidden by all the banners and displays.

Approaching an opening big enough for one of the large boxes, he walks to the tower where he sees two vertical doors, one opens up and the other opens down. Karl opens the doors revealing a dumb waiter within. This one is electronic with buttons for up or down within the inner chamber. It is fairly large for a dumb waiter allowing more packages to be carried.

The material appears to the metallic but it does not feel that way when he touches the surface. The buttons appear to be part of the same material slightly indented without a seam or indentation.

It has several small and one medium sized unopened boxes waiting to be offloaded with the store's name on the packing slips of each of the boxes. The space is big enough for him to easily crawl into and out of. He pounds on the bottom surface to gauge its strength, and it rewards him with a deep bass sound. He decides it is strong enough for his weight.

The outer door is divided in half with the top half moving upward and the bottom half moving downward when the door is opened. It has a catch on the inside and it is counter weighted to stay closed unless forced open.

Karl asks, "That's two. Do all of the sections have dumb waiters to the maze?

"But why are they in secret locations in the shopping centers? There must be some reason."

* * *

Robert's office is almost filled with officers standing at attention. The rest of the officers sit at their desks trying hard not to look up into Robert's office. His monitor displays, "Saturday, June 12, 2483 4:00 P.M. Bridget, Diversity."

Robert sits wearing his standard uniform at his desk checking a to-do list on the screen of his pilo. His white tie is loose around his neck and the top button on his shirt is unbuttoned. The long sleeves of his shirt are wound up to his elbows. His hair is slightly ruffled and he needs a shave. His explanation would involve a flighter that tried to run him down, but it is only the stress of his duty. No one would believe that story, even though he saw it in a movie.

Six officers stand in a semicircle in front of him around his desk with every tie, shirt and pants crisp and newly pressed. Their black shoes are highly polished. Every hair is in place and the men have recently shaved.

Looking up at his officers, coughing once to clear his throat, Robert says, "I've passed the routes to your individual pilos. Be sure to review the material. Each of you will be leading a group of men and women from diverse regions."

He lowers his head to peek at his pilo before continuing, "You have eighteen portable devices total between you which enable us to sleep induce anyone with a GHD. By all indicators, the acolytes and the guards have them, but the red sashes are suspect and Ingrider is suspect due to aliases.

"Use them on the guards at the gates especially. The rest of the guards will be near the habitats that are by to the terrace steps.

"The only exception is the guards on the top terrace who guard the cardinal exits. Because of their position, the devices will have to be ready before starting up those steps. After we have the guards, the white acolytes are next. Most of the white acolytes will come quietly.

"However, the older white habited acolytes will need the device and maybe more. There will be a few exceptions which we will have to handle quickly.

"Any questions?"

He looks up at his officers which all stand at attention with their eyes firmly focused on the wall of books behind him.

Smiling, Robert says, "Head for your staging areas. Don't capture the gate guards until you get the signal from me. Under no circumstances, try to take a red sash or a guard by yourself. They may claim to come quietly, but the first chance they get they will turn on you.

"Dismissed!"

The officers turn and march out of Robert's office.

Robert looks at the dummy on the left side of his desk. It has a black helmet covering the head, showing the chin and neck, and a black habit with a white emblem on the chest. Pink legs, feet and hands stick out of the habit and sleeves respectively.

Robert says, "The hands and feet look so life like. Even up close, it would be hard to tell the difference without touching to make sure. I keep expecting it to get up and walk out the door on its own. I have to remind myself that it is a dummy otherwise I would start talking to it and expecting an answer. And then I would lose my position as Police Chief. Well, we can't have that happening, so I won't even think about it.

"Tarcey did a good job. If I didn't know better, this could be one of his tricks. It would surprise me though, if Cliff wasn't playing around so much. I don't actually know where that boy is heading, but it will certainly be interesting."

* * *

Near the stairs at the top of the hub, Ingrider points to two of the red sash acolytes gathered around the central stone.

All of the rest of the red sash acolytes keep their heads bowed while the two in question quickly kneel.

Ingrider says, "You two are out of sync. I know you have practiced this many times, so you have no reason to do this. When you get back into position, I'm expecting perfection.

"The crescendo must build slowly and reach its peak when the bell chimes. We must have coordination to pull this off.

"I will not stand insubordination. You most of all are aware of my duties. If we show even the slightest miscarriage, all of the rest of the red sash acolytes would throw you from the tower walls.

"Let's try it again."

Ingrider checks his pilo looking for messages that are not coming. He turns it off and puts it back in his pants pocket.

The two red sash acolytes, whose faces, although hidden behind by their hoods, are almost as red as their sashes, rise back into position, but every other red sash know who they are and what they have done.

Ingrider's pilo displays, "Saturday, June 12, 2483 4:00 P.M. Bridget, Diversity."

The red sash acolytes begin to hum, and opening their mouths wide, they chant slowly at first, steadily increasing the tempo and the volume. The level slowly increases to a higher and higher degree in perfect pitch and tempo.

They reach the highest point, holding it for mere moments, and the bell chimes. The chant stops and each acolyte keeps his/her head bowed while continuing to stand still waiting for Ingrider to pronounce judgment. And the wait takes longer than any of them could imagine.

Ingrider claps his hands in delight with a grin from ear to ear. The red sash acolytes, from the tallest to the shortest, wait before responding.

Ingrider says, "Very good, very good.

"You do that tonight and all the gods will glorify you.

"Take a fifteen minute break and we'll do it again."

Grinning, but staying in position without any other movement, they thank their lucky stars especially the two acolytes recently reprimanded.

While each of them hears a guard walking up the outer steps, none move as if they didn't notice. The guard steps over to Ingrider, stopping at one meter from his position. After bowing and kneeling, he waits for Ingrider to allow him to speak.

Turning towards the guard, Ingrider signals his permission, reluctantly. The guard whispers his message. Ingrider doesn't understand, until he realizes the guard is whispering. He leans forward to hear the guard.

The guard repeats his statement. Ingrider straightens up in amazement looking out over the entourage. The red sash acolytes stiffen as one, waiting for his usual response which has known to be devastatingly quick.

Ingrider says, "He did it again!   That man is going to destroy me.

"Keep the men on guard at the entrances to the city.

"We have to maintain security within our outer walls and the lower terrace stairwell. How can he be so devious and cunningly mischievous to escape sixty-plus guards in the maze of all places?

"Send every guard to the shopping center. He can't leave; he has no fuel."

* * *

Facing a stone wall within the maze, Karl closes the door to the dumb waiter. The outer stone door slides into place along the curve of the wall. The stone door meshes into the curved stone wall leaving no trace of a seam or edge. The outside lever moves between two stones hiding its location.

It matches the color of the clay between the stones, except for the several patches of chrome. Otherwise the door seam disappears leaving no trace of its existence. He checks his pilo.

Karl's pilo displays, "Saturday, June 12, 2483 4:00 P.M. Bridget, Diversity."

Karl pushes buttons on his pilo.

Karl says, "That takes care of all the secret locations of the dumb waiters."

Karl turns on his pilo light, walks towards the next intersection and turns left. He walks past several other intersections. At the next intersection, he turns right. He turns off his pilo light before exiting the intersection. The dimly lit steps to the rectangular room appear ahead.

Three red lights flash on his pilo indicating heat signatures. He immediately stops and increases the gain on his pilo until he can clearly see the guards. Three guards stand in the shadows of the passageways out of the light of the intersection. They don't act as if they have seen him yet.

After making a notation in his pilo, saving it and forwarding it to Robert, Karl turns around and heads back to the intersection that brought him to this passageway and turns left. Walking only a few meters, the next intersection looms ahead. He turns right staying in the shadows between light panels near the walls and turns on his pilo light after listening to make sure the passageway was empty.

After coming to a stop, he looks at his pilo, holding it out in front of him, and slowly walks forward.

He stops, finds a lever on the wall and pulls it. The curved outer door, not thicker than two point five centimeters, of stone like material regresses into the passageway and slides up into the ceiling disappearing leaving no trace.

Karl slides the two halves of the door of the dumb waiter apart and climbs in. He closes the two halves and pushes the up button. After a few seconds the lift moves up. Half a minute later, it stops. Karl opens the dumb waiter doors slightly and looks beyond the displays and boxes.

Three guards are leaving the sporting goods store, except for the last guard who decides to turn around and walk back to the central tower for further investigation. Karl closes the dumb waiter doors. The guard comes closer to Karl's location. Finally the dumb waiter moves down. Karl breathes again. It's not easy to stay away from so many guards, but his luck is holding. At the bottom, he opens the doors and gets out.

Putting one foot on the dirt covered stones of the passageway in the maze and after easing the other foot, he steps away from the opening.

After closing the dumb waiter doors, he pushes the outer lever, the stone door slides into position disappearing into the wall as if no opening had ever existed at this location.

After standing for a moment to regain his thoughts, Karl asks, "Now what do I do?" Several seconds later it comes to him. He smiles as his head checks out all of the possibilities, pitfalls, escape plans and other challenges.

"Behind the free-standing stairwell of the generator room is a cold-storage room," he says.

Karl checks his pilo and pushes buttons until the lower terrace stairwell appears on his display rotating to a side view to show the nearby lower door in the protuberance and three way intersection. The display zooms through the doorway to the stairwell. Continuing on past the stairwell to underneath it, a dotted line appears for the supposed doorway to a storage locker. The storage locker looks big enough for two or three weeks of food, leaving room to move around.

Karl says, "The stairwell at the lower terrace in the old city has a free-standing stairwell with room to spare beside and behind it. However, it doesn't look promising. If they have established guards at each exit, I could have my hands full. That particular location also has more guards instantly available on the lower terraces and in the habitats nearby. It would be impossible. These are the times I wish I could be invisible; even an invisibility cloak would work, but that's not going to happen any time soon. I still have enough time to figure out something that will work."

* * *

The guards whisper among themselves about their duties, pay rates, family problems and the usual financial crises. The shopping center's corridor monitor displays, "Saturday, June 12, 2483 4:30 P.M. Bridget, Diversity."

The first guard paces back and forth in the rectangular room, mumbling with a few curses thrown around for good effect.

He wants the rest of the guards outside the room to be wary. The six turbine generators hum in sync with the excess steam drawn downward by the fans below the base. The door behind him opens and a guard steps through, coming to attention inside the room. The first guard stops walking and turns to face the other.

After saluting, the other guard says, "Reporting as ordered, Sir. We have searched each sector of all the hexagons west of the center twice, including aisles, restrooms, closets, changing rooms and storage areas. We've looked in every single box from the empty to the full centrally located. All displays in aisles or along walls with room to hide have been checked out. Nothing has been left unturned or inspected.

"He is not in the shopping center on the west side. My men are tired and cranky, but well fed by the stores in the shopping center. We need a little more sleep and another good meal in order to continue."

The first guard asks, "You have been a faithful and competent guard for some time now. Have you forgotten how to be a leader, especially under the leadership of Ingrider? How long have you served our leader?"

Smiling, the other guard says, "Two years, sir."

The first guard asks, "In the last year, you have been on several excursions as a leader starting with small groups and ending with the group you have now.

"And how many times have you returned to our leader with empty hands?"

The other guard says, "Sir, I'm very sorry, but, after we take a short break, we are going to have to search at least two more times if we are to return to our leader with empty hands. Our leader will not be satisfied until we have turned over everything four times. I have seen too many former leaders lose their lives, because they did not explicitly follow our leader's orders.

"He has an uncanny way of always being right."

The first guard says, "You're incredibly right about Ingrider's pronouncements. His information is always correct, irrefutable and infallible. The only reason I can stand before you as first guard is because I have no doubts in the abilities of my leader and my master. By following his lead and every command, I have kept my head on my shoulders. I have seen my share of good guards make just one mistake. Dismissed!"

The first guard turns his back to the other guard. The door closes behind him. The first guard smiles as he remembers his first and only mistake with Ingrider. Luckily, he learned his lesson.

The first guard paces again, in the opposite direction, only faster at the beginning and slowing down to a regular place as he vents his frustrations on the stones beneath his feet. He occasionally peeks at his pilo to check the time.

Eventually, he tires enough to sit down with this back against the wall and falls deeply asleep. The pumps and generators cycle to a quieter mode with the fans coming to a halt. The generators barely hum keeping a steady current through the large cables. Every few moments, steam escapes and disappears into the colder air coming from the maze through the stairway. The mouse comes out from the far wall and sniffs the air before returning.

* * *

R obert's frustration diminishes as he walks back and forth in front of his desk. His monitor displays, "Saturday, June 8, 2483 4:30 P.M. Bridget, Diversity."

Robert, still ruffled, but no longer concerned, stands in front of his monitor focusing his thoughts on a current view of the old city.

His desk is behind him with several piles of reports from his officers.

On the display, two kilometers from each gate, men and women set up staging areas on the outer edge of the forested area surrounding the old city. Equipment is rechecked and confirmed by officers from other regions.

Outside the city wall, six guards, two on watch, two on standby and two sleeping, on rotating shifts man each of the lower gates. Standing outside two meters from the gate and at opposite ends, facing outward, two guards watch the forest intently after hearing unusual noises. Within the forest, two officers who had recently dropped a device to the ground, quietly pick it back up and move to their destination. At the gate after shrugging their shoulders, the two other guards approach each other coming across the open gate from the inner perimeter. They march together through the gate where a guard waits and watches for any activity beyond the wall.

The guard at the other end of the gate on the outer wall comes across. After the guards exchange positions and last minute information with the other two, the off duty guards march in step to the center of the gate, march through the gate and enter the old city. Before the gate closes, one of the outer guards marches to the other side where she moves to her position facing outward from the wall. They both diligently watch and wait for the next two hours the field, forest and as far as they can see around the wall of the city. Every twenty minutes they trade positions.

Inside the city wall, several white habited acolytes mill about on each level of the terraced city, some pairs walking through the gardens, while most of the others gather in groups for lively and spirited discussions. A few quietly tend the gardens and clean up after their brethren. Otherwise, everyone on the terraces is relaxed, awaiting the start of the ceremony.

Lights blaze on the top of the hub with two highlighting each pole slightly below the top where the banners are connected. Others light the banners and flags at every cardinal position.

Red sash acolytes clean the short walls, the floor and the central stone alter, including all the crevasses for tools and the rivulets etched in the surface of the top stone. Garbage is placed in plastic bags and white habited acolytes gladly take them down the outer stairs. Loose stones which have fallen off the face work are removed. The stones are patched into place with new stone.

The hole in the wall near the hollowed out space in a large stone block for the bell boy's station and his chair are cleaned of dried leaves, needles and bird nests. Lastly all the surfaces are swept clean followed by a rinse of vinegar to whiten the stone work making it look brighter. Everything is gathered together and taken off the top of the hub down the outer stairs. One red sash acolyte makes a final inspection.

Lights below the surface of the upper terrace at the base of the hub, shining up the sides of the hub, make it look even larger and almost alive with their changing colors highlighting the many crystal prisms along its surface. Every other moment, a different crystal will shine as it reacts to color display throwing out many hues of the same or alternate colors.

Robert increases the gain until individuals can be identified.

Ingrider walks around the base of the hub with several white habited acolytes in attendance staying a respectable distance behind at all times. He checks that each base light has a clear undisturbed view to the outer hub wall. After removing a white Frisbee blocking one of the lights, a white habited acolyte comes forward kneeling and removes the Frisbee with apologies.

Another group of red sash acolytes sit on the east terrace steps below the upper terrace, practicing their timing and pitch for the ceremonial chant. They do a round to loosen up and then go right into the chant. Soon they all are together and then the lack of training takes over. They stop and try several more times until finally, they are all in sync.

Two voices have not yet found the right key and struggle to keep up with the rest of their peers.

A guard starts walking up the last of the east terrace steps to the upper terrace. The red sashes regroup around the east terrace steps to allow him to pass. Out of the corner of his eye, Ingrider spots the guard on the east terrace steps before he has reached the upper terrace.

Ingrider rushes to the edge of the upper terrace, almost knocking over several white habited acolytes trying to get out of his way and puts his hands on his hips with a disconcerting look on his face. The guard takes one look and quickly turns around as if he had made a mistake. The red sashes and the white habited sashes bow their heads and don't look up until they hear Ingrider's steps coming back and the guard's steps retreating down the east terrace stairway.

The tension among the white acolytes increases to a new level of anxiety. Each remains quite still almost afraid that any movement will attract Ingrider's wrath. Only when Ingrider is firmly seated at his throne, do the white acolytes return to their normal activities. The red sashes confer to reach a consensus to assuage Ingrider's anger.

* * *

The maze's cold locker monitor still displays a temperature only slightly above 0 degrees Centigrade and displays,

"Saturday, June 12, 2483 4:45 P.M. Bridget, Diversity." The fan has cycled off, leaving the moisture to start accumulating.

Cliff awakens shivering all over, stirring the dirt around him into a small cloud of ice crystals which quickly settle down melting into the floor before evaporating into the air. As he stiffly moves, he feels like the very air he breathes has turned into gelatin which he is forced to move against. Every joint feels distant, noisy and no longer his. He remains still for a moment flexing every muscle.

He checks if all his limbs are still there and he is not in a thousand pieces.

Sitting up, he feels slightly groggy from lack of sleep and the cold dirt floor which he almost feels a part of. Flakes of ice fall off his habit, breaking into tinier pieces as they hit the floor, begin to melt and then evaporate. The rush of cold air goes through him as if he wasn't even wearing a habit.

He stands getting up on one hand and his knees feeling the coldness of the floor through his right hand, which he quickly removes, and his feet of ice. Ice sheets cover his helmet and begin to break apart falling to the floor with his movement to warmer air. Similarly, more ice sheets on his habit fall off onto the floor, break into smaller pieces, begin to melt and disappear into the air. Smaller ice sheets slide off his habit falling farther from his position, leaving smaller puddles against the wall and in his corner, but they also are the first to disappear. Puddles begin to appear around the walls and moisture coalesces gathering speed.

A puddle forms around him as the ice meets the slightly warmer floor. However, the puddle quickly disappears creating a fog within the room especially around his body and the rest of the floor. His movements alter the fog's position causing the fog to imitate his every move.

Barely flexing his fingers, he feels stiff all over. Standing is almost painful. He puts out his left leg to take a step and almost falls over. He rubs his hands up and down both legs until they begin to feel warmer. He starts walking around the perimeter, legs together taking baby steps from his knees and upper arms next to his body, shivering as he barely walks.

He cups his hands as he blows on his fingers. His breath is ragged and he coughs to clear his throat. After warming all over even more, he begins to jog. He puts his hands under his armpits. The fan goes off and comes back on every other time he goes around the cell.

Warming up, he increases the jog to a full run being careful to avoid the walls of the cold locker which because of the helmet he can't see. He returns to blowing on his fingers and palms trying to get more warmth into them. With his mind getting clearer, he decreases the run to a jog and then finally to a couple walks around the perimeter of the cold locker. He walks at a fair pace, trying to keep his body warm. The last time he walks around, he pays special attention to the noises outside the cold locker room.

Startled by muffled voices above him, he stops blowing on his fingers and puts each hand under his armpits again. Cliff stops walking. The voices get louder and then softer. Footsteps go up the stairway. Gears turn and stop. More voices come from the top of the stairwell and footsteps go down the stairs. Gears turn and stop. The voices disappear as they walk farther through a passageway from the location. Gears turn and stop. For a moment the noises have stopped.

His breath still comes out in a fog, but his breathing is easier and no longer ragged as he feels warmer and more relaxed. He takes several deep breaths. The shivering has stopped. The only parts of his body still cold are his bare feet, but there is very little he can do about that.

He returns to his corner and sits down on the cold floor as the fan blows air through the room. The fog slowly disappears leaving clear air. Water flows through pipes and then just as suddenly, it stops.

His habit now is clear of all ice, but he knows that won't last long. Before long, ice begins to form on the top of his helmet and the top of his shoulders. Within a few minutes, he is once again covered in ice.

Cliff says, "If I-I-I don't get ou-ou-out of here soon, I'll b-b-be a frozen tr-tr-treat. My mo-mo-mom can keep m-m-me in cold storage for the res-res-rest of her life. That's o-o-one way to sti-sti-stick around. Someone wi-wi-will come and get m-m-me ou-ou-out of this. I-I-I hope it's soon."

He shrugs off the accumulated ice and begins walking around the cell, trying to take his mind off the cold air. At that same time, the fan cycles on and begins removing the moisture from the walls and floor. Soon the very air is dry.

* * *

Karl walks slowly towards the secret stairway staying in the shadows watching his pilo for heat signatures. He stops as three dots appear on his screen at the intersection and increases the gain.

Karl's pilo displays, "Saturday, June 12, 2483 4:45 P.M. Bridget, Diversity."

It shows three guards standing in shadow depressions along the stone walls, each watching two directions, walking back and forth trying to keep warm in the cool atmosphere of the maze.

One stands on the south wall, overlooking the east passageway and the intersection except for the protuberance of the off-set door. Another stands on the east wall watching the north part of the "T" passageway as far as possible and the intersection without being able to see into the west passage. The third guard stands on the northern side covering the intersection, the door and the west passageway. This guard cannot see the other two because of the protuberance and, likewise, they can't see him. The guards only watch the area of the passageway they can see.

Karl says, "Not this way. I'll have to backtrack to the right passage and use the secret passageway. I'll have a more protected angle that way."

Karl turns around and walks to the next intersection and turns left.

Karl asks, "Now where is that secret passage?"

Walking slowly watching his pilo, Karl stops, finds the lever and pulls.

The stone door regresses from the wall of the passageway and slides up into the ceiling, leaving a dark opening to another passageway. He walks through as the door closes behind him.

Karl walks through to the other dark end using his pilo's light for guidance. He finds another lever and pulls.

The stone door regresses and quietly slides up into the ceiling. Before walking through the door, he turns around to make sure the other door has closed automatically. He walks into the passage and turns left. The guard stands mere meters ahead with his back to Karl.

Stealthily approaching the guard, Karl hammers his right hand into the right side of the guard's neck as the guard's head begins to turn to his left. The guard stiffens with every part of his body flailing as if struck by lightning.

The guard's head moves to the right. "Crack." The guard crumples onto the dirt floor with one arm draped over his body and his legs twisted as he was trying to turn around. His head is at an awkward angle.

Removing his backpack, Karl sets it beside the guard's body. With his back against the north wall, he hugs the north wall staying away from the view of the other guards watching his pilo with every step he takes, not making any unnecessary noises that would alert the other two guards.

Karl approaches the sealed doorway and looks quickly at his pilo to look at the guards in the other two passages. They haven't moved from their last positions after he had knocked out the guard.

The other guards stand around the corner hidden in shadow by the protuberance from his viewpoint, so he continues across the doorway which luckily hasn't opened. He pulls the guard's feet up to the doorway. Turning around he takes a look at the doorway.

A small depression cuts into the wall on the left side at eye height. It has many ridges within as if something precise went into the depression.

Removing his belt from his pants, Karl clicks open the clasp with his right hand.

He places the clasp near the depression, holding it there for the moment. Slowly, something like yellow foam fills the space of the depression and increases its density once it has completely covered the ridges, changing to a darker color.

After a few seconds, Karl turns the now solid brownish yellow foam clockwise until it stops. The stone doorway quietly moves back and up from the ground floor into the ceiling above with gears and levers turning in the background. When the sounds stop, the doorway is fully open.

Karl checks his pilo again. The guards on the other side have not altered their positions and no one is approaching or already on the steps coming down. He removes the solid foam emblem key and enters the doorway, moving quickly to the side of the stairwell where he can see to the back. He pulls the guard further through the doorway and into the area beside the stairwell. He positions the guard under the stairwell hidden from anyone walking up or down the stairs.

Walking past the stairway, he watches and listens for anyone on the stairs or the lower terrace above.

Getting under the stairwell, Karl turns on his pilo's light. A similar blank wall greets him as under the rectangular room stairway. The stones even look similar in appearance, size and position as if they were made from the same mold. Even the smell is the same probably from the fan motor and the compressor. He can smell ozone which tickles his nose.

Karl finds a metallic lever in the same place as the other storage locker and pulls it. The door opens out into the passage and a small boy in a black habit and black helmet falls at his feet.

The boy shivers, covered in frost which falls from his helmet and his habit onto the ground breaking into many pieces.

* * *

Ingrider paces back and forth from his throne to the edge of the east terrace in an oval pattern alternating directions every time he returns to his throne, trying to make up his mind about something that continues to nag at him. In less than three hours, the ceremony will begin. He's worried that it won't happen and not entirely sure why he feels that way.

The rest of the white habited acolytes and red sash acolytes have vacated the upper terrace to practice their parts in the ceremony somewhere else where they can't be so easily cornered.

They help the rest of the members if they ask any questions about the ceremony although most are concerned about the way Ingrider is currently acting.

Stopping for a moment at the outer edge of the upper terrace near the east terrace steps, Ingrider looks out over the eastern part of the lower terraces and sees all of the acolytes in the city engaged in some activity centered on the upcoming ceremony. They look so busy that they couldn't possibly have a care in the world.

Some are teaching younger students while others are working on uniforms, doing various repairs, washing clothing in the water, drying lines between terraces and habitats, and sewing to a smaller size to fit a younger acolyte.

Others are practicing their parts in the upcoming ceremony. Ingrider shakes his head in amazement that he could lead all of these acolytes into a battle and know that they would perform to their deaths.

He admonishes himself for being so selfish when his followers are so devoted. He recognizes the strain he is under and that he should delegate more of the workload, but he is too selfish to release his hold. He doesn't trust himself to trust them.

After several trips back and forth, he arrives at his throne, free of his frustrations for the time being. He shakes his limbs as he walks along back to his throne. He stops and checks his pilo.

Ingrider's pilo displays, "Saturday, June 12, 2483 4:45 P.M. Bridget, Diversity."

Ingrider asks, "No one is reporting in. Where could he be?

"What has he got planned?

"I should have had a report from the shopping center by now. What are they doing up there?"

With his dire thoughts now returning to the forefront of his mind, Ingrider resumes pacing through a tighter ellipse at a slightly faster rate as if trying to burn away his troubles into the very air around him. The white habited acolytes watching their leader's actions on lower terraces are amazed at the stamina of their leader and master at his age.

He's acting like many of the younger children due when they are agitated usually about something they can't have.

How he can keep going round and round without uttering a single word astonishes them as they return to their individual duties. They discuss it, but don't reach any profound conclusions.

Continuing to pace, he moves slower and slower as he comes to a realization. He stops with a look of enlightenment on his face and a smile begins to take shape. Now, even more afraid, the white habited acolytes scatter to the far corners of the upper hub where they can be out of sight of Ingrider behind the larger habitats. Ingrider doesn't notice as the hub now looks empty with him being the only person on the upper level, except for a few taller acolytes. Peeking out from behind their taller companions, they slowly return to their duties.

* * *

Ingrider stands next to one of the white habited acolytes at the base of the hub near his throne. The upper terrace is almost empty except for a few white habited acolytes reading e-books and pilos, while they sit next to the outer gardens, occasionally watching birds fly from the top of the hub to the forest and back again. Red sashes have retreated to the habitats on the upper terrace to practice and exercise. Very few children are on the upper terrace and if they get to rowdy they are quickly moved off the upper terrace. One of the white habited acolytes reading an e-book looks up at Ingrider and the acolyte standing next to him.

Ingrider consults his pilo.

Ingrider's pilo displays, "Saturday, June 12, 2483 4:50 P.M. Bridget, Diversity."

The acolyte and Ingrider walk to the east end of the upper terrace with Diversity's sun rushing for the horizon behind them. A few clouds on the western horizon thin out and dissipate. The sky in the east remains clear without a cloud on the horizon nor south or north.

When they reach the gardens, the acolyte kneels and bows his head. Ingrider turns around and faces the hub, looking back over the area he loves the most and is very dear to his heart. After all the garden was his design in the first place. It makes the place peaceful, and yet, a work in progress.

Ingrider says, "Position them at the bottom of the northeast and southeast steps near the inside channel. Have them check the troughs for obstructions and keep the children out of the area until after the test has been completed. Be sure you have a clear line of sight along the trough. Keep the younger children away from the trough. They have been known to stop the flow with their toys."

Ingrider points to the two other ends of the terrace before continuing, "As the water runs down the oval stone it enters the hub traveling down through the walls picking up a tremendous amount of speed.

It comes out through special piping at the northeast and southeast terraces, especially gushing on the upper terraces where it comes to the surface along a special channel beside the stairs. When the water gets to their respective positions, each acolyte will raise their right arm. The waters speed will diminish as it gets further down the terraces. Since it is later in the day, the heat has diminished enough that evaporation will not be a problem.

"If for any reason the water does not flow as it should, the acolyte shall raise their left arm at the allotted time. All the troughs have been double-checked, so I'm not anticipating any problems, but you never know which child might leave some large object in one of the trenches. I have personally seen some of the most outrageous ways to block the troughs.

"Since this is water and not blood, the amount of time it takes to get to each acolyte will be noticeably faster in this test. Make sure the rest of the acolytes understand this or they will miss the passage of water and they might think that the test has failed with them being responsible.

"Is this understood?"

Acolyte says, "Yes, master, we understand. Your command will be obeyed."

The acolyte bows, rises from kneeling and walks to the southeast point near two other white habited acolytes on the top terrace. They confer for mere moments before one of the acolytes walks around to the northeast point on the same terrace while the other two remain in place conferring on other subjects.

Other activities take place, i.e. games, lessons, practicing, cleaning gardens and grounds, and decorating the outside walls of the terraces and habitats. More mature acolytes engage in lively discussions about life, liberty and the pursuit of happiness.

After conferring, one acolyte walks down the terrace to the next lower southeast point where she meets two other acolytes where the same actions occur on that level. The acolyte which had conferred with Ingrider quickly checks the trough from the base of the hub to the hole where it exits to the next terrace level. Afterwards he remains at the southeast point of the upper terrace dividing his time between watching the channel from the base of the hub to the edge of the terrace and the top of the hub. Every once and a while, he shoos a younger acolyte out of the area.

Soon eighteen white habited acolytes on all nine terraces patiently wait for the beginning of the test, keeping their view of the trough clear from children playing on the terraces. Some younger acolytes, not understanding the significance of their friend's task, try to run up to them to play games, but older acolytes pull them back. Since not all of them know what is going on, lessons in responsibility and growing up soon follow. After certain borders are established, the children play quietly while some continue to test making it into a game.

The rest of the red sash and white habited acolytes remain at their proper duties mindful to not bother the acolytes on the southeast and northeast positions. Preparations inside the habitats on each terrace produce flower arrangements, sort forks, spoons and knives, and check the cooking on the ranges and in the ovens. Older acolytes bring out tables and chairs which are set up beside the habitats and the other side of the terrace steps. Usually six chairs surround each table.

Others bring out table clothes and napkins using the proper color from boxes that have been stored in lockers along the side walls. Tables are cleaned and repaired when necessary as well as any chairs especially those that have the most wear and tear. Usually, one or two chairs from each terrace are discarded and replaced with new ones. Before long, all preparations are finished, leaving almost every acolyte sweating with their habits clinging to their bodies. The females are the most embarrassed and quickly return to their usual habitat.

When one obligation is completed, the crew rushes to the back of their habitat for showers and clean habits.

* * *

The activity around the secret stairwell remains quiet with nary a sound. The cold locker's monitor displays, "Saturday, June 12, 2483 5:00 P.M. Bridget, Diversity."

Karl holds Cliff tightly in his arms and between his legs. A space blanket wraps around Cliff, but the boy shivers almost constantly. Hoping that the boy will soon be warm, Karl continues to keep holding him, transferring as much of his own warmth as possible under the conditions.

A small puddle of water soon dissolves into the ground at the bottom of Cliff's feet making mud out of the dirt covered stones. The door of the storage locker is closed and only the light from Karl's pilo, on the ground between the left wall and Karl's right side, provides any light through the darkness behind the stairs. Luckily no one has come up or down since Karl opened the storage locker door.

The helmet rests in the dirt nearby to Karl's right with a trough of water around the edge. Water drips from the helmet into the trough with one small sheet of ice on the very top of helmet slowly sliding off the top hitting the ground, breaking up into several pieces before slowly melting into the dirt. The black habit is thoroughly drenched.

Karl holds Cliff's hands and then gently massages them. Cliff's shivering diminishes and finally stops. Cliff awakens. He opens his eyes looking straight up at Karl's face.

Cliff asks, "Who are you?"

Karl says, "A friend. Your mother sent for me.

"I've come to get you out of this, but unfortunately not at this present moment."

Cliff's countenance brightens and then wanes.

He lays his head on Karl's chest. Karl ruffles the boy's hair and remembers the first time he saw the boy in the shopping center. He didn't get him out of that dilemma either, but that doesn't mean he won't be rescued.

Karl says, "Unfortunately, there are too many guards and acolytes around for the foreseeable future. The risk is too high for both of us. Someone would see us and alert the others. Then we would both be caught. Since we have both met Ingrider, I think you can understand what kind of predicament we are in.

"You have to hang in there and do exactly as they say. Be strong and I will get you out of this.

"You have to believe me. Your mother is counting on having you back and I don't want to disappoint her.

"I know you might think that you're going to die, but that is not the case. You'll have a long and fruitful life.

"I'm sure we'll see each other again long after this is over.

"Someone will come to get you very soon, so keep walking around to stay warm. Don't go to sleep.

"You'll need to keep your wits about you."

Karl removes the space blanket from around Cliff's body, putting it behind him, and massages his arms and legs. Cliff stands, not yet sure of himself, but steadying his wooziness by placing his hand on Karl's shoulder.

Karl gets on to his feet with Cliff's hand coming off his shoulder. Karl reaches down and picks up the helmet. The last sheet of ice falls off. He replaces it on Cliff's head and locks it.

Karl pulls the lever out of the wall. The door opens releasing more cold air. Cliff looks up at Karl. A tear falls from Cliff's right eye and off his cheek. Karl pats the helmet holding back his own tears. Cliff walks into the storage locker. Karl turns, reaching towards the lever.

Cliff sticks his arm out and Karl grabs Cliff's hand with his right. They hold for several seconds and then Karl releases. Cliff's hand pulls inside. The door swings closed as Karl pushes the lever into the wall. He waits for a moment to listen for any activity from the guards, but the stairwell remains closed and quiet.

* * *

Ingrider walks up the inner stairs of the hub from the upper terraces. Candles light the stairway every three meters. The yellow and red flames leap straight up revealing the lack of wind in the hub. Except for the candles, the hub entrance and the upper stairway exit to the hub top, darkness engulfs the hub from the top to the terrace bottom. The candles don't penetrate the darkness more than half a meter from the hub's other side while the hub's diameter is only twenty meters.

As Ingrider completes one round and continues up the stairs the candles behind him recede into the darkness with only the three candles behind him and in front of him lighting his way.

What lies in the middle of the hub is unknown. No one has ever dared to shine their pilo light or use a mirror in the central area of the hub. Stories make their rounds from every uninitiated acolyte to any who has been on the inner steps.

The white habited acolytes remain frightful, while the red sash acolytes would rather take the outer stairs even in the middle of an ice storm than brave the supposedly inner demons within the inner stairs.

Ingrider stops for a minute and faces the inner darkness of the hub. He puts his right arm straight out into the darkness and watches as his hand and lower arm vanish before his eyes.

He doesn't feel anything different this time, but, as always, the same little chill runs along his hand and arm. He almost feels the utter coldness of the darkness. He pulls his right arm back, whole, looking perfectly normal in the candle light. The coldness, that he felt moments before, disappears and his hand and arm are perfectly normal. He flexes his fingers and rotates his wrist just to make sure.

Pilo lights cannot illuminate beyond the stairs. He had tried it the first time he arrived. Ingrider remembers the time they brought in a large light on wheels with enough candle power to light up the outside of the hub on the darkest nights, but inside it could not penetrate the darkness beyond the stairs even at the highest level. They had a devil of a time getting it up the stairs from the maze level. Luckily only his closest red sash acolytes knew anything about it, so the regular dire stories continued with no one else daring to try to light the inner darkness.

Ingrider returns to walking up the stairs, mindful of the darkness so close which strangely warms him. Even as Ingrider continues up to the middle of the stairway, the bottom part of the stairs are engulfed in black. As he nears the top, only the last three candles are visible. Here the movement of the air around the top of the hub becomes visible with the dancing of the flames.

Daylight from the hub top shines on the inner wall and the upper inner stairs, but doesn't penetrate the darkness of the inner hub anymore than the candles. Direct sunlight doesn't do any better as they have tried with mirrors.

As he walks into the outside light several steps from the top, he pauses for minute to let his eyes adjust to the direct sunlight. He turns around to look down through the inner stairs of the hub. The breeze feels fresh and lively barely stirring the few leaves and seeds left after the most recent cleaning.

Only three candles can be seen along the disappearing stairs. The rest of the hub inside is completely black.

Light from the low sun barely highlights the upper half of the inside wall of the hub top on the east side. A deep dark shadow appears on the eastern inside wall from the large oval stone in the center of the hub top. The rest of the top of the hub is empty with side cutaways in the central stone and along the walls for implements and instruments mostly used during ceremonies.

* * *

Ingrider reaches the top surface of the hub and walks to his appointed place at the head of the stone two meters away in a slight depression. Two acolytes, one male, carrying a medium wooden stave barrel with rope handles, walk slowly up the outer stairway with their heads bowed trying to keep the water from sloshing as they move up the stairs one step at a time.

They reach the top of the hub and walk between Ingrider and the stone.

They move over to the head of the stone with the male acolyte on the east side and the female on the west holding the barrel between them. The water continues to slosh within the barrel.

Without making a sound, using both hands, they place the barrel between them on the hub floor, kneeling for only a moment, quickly lifting, and place the barrel in the center of the stone, moving slightly back from the stone with their heads bowed and their hands clasped behind them.

Keeping their heads bowed, without moving their heads, they still rivet their eyes on Ingrider to await his next order. They wait patiently.

Ignoring the two acolytes at the stone, for the moment, Ingrider walks over to the southeast side of the hub and looks out over the city terraces below. The acolytes stand in their appointed places on the southeast side of each terrace. Walking over to the northeast side and seeing the same, he smiles, knowing everyone is in place. Walking back to the southeast side, he signals to the acolyte on the west side by the central stone, who keeps her head bowed with her hood back far enough to see Ingrider's signal.

The female acolyte on the west side of the stone steps forward to the edge of the stone and reaches up to the cork.

She removes the cork from the bottom of one of the staves. Colored water flows over the rounded top of the stone, moving through impressions carved into the stone till it gets to the raised edge. After placing the cork on the stone away from the stream of water, she steps back and stands solemnly with her head bowed.

With only the slightest upward turn of his head, Ingrider watches the liquid flow out of the barrel over the face of the stone and down through six holes into the hub.

The liquid meanders across the top of the stone until it reaches an oval depression before reaching six small holes spread equally apart that go down through the edge of the stone and into the hub, through the dome top to the outer walls. Soon all six holes have rivulets of a dark liquid reaching them.

Small rivulets cut into the surface of the top of the oval stone guide the water from the depression to each hole arriving at the same time.

Moments later, red colored water pours from a spout in the hub outer wall ten centimeters above the upper terrace. Even though the acolyte watching had anticipated the flow, he was still surprised at its volume.

It drops into a slight trough within the upper terrace and runs to the southeast edge where it drops into another hole, exiting from the wall onto the next terrace.

It continues through all the terraces until it reaches the lower terrace where the liquid is routed to the nearest drain where it is collected for other uses.

The two acolytes on either side of the top terrace raise their right arms and it goes down each terrace until the last two acolytes on the lowest terrace raise their right arms. By this time the water gushes from the terrace wall on the lower level over shooting the trough, but being contained by the slight slope on both sides of the wider trough. It slows down to a crawl until it reaches the drain.

After checking both sides, Ingrider smiles and dismisses the two acolytes at the oval stone. The female acolyte steps forward and puts the cork back into the hole in the stave. The male acolyte steps forward. Using only one hand each, they take the empty barrel off the stone and back down the outer stairway.

He's almost giddy with the excitement only he could imagine. Ingrider looks out over the east side of the terraces, caught in the magic that will soon be happening within the next three hours. The sun dips closer to the horizon as it races the clouds across the sky. He consults his pilo.

Ingrider's pilo displays, "Saturday, June 12, 2483 5:00 P.M. Bridget, Diversity"

* * *

Walking west through a long passage in the maze that seems to go on forever, Karl approaches an intersection right after the intersection leading to the hub entrance. Feeling confident, but staying vigilant, he's glad he hasn't run into any guards, but he knows deep down inside that his troubles are not yet over. He has to be extra thorough in order to be able to come back and get the child. He stops and checks his pilo.

Karl's pilo displays, "Saturday, June 12, 2483 5:30 P.M. Bridget, Diversity."

A red dot flashes on the pilo a meter before Karl walks into the intersection, but Karl fails to notice, caught up thinking about how he will get the boy out of the maze. The first guard steps out of the shadows from the left passage into the middle of the intersection under the single light panel blocking Karl's way.

The first guard says, "You may have gotten by my second, but you won't make it by me. I taught him a few of my tricks, but not all."

As the guard talks, Karl gauges his ability. The younger man has strength beyond Karl's, but not experience, quickness, stamina nor training. It is not an even match, but then the guard doesn't know that.

"Ingrider taught both of us, but I was always his brightest pupil and that is why I am the first guard. Only my master is better than me," continues the first guard.

While the guard continues to talk, Karl pockets his pilo in his right pants pocket, but it only goes in half way.

The guard swings with his right into Karl's face, but Karl shifts away from the blow, grabs the guard's outstretched right arm and throws him against the stone wall. Putting out both hands, the guard quickly stops his head long fall towards the passage wall before his head would have impacted.

He recovers, facing Karl, as Karl plants a left into his jaw spinning him around in the same direction. Coming out of the spin, the guard lunges for Karl, landing his head on Karl's solar plexus, throwing punch after punch into Karl's midsection.   He backs away from Karl swinging a left at Karl who takes it on the chin turning his head at the same time to lessen the impact. Karl and the guard struggle with hits and misses gauging each other's strengths and weaknesses.

Karl falls to the dirt floor with the guard's full weight on him as Karl twists and turns trying to extract himself. With his arms pinned, Karl brings his knees into the first guard's back right into his kidneys.

The guard winces, but doesn't break his hold on Karl. Karl gives a mighty push with his legs and hips and rolls the guard over as Karl gets on top. Karl sends fist after fist into the guards face leaving blood splashing in every direction. Soon, his hands and lower arms have streaks of blood. Karl's pilo drops onto the floor of the passageway, out of his pants pocket. He stops fighting.

Moments after the guard recovers his breath, Karl says, "We could make this much easier for both of us.

"All you have to do is come with me to the police station.

"You will be held in a cell until we can get you to a rehabilitation center."

The first guard says, "Never happen. I can tell you're getting tired. Don't worry; I'll try to make it relatively quick."

* * *

Ingrider sits on his throne looking over his pilo with a worried face hidden by his hood from the red sash acolytes around him. They wear red sashes over their white habits.

The only sounds come from the breeze turning through the habitats and the few birds at the top of the trees in the nearby forest. Within the forest animals are still asleep waiting for darkness to fall so they may forage outside of the forest. He consults his pilo.

Ingrider's pilo displays, "Saturday, June 12, 2483 5:50 P.M. Bridget, Diversity."

Breaking out of his thoughts, Ingrider says, "You are my last defense. No matter what else may transpire, that child's blood shall run. It is ordained.

"I want you to guard the steps to the hub, the hub base and the inside steps from the maze. Absolutely no one gets to the hub top without proper authorization and I am the only authorization. This will continue until seven tonight."

Seeking their absolute obedience, Ingrider asks, "Is this completely understood?"

The red sash acolytes bow forward in one motion to signify their understanding.

The acolytes say as one, "We hear and obey."

Ingrider claps his hands, in appreciation. The red sash acolytes rise together and head into the hub in an orderly fashion, keeping their heads bowed until they are well inside the hub going down the inside stairs where they burst into the latest gossip.

Returning to his worried state, Ingrider consults his pilo again, keeping his head bowed. He taps the screen more than once. After reading several updates on the preparation of the ceremony from white habited acolytes, he gets to the last message and looks up from his pilo. The entire upper terrace has been vacated leaving only the scent of the nearby forest.

"I haven't heard anything from my first. He should have reported by know. What could possibly be keeping him?

"He has already transferred the boy to the cold storage locker on the lower level, but that was reported by another guard.

"Well, he'll report before the ceremony. He either has Karl or is sufficiently certain that he is not in the maze. Either way, Karl can't do anything from now to the ceremony without trying to get past my guards or red sashes. It cannot be stopped. They don't have enough officers to stop us."

Evening

Karl and the first guard continue to fight with less vigor and more sweating both exhibiting cuts and bruises. Half the punches or jibes miss entirely. Karl doesn't maintain his stance, losing his balance for the moment. The guard's sudden left upper-cut catches Karl in the chin, surprising him.

Karl's feet leave the dirt floor and he flies backward through the center of the passage, landing on his back in the dirt. Only for a couple of seconds, Karl's senses are rattled. Karl sits up and brushes the dirt from his shirt and hair.

Karl gets up on his feet and touches his chin as he steps towards the guard.

He says, "Good shot!" He moves his jaw left and right. " You're not as tired as you have been playing."

The first guard says, "I'm full of surprises."

Karl's left foot impacts the guard in the face as Karl suddenly twists. The guard falls backward, hitting his head on the stone wall, bouncing off and landing on his right side. For a moment he doesn't move. Then slowly he pushes himself off the dirt, shaking the dirt off his habit and sits up.

"So am I," says Karl.

The guard touches his nose with his right hand and the back of his head with his left. Both come back with fresh blood all over his fingers and hands. His nose bleeds and he can feel blood running down the back of his neck. He wipes his nose on his left arm, grimacing. The guard rushes Karl slamming blow after blow into Karl's stomach and lower chest like a madman, flinging blood everywhere as the air around them becomes a red mist. As the blows become less and less, Karl pushes the guard back away from him as he breaths again.

Karl and the guard begin again with Karl landing more hits than the guard, ducking quicker and recovering faster. The first guard rarely connects and when he does the blow has very little effective power.

Karl lands his right fist in the guard's solar plexus. The guard gasps for air, instantly frozen with his arms hanging by his sides. His eyes dart from side to side coming to rest looking straight at Karl. Karl lands a chopping blow to the right side of the guard's neck. The guard's head snaps to the right. The guard collapses to the dirt floor with his head at an awkward angle. The broken nose snaps back into place and stops bleeding. The bleeding of his cheek cuts and hand cuts also stop. However, no breathe comes in or out of his half open mouth.

Karl checks the guard's pulse at the neck.

Karl says, "No more fighting for you. At least, not on this world."

Karl finds his pilo in the dirt in the center of the intersection. He blows off as much of the dirt as possible and runs a diagnostic to make sure the device is operational. The diagnostic responds with an OK. He runs a diagnostic on himself revealing no broken bones with lacerations and bruises already healing. Several bruised ribs and a number of bruises show up on the display. Karl checks his pilo for messages.

Karl's pilo displays "Saturday, June 12, 2483 6:00 P.M. Bridget, Diversity."

* * *

After dodging several encounters with other guards walking through the maze, Karl continues through the maze heading for the shopping center. He avoids, if at all possible, any entrance/exit defended by guards. He keeps a wary eye on his pilo so as not to get surprised this time. Thankfully that has saved him many a time from unfortunate encounters with guards patrolling the maze.

At several intersections, he stops, gets down on his stomach, and eases up to the edge of the corner, especially when he hears noises. He looks both ways not only to protect himself from patrolling guards, but also to check for guards defending entrances/exits close enough to hear or see him.

Only the maze entrance from the small meadow, that Karl and Robert first used, crosses over Karl's current position, having passed several more intersections. After walking through several more intersections, Karl arrives at the intersection with the cross over passageway where two guards in shadow guard the stairwell from the rectangular room where only the upper steps are visible from the light in the room.

Using his pilo, he monitors the two guards for some time watching their routine movements and to see if they get relieved, but after several minutes nothing happens. The guards get occasionally spooked by sounds emanating from the circular room where they both turn at once. They laugh about it together trying their best to not be discouraged or frightened after all the stories they have heard about their enemy. During the time, Karl watches the pair of guards on his pilo's screen, no one comes to relive them and no messages are exchanged.

He goes through all the advantages and annoyance that he has available, trying to find a timely one.

He waits until he sees both turn towards the stairway. While they stay turned away from him, Karl quickly walks into the intersection turning to the right into the cross passageway to the staircase, careful not to make any sounds to attract the guards. At the very next intersection, he turns left heading back towards the shopping center. Stopping for the moment, he listens for any sounds within the maze.

He doesn't start breathing again until he is well past the last intersection and then only quick breaths.

Arriving at the next intersection of the maze, Karl turns to the right, walks several meters, and stops facing the left wall in the passageway. Finding the lever between two stones, he pulls on it. The outer stone door regresses, moving upward, leaving an empty dumb waiter shaft with a rope hanging on the left. Each dumb waiter is different from any other.

Karl checks his pilo one more time for any anomalies within the maze. He pilo reports that the maze is clear for many intersections from his present position. Sound analysis indicates several guards beyond infrared range. Breathing a sigh of relief, he only hopes that the guards have finished their shopping center search, but he is well aware that some guards could still be lingering within the shopping center waiting for him to come by.

Karl pulls down on the rope flipping the switch to bring the dumb waiter to the maze level. The sound of the dumb waiter moving through the shaft breaks the silence within the maze passageway. While he waits for the dumb waiter to arrive, he watches the passageway and listens for any sounds keeping one eye on his pilo's reports.

Seconds later, the dumb waiter arrives with a thud. After opening the dumb waiter's double doors, Karl climbs in, pushes the lever for the outer stone door and closes the dumb waiter's double doors.

* * *

Karl steps out of the dumb waiter and closes the hidden door in the tower. After putting several boxes around the tower to hide it, he looks around the outdoor equipment store and then walks to the store's entrance. Checking the corridor once more, he checks his pilo on its widest gain, but it comes back clear. Satisfied, he looks through the window of the store to be sure.

Karl's pilo displays, "Saturday, June 12, 2483 6:30 P.M. Bridget, Diversity."

When he gets to the entrance door, he stops, expecting footsteps and idle chatter.

Not hearing anything, he opens the door very slightly, keeping it barely open with his fingers. Moving his fingers lower, he crouches and finally lies on the floor. Karl opens the door wide enough for his head and sticks it out into the corridor. Twisting around using his chin to keep the door open, he quickly surveys the corridor both ways.

The corridor is clear of any guards, no doors are opening or closing, and he doesn't hear their usual grumbling noises. Getting to his feet, he opens the door wider, but he remains cautious. He walks out into the corridor carefully watching for any other activity.

Walking along the corridor, Karl heads for the center of the shopping center. Stopping at each store's entrance along the corridor, he doesn't walk past without listening for any activity within the store and checking his pilo.

Satisfied without hearing anything, he reaches the last open barricade, turns right and enters the corridor around the circular room in the center of the shopping center. The inner wall is free standing without any additional support.

Walking along the curved corridor, Karl comes to the circular room's door. Before opening the door he puts his left ear up against it. Satisfied by its lack of people noises and the reassuring rumble of the turbines and compressors felt mostly through his feet, he opens the door and walks to the central tower of geothermal steam, turbines, high pressure steam piping, compressors, the cooling tower and associated framework along with gauges, fire suppressing equipment, first aid kits, basins and testing counters with cabinets.

He climbs the ladders and walks the walkways, watching for any other activity either above or below. He finally reaches the ladder for the cone tower.

He takes a look around to be sure there aren't any traps lying in wait for him. He climbs that ladder to the top of the central cone, sneaking a quick look above the opening to look outside.

* * *

The sky, clear with only a few clouds, turns from light blue in the west to a darker blue in the east. Stars begin to appear in the eastern sky. The sun has set leaving a glow on the western horizon with the few clouds along the western horizon tinted orange and pink with streaks of gray.

Karl climbs out and slides down the cone along the seam using the bolt heads and nuts to keep from sliding until he arrives on the regular roof of the shopping center. Walking gingerly between cones using the sides of his feet, he tries not to make any noise while he is quite visible through the transparencies around each cone including the central one. Luckily, the guards do not notice his movement above them.

Reaching the northwest perimeter of the west hexagon, Karl gets on his belly watching through the transparency the main western corridor and the west entrance. As he looks out over the perimeter to the short grass field, one guard stands beside Karl's flighter at the end of the left wing. Looking back, other guards stand still at the main west entrance to the shopping center. As Karl watches, they enter the main west corridor leaving the entrance clear of guards.

Inching back carefully not making any noise until he reaches the next cone intersection, he gets to his feet.

He heads for the same tree arching over the perimeter he used last time. After checking through the transparency, he starts his run for the tree limb, jumping off the edge and landing with his hands around the limb.

When Karl gets to the ground, he circles around his flighter through the tall grasses and trees, coming up behind the guard. He keeps a sharp eye and uses his pilo as well to keep out of any traps that may have been set.

While still in the tall grasses and trees, Karl fashions a noose out of a green branch which he tears off of a young tree. He finds a straighter longer branch entwined in flotsam not far from the young tree.

After removing it from the strangle hold of the vines and undergrowth prevalent in meadows, he removes all of its smaller branches and the outer bark which he uses for strapping. After it is free from smaller branches, Karl ties the noose to the end of the branch, using a strip of bark from the same deciduous tree. He pulls the noose several times before he is satisfied it will hold.

Approaching the guard, Karl carefully holds the noose branch in front of him as his walks out of the tall grasses. He watches where he steps and the guard alternately as he gets closer to the flighter.

The guard coughs as Karl gets nearer causing Karl to stop moving. The guard turns his head to his left, watching a flock of geese take to the air. Karl ducks behind the flighter's left tail fin and waits patiently for the guard to return to his position, watching his every move.

The guard's head turns back, facing the entrance once more.

Karl comes out from behind the tail, still holding the noose branch in front of him watching the guard's every move.

After three steps, he's about a meter from the guard; Karl places the noose right over the guard's head. The guard flicks at his cheek with his left hand thinking a bug had hit him not feeling the noose around his neck because of his flighter jacket.

He quickly brings it down on the guard's neck and pulls hard on the branch, tightening the noose around the guard's throat.

The guard struggles and then collapses to the ground at the end of the left wing. Karl throws the branch towards the guard. It swings in an arc over the guard, landing in the short grass on the opposite side of the guard.

Returning to the side of the fuselage, Karl removes his backpack setting it on the left wing. Taking the two fuel cubes out of his backpack, he puts them in the side of the flighter. Leaning into the cockpit, he checks the fuel level is topped off. Karl closes the outer fuel door latching it in place for flight. He takes one more look around carefully watching the main west corridor for any activity. He picks up his backpack.

Returning to the front of the flighter, carrying his backpack in his right hand, he puts his backpack in the front storage area, fastening it to the back board and securing the nose cone for flight. After returning past the canard and left wing, he climbs in the cockpit, starts the engine and takes off vertically. The flighter twists in mid-air until it faces the direction desired. The rear props are engaged. The flighter vanishes into the clouds without a sound. The entrance to the shopping center remains empty.

* * *

Acolytes scurry about cleaning, moving chairs and tables into place. Purple table clothes cover each table on the terraces lower than the upper. Silver serving spoons and forks are set on the tables. Occasionally, two acolytes will bump into each other with the undesired effect of plates and silverware going every which way and the resultant clamoring as they clean up the mess.

Taller white habited acolytes bring out platters of vegetables, pitchers of juices and sliced bread on platters. Plates of steaming rump roasts come next. Condiments, butter, salt and pepper and steak sauce come next. Heads turn and noses rise out of every habitat to the various smells from elementary children finishing classes to middle school children washing pots, pans and various cooking utensils while various guards not on duty smile as they remember past ceremonies.

The smells reach Ingrider, who turns his head and smiles.

Next, a flower arrangement of three medium stem daffodils separated by ferns with a base enveloped in six freesia separated by moss is set centered on the tables. Each centerpiece has a different color with the bases complimenting the color of the daffodils creating a kaleidoscope of color on each table.

Watching from his throne, Ingrider grins at the activity. Like a well-oiled machine, they perform expertly. Marveling at their ingenuity and creativity, he consults his pilo.

Ingrider's pilo displays, "Saturday, June 12, 2483 7:00 P.M. Bridget, Diversity."

Two red sashes bring out Ingrider's ceremonial habit of scarlet stripes against a pale blue background. They remove his current habit, exposing the remarkable tattooing of snakes and dragons all over his back and arms and the white pants he normally wears under his habit.

Ingrider stands before the throne as the red sashes put his pale blue habit on over his head. They adjust it around his shoulders and tie a white rope with crimson threads around his waist so the hem barely touches the ground.

As the rest of the acolytes on the upper terrace try to get a peek at Ingrider's new wardrobe, two other red sash acolytes bring a full mirror with a carved cherry burl frame out of the hub. They walk slowly through the other acolytes carefully holding the mirror as they walk past each acolyte.

Some of the white habited acolytes are astonished at the sight of the full mirror which is taller and wider than most of them.

Slowly walking with it towards the throne, they place it a meter from the front of the throne, turning it towards Ingrider and holding it at a slight slant away from him. He doesn't even notice until the acolytes step away from him.

Ingrider turns around, seeing himself in all his splendor in the mirror. He smiles. Turning sideways, he likes what he sees, smiling from ear to ear. Another red sash acolyte brings out a large hand mirror framed in the same wood.

Taking the hand mirror from the red sash acolyte, Ingrider turns his back to the full mirror and looks through the hand mirror at his back reflected in the full mirror, seeing the intricate pattern squares, triangles and circles in the weaving with another geometric pattern interlocking circles of silver threads.

Ingrider says, "Wonderful, simply wonderful."

The rest of the red sashes always show a neutral face around their leader, but are literally bursting inside with consummate joy. Ingrider hands the hand mirror back to the red sash.

The two red sash acolytes take the full and hand mirror away from the throne and return with them through the rest of the acolytes and the hub entrance. Taking turns, white habited acolytes from all the lower terraces form a circle approaching one at a time to see their leader's new clothes.

* * *

K arl accepts the dummy from Robert and walks to the nose cone of his flighter. His cockpit monitor displays, "Saturday, June 12, 2483 7:00 P.M. Bridget, Diversity."

Karl places the helmeted dummy in the forward storage area of his flighter securing it with a Velcro strap from the bottom of the locker.

He adjusts it so it won't get loose and bang around in the locker during flight.

He secures it with a Velcro strap that he can undo with one hand. He closes the nose cone, latching it for flight. Karl wears a one piece black outfit with dull black boots and gloves. His face is masked in dull black making him look ghostly without any defining features. And he wears a dull black cap covering his forehead, brown hair and white ears.

Robert stands three meters away, looking at his pilo reading the last of the messages from his officers setting up the camps.

Robert says, "The two moons rise at 7:55 P.M. At eight o'clock they will be above the horizon.

"The ceremony begins about 7:30 P.M. They circle the hub three times on their way up. They stop at the eastern end each time for prayers.

"Sometime before eight, the two moons will be above the horizon and that's when the activity really begins.

"The crescendo ends, the bell rings and Indiger drives the knife into the torso of the sacrifice."

Karl says, "Thanks for installing the winch and making the ladder. It's going to come in very handy for what I have planned.

"I can't say I like the dull black paint scheme. It will definitely keep the flighter out of sight and mind. Ingrider won't be expecting this."

Robert asks, "You don't look all that much different from your flighter. Per your request, the storage area will turn transparent and non-reflective when you start the winch. The inside of the nose cone, especially the storage locker has been painted dull black as well, which, I suspect, you'd want it that way when the nose cone is open."

Karl smiles.

"Once the winch is secured and power cut off, the nose cone will return to dull black," continues Robert.

"You wanted the flares to be short?"

Karl says, "I don't want Ingrider to see the flares, only the acolytes on the terraces and the guards on the south side of the terraces. That will be enough to excite the acolytes, but not enough for the guards to become worried.

"I suspect everyone except Ingrider will accept the flares as part of the ceremony since my timing depends on when he comes around the hub from the north side.

"When your men are in place, I'll send up the appropriate flares. Hopefully, this will go off as planned."

* * *

One red sash stands guard within the room at the bottom of the hub. He watches the other guard walk around the room. The red sash guards the door between the bottom of the stairs and the maze exit. The other doesn't have a red sash on his white habit. He busily scurries around the room desperately looking for it. The hub chamber's monitor displays, "Saturday, June 12, 2483 7:15 P.M. Bridget, Diversity."

Cliff sits on the edge of the bare oval stone in the center of the room. All of the red stains from Karl's earlier encounter with Ingrider have been cleaned leaving the stone pristine.

The bare sash acolyte asks, "Where could it be?

"I came in here with it on. You saw me. We both checked each other before picking up the boy.

"The collar of my habit was not lying correctly, so I took off the red sash to adjust it. I laid it down somewhere in this room. I just don't remember where. If I hadn't left to get to the restroom, my mind wouldn't be so jumbled right now."

The other red sash acolyte nods in agreement and quickly returns to attention looking straight ahead at Cliff who's looking straight ahead at the maze opening trying hard not to give away any knowledge of its current position.

The non-red acolyte starts looking under every box on the floor and in every cabinet attached to the wall. After moving everything off the counter, he comes up empty handed. He almost slams his hands on the counter in frustration, but he stops suddenly, turns around and faces Cliff. Cliff sits quietly not saying anything or moving his hands or his feet.

With a discerning face and tilting his head, the non-red acolyte looks over at where Cliff sits. He points his right arm towards the left of Cliff and then back to his current position on the end of the stone.

The bare acolyte says, "I remember, now. I placed it neatly folded on the end of the oval stone right next to where the kid is sitting now.

"The kid was more away from the end when we first set him on the stone."

He walks over to the other side of the central stone and lifts Cliff off. There on the stone, neatly folded, lies his red sash.

The bare sash acolyte says, "So, you little brat!" He almost drops Cliff on to the stone next to his sash.

"If my master doesn't happen to kill you, you will live all right but never the same with the wounds I will inflict."

The red sash flattens his habit's white collar and carefully places the red sash under the collar and adjusts the two ends to match. Satisfied, but still angry, he takes his place beside the maze doorway opposite the other red sash. He continues to stare at Cliff, but Cliff doesn't even notice.

Cliff remains sitting on the stone watching the dirty feet of the guards at the maze entrance.

* * *

S tanding outside of the Police Station near his flighter, Robert watches flight after flight of officers leave from Bridget flying southeast. Officers stream out of the dual doors, down the steps and across the east field to their respective flighter. Some take off in groups and others take off alone. Like a puzzle losing pieces, the field gets emptier bit by bit.

Row after row gets smaller and more of the east field is exposed, looking like something was missing. Soon, only a few flighters remain scattered from one end of the field to the other. The few officers that remain behind will file the usual reports, keeping them busy for the next week. He checks his pilo.

Robert's pilo displays, "Saturday, June 12, 2483 7:15 P.M. Bridget, Diversity."

Robert says, "That was the last wave. Since this morning we've had officers from all over the northern regions arriving and departing after getting their orders. The logistics have been remarkable. We'll have enough officers and flighters to evacuate everyone. I've pulled about every regional officer from the northern regions, leaving skeleton crews to manage the day to day affairs of each region. Hopefully, we won't have any other major problem facing the northern regions.

"I hope it's enough. As Karl has said, only sufficient numbers will matter to these guys. Every single guard and the red sash acolytes will require two officers each. Anything less and we would have been overwhelmed.

"They can handle the individuals and the small groups, but anything bigger in number will sufficiently intimidate them.

"I'm glad the northern regions could help out, although we had major problems getting them here quietly and housed so as not to attract undo attention. The sheer numbers of people has been mind-boggling.

"Luckily the deceptive northern conference took care of all the questions about their movements.

"The families visiting relatives provided most of the logistical problems, but they also masked the tens of individuals that arrived in bunches. We had to arrange spurious conventions to contain the onslaught.

"And Karl was right about this timing, the guards and acolytes will not even notice all the flighters coming their way. They will be too involved in getting ready for their ceremony."

As the last flighter leaves the field, Robert rechecks the numbers on his pilo before finally putting it away in his pants pocket. He looks out over the field one more time before climbing into his distinctive flighter. He starts the engine and the wing turbines, lifting into the air.

At an appropriate altitude, he engages the dual rear props and heads southeast, following the stream of flighters already in the sky. They travel in formation leaving room between each of the groups. Robert joins the trailing group taking the lead position. He checks his GPS and gets an estimate of travel time.

* * *

Scurrying in and out of the hub, Ingrider talks with one white acolyte who then walks off to the lower terraces. Activities around all the terraces continue at a frantic pace with everyone busy getting ready for the ceremony. Ingrider consults his pilo.

Ingrider's pilo displays, "Saturday, June 12, 2483 7:30 P.M. Bridget, Diversity."

The white acolytes in the northeast and southeast position on each terrace busily put on outer garments of lavender with light yellow streaks throughout, helped by younger acolytes grooming their hair, hands and feet. The older acolytes appreciate the helpfulness of their consorts as they remember their own days of grooming their mentors.

Other unadorned white habited acolytes set up tables near the steps on either side of the habitats. They place crimson table cloths on each. Yellow "Impatiens" and lavender "Geraniums" with ornate white vases adorn the centers. Table settings and plates with napkins all in bright red come next.

Acolytes, dressed in now clean white habits come by twos out of the habitats on each terrace and surround the tables, standing at attention until the ceremony is finished. The acolytes have crimson straps tied around their necks as omega symbols. They wear no shoes or sandals. The older acolytes gather around the tables near the terrace steps. While the smells of the food on tables reaches their noses, their eyes remain fixated on the hub.

Coming out of the hub, Ingrider talks to another waiting young acolyte. The acolyte wears a lavender habit with the emblem on his chest in yellow. The young acolyte fidgets from foot to foot looking around as if someone were going to clobber him without a moment's hesitation.

Ingrider says, "The two moons are indeed duality.

"This was in the second or third lesson."

The lavender acolyte says, "Honored sir, this pupil does not always understand your great teachings. My head is too thick."

Ingrider says, "The large moon represents me. You are the small moon.

"Likewise, the great master is the large moon while I am the small moon. We all have our place where we are both master and student.

"You are the bell ringer, when the two full moons clear the horizon, you ring the bell. You are our guide."

Ingrider watches as the child's face turns from questioning to amazement.

Lavender acolyte says, "As you command!"

The acolyte bows deeply and takes his position on the upper terrace below the eastern face of the hub behind Ingrider's throne. Ingrider returns to his throne and sits down trying to gain a moment of peace, but several acolytes approach kneeling and bowing asking for counsel.

Ingrider ignores them for the moment knowing their requests will be primarily questions of minor importance.

* * *

K arl adjusts the power level for his current maneuver. His cockpit monitor displays, "Saturday, June 12, 2483 7:45 P.M. Bridget, Diversity."

Circling above the city at a fifteen degree angle keeping his altitude consistent, Karl's dark flighter flies above the central hub barely visible to the naked eye. Anyone looking up would have to have known his exact position, otherwise stars winked out and back continually without any pattern. The procession from behind the hub begins moving with Ingrider leading the way.

Tightening his turning radius and then leveling out, Karl lights two flares and tosses them above the tower over the city as he files directly over the hub.

Karl eases back to level flight until he is past the west end of the city. He does a tight turn to the left to reverse his path.

Nearing the hub once more, Karl initiates silent mode of the flighter.

The turbo fans in the wing spin up to speed. The wings tilt backwards stopping the flight in midair. The fuselage turns to vertical as the wings return to horizontal, keeping the flighter at the same altitude, until the nose is pointed directly down. Wing flaps keep the fuselage within a small circle horizontally.

The dual rear props slow to almost a stop. The dual props widen and lengthen as they take over the load. The wings now turn vertical with the turbo fans providing reverse pitch to keep the flighter from wobbling with the slower turn of the dual props.

As the nose heads down, Karl adjusts his seat backwards forty-five degrees.

Once the nose is down, he sets the autopilot with the GPS coordinates. He unfastens the straps and opens the nose cone from the cockpit. The nose cone pops open turning translucent.

Getting the rope ladder from the back of his seat, he hooks it over the cockpit. Turning around, he puts both feet on the edge of the cockpit window. Holding the back of the seat, he puts his right foot in the next rail and tests the ladder by putting his full wait on it. The ladder holds and Karl descends down the ladder.

The dual props turn above him in silent mode with only a whisper of sound as they counter rotate as the equally quiet turbo fans reverse their pitch as necessary. At his present height, the hub appears to be like a large pencil with a missing eraser. The red sashes are red ants. The white habited acolytes and the guards are barely visible.

As his chest passes the back of the nose cone storage locker, he checks his pilo which reports his current altitude and latitude and longitude coordinates. So far, he hasn't moved out of position. Hopefully, Robert's coordinates are correct. The variance is within limits and with the light wind it should remain so during the entire rescue operation.

* * *

L eading two red sashes in single file with Cliff between them, Ingrider walks around the northern part of the hub to the east on the upper terrace. The other red sashes follow in twos. Their footsteps on the terrace make the only sound for the time being. Everyone on the other terraces respects the quiet remaining completely aware of talking, mumbling, humming or singing.

The white habited acolytes on the terraces clap as the short flares arc over the city into the forest on the south, knowing that if they didn't they would be punished. Even the guards on the south side clap in wonderment.

They ask themselves how Ingrider pulled that off without telling them.

Ingrider smiles and raises his arms and hands high, acknowledging the acolytes and guards applause. Placing his hands by his side, Ingrider puts his right foot on the ground at the base of the outer stairway as he gets to the eastern part of the hub. Putting his left knee to the ground, Ingrider brings his two hands together below his chin.

A red sash acolyte pushes Cliff into kneeling. Cliff falls to his knees, but he does not bow. Cliff gets the bottom of his habit between the stone of the terrace and the skin of his knee. He can feel the surface of the upper terrace through his knee and it doesn't feel good. The red sashes bow together.

Ingrider mutters a prayer of thanksgiving and repentance. He consults his pilo.

Ingrider's pilo displays, "Saturday, June 12, 2483 7:45 P.M. Bridget, Diversity."

The night sky darkens, filling with more stars and groups of stars especially on either side of the Milky Way. The Milky Way itself is so bright; it masks the stars that are closest to it.

The light from the two full moons brightens the eastern sky like the two flares Karl sent over the hub. The lights at the bottom of the hub base go out, making Ingrider's ethereal shadow and the procession's ethereal shadows appear against the hub.

All of the lights throughout the city go out, leaving long tentative shadows throughout the terraces, frightening some of the younger children who cower behind their bigger peers and adults.

Those who burst into crying are rushed into the nearest habitat. Older acolytes rush to their sides and comfort the most disturbed. Other children not as traumatized are comforted by the sounds of the older acolytes.

Some are hugging, while others are only holding hands, quietly talking and listening, waiting for the procession to start up the stairs. Those who were crying now come out of the habitats with redder faces without tears. The cowering ones come out from behind their peers or adults to see for themselves. The lights surrounding the hub ignite, delighting every acolyte.

Ingrider rises and starts an incantation which the red sashes repeat. He puts his right foot on the first step. He raises his habit slightly, exposing his ankle and lower leg. The incantation builds. A young acolyte wearing a red habit dashes by the red sashes and Ingrider, turns in front of Ingrider with a white towel over his shoulder and a small bucket of soapy water. Sitting on the step above Ingrider's foot, he washes the right foot, places the wash cloth in the bucket and dries the foot with a towel.

Ingrider puts his left foot on the next step, rising up the steps and raising his habit like before. He takes a peak from under his hood. The upper terrace is populated with white and lavender acolytes standing at attention around the tables near the habitats. A few tables have empty chairs where they are away from their table performing other duties which for the moment are more critical.

The incantation reaches a climax and holds.

The red habited acolyte backs up a step and washes Ingrider's left foot. When done, the acolyte dashes past Ingrider down to the upper terrace past the procession which separates allowing him into the hub entrance with the bucket sloshing water drops into the air falling on the terrace.

The incantation abruptly ends and the chant by the red sash acolytes begins at a low guttural level repeating each verse three times. At the end of the third verse, Ingrider walks up the steps followed by the red sash acolytes.

They sing the chant again at a slightly higher volume. They keep their tone the same as their neighbor.

Continuing up the steps, Ingrider walks solemnly keeping his head bowed with the acolytes following in step behind, maintaining an arm's space between them. Once all of the acolytes are on the steps, the young lavender acolyte runs from the back of the throne to the foot of the stairs where he starts to climb. He misses the second step and has to slow down. While getting past the two steps without problems, he flounders on the next step. He watches the last of the red sash acolytes go around the hub to the south side as he struggles to keep up.

He takes a great big gulp of breath and brings out more effort to catch up with the rest of the group. The results show as his pace increases, his missteps become fewer and his outlook brightens. He feels much better going up the steps.

* * *

With his back against an evergreen tree, partially hidden by low hanging branches, Robert checks his pilo.

Robert's pilo displays, "Saturday, June 12, 2483 7:45 P.M. Bridget, Diversity."

On the edge of the forest, Robert watches two short flares ignite directly above the hub and arc over the city's south side away from the procession, flaring out over the forest proper. He hears the roar of the acolytes clapping on the terraces as he watches the procession come from the northern side behind the central hub.

Robert says, "It's a go. Leave the shopping center last and concentrate only on the old city. Let's start moving."

Robert sends the same message to each of the other groups. The startled animals within stop moving and silently watch the procession move through the forest

Six groups of three hundred officers each march toward the city moving silently through the surrounding forest each watching their step and keeping quiet. The northwest group move out of the forest towards their assigned gate.

The people holding the sleep devices move first.

They are immediately followed by their assigned security officers guarding their flanks and rear end.

Waiting at the edge of the forest and the perimeter around the old city, the rest of the groups at the other indices follow the procession around the hub with each group moving forward in turn.

After Ingrider has completed one circumference, all of the groups will be approaching the gates. Whenever Ingrider stops on the east side, the northeast group through the southwest group will hold its position, until the procession is moving again before progressing any further. They will try to keep the noise level low which isn't hard to do with the chanting being so loud even at the lower levels.

Even if someone runs into another officer or trips on a stone or hump, it doesn't break the focus of the guards or acolytes on all the levels. Even with some doubters among them, the guards and acolytes know to keep their full attention on only the ceremony. Their other duties are forgotten. Even the youngest white habited acolyte stays focused on the procession going around the hub and the chanting.

Robert's group waits until the last of the procession is heading into the west side of the hub. His leading officers carefully watch the guards who are in turn watching the procession as best they can over the outer wall of the city. For the present time, the guards can only hear the chant.

They will have to wait for the procession to reach the middle of the hub before they will be able to see it from their position outside the gates. Of course, Robert officers will change those plans.

The rest of Robert's officers watch the people in the old city mindful that one or two strays might not be watching the procession and give them away, but Ingrider's followers are well trained and they wouldn't be caught breaking their attention from the ongoing ceremony. Every single head is facing towards the central hub.

Robert watches Ingrider approach the first step with all of the red sash acolytes behind him. He can barely see the boy in black between two acolytes walking along with them. When they kneel the boy's blackness stands out against all the red sashes. With the boy's presence, the procession is broken into two. Ingrider and the acolyte behind him with the second being the rest of acolytes.

Robert isn't surprised to see the boy not bow his head.

That helmet weighs too much; he'd fall over onto the steps. The red sash acolytes must know this and that is why they don't insist on him bowing his head.

* * *

With the sound of the incantation and the subsequent chant pounding his ears, Cliff still hears something else beyond the city. The rest of the birds and animals have fled the area with the unnatural sounds from the red sash acolytes. In his mind's eye, he pictures something black above him getting larger by the moment, but he can't figure out what it is.

Cliff isn't quite sure if maybe he is dreaming this, but everything has been so real up to this point. If it is a dream, he hopes it ends soon. It is certainly unlike any of his other dreams especially his recurring dreams of tunnels and ancient computers. But that is not on his mind now.

He almost feels the steps of many people coming towards him and it's different from the sounds the red sash acolytes make behind him around the hub or up the steps.

Cliff can't quite understand what could be happening.

He knows there is no guard rail on the outer steps and the surface of the terraces is stone, yet the fear of falling is not at the forefront of his mind. He can't escape from their grip. He begins to lose all hope and then he remembers what Karl had said, "You will have a long life." Cliff smiles under the helmet with renewed vigor.

Somehow he senses something else is happening. His mother would discount it as some unusual dream. But he knows it is something much different.

* * *

Robert's men and women approach the edge of the perimeter mere meters from the gate. The main group stops before entering the perimeter. The three officers in each group with the sleep devices move slightly forward and wait. The security officers do likewise. Robert checks his pilo.

Robert's pilo displays, "Saturday, June 12, 2483 7:50 P.M. Bridget, Diversity."

Robert says, "Everyone is ready.

"Now, it's a waiting game.

"If my timing is right, we should have this gate and the three lower terraces under control before Ingrider and the procession come around to the east again."

Disappearing behind the hub, the last of the procession of red sash acolytes will be gone for a while as they journey around the back side of the hub.

He looks east. The sky gets brighter and the shadows against the hub and on the terrace levels get blacker and sharper in definition. The sound of the chant echoes off the western forest. Around him the forest is quiet without the normal sounds of wilderness animals foraging or playing in the forest.

The stars above him become brighter and more numerous with galaxies and clusters scattered throughout.

The known constellations become visible against the black background becoming the brightest objects in the sky next to the Milky Way.

Robert asks, "I still haven't figured how he is going to get the kid without being chased all over. And what is that dummy for? I can't even see him in the sky above the hub. He must be there doing whatever he intends to do. I wish him the best of luck."

He checks with the last of the group. They no longer see the procession. Robert motions the sleep device officers forward. They and their security guards march forward toward the gate.

The rest of the group follows spreading out to cover their flanks as they also watch their comrades at the other gates to their left and right. Half of the groups have reached the gates while the other half are quickly approaching watching the guards at the gates for any sudden movement of recognition.

Everyone remains quite, making sure that any sounds they make are natural to the perimeter and the forest beyond. The sound of birds chirping, flying from a branch of one tree to a branch of another, occasionally flying in formation south of the city, are overwhelmed as the chant heads up the outer stairs.

An owl hoots and a wolf howls at the light of the two moons on the horizon as the regular noises of the surrounding forest return. Moments later more wolves join in herding deer, sheep and antelope out of the prairie where they are free to run and evade and back into the refuge of the forest where they can easily be picked off by the pack of wolves, but the quick ones can dart between trees.

However the loud chant from the red sash acolytes reigns over all the other sounds, keeping all the animals on guard so that even on the edge of the forest nearest the old city, quietness reigns while beyond nocturnal activities continue except close-by the staging areas on the other side of the forest.

* * *

Ingrider and the rest of the red sash acolytes come out from behind the north side of the hub, like long lost travelers returning. Their marching is not quite synchronized, but their chant is still strong and jubilant.

The faces on all the acolytes and guards who can see the procession, brightens as they look east to the two moons rising from the horizon. A few of the white habited acolytes on the upper terrace turn to face the two moons enjoying the sight along with the red sash acolytes on the outer stairs of the hub, but they fail to see the officers at the gates or on the first three levels. Only the acolytes on the west side cannot see the two moons, but they keep their faces turned that way and watch the acolytes and guards on the northwest and southwest for clues.

Ingrider stops for the first time as he gets to the eastern step, kneels on his right knee and mutters a prayer of repentance and forgiveness. The rest of the red sash acolytes kneel and bow keeping their chant, but toning it down during Ingrider's prayer. Again Cliff kneels but he does not bow his head.

The two full moons barely peek above the horizon. Pale shadows of twisted trees, sagebrush and tall grasses begin to appear against the outer wall of the old city, but not the multitude shadows of the officers who keep back far enough so the guards can't see and be distracted to look around them.

Before walking up the next round of steps, Ingrider consults his pilo almost certain that Karl has somehow found a way to get to the boy behind him. He doesn't even want to look almost afraid that Robert has sent his contingent of officers through the maze to the hub entrance and are now making their way up the inner steps.

He shudders at the thought of what awaits him at the top.

I must proceed as if everything is in order. My red sashes will protect me if it comes to that.

Ingrider's pilo displays, "Saturday, June 12, 2483 7:55 P.M. Bridget, Diversity."

The red sashes continue their chant at a low level waiting for Ingrider to resume walking up the outer steps. Some of the red sashes near the rear of the procession take a peek at the upper terrace which is now below them. Being the newest to the red sashes, this is the first time they have ever participated in the ceremony. Some are cautious of their every movement. They keep wary eyes on the edge of the stairs, knowing of the horror stories of those that have fallen to their deaths as told by older red sash acolytes. They say their individual prayers, hoping that they will not be the latest statistic.

Ingrider rises and continues walking up the stairs.

The red sashes follow raising the level of the chant still higher, but saving plenty of room for the next levels. Much like a train, the beginning of the procession lengthens until they are an arm apart while the middle and then the end play catch-up with the first of the procession.

The young lavender acolyte comes out of the north side of the hub as the last red sash acolyte walks past the east step. Holding the bell in one hand and the striker in another, his short legs barely reach the next step. He misses that step and scrapes his shin on the edge of the step. A tear comes out of his left eye running down his cheek and off his face, landing on the step before him. He brushes the stone off his shin.

Ignoring the pain in his legs, he continues up the steps falling farther and farther behind. However, his concentration is so strong, even he doesn't notice the officers at the gates and on the lower terraces. He tries switching which leg goes first up the next step, but even that doesn't improve his speed.

* * *

Everyone, including the guards watch the procession up the hub. No one sees the men and women marching out of the forest approaching the gates, some with devices strapped to their chests. Even as they get closer to the gates, the guards remain unaware of their existence.

At each gate, three of the men and women wear harnesses which hold the devices on their chests. The two guards outside the gate still watch the procession as it heads around behind the hub. The two guards closest to the devices start collapsing one by one.

Soon all the guards outside the gates are asleep on the ground. White habited acolytes don't even rush to their aid when they see the officers nearby. They wait quietly until they are summoned by the officers.

Two officers grab the first downed guard and escort him away from the gate. Other officers gather the rest of the guards and gingerly walk the sleepy guards back to holding cells within the forest edge.

Once all the guards are removed from outside the gate, an officer removes her pack, takes a box from a side compartment and opens the corner of the box. She taps it into the door's lock. Soon all six doors, one after the other, open to the old city. The primary regional officers enter the city first to ascertain the number of acolytes and guards.

The primary and several secondary officers spread across the terrace level to direct the people with sleep devices to appropriate places where they can catch guards and older acolytes off guard. The primary stays near the terrace steps and positions the secondary officers near the other side of the habitats.

The men and women carrying the sleep devices enter the old city next. Officers locate every guard and older acolyte on the lower terrace in their vicinity. Soon on the lower three levels, acolytes and guards are removed to the forest staging areas in a steady stream of officers, guards and acolytes.

While some officers guard their prisoners, most return to the terraces to gather even more guards and acolytes. Guards are usually found around the habitats closest to the terrace steps near the gates. Two guards are up and eating a snack waiting for the ceremonial meal while two others sleep off their last guard duty.

As the last of the guards and acolytes are removed from the lower three levels an officer approaches Robert and reports, "Resistance from the acolytes remains minimal except for a few older mentors. Guards on the other hand have been more aggressive except for one or two who simply gave up and complied with our officers."

Robert says, "Get back as soon as possible. All officers will be needed for the next six levels.

"Our information on the next three levels indicates many more acolytes and the same number of guards, but these will be much more experienced, so I will wait. I want all the officers for the next six levels."

Secondary officers mill about on the lower terraces talking with the sleep device carriers. As they talk they move into position against the terrace walls where they are out of sight of any guards or acolytes on the upper floors. At the same time, other officers trickle through the gates and up the terrace steps. And one by one they come out of the forest to the gates.

* * *

Ingrider and the rest of the red sash acolytes come out from behind the north side of the hub for the third time, trying to maintain their timing and pitch, but some are simply dragging along keeping up through sheer determination. Only their spirit keeps them going. While their chant remains strong and vital, their cadence is showing signs of wear. The procession's march is no longer crisp or smooth.

The two full moons are half above the horizon. Shadows of twisted trees, sagebrush and tall grasses appear darker against the outer wall of the old city. Ingrider stops and prays again as he gets to the most eastern step, kneels on his right knee and mutters a prayer of severance and unification.

The entire procession kneels and bows their heads except for Cliff, thankful for the moment of rest. The chant stays at a low level until Ingrider resumes walking up the stairs. Ingrider consults his pilo almost certain that Karl can no longer do anything to get the boy.

I can continue, because it is now too late. My guards have the hub secured. No one can enter the hub through the maze. My enemies have lost. The ceremony will continue to the end. It will be a glorious night and we will celebrate into the wee hours of the morning. My red sashes will bestow on me their best wishes and heartfelt thanks. My guards will rotate through their guard duties even faster to enjoy the festivities.

Ingrider's pilo displays, "Saturday, June 12, 2483 7:57 P.M. Bridget, Diversity."

The red sashes continue their chant at a lower level waiting for Ingrider to resume walking up the stairway.

Ingrider rises and continues walking up the stairs. The red sashes follow increasing the level of the chant raising it up a notch with Cliff staying in step even though he can barely see the next step. The first third of the procession remains fresh and smooth in their march while the rest of the procession now exhibit an entirely different cadence as they try to catch up to the first third of the procession with several steps between them.

The young lavender acolyte comes out of the north side of the hub as the last red sash acolyte walks past the southeast step. Holding the bell in one hand and the striker in another, he gets to the east step. Putting the bell and striker on the that step, he continues up the steps, picking up the bell and striker staying the same distance behind, but he never stops, knowing the importance of his duty to his master.

His concentration never varies. He keeps his eyes on the steps before him, trying very hard to make the steps fewer than they already are, but knowing that will not happen in his lifetime. He shrugs off his dourness returning to trying to catch up to the last of the read sashes as they go around the hub out of sight. He tries to speed up the steps, but it always catches him when he stumbles.

He tries using his right leg first up the steps but it doesn't work any better than his left.

* * *

Everyone on the upper six levels, including the guards watch the procession up the hub mindful of the closing ceremony. No one sees the men and women moving up the terrace steps on the east, southeast and southwest sides.

At each of the next three levels, three of the men and women wearing harnesses move up the terrace steps after the primary and several secondary officers have moved into position. The guards closest to the devices start collapsing one by one. Soon all the guards are asleep on the ground on the fourth level. The remaining white habited acolytes remain calm next to the fallen guards and follow the instructions of the officers with very little scuffling and concern for the younger acolytes who don't quite understand what is happening, but even they remain quiet when guided by their mentors. Some begin crying and soon are carried by other more responsible acolytes.

Two officers grab a guard from the fourth level and escort him down the terrace steps to the appropriate gate and off into the appropriate forest staging area. Other officers gather the rest of the guards on that level. After the officers have handed over their prisoners to the staging areas, they quickly return to the old city to gather even more prisoners off the terrace levels.

When the level is clear of acolytes and guards, the primary and secondary officers move to the next level and the process continues capturing even more acolytes along with the guards.

This time, the primary and secondary officers assign the sleep devices closer to the guards when the regular officers are within range, which results in faster processing and a quicker turnaround for the officers. Processing becomes more productive and proficient with fewer guards required for escort of the acolytes.

More trouble occurs on the east side on the next two levels with the older and more experienced guards not being caught as easily as on the four lower levels. The sleep devices silence the guards before they get the opportunity to speak and the older acolytes are easily subdued, because they do not have the training of the guards. The rest of the younger acolytes come peacefully, but not all understand what is happening. They look from one acolyte to another trying to gauge other's reactions. Failing that they notice the smiles on the faces of the adults in uniform.

On the sixth level, a fight breaks out inside one of the habitats between a guard and several officers. A sleep device comes quickly to their aid and the officers practically drag the guard out of the habitat.

The pressure is kept up though until the middle three terraces are clear before Ingrider and his procession of red sash acolytes make their fourth appearance on the east steps. The first third of the procession of red sashes is beginning to show signs of wear. They all can keep the chant going, but their legs are no longer synchronized. They look forward to the last of the steps.

Robert looks out over the lower terraces waiting for the return of his officers. From his viewpoint on the east edge of the fourth terrace from the top, he watches the officers coming up the steps to the fourth level for their assault on the final three levels.

Robert says, "Well that was fairly easy. Now comes the exciting part. I'm hoping the upper terraces have fewer guards and acolytes, but based on previous surveys, they'll have the most."

* * *

Stopping for the final time on the eastern side, Ingrider bends his knee, mutters a pray of redemption and disgrace. He consults his pilo.

Ingrider's pilo displays, "Saturday, June 12, 2483 7:59 P.M. Bridget, Diversity."

The red sash acolytes lower their chant for Ingrider's prayer while most massage the cramps in their legs and do stretching to increase their stamina for the final steps. Many of the red sashes at the end of the procession are barely able to move, but they are ready and willing when they restart again.

The two moons hover at three quarters above the horizon. Almost all the stars on the eastern horizon are blotted out by the brilliance of the two moons. The entire hub area is cast in the light.

The shadows against the wall and on all the terraces are crisp and well defined.

Ingrider rises from his position on the east step with a smile on his face hidden by the hood he wears over his head. Keeping their heads bowed except for Cliff, the procession continues to the top. The procession seems excitable with the top of the hub so close. Everyone in the procession is revitalized and they have returned to their original cadence with renewed vigor. Each step they take up the stairs reverberates along the stairway causing another moan to echo off the outer wall of the hub.

The red sash acolytes' chant gets much louder. The last quarter turn of stairs lies ahead around the corner. Stars can be seen through the opening where the stairs reach the top of the hub.

The younger lavender acolyte finally comes out of the back of the hub still struggling up the steps, but obviously catching up with his new method. The last part of the procession is finally within reach. He will after all be able to join them as they reach their destination. Then he will finally be able to do his part, which gladdens his heart.

The last of the red sash acolytes haven't passed the east step let alone the southern end. He holds the bell and the striker in his right hand and uses his left for balance and thrust to get him on to the next step. The process is much easier as he practically rolls onto the step faster than the procession is marching.

Ingrider's head appears above the waist high wall around the upper part of the hub as he gets to the last of the steps before the top. His fears are relieved at the sight of the emptiness of the hub top with the central stone clearing visible. The top of the hub is pristine almost entirely white with only shadows on the far wall.

The rest of the red sash acolytes keep their heads bowed, yet each one knows exactly where they are relative to the top of the hub. The rhythm strengthens; their bodies straighten; their steps are crisp and more certain the closer they get to the top. The chant reaches a new level, but not yet at the top of their ability.

Ingrider is absolutely sure of his success and almost giddy with joy for his success over his adversary. Nothing can get in his way. The ceremony will continue to the end and his message will reach the four planets. There will be a new order.

Now nothing can stop me. For certain the boy will die.

The young lavender acolyte catches up to the last red sash still on the stairs and stays behind in step with the red sash acolytes as they enter the top level of the hub.

The two moons edge up so very little as to almost be unnoticeable only getting larger in appearance.

* * *

On the east side, only the top terrace has any acolytes or guards standing or walking around the fewer habitats. Their intention is rooted to the top of the hub even though they can no longer see what is happening. They are certain the ceremony will continue and they will soon see blood come down the hub onto the terraces to bless each level. They wait for the sound of the bell and the usual jubilation that follows.

All the rest of the terrace levels have been quietly removed to the forest staging areas with remaining officers growing in rank with the increasing number of detainees. Robert's forces are down to one third of what he started out with, but they still outnumber all of the acolytes and guards on the top terrace.

The remaining officers silently move up to the top terrace. All the rest are either in transit to or from the forest staging areas or on guard duty within the forest.

Robert, as the primary officer for his group, cautions his secondary officers to be especially watchful for any backlashes as the guards or acolytes become more daring. He expects more trouble to occur on this upper level since it is Ingrider's special venue and the highest with the only inner access to the hub's spaces. It also houses the elite guards which act as the front guard for Ingrider.

As on the other levels, the officers with sleep devices move up the terrace steps to the upper level. Using the habitats for cover, they silently approach the gatherings of white habited older acolytes and the most experienced guards. Most of the guards have moved away from their stations at the steps.

The sleep devices skillfully remove the outer rear acolytes of the group with regular officers catching the acolytes before they crumple to the floor. Occasionally an acolyte will notice and tap on the shoulder of the nearest guard.

The two closest security officers subdue the guard with extra help from a sleep device nearby. The sleep device people expect that kind of response and try to catch the guard before he has a chance to react and alert others.

The guard is escorted off the upper terrace to a staging area. With the only unknown being the hub itself, the officers hurry their prisoners along in order to return as fast as possible.

Slowly, one by one the acolytes and guards are removed from the upper terrace. Altercations have occurred but they have been quickly subdued by security officers without alerting any acolyte or guard on the same level.

Robert gathers his secondary officers around him.

When they have all returned from escorting prisoners or other duties, Robert begins.

"Get a few more officers and search the inner lower section of the hub, but don't enter the maze. Be careful for any traps, hidden equipment, false doors or hidden explosives. I don't want to send any other officers to rescue you, especially if you get lost in any of these secret passageways which I hope are limited to the maze," says Robert.

The secondary officers grab a half a dozen other officers, including one with a sleep device, and head into the hub entrance. The rest of the officers search the habitats finding more than one hideaway with a younger acolyte cowering before them. They bring in their best counselors and soon have the children safely off the terrace out the gate to the forest sanctuary. The smaller children do not understand where they are going and ask questions along the way.

* * *

Karl adjusts the position of the dummy at his waist and checks the display inside the cone for any drift from his position. For a moment, he watches the stars high above him. He consults his pilo. His pilo displays, "Saturday, June 12, 2483 7:58 P.M. Bridget, Diversity."

The dull black flighter hovers nose down and the long wide dual props spin above. The thin twelve meter long props silently rotate and pull into the air maintaining their altitude above the central hub of the old city.

The seat position has rotated backwards forty-five degrees. Turbo fans in the now vertical wings keep the fuselage from spinning. There is no persisting circular movement. The position is accurate to a millimeter.

The flighter's open storage area displays a winch inside lowering a taut black carbon cable by steps, going down away from the nose of the flighter.

A small black ladder comes out of the cockpit over the open nose cone ending a third of a meter below the storage locker. The transparent nose cone itself is hanging off to the left of the fuselage and cannot be seen from a distance. The flighter appears to be stationary with very little movement from the turbo fans.

Barely highlighted by the light of the two moons, Karl has one foot in the hook at the end of the black carbon cable with his left arm around it. Two meters from the flighter, Karl's head tilts downward, watching the procession enter the top of the hub. As Karl descends; the flighter recedes into the dark above him.

Attached to his waist, the dummy's arms and legs bob with each stepped descent of the hook. Karl look's at the gloved left hand which is holding the cable. It isn't wearing through.

Karl watches Robert's officers remove the acolytes and guards from the levels including the upper level where with some tricks and feints of their own, they overcome the guards and acolytes. Officers with prisoners in hand walk down the terrace steps while other officers are returning walking up the terrace steps.

Quietness comes over the entire city with Ingrider and the red sash acolytes getting into position. Birds have stopped singing, owls don't hoot and the wolves have stopped howling. All the animals have retreated to the depths of the forest to hide until the upcoming noise has quieted down. They've been through this before and they want to stay away from the humans who have repeatedly destroyed their habitats.

Even the slight wind that was blowing the banners and flags around the top of the hub has suddenly come to an end.

Any clouds along the horizons have also come to a stop as if everything was watching to see what was going to happen next. Of course, the two moons appear to be glued to the horizon. Even the animals and birds in the surrounding forest are quiet.

Karl drops further through the sky over the top of the hub. Almost at once, he's right where he wants to be and everything is, once again, normal size.

While off to the side, he is right above the stone with his feet only centimeters away from touching it. He can see the boy lying on the stone. He has to look twice before he sees the up and down movement of the chest. He glances over to the dummy attached to his waist. The likeness is remarkable. The hands, the feet, the habit and the helmet are interchangeable. He looks back at the boy who continues to breath while the red sashes continue their chant. He seconds away from pulling the boy out of this jamb.

*   *   *

Ingrider moves to his appointed place two steps back from the head of the stone. The two acolytes, escorting Cliff, head directly to the stone, lift him onto it and place him on his back with the helmet at the head of the stone ten centimeters from the edge.

Long moon shadows cover the hub area casting large dark shadows of Ingrider and the acolytes on the inside west wall of the hub. The acolyte's torsos appear in shadow on the inside wall with their heads cut off. Cliff's hands are placed by his side and his feet put together. Cliff breathes regularly and doesn't move any other muscle. The two red sash acolytes return to each side of Ingrider a half step behind. While they don't participate in the chant, nevertheless they keep their heads bowed and await the bell.

After waiting for the boy to be placed on the stone, the head acolyte of the outer circle of red sashes moves away from the stairs and goes around the western side of the stone until he gets to the foot of the stone and stops with two rows of acolytes behind him. All of the acolytes on the west side take a half a step back away from the stone, spreading farther apart to allow the inner circle to move to the east side of the stone.

The head acolyte of the inner circle continues around the foot until he reaches the head of the stone completing a circle of red sashes. The red sashes adjust their positions relative to each other until the circle is perfect with the west side moving inward and the east side moving outward. The circle of red sash acolytes surrounds the oval stone. Quickly checking their hoods and red sashes are in position, they remain still.

Everyone's head bows as the chant's volume increases. The two full moons hold their position at three-quarters above the horizon. More stars appear in the dark sky above the old city. The Milky Way becomes brighter as well. The galaxies and clusters brighten and more of them come into view.

Coming up last, the lavender acolyte turns around and stands on the last step intently watching the two rising moons with the bell in his right hand and the striker in his left before turning back and entering the top level of the hub.

After the red sash acolytes encircle the oval stone, the lavender acolyte walks up the last of the steps. He loses sight of the two moons as he reaches the top level of the hub since the outer wall above the hub's top level is over his head. After walking a circular path around the wall to a small opening, he tenses within the compartment which shields him from the sound of the rest of the red sash acolytes as he looks out through the ten centimeter hole in the east wall.

The two moons sit on the edge of the horizon, seemingly unable to move up into the sky. The chant continues from all of the acolytes and Ingrider trying their best to somehow bring the two moons off of the horizon. They all tense willing the two moons to rise so that the ceremony can begin.

The young lavender acolyte holds the bell in his right hand and the striker in his left holding his breath as he watches out the hole in the east wall for the two moons to rise above the horizon. The knuckles of both hands are white as his grip tightens on the striker and the bell.

* * *

K arl drifts closer to the stone now almost within touch. High above him, his cockpit monitor displays, "Saturday, June 12, 2483 7:59 P.M. Bridget, Diversity."

The cable's hook with Karl's foot in it passes next to the stone a meter from the bowing and chanting acolytes who remain unaware of his nearness. His torso is only five centimeters from the edge of the stone halfway along the longer axis of the oval stone. Cliff rests on the stone remaining calm as Karl comes into position.

Karl's downward motion stops when his knee drops below the height of the stone. The cable above him disappears into the night sky almost invisible.

He reaches out with his right hand and grabs Cliff's ight hand. Cliff smiles at the touch and stifles a laugh with his left hand. The boy rises silently following Karl's arm and shoulder, climbing onto Karl's back with his right hand. His arms and hands around Karl's forehead hold tightly. His legs don't quite wrap around Karl's upper torso.

Holding the dummy with his right arm, Karl pulls the Velcro strap. It starts to fall out of his hand, but he quickly grabs it before it hits anything. He grabs the helmet and turns it around into the position he wants.

Ingrider and the acolytes continue to chant, trying to will the two moons above the horizon and not wanting to wait. They all keep their heads bowed with their hoods covering their determined faces. They can't see the top of the stone or the base. Everyone around the stone is totally engrossed with their chant and are completely unaware that Karl in within their grasp.

Even Ingrider is too far back from the stone to see Karl's rescue. The young lavender acolyte remains focused on the two moons and his bell.

The two moons continue to sit on the horizon. Only the sound of the chant can be heard, but nothing else is even trying to compete. The banners and flags around the top of the hub are listless. Every red sash acolyte remains in position.

With his right hand, Karl places the dummy into position carefully placing the helmeted head, the arms and legs to match the way Cliff was situated. Karl puts his hand in his right pants pocket. The winch reverses direction and pulls up at a slightly quicker step, but at a still quiet pace. Soon they are far above the hub out of reach of the red sashes and Ingrider. All they have left is a dummy and they aren't even aware of that. Karl wishes he could see the look on Ingrider's face when he finds out.

The dummy lies on the stone not moving looking exactly as Cliff did only moments before. The chant continues and the two moons sit on the horizon. The officers on all the terrace levels remain quietly performing leading guards down the terrace steps and keeping a record of everything they can get their hands on.

The image of the dummy, the red sash acolytes and the top of the hub diminish as Karl and Cliff are pulled farther into the sky. The black flighter above them remains allusive until they reach an even higher elevation.

Karl watches Ingrider move into position next to the head of the stone. He is almost sure that Ingrider takes a peek by raising his head towards the head of the stone as he moves closer.

Above Karl, the flighter becomes much bigger almost as if a giant fly was going to eat him and the boy. Cliff watches the flighter for a little while and then the top of the hub. He can't remember ever being this high in his short life. This is turning into a very interesting journey. He wonders if this will be the last or are there more in store.

Very little movement occurs on the top of the hub. He can still here the red sashes chant although it's not as loud.

* * *

Keeping his head bowed Ingrider moves to the head of the stone as the chant continues now holding the last note for what seems like an eternity. The two acolytes behind him remain in position ready to remove the sacrificed body. They only watch Ingrider for the moment waiting for their turn. When he is halfway to the stone, he peeks under his hood and sees the helmet on the head of the stone.

He smiles and lowers his head as he arrives at the head of the stone. After composing himself, he says a silent prayer. He thinks that he has finally completed his task.

Taking a knife from a hollow in the stone face, he raises it above his head, holding the hilt with both hands. The blade of the knife points south. The chant reaches a tone almost felt. He closes his eyes and waits for the bell to ring.

The two full moons continue to sit forever on the horizon.

With the moment near, the young lavender acolyte tenses with his entire body starting to shake. Not seeing the moons above the horizon, he becomes worried. Finally, he relaxes and takes a deep breath knowing that they are rising, but it will happen when he least expects it. He blinks and almost senses that the two moons are ready to pounce, but not enough to clear the horizon. However, they stay in position. No longer anxious, he brings the bell and the striker closer together.

Some officers on the upper terrace look back at the eastern horizon. Many do not have the time to get out and watch the two moons rise together since it only occurs twice a year. The rest of the officers are either, returning from the forest staging areas or taking guards or acolytes to the forest staging areas.

Everything around the top of the hub hangs in suspension as if a picture had been taken. The air is still with a slight ozone smell, a combination of the forest, everyone's sweat and the bountiful flower gardens on every terrace. Even the surrounding forest remains quite waiting in suspense.

Nothing moves; the banners and flags are limping; the forest remains quiet; no one moves around the stone or anywhere nearby. The chant continues holding the note for as long as it takes. The waiting red sash acolytes wonder how long they can keep going, but they are so high on adrenaline they continue. The seconds go by so slowly.

Ingrider's arms are getting tired. He's beginning to think that time has stopped and he can't figure out why. He peeks from under his hood at the black helmet lying on the stone unknowing of its fate.

A turn of air passes through the red sash acolyte's habits, tossing the banners and flags into the sky while every red sash acolyte keeps their eyes closed waiting for that bell to ring. Some of the red sashes begin to fidget even as they continue the chant.

Others have to scratch their bodies where the habits rub against their skin.

* * *

K arl pushes Cliff into the cockpit and directs him to the nose cone. Karl climbs into the cockpit securing his harness and retrieving the cable and hook. His cockpit monitor displays, "Saturday, June 12, 2483 8:00 P.M. Bridget, Diversity."

Karl releases the cable and hook, engaging the winch which pulls the cable and hook inside the nose cone. He closes the nose cone, which turns back to the same color as the flighter. Karl sits in the cockpit while Cliff rests without the helmet on in the dark storage area. The nose cone is closed and locked in place for flight. The cable is wound on the winch with the hook in its holder. With Cliff in the compartment, there is barely enough room to breathe, but he manages to fit opposite the winch.

Not satisfied with holding the helmet, Cliff turns around easily in the small quarters and finds an empty strap on the rear wall separating the locker from the cockpit. He straps the helmet to the wall and looks up at Karl.

Cliff asks, "Have they done it yet? I can't see that far; they all look like ants."

Karl says, "They're about to. The moons will be above the horizon in only a few more seconds. I wish we could be closer, but we can't take that chance. There are too many of them."

Cliff wears brown corduroys and a pale blue shirt with white socks and black sneakers. He's excited to be off that stone and out of that habit. He scratches his arms and legs trying to get rid of the touch of the black habit. After a few seconds, he stops scratching and looks through the clear nose cone at the tiny scene below. He sees a circle of red and white with black on stone.

Taking very little space in the right rear corner, the black habit lies crumpled. The silent winch has the black line coiled around it with the hook folded between the wire guides.

Still in silent mode the blades turn swiftly above them keeping the flighter vertical while the turbo fans in the vertical wings keep the fuselage from spinning. The ladder is safely stowed behind Karl's seat. From the hub, the flighter would be hard to pick out with its blackness barely hiding only a few stars behind it.

Karl motions for Cliff to move into the cockpit from the storage locker. The storage locker's thick rear wall only goes up three quarters of the way, leaving an opening between the locker and the cockpit. Normally this would be for quick access to something stowed in the storage locker.

Cliff easily climbs out of the storage locker into the cockpit grabbing on to Karl's legs to steady him. He arches his back and pushes down on Karl's thighs to bring his legs out past the storage locker wall.

He twists his body around and gets up on Karl's lap. Cliff sits high enough to see, over the edge of the cockpit, the small hub scene below them. The red sash acolytes are gathered around the oval stone with the black figure on it. Ingrider has his arms above him holding something between his fingers.

"Wow, they look so small," says Cliff. "Almost the same size as my space figures that I play with out on the prairie or in the foot hills."

"I would love to be down there to watch his reaction to the dummy. Even if they knew we were up here, they wouldn't be able to do anything. See all the officers on all the nine levels. Ingrider and his red sash acolytes are the only ones still on the terraces. Robert probably has the inside steps well-guarded. Ingrider and his red sashes don't stand a chance of getting away. He's going to have one heck of a time trying to get down to the terraces without running into Robert's officers," says Karl as he points to the hub again.

"Watch, here comes the knife."

Cliff looks out over the edge of the cockpit and watches as Ingrider raises his hands above his head. He waits momentarily and begins to bring the knife down. Cliff watches intently as the knife enters the dummy's chest. The feathers come out up into the air around the dummy and the stone. No one notices even when the feathers land at some of the feet of the red sashes. Most of the litter congregates around the placement of the tables. Only a few spillages from hurrying with pitchers or dropped food items litter the terrace levels and they are quickly cleaned up. Mops remove the liquid spills and sweepers take care of the rest. Bit by bit the terraces are cleaned of litter, leaving each empty.

Robert stands next to Ingrider's throne, making notations into his pilo with his dark distinct shadow on the wall of the hub. Officers mill about after finishing their duties and after waiting for their next assignment, talking about their current exploits, home disasters with kids or their last vacation encounters.

The lights around the base of the hub remain off. Robert looks up from his pilo towards the eastern horizon. The two moons are still glued to the horizon and seem to be taking their time about rising above it. He knows it is only a matter of time and part of an illusion of the horizon.

After turning away for only a minute, Robert notices the chant's conclusion and the ringing of the bell. Without looking, he senses a change in the air around him.

He cautions the rest of the officers on the top terrace to remain quiet.

The officers quickly stop doing anything that makes even the slightest noise.

"I hope Karl got the boy, there's very little I can do. No way to rush a hundred officers up those stairs. We could have scaled the walls with hooks and ropes, but that would take to long as well and we would be definitely noticed.

"Whatever Karl did was a very careful maneuver around all of those red sash acolytes," says Robert,. "He has pulled off something I could never have done. I will be in his debt for a long time coming. I only wish he was on my staff instead of rescuing children and adults on the other planets. There is still a lot of work to be done. The acolytes, red sashes and the guards still have to be transported. And that will take most of the night."

* * *

The two moons rise above the horizon. The crescendo arrives and the red sash acolytes take deep breaths. The bell chimes. For a moment no other sound arises.

Ingrider brings the knife down quickly. It enters the dummy's body right through the center of the white emblem, impacting on the oval stone with a sharp ping. The red sashes cheer, tossing their hoods off of their heads as a dark liquid meanders over the stone to the edge and down the six holes.

The red sashes dance with each other and separately to music only they can hear. Laughing, they throw their arms above their heads and twist their heads back and forth. They are as children delighting in a moment of grandeur.

The young lavender acolyte comes out from his cubbyhole to see what he is hearing. He doesn't understand what is going on with the red sashes and Ingrider.

He stands and watches the activities of the red sash acolytes around the oval stone. They dance around each other; a few laugh loudly at the antics of some of their peers; others kneel down with a prayer of thanksgiving.

Watching Ingrider's solemn pray against the backdrop of the red sash acolytes frolicking, the young lavender acolyte wonders about indiscretion at times of celebration. As his gaze turns to the child on the stone, the young acolyte struggles for breath when he sees the shrunken form and the feathers flying through the air.

When the liquid reaches the middle of the eastern face below the second eastern step of the outer stairway of the hub, two coincident circles fill with the liquid, the outer with a one meter diameter. The inner is twenty centimeters smaller.

Next, between the circles, arrangements of five centimeter triangles, squares and circles coincidently stacked or as separate items appear randomly.

Lastly, inside the inner circle, an elliptical alpha symbol appears over an elliptical omega symbol positioned so that one end of the alpha symbol matches an end of the omega symbol. The inner circle and the alpha and omega symbols finish filling with the liquid, as do the lower symbols between the inner and outer circles and the bottom of the outer circle next.

Ingrider removes his hood and opens his eyes very wide. Hearing the young lavender catch his breath, he is amazed to find feathers float in the air before him. Most land around the dummy and the stone in a random manner. He grabs one and puts it to his nose tossing it away briskly.

Ingrider asks, "Chicken feathers. What is this?"

Ingrider pulls out the knife and smells it. He wipes it off tossing it to the ground. When it hits the stone floor of the upper hub, the red sash acolytes stop doing whatever and quickly return to look at the figure on the stone. A few reach out to touch the dummies body. Many gasp and cry out when they see the feathers and the dark grape juice.

Ingrider asks, "Grape juice. How did this happen?"

Ingrider tears open the habit and tears into the wound. His fingers turn purple. More feathers fly through the air. He picks up the dummy and throws it over the edge of the hub. The helmet comes off along with one of the legs spewing more feathers into the air above the upper terrace.

At this time the red sashes realize that something is wrong, so they carefully and quietly return to their positions around the stone, bringing their hoods over their heads and their hands clasped together in front of their chests as a solemn gesture.

They instinctively hum a lament to ward away evil spirits.

The dummy falls on the top of Ingrider's throne where the plaster helmet shatters into several pieces scattering feathers from the torso over his throne. The loose leg lands at the foot of the throne bouncing twice recoiling as if it were alive. Feathers shower all over the east terrace. Most land around the throne with the rest forming an irregular pattern on the upper terrace.

Ingrider looks out over the old city. All acolytes and guards have disappeared from the terraces below. He looks at the base of the hub. Regional officers mill about at the base of the hub.

Ingrider steps over to the head of the stone and removes another knife. He puts it in his inside left ankle sheath. Ingrider turns to the red sashes.

Ingrider says, "You must ensure my safe exit in these next few critical moments. I cannot be caught. These are perilous times and our work needs to go on."

After quickly ending the lament, one of the red sashes steps forward and exchanges habits with Ingrider. The two red sash acolytes behind Ingrider help him remove his habit and the other red sashes habit. Several of the acolytes gather around to provide some privacy while the habits are exchanged.

The two leaders of the red sash acolytes confer for a few moments before reaching a decision.

Half the red sashes take the outer stairway while the rest take the inner surrounding the fake Ingrider. The young lavender acolyte wisely takes the outer stairs, knowing that Ingrider intends to fight.

Ingrider walks towards the front as one of the red sashes guarding his replacement. He works his way to the rear as they reach the halfway point.

They proceed down the inner stairway. The darkness keeps them from seeing more than three candles in front of them. They slow their rate to arrive after the other red sash acolytes on the outer steps. Reaching the bottom, they meet several officers which command them to come off the stairs.

Outside the hub, the red sash acolytes file down the steps into the arms of officers waiting for them. All of the red sashes watch the entrance of the hub waiting for the other red sashes. When the inner red sashes appear a signal is given by raising a right hand. A scuffle breaks out between several of the red sash near the end of the outer procession.

Before the officers attempt to take the fake Ingrider, the officer's attention is diverted by the last of the red sashes on the outer steps outside creating a disturbance. Turning their heads toward the entrance, they keep a grip on the fake Ingrider, not noticing the regrouping of the red sash acolytes.

The real Ingrider slips by further down the stairway as the red sashes close ranks. He blows out each candle on the inner stairs as he goes by putting himself in darkness sooner. He walks down the stairs to the maze entrance below. Tossing his sash aside in the knife room, he runs into the maze. The sash floats through the air and lands at the base of the central stone.

* * *

Karl checks his GPS position and adjusts the power level slightly. The flighter is in its normal configuration with the dual props pushing from the back and the turbo fans providing additional lift when necessary. The props have returned to their flighter length. The sky is clear and dark with most of the light coming from the two moons. His cockpit monitor displays, "Saturday, June 12, 2483 8:30 P.M. Bridget, Diversity."

His flighter flies over a forest which ends at a prairie with Bridget in the far distance. The forest consists primarily of evergreens with a few deciduous interspersed. Before long, the flighter approaches the city. Karl checks his coordinates on his GPS, spotting Tarcey's house straight ahead.

He points to the house a couple kilometers ahead. Still excited about his escape, Cliff breaks away from his thoughts, realizes where he is, and that Karl is pointing at something in the far distance.

Cliff slides upward along Karl's torso until he can see over the edge of the cockpit. He sees his mother's house and quickly finds her near her garden where she usually spends most of her time. The wind quickly dries out his damp hair, tousling it wildly.

"She's working in her garden again. I don't believe I've seen a garden so big. It takes up a good portion of the front lawn, the side lawn and the back lawn." Karl remarks as Cliff sits up further to follow Karl's arm. Cliff's hair begins to loosen, to dry out and to get tousled every which way.

"She's working on the roses again. I've helped her plant and weed, but sometimes I get the plants and weeds mixed up. That's when my mother sends me into the house to play on my video games." Cliff shifts downward to get out of the airflow. He thinks about all the things he has done which at one time or another have upset his mother. He's grateful that he will be able to see and appreciate her.

Tarcey sits near her garden trimming a row of flowers with pruning scissors. Her pilo light attached to a tree provides light for her work. She snips off another branch above a bud with her pruning shears.

As she reaches for another branch, Karl honks the horn on the flighter and Tarcey turns around and in one fluid motion stands, dropping her tools and gloves on the grass as she rushes towards the street. She passes the oak tree as she tries to glimpse where the flighter would be coming down. Moving past the oak tree towards the street, she spots the flighter almost directly above her.

The flighter moves over Tarcey's house hovering as it drops slowly down to the driveway alongside her house. Before touching down, the flighter's wings rotate in different directions, spinning the flighter around till it's facing south. The turbo fans wind down. Karl secures the cockpit controls. The turbo fans spin down. Karl sets Cliff outside of the cockpit on the left wing.

* * *

Karl spends a moment going over the entire episode once more. He can't find any errors. His cockpit monitor displays, "Saturday, June 12, 2483 8:40 P.M. Bridget, Diversity."

Cliff hops off of the wing and runs to his mother. Two dogs bark from inside the house for only a moment and then a commotion in the kitchen alerts Tarcey that the dogs are on their way. At that same moment, Cliff's head impacts his mother's stomach as he stumbles into her arms.

She gathers him in her arms and holds tight, twirling around, kissing his forehead and brushing his hair. She tells him how happy she is to see him and how much she has missed him.

She lets him know the dogs feel the same way, but they will have their own way of showing their happiness.

Karl steps out of his flighter, checks his pilo and walks over to Tarcey and Cliff. Tarcey allows Cliff to stand.

Cliff says, "You should have been there Mom. Karl was brilliant. He took me right out of there in front of all those people. And they didn't even notice."

Tarcey says, "You'll have to tell me all about it later.

"You need to get to bed and get some rest; your birthday celebration will be tomorrow.

"Thank you, Karl for bringing my boy back to me.

"I don't know how I can repay you. You probably have done this so many times, you're immune."

Karl says, "It tears at my heartstrings every time. I'll have to tell you about it, perhaps another time."

The two black female Labrador retrievers come out the front door opening, jump over the porch steps onto the meandering path and practically push Cliff to the ground where they all wrestle. Cliff laughs and the dogs bark and whimper.

Karl asks, "My, they're as big as he is. What are their names?"

Tarcey says, "Thelma and Louise, but we usually call them T and L."

Karl replies, "Interesting names, certainly nonstandard. I'll guess they grew up together. Wait, wasn't there a movie about two women on the run using those names?"

Tarcey asks, "Will you stay with us tonight? I have an extra bed. You would certainly be welcome for Cliff's birthday.

"Between you and Cliff there won't be anything else to talk about."

Karl asks, "Something has come up and I have to get back to the maze.

"I will certainly try to make it to Cliff's birthday.

"Will it be in the afternoon?"

Tarcey says, "Yes, about two P.M. I hope to see you there. We have enough food to feed the entire city, so you have to come to get your fair share."

Tarcey extends her hand. Karl reaches out and gives a firm grip. Their eyes meet momentarily. Neither says a word with only the hint of a smile on each face.

Releasing his grip, Karl turns and walks back to the flighter, climbs in, starts the engine, engages the turbo fans and flies into the air.

Tarcey watches Karl's flighter quickly shrink to a spec.

She rustles Cliff's hair and escorts him into the house, holding his shoulder.

The two retrievers follow. Along the way:

Tarcey says, "You need a bath, my young man. I'm so proud of you. After you have rested and ready to talk, we'll discuss everything that happened to you and I will let you know what transpired while you were in the maze. I think you will be amazed at all of the activity that took place to rescue you. It will take you more than a month of writing thank you notes to just about every child in your school.

* * *

Robert assigns tasks to several officers as Karl approaches up the eastern steps to the top terrace. The officers leave and Karl steps onto the upper terrace. Another officer comes towards Robert and asks a quick question before returning to his duties. Karl checks his pilo.

Karl's pilo displays, "Saturday, June 12, 2483 9:30 P.M. Bridget, Diversity."

After walking up to Robert near Ingrider's throne, Karl asks, "So, he got away?"

Robert says, "Slipped by us during an altercation outside of the hub. I believe it was staged for his benefit."

Karl walks towards Robert until he stands a meter away. Robert looks tired with his blue pants covered in the dust of the terraces. His hair is disheveled and discolored. Karl wears his black pants and shirt although he has washed off the black face. Karl's brown hair is equally disheveled from the wind of flight, but not discolored.

Karl asks, "He entered the maze through the hub entrance?"

Robert says, "We had all of the exits/entrances closed, including the dumb waiters in the shopping center. I didn't pay any attention to the maze entrances. With the lower terrace empty, it didn't occur to me. I should have had the maze entrance at the bottom of the hub secured before the red sashes and Ingrider came down."

Karl says, "Don't let it get to you. Ingrider is very resourceful and suspicious."

"I know that, but it will still be in my report that I let him get away. He's had a good head start, but he is not in any of the main passageways. We have checked with our pilos. He could be all the way to the tunnels by now," says Robert.

"Then there's, at least, one other secret passage that I haven't found. He has a good hour on me, so I better get going. Although knowing him, he will not be in any hurry to get away. He's way too confident.

"I have a funny feeling that he is going to be one of my slippery opponents. They're the hardest ones to catch."

Robert says, "With the notoriety that he has created, he won't be able to go into any city on the planet. The word is passing around the world fairly fast."

Karl says, "That's why he is probably holding up somewhere underground waiting for the appropriate time. He still has his pilo so he can be in contact with any of his other cohorts.

"If he gets to those tunnels, we'll never find him."

Robert asks, "He won't be getting any help. Every associate, acolyte and guard have been rounded up in all the cities on this planet. Do you want any of these fine regional officers from my region?"

Karl says, "I have to do this by myself. He owes me that."

Karl walks by Robert and several other officers through the hub entrance. After Karl leaves, the other officers begin talking about his exploits.

Karl walks down the stairs. The candles are all aglow, having been ignited by Robert's officers.

* * *

Tarcey walks with Cliff towards his room through the hallway. Above them the breakfast table monitor displays and beeps, "Saturday, June 13, 2483 9:30 P.M. Bridget, Diversity."

Tarcey tucks Cliff into bed. Pulling the top blanket up to his chin, she kneels by the bed and flattens Cliff's tangled hair.

Cliff asks, "Mom you are not going to believe this?

"I thought you were giving me a really big birthday surprise, until they put me in that freezer. I don't ever remember when I have been so cold that I could feel it down to my bones.

"I knew you wouldn't do that."

Tarcey says, "We can talk about it in the morning. You've had a big week and tomorrow will be a big day. You're going to need some sleep and you haven't the foggiest idea of what is going to happen tomorrow.

"Half the school is coming here."

Cliff asks, "How did they know?"

"Karl didn't do this all by himself.

"He had lots of help. For many of these people, I will never be able to thank them for they will have long gone back to their own homes."

"Lots of parents and teachers were out there as officers to help round up those nasty people. They spread the word much better than I could have from my place.

"They all got to watch you being rescued on their pilos from Robert's automatic fly over the old city. I had to disconnect the phone and disable my pilo so I wouldn't be inundated with calls and messages about your rescue.

"In fact, I'm sure it will be plastered all over the city and maybe all over Diversity by ten o'clock in the morning." Tarcey brushes a stubborn hair from Cliff's forehead before she kisses it. Standing, she walks to the door, turns off the light and closes the door behind her as she leaves.

She walks down the hallway to the stairs. Arriving in the kitchen, she goes over all the preparations, checking off who's bringing what and who's doing what. The kitchen console monitor offers several suggestions to improve the work flow. She considers all of them.

* * *

Walking west along a passageway, Karl reaches a dead end. *These passages can certainly be confusing.* After searching for hidden passages, he checks his pilo.

Karl's pilo displays, "Saturday, June 12, 2483 10:00 P.M. Bridget, Diversity."

Karl says, "That takes care of the eastern route, for the time being. Only the stairwell entrance to the lower terrace was anywhere near secret and that was because it was open most of the time. This western passage is certainly long enough to have several intersections, but it does not seem too. There's no symmetry to these stones.

"They are all random. That means I'm going to have a devilish time trying to find metallic levers between stones. In this area, they could have used some other means, like moving or rotating stones."

Karl punches buttons on his pilo.

Karl says, "I hadn't even noticed that."

Karl looks up at the ceiling of the passage and shines his pilo light on it. An isosceles triangle points down the passage in the same direction Karl was headed. After pointing his pilo light further along the ceiling, he finds more triangles further down the passageway. They all point in the same direction.

Several meters later, Karl's brings his head back to vertical and rubs the back of his neck as he continues to walk.

He stops and backs up a meter and shines the light on a triangle pointing north.

Karl begins a search, using his pilo, on the north wall of the passage. He puts a grid on his pilo's screen and using it and the light, he moves the pilo along the grid. It analyzes all light frequencies not just the visible light from the light panels that shines on the passageway walls.

* * *

Ingrider walks confidently through a passageway, humming a happy song. Now that he has escaped from his enemies, he can relax. He consults his pilo.

Ingrider's pilo displays, "Saturday, June 12, 2483 10:00 P.M. Bridget, Diversity."

Approximately ten meters ahead appears an intersection. Before Ingrider gets to the intersection, he stops and turns to his right and pulls a lever between two stones. The lever was well hidden and would not have been noticeable even in a close look. The stone door regresses and slides up, revealing a large room. Ingrider walks in.

Ingrider says, "Not a bad hideaway. I've been in worse. A few days here and then off to the south. I can disappear amongst some of my followers. My enemies will be back in their contented homes thinking that I am out of their hair, but little do they know of my resources in the south."

The door closes automatically several seconds after Ingrider enters the room. Its almost square with tile around the kitchenette and a corner bath with shower. The room has a dining table and chairs with a lounge chair next to an end table. No large screen monitor exists for it could be easily traced.

Light panels from above warm the room although several are dark. Under the kitchen cabinets, row lights bring out the details of the marble cook top. A single panel in the bathroom provides enough light for the shower, sink and toilet. A single light panel glows above the lounge chair providing light for reading.

Getting comfortable in the lounge chair, he takes an e-book from the end table and starts reading. He asks the room for background music with light jazz instrumentation to start. He'll probably switch to classical later on.

* * *

Coming to the north passage's end, Karl checks his pilo. His pilo displays, "Saturday, June 12, 2483 10:30 P.M. Bridget, Diversity."

Karl says, "Wishful thinking. All of these passages are dead ends except for the other hidden passageway. Ingrider has to be in here somewhere."

Karl turns around and heads back to the next intersection.

Later, Karl gets to the intersection.

Karl asks, "Ahead is the passage I came in here on. Straight ahead leads to the tunnels and the passageway shows no signs of any footprints in that direction.

"Now I have two choices, west or east. If I were Ingrider, where would I go? Or maybe I shouldn't think that way. He could only be trying to get out of the maze.

"East is back towards the old city, while west is towards the shopping center and the other tunnel exit. Which would Ingrider take?"

Karl looks west and then east. He looks back west and starts to pull something out of his pocket. He stops and pulls his hand out empty. Karl turns left heading east. He begins to walk faster and then he breaks into a run passing intersection after intersection. He carefully watches his pilo and the ceiling above him for the signs he knows are there. But no other secret passageways are visible and so he keeps going stopping occasionally to catch his breath and recheck his pilo.

* * *

R obert leads a group of officers through a forest glade. Beyond other gates more officers are moving through the forest as well. The last of the terraces are secure for now. Most officers will be headed home to their own regions after securing the acolytes.

Robert checks his pilo.

Robert's pilo displays, "Saturday, June 12, 2483 11:00 P.M. Bridget, Diversity."

Behind them come several groups of ten acolytes each followed by the red sashes marching by twos.

Four rows of top officers from different districts as signified by their shoulder patches surround the red sashes.

Robert meets up with another group who has the rest of the guards. Everyone else heads for the staging area south of the old terraced city.

Robert's group and the rest arrive at the staging area. Several hundred flighters with regional designations land onto the small grass field one at a time.

One group of white habited acolytes heads for the first landing flighters. By pairs they climb into the nose cone of an aircraft. The nose cone is closed and secured for flight by one of the officers.

The red sashes are broken into pairs matching taller with shorter by the officers. Each pair squeezes into the next set of landing flighters. As soon as the first set of aircraft take off with the white habited acolytes another set of flighters lands and the process continues until all the white habited or red sash acolytes and guards are away.

One of the officers walks over to Robert as acolytes and guards load into flighter storage areas behind him. After Robert finishes with another officer, he acknowledges his presence. They shake hands.

The officer asks, "Where will the red sashes and Ingrider eventually go for rehabilitation? I'm not aware of our planet even having a rehabilitation facility."

Robert responds, "We'll send the leaders to New Banque. The first planet discovered in this area of space. They were the first to recognize the types of problems that would occur.

"They have a first rate rehabilitation program with twenty-four hour security and the facilities are well away from the general population.

"Even though it is not perfect; getting these noncompliant members off this planet is paramount."

* * *

Checking one side of the dead end and then the other as well as the ceiling, Karl sits in the dirt exasperated. He feels he has checked every single wall of this passageway for the intersection to the lower terrace. He checks his pilo.

Karl's pilo displays, "Saturday, June 12, 2483 11:00 P.M. Bridget, Diversity."

Karl says, "If he isn't at the dead end, he must be somewhere in between.

"Of course, he would be near the last western intersection for a quick getaway!

"And I was right there and missed it."

Karl stands and starts to jog, increasing to a full run. Light panel after light panel brightens and fades until he reaches the next intersection at the lower end of the east terrace many meters ahead. He can almost count the seconds until he will reach the intersection.

He slows to a walk as he gets to the secret stairway protuberance where he walks around and then picks up the pace. He zips by several intersections, some going through while others only go north or south. Still running, he comes on the hub crossover intersection where two officers guard the maze entrance at the hub about forty meters from the intersection. Running past the only other through intersection, the far intersection comes into view. He slows down to a walk.

It is the last north/south passageway before the western end which goes under the shopping center. As he passes the secret passageway on his right that he discovered earlier, he starts to slow, checking the ceiling more often.

After reaching the last intersection, Karl walks away from the last intersection heading east, shinning his pilo light on each wall and the ceiling.

Ten meters from the intersection, the light glances off a metallic lever on the north wall. He checks the ceiling where a line goes through several stones to become an isosceles triangle pointing to a secret room. After putting his pilo away, Karl stops and puts his ear against the wall. He hears the sounds of movement within the room. He doesn't move the lever right away. He wants to gauge what Ingrider might be doing within the walls of that room and what other exits might exist on the other side. After checking his pilo, he finds a corresponding passage on the opposite side which just happens to intersect with the secret passageway which crosses between the two. He makes a notation concerning the time factor and his best option or opportunity. *Ingrider obviously has a plan to escape back towards the space port. This is only a staging area which he prepared long ago or had his guards prepare the facilities. I'll bet he has others as well.* He puts the pilo away and continues to listen.

* * *

Ingrider looks over the room remembering the hidden places and escape routines. The hidden maze room's monitor displays, "Saturday, June 12, 2483 11:30 P.M. Bridget, Diversity."

Light classical music from hidden speakers within the room makes Ingrider's sandwich making a command performance. Standing by the kitchen counter, he prepares a sandwich when the lever moves out of the wall. Hearing the stone door regressing, Ingrider instinctively jumps quickly to the far side of the room and rotates the smaller picture clockwise. A door regresses into the wall and slides up into the stone wall.

Ingrider jumps through, tumbling and landing on his back. He quickly gets up and pushes the lever back in on the passageway side. The door comes down. Not waiting for it to seal, he starts walking east, counting his blessings.

Karl watches the stone door on his side regress into the stone wall and slide upwards into the ceiling. He looks into the room and notices the kitchenette, lounge chair and bathroom.

He walks into the room and immediately sees the door on the other side of the room close, leaving no trace on the wall. He looks at the two pictures on the wall and notices that there are no other protuberances like a lever on that smooth surface.

Walking to the kitchen counter, Karl finds a half made sandwich. He finishes making the sandwich and eats it. The room certainly is simple enough with a small kitchen and restroom. Karl opens the small refrigerator in the corner of the counter and selects a box of mineral water.

Finally noticing the music, he cancels it.

He opens the corner and takes a large gulp, savoring the taste. Once that settles, he gulps another before putting the water box on the counter.

Karl says, "Thanks, Ingrider. I didn't know I was so hungry or thirsty. You've led me on a merry chase, but I will find you. You can't hide forever and I'm beginning to believe that I know as much about the secret passages as you do."

Karl finishes the sandwich and the water. He carefully cleans the counter and tosses the water box and crumbs into a trash receptacle. He puts the plate and utensils in the dishwasher. He turns around and surveys the rooms once more.

He walks over to the opposite wall from the entry door. Two pictures hang on the wall with the one on the right bigger than the one on the left. The smaller once is slightly askew.

Reaching for the smaller picture frame, he withdraws his hands. Turning, he walks back to the other side and opens the entry door. He steps out the door and heads down the southern passage at a fast trot without making enough noise for Ingrider to hear him. Before long he arrives at the secret passage. He engages the lever and enters the passageway. It is dark inside like all of the other secret passageways, but he hasn't gotten used to it and his pilo

light guides him along.

SUNDAY

Morning

Walking casually towards an intersection, Ingrider smiles with a skip to his step as he feels giddy with pleasure. Watching the ceiling as he walks, he feels like a person who has escaped the jaws of death. He consults his pilo.

Ingrider's pilo displays, "Sunday, June 13, 2483 12:00 A.M. Bridget, Diversity."

Ingrider asks, "Barely escaped that one. How does he do it? Such talent."

As Ingrider nears the intersection, Karl steps from the right passage into Ingrider's path. Ingrider steps back, surprised and repulsed.

Ingrider asks, "How did you do that?"

Karl asks, "Aren't you the one who is supposed to know all about the secret passages and rooms in this maze?

"I used a secret passage I found while I looked for you."

Karl looks in Ingrider's eyes. Ingrider's head moves with each word as if deemphasizing his words. Thinking of him as a clown, Karl keeps an eye out for any mischievous deeds.

Ingrider asks, "Now that you have found me, you even think I am going to go with you obligingly?"

Karl asks, "You would be true to form now wouldn't you? You've been fighting way too long. Can we really consider ourselves to be free, or even fully human, when we have lost the ability to survive on our own?

"Weapons were outlawed long ago to prevent people like you from creating hysteria and murder.

"The GHD accomplished the emotional turnaround. Separating weapons and humans accomplished the rest."

Ingrider says, "That is why you do not have any fear.

"You've learned to stay calm and face your difficulties."

Karl says, "Oh, I was afraid. Especially, when I didn't have this vest to protect me. It has a grid in it which prevents any signals getting to my GHD.

"You could touch me with your knives, but I knew my nanos would abate the pain and help heal the wounds.

"Look at my hands."

Karl holds out his hands, palms up, and turns them over.

Ingrider says, "But it would take three days for those cuts to heal. You almost have eliminated the cuts without any scars."

Karl returns his hands to his sides and keeps looking Ingrider in the eye.

Karl says, "Whoever is messing with your GHD is making you forget who you are and your origin. You are not part of the last civilization. Your ancestors came from Earth. Earth populated this planet two hundred years ago."

Ingrider says, "My great master says otherwise. He has provided us with everything we need. He will provide us with everything we need to bring you into his power.

"He gives us food from the automated farms and clothes from the automated shopping center."

Karl says "This is not getting anywhere. Are you going to come quietly or do I have to drag you by the hair. I can do either. It will take about the same amount of time because I seriously doubt your conviction."

Ingrider says, "I will go quietly. I don't have that much hair left. I'd like to keep whatever remaining hair I have. I don't know why my hair is thinning so rapidly. I'm not that old."

Karl points down the passage to the east and Ingrider takes the lead, but not in any hurry to reach the old city. They walk past several intersections. Karl continues to carefully watch Ingrider, keeping his eyes rooted to Ingrider's head waiting for that slight movement that will give away his next thrust.

Nearing the next illuminated intersection, Ingrider bends forward and pulls a knife from his left ankle. He spins to the left and shoves the knife into Karl's heart, except Karl isn't there.

Karl asks, "Were you expecting me to fall for that?"

Ingrider spins to his right. Karl stays behind him. Ingrider sees only a blur whip past him.

Ingrider asks, "I was hoping you would stay in one place. Where did you learn to anticipate like that?"

Karl says, "My foster father taught me."

Ingrider stands straight with his hands by his side. Karl moves around him until he is in front of Ingrider. As Ingrider faces him, Ingrider switches the position of the blade so that instead of pointing towards Karl, it lies along Ingrider's wrist. He watches Karl eyes for any distraction, but his enemy doesn't break concentration or even move.

Ingrider says, "From what I heard about the guards, especially my first and second, you must be very good. I guess I am going to find out."

Ingrider quickly crouches and lunges at Karl leaving a diagonal cut through Karl's vest. Karl and Ingrider trade hits and misses evenly.

Eventually Karl knocks the knife out of Ingrider's hand and knocks Ingrider onto the dirt path. Ingrider rolls over. Ingrider sits up and looks at Karl.

Ingrider says, "That was quick."

Keeping his eyes on Karl, Ingrider uses his right hand to search through the dirt for the knife. Karl spins again hitting Ingrider's face and knocking him sideways.

Karl and Ingrider continue to exchange jabs, each watching the other for strengths and weaknesses. Karl recognizes Ingrider's need for the knife and so he tries to keep his attention away from it. But finally Ingrider finds enough time as his right hand finds the knife. He quickly gets to his feet. Staying within a half meter, Karl and Ingrider circle with Ingrider taking several swipes.

Karl evades each time twisting left or right as necessary. Karl switches directions and Ingrider loses his balance almost falling to the ground. But Karl takes advantage of the moment, before Ingrider has the time to recover.

Karl spins and knocks the knife out of Ingrider's hand again with his left foot. The knife falls several meters behind Ingrider. Ingrider lunges at Karl grabbing him around the waist and throwing him against the intersection's corner. He hits the corner hard with a sharp pain going through his back.

Karl loses his breath for the moment as Ingrider tries to push him into the stone. Karl brings his hands together and pounds them down on Ingrider's back. Ingrider winces and releases Karl. Karl swings with a right upper cut and catches Ingrider's chin.

Ingrider lands against the opposite corner. Quickly rising, Ingrider hastily searches for the knife. Moving back and forth, he stays between the knife and Karl. Ingrider swings at Karl with his left and quickly returns a right hook.

Karl diverts both, losing sight of Ingrider. His eyes are blurry from the dust that they have stirred up and around them

Bending right, Ingrider swings his left foot into the air. He shoves it into Karl's right knee. Karl goes down clutching his knee. Even though he is very tired, Ingrider stands with his hands on his hips convinced he has won.

Ingrider jumps onto Karl's left leg, but Karl moves it out of the way. Karl stands obviously tender on his right leg. Ingrider lunges for Karl. Karl spins out of the way and pushes Ingrider's head into the corner. Ingrider hits hard and bounces off. He collapses in the dirt path.

Karl says, "You were tough, but not tough enough. Now all I have to do is drag you up those stairs."

Using a few plastic ties, he ties Ingrider's wrists behind him and sits him up against the wall of the passageway. Ingrider's head lies back against the sloping side of the passageway. Karl runs his pilo's diagnostic routine on himself and Ingrider.

* * *

Outside Robert's office, officers are engaged in dialog and work diligently at their pilos filling out report after report. Inside Robert's office, Robert works just like his officers using his pilo and the larger monitor. His monitor displays, "Sunday, June 13, 2483 1:00 A.M. Bridget, Diversity."

Robert sits at his desk looking over the view on the monitor of the old city. After all that has happened, he's enjoying the lack of activity at the gates or on the terraces. Karl walks into his office favoring his right leg and sits on the closest chair. He looks at Robert's uncluttered desk realizing for the first time that this is probably how his desk looks normally.

Robert asks, "Is he awake yet?"

Karl says, "And screaming for a lawyer at the top of his lungs. Your officers are looking for ear plugs"

Robert says, "Seems perfect. I'll get right on it come Monday."

Karl asks, "Are you still cleaning up out there? How much longer will you be guarding that complex? There can't be that many hiding places."

Robert says, "I left a few hundred officers to search the habitats and go through the maze. They'll love the overtime. With your information and their input, we will finally have a detailed map of that maze.

"I'll send another hundred for the derelict shopping center. I don't want any more unwanted surprises."

Karl asks, "This was a difficult case. I don't think I've ever been up against so many conspirators. Do you mind if I use one of your cell beds?"

Robert says, "Go right ahead. I'll let the crew know, but I would imagine the word has gotten out."

Karl trudges out of Robert's office still favoring his right knee. He turns left out the door and left again at the corner. He walks as well as he can to the rear of the police station where the cells are located.

* * *

Robert watches Karl leave his office as his thoughts return to the more recent events. His monitor displays, "Sunday, June 13, 2483 1:30 A.M. Bridget, Diversity."

Robert stands behind his desk, walks over to his wall monitor and watches the old city looking at the base of the hub. He notices something around the base of the hub that he hadn't noticed before. He returns to his desk. He picks up his pilo. Pushing several buttons on his pilo, he pockets it.

Robert says, "Magnify the hub base."

The image on the monitor zooms to the hub base and enlarges the area displaying the throne at one end and the entrance to the hub on the right.

Robert says, "That's interesting. The base has a band that circles the hub and another above it.

"Between the two bands are triangles, squares and circles all based on the horizontal base of the triangle.

"Like the emblem, the triangle, square and circle are on top of each other after every three symbols."

Robert says, "All reports are in, except for the follow up and that will take weeks. Time for me to get some sleep."

Robert stands and walks out his office doorway.

* * *

Cliff lies face up in his bed with a light blue blanket up to his chin. He shudders. Then he screams.

A night sky full of stars projects through a faux window into his room. The stars rotate past the window from far off center.

Tarcey races into the darkness of Cliff's bedroom.

Tarcey says, "Wake up Cliff! Lights!"

Light panels quickly flood the room. A black wall with posters of spaceships and spacemen working on them is opposite the door. The other three walls are pale tan with white trim around the baseboards and the doors. The door is bright red. Cliff sleeps with his nightmare on a twin bed with light green sheets and a quilted comforter.

She nudges his shoulder. Her right hand touches his forehead.

Tarcey says, "Hot, but not feverish. Pobably a bad dream. What with all he went through, it would seem natural."

She nudges him again. He screams once more. She grabs him by both shoulders and shakes him. Cliff awakens. Tears form in his eyes and his forehead becomes wet. His face turns pale white.

Cliff says, "I was being held in that freezer and they weren't going to let me out. I didn't know what to do. I was afraid."

Tarcey says, "It was only a nightmare. You're here in your own bed and I'm here to be with you. You don't have to be afraid."

Cliff says, "I'm so sorry mom."

Tarcey says, "It wasn't your fault."

Tarcey smoothes the blanket over Cliff. She kisses his forehead twice.

Tarcey says, "I'll go get you a glass of water. That will make you feel better."

* * *

Lights get brighter throughout Tarcey's house as congratulations appear one after the other on the kitchen console monitor. Some come as videos while others display only text. At the same time her pilo beeps and beeps for several minutes.

Her kitchen console displays, "Sunday, June 13, 2483 7:00 A.M. Bridget, Diversity."

Outside, through the kitchen bay window, with the Diversity's sun less than halfway above the horizon, the clouds dissipate. Through the trees, the wind dies on its last breath. Dogs bark and yap. People walk along the sidewalk heading straight for Tarcey's house.

Tarcey busily washes some fruit in her double sink putting each item on a towel covered rack sitting on the right counter. The kitchen hums efficiently with various people preparing sauces, flowered center pieces, decorations, cupcakes, strudels and the finishing touches to a four tier birthday cake. Over by the larger dining table, several seamstresses sew bows with Velcro attachments. Others make hems around banners and flags decorating each with birthday themed needlework.

In the rest of the house, decorations hang on the walls and ceilings and over every chair or sofa. Balloons stick to the ceiling and every wall saying 'Happy Birthday'.

Any table of any sort has a center piece of flower arrangements of three medium stem carnations separated by ferns with a base of six groups of astromelia separated by moss. Each centerpiece with different base color compliments the various colors of the carnations.

Outside, a big banner announcing Cliff's birthday hangs from the fascia boards along the front of the house. Various colored balloons rise every ten centimeters from the top edge of the banner. As the banner waves with the light wind, the balloons follow along in a sporadic fashion.

A trellis covered with a rainbow color of daffodils and honeysuckle intertwined over the walkway from the house to the street brightens the entire entrance. Even the posts have large ribbon bows on the inside and the outside.

A horse's clop clop pounds the street from the nearest intersection. The creaks of the wagon and its wheels fill the air along with a hundred kids talking and laughing. Soon a horse drawn wagon pulls into Tarcey's driveway.

It heads to the back of the house with a sign claiming ninety-seven different flavors of ice-cream along with chocolate and fudge bars, popsicle bars and various cups of ice cream with wooden spoons.

Hundreds of kids ignore the driveway and the walkway. They head to the back of the house every which way they can. Carefully staying away from the garden along the fence, some go through the trellis carrying presents into the house.

Afternoon

B y noon most of the activity outside has died down with only a few items left to be done while more guests arrive. Inside, the kitchen console displays, "Sunday, June 13, 2483 12:00 P.M. Bridget, Diversity."

Through the bay window, on the left side of the front yard, between the trellis and the garden, three tables are decorated with purple table cloths.

Half of each table is piled with bananas, apples, cherries, grapes, slices of kiwi, cantaloupe or honeydew in three bowls of ice encased in clear plastic.

The other half of each table comes filled with box drinks of water, juices and sodas also sitting in three bowls of ice. The selix bowls are equally spaced around the flowered centerpiece in the middle of the table.

People gather around the other twelve tables, some sitting in chairs, the rest standing or milling about sipping water bottles, cups of the latest coffee flavors, glasses of various soft drinks, cups of hot tea or glasses of iced tea with lemon slices.

In the backyard close to the house, five barbeques busily grill hotdogs and hamburgers along with veggie-sticks on gas fired burners with warming ovens and plates of fresh ground beef, hotdogs and vegetables already cut to size nearby.

Adults grill and watch a hundred children playing on the swing sets, the horizontal bars and the horizontal ladder and, for those in swimsuits, the four small pools and water slides. They know that there are as many in the house either playing video games or helping the adults.

The adults wear earplugs. Kids scream louder each moment with deafening accounts of victory or defeat. Every so often a child gets injured and cries out for its mother or father, but within minutes, the injury is forgotten and the child returns to the same kind of game.

One child comes out of the middle of the yard brushing grass off her flowered pink dress and heads for one of the adults at the grills.

When she gets there, she tugs on his pants. He looks down, smiles and removes his earplugs.

The little girl asks, "Is he awake yet?"

The man says, "Tarcey said she would wake him about one o'clock. Remember, he had a big day yesterday."

The little girl turns and runs back into the middle of a bunch of kids.

Every so often a child's voice rises above the clamor, from one corner or the middle or one side in their usual high voices. What is heard rises above the din and is clearly stated as if trying to make a point.

Various kids say, "He swooped him up in a saucer and put the dummy in his place.

"He was transported and then the dummy was transported in his place.

"I heard that Karl grabbed him running right through the red sashes.

"He didn't run he was swinging on a pendulum attached to a hovering flighter only meters above the hub.

"He used a ray gun to make Cliff disappear.

"The same ray gun put the dummy on the stone.

"It wasn't a stone; it was a pedestal of gold.

"Cliff climbed into the cockpit of the flighter as it hovered next to the stone. Karl placed the dummy on the stone and the flighter swooped them up into the sky away from the hub before the mad priest could do anything.

"Cliff placed the dummy and then he got into the cockpit."

Meanwhile similar conversations occur in the front yard where all the adults are gathered for a moment of tranquility from the raucous routine in the backyard.

Various adults say, "Karl was so badly burned it took two days for him to heal.

"Karl hit Ingrider with his knee, that's why he limps.

"It took him two days to find Ingrider.

"We now have a complete map of the maze including secret passages and rooms.

"He actually ran out of fuel running from that other enemy's flighter.

"He found dumb waiters in the shopping center.

"What's a dumb waiter?

"A winch in a flighter, I suppose it's possible.

"We had two hundred thousand to their four thousand.

"I didn't know we had that many officers.

"They could have stormed the old city and disrupted the ceremony.

"That still might have resulted in the death of the boy.

"How can you talk about death, Karl had this so well planned? He didn't leave anything untouched. It was the only way."

* * *

A ctivity inside the house has returned to less than a fever pitch with some items still being worked on. Most decorations are in place. A few food items have not yet been distributed. The kitchen console monitor displays, "Sunday, June 13, 2483 1:00 P.M. Bridget, Diversity."

Tarcey leaves the kitchen and walks towards the stairs on the other side of the breakfast table. She stops near the middle of the table remembering something she'd forgotten to do as she looks at the decorations on the table top.

Tarcey says, "Someone check the roast in the top oven.

"Let me know the temperature. It will say it right on the screen panel."

A female voice answers, "It's fifty-five degrees centigrade, Tarcey. Smells wonderful."

Tarcey says, "Check the lower one too.

"Time to wake ole sleepy head. He'll have recovered by now, hopefully."

Tarcey takes another step. Cliff comes bouncing up the stairs wearing blue jeans and a green shirt. Tarcey stops in mid stride. Cliff waves and turns to go out the back.

Cliff says, "I made the bed, put my dirty clothes in the hamper and put all my toys in the toy locker."

Cliff pushes the backdoor open and runs into the middle of the backyard.

Tarcey asks, "You made the bed, put your dirty clothes in the hamper and put your toys in the toy locker. Will wonders never cease? How long have I been trying to get you to do that? After all these years and now you decide?"

* * *

Aprons come off, workers grab glasses of drinks and head outside to join with their friends and associates. The breakfast table monitor displays and beeps, "Saturday, June 13, 2483 1:30 P.M. Bridget, Diversity."

Tarcey bastes the upper roast and closes the oven door. Cliff runs from the back door, past the breakfast table not even noticing the decorations and slides to a stop on the kitchen floor.

Cliff blurts out, "Bryan's not here. Some kids say he isn't coming back. He was supposed to be here. I have so much to tell him. He's not going to believe any of it."

Tarcey says, "Let's both sit down at the breakfast table for a brief moment."

Cliff walks to a chair on the longer side of the oval table and pulls it away from the breakfast table. He sits in the chair with his hands on the table. His mom sits in a chair on the short side of the table closest to the kitchen.

Tarcey says, "I know you and Bryan are the best of buddies and I'm sure that will continue for a long time.

"However, Bryan's parents made a decision to put Bryan in the military academy.

"You'll be able to see him on some weekends."

Cliff asks, "He won't be coming to our school ever again?"

Tarcey says, "He'll be in the academy until he is sixteen.

"After that, you two can go to college together.

"But time changes, especially close friendships. So keep that in mind."

* * *

Through the bay window of the dining room, two flighters approach Tarcey's house flying low over the ground.

Kitchen console monitor displays, "Sunday, June 13, 2483 1:45 P.M. Bridget, Diversity."

Karl and Robert land their respective flighters in a neighbor's yard across the roadway. After shutting down his flighter, Karl gets out of the cockpit, brushes off his suit and shoes until he is satisfied. He wears a royal blue suit with a pale orange shirt and no tie.

After shutting down his flighter, Robert exits the cockpit. He wears his whites with a blue stripe on the outside of each leg and a light blue shirt with a pastel yellow tie. His black shoes practically shine with a glow from within.

Karl walks, favoring his right leg, across the roadway and enters the trellis. Robert follows limping on his right leg. After noting the decorations on the house and trellis, Karl gets to about the middle of the trellis when Cliff runs out the open door of the house, down the path and literally jumps into Karl's arms.

Karl says, "Hi, there partner. Happy Birthday!"

Cliff says, "You have to see the pile of gifts in the living room. Mom says I have enough for my next seven birthdays. There are three piles already. It's going to take me weeks to open every single one."

Karl says, "And I bet she's only going to let you open a few each day."

Cliff asks, "How did you know that?"

Karl says, "I believe your mother might know that answer."

* * *

They finally make it through the crowd along the walkway and on the porch before getting through the front door. They head directly for the two large piles of presents in the living room. The breakfast table monitor displays and beeps, "Sunday, June 13, 2483 2:00 P.M. Bridget, Diversity."

Coming up the stairs into the living room, Tarcey wears a silver sleeveless evening dress and black stilettoes. Cliff stands in the living room along with Robert and Karl shaking gift boxes and announcing their best guesses. All three notice Tarcey's entrance, at once.

Cliff says, "Mom! Wow, you're beautiful."

Karl says, "I believe the boy has said it best. You are absolutely magnificent."

Robert says, "I should have known. I should never have let you go."

Tarcey rushes Karl, plants a kiss on his lips and backs up. Tarcey grins from cheek to cheek.

Tarcey says, "My Hero!"

Karl moves his head to his left side and stops a tear in his left eye with his left hand. He turns back and looks deeply into Tarcey's eyes.

Karl says, "You took by breath away for a moment.

"Remember, it is my job to find lost children. Robert will get my bill."

Robert says, "And worth every penny."

Acknowledgements

I would like to thank the following people for their contribution to the writing of this novel: my editor: Ileah, my readers: Jeff, Judy, Anthony, Marsha, Richard, Mr. Brown, Larry, Dorothy and several others who only read parts of the story. A special thanks to my photo editor, Jacqueline Smith, for the front cover, spine and back photo.